Old Bahama

Old Baham

The Fifteenth Carlisle & Holbrooke Naval Adventure

Chris Durbin

Chris Durbin

To Nicholas

Our eldest grandson

Old Bahama Straits

Copyright © 2024 by Chris Durbin. All Rights Reserved.

Chris Durbin has asserted his rights under the Copyright, Design and Patents Act, 1988, to be identified as the author of this work.

No part of this book may be reproduced in any form or by any electronic or mechanical means including information storage and retrieval systems, without permission in writing from the author. The only exception is by a reviewer, who may quote short excerpts in a review.

Editor: Lucia Durbin

Cover Artwork: Bob Payne

Cover Design: Book Beaver

This book is a work of historical fiction. Characters, places, and incidents either are products of the author's imagination or are used fictitiously. For further information on actual historical events, see the bibliography at the end of the book.

First Edition: May 2024

Chris Durbin

CONTENTS

	Nautical Terms	vii
	Principal Characters	viii
	Charts	x
	Introduction	1
Prologue		4
Chapter 1	Guarda-Costa	12
Chapter 2	The Emissary	23
Chapter 3	Flagship	34
Chapter 4	A Shipless Sea	45
Chapter 5	The Picket	55
Chapter 6	Brave Fool	63
Chapter 7	The Step	73
Chapter 8	Dire Straits	83
Chapter 9	The Chase	91
Chapter 10	Timber Convoy	101
Chapter 11	Denial	111
Chapter 12	Three Brothers	121
Chapter 13	The Landing	130
Chapter 14	Marines and Seamen	138
Chapter 15	Misgivings	149
Chapter 16	Soundings	159

Chapter 17	Red Ensign	169
Chapter 18	Gresham's Day	179
Chapter 19	Three Decker	188
Chapter 20	Malaga Wine	196
Chapter 21	A Contrast in Characters	208
Chapter 22	The Convoy	217
Chapter 23	The Batteries	225
Chapter 24	Shot in the Dark	235
Chapter 25	Les Enfants Perdus	246
Chapter 26	A Quixotic Hero	255
Chapter 27	Obstinacy	266
Chapter 28	Capitulation	276
Chapter 29	A Lee Shore	287
Chapter 30	Home At Last	298
	Historical Epilogue	303
	Fact Meets Fiction	306
	The Series	310
	Bibliography	312
	The Author	314
	Feedback	316

LIST OF CHARTS

1	Caribbean Sea	x
2	Old Bahama Straits	xi
3	Havana	xii
4	Middle Colonies	xiii

NAUTICAL TERMS

Throughout the centuries, sailors have created their own language to describe the highly technical equipment and processes that they use to live and work at sea. This still holds true in the twenty-first century.

While counting the number of nautical terms that I've used in this series of novels, it became evident that a printed book wasn't the best place for them. I've therefore created a glossary of nautical terms on my website:

https://chris-durbin.com/glossary/

My nautical glossary is limited to those terms that I've mentioned in this series of novels as they were used in the middle of the eighteenth century. It's intended as a work of reference to accompany the Carlisle & Holbrooke series of naval adventure novels.

Some of the usages of these terms have changed over the years, so this glossary should be used with caution when referring to periods before 1740 or after 1780.

The glossary isn't exhaustive; Falconer's *Universal Dictionary of the Marine*, first published in 1769, contains a more comprehensive list. I haven't counted the number of terms that Falconer has defined, but he fills 328 pages with English language terms, followed by an additional eighty-three pages of French translations. It's a monumental work.

There is an online version of the 1769 edition of *The Universal Dictionary* that includes all the excellent diagrams that are in the print version. You can view it at this website:

https://archive.org/details/universaldiction00will/

***

PRINCIPAL CHARACTERS
Fictional

Edward Carlisle: Commanding Officer, *Dartmouth*

Matthew Gresham: First Lieutenant, *Dartmouth*

David Wishart: Second Lieutenant, *Dartmouth*

Joseph Hooper: Second Lieutenant, *Dartmouth*

Francis Pentland: Third Lieutenant, *Dartmouth*

Arthur Beazley: Sailing Master, *Dartmouth*

Alfred Pontneuf: Marine First Lieutenant, *Dartmouth*

Frederick Simmonds: Captain's Clerk, *Dartmouth*

Jack Souter: Captain's Coxswain, *Dartmouth*

Old Eli: Quartermaster, *Dartmouth*

Nathaniel Whittle: Able Seaman, *Dartmouth*

Lady Chiara Angelini: Captain Carlisle's wife

Capitán de Fragata Ramon de Laredo: Spanish naval commander

Historical

Admiral Sir George Pocock: Commander of the naval forces at Havana

George Keppel, 3rd Earl of Albemarle: Commander of the land forces at Havana

Major General William Keppel: Commander at the storming of the Morro Castle

Commodore Augustus Keppel: Second in command of the naval forces at Havana

Juan de Prado Mayera Portocarrero y Luna: Governor-General of Cuba

Almirante Gutierre de Hevia y Valdés: Commander of the Barlovento Squadron

Charles de Courbon, Comte de Blénac: Commander of a French squadron

Luis Vicente de Velasco e Isla: Commander of the Morro Castle

The Honourable Augustus Hervey: Commanding Officer *Dragon*

Elias Durnford: Ensign, Corps of Engineers

***

Chris Durbin

CARIBBEAN SEA

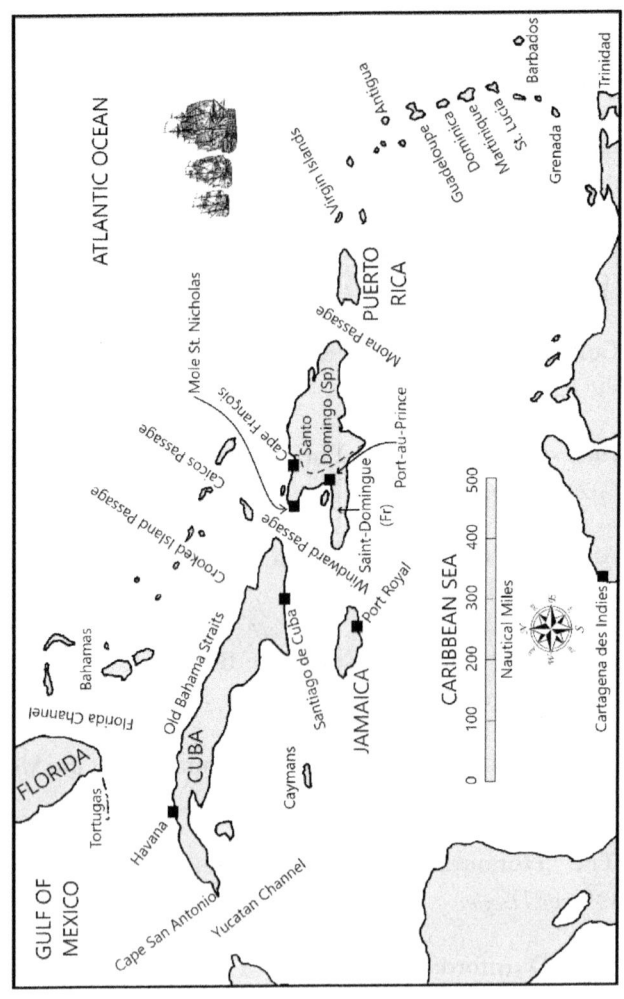

OLD BAHAMA STRAITS

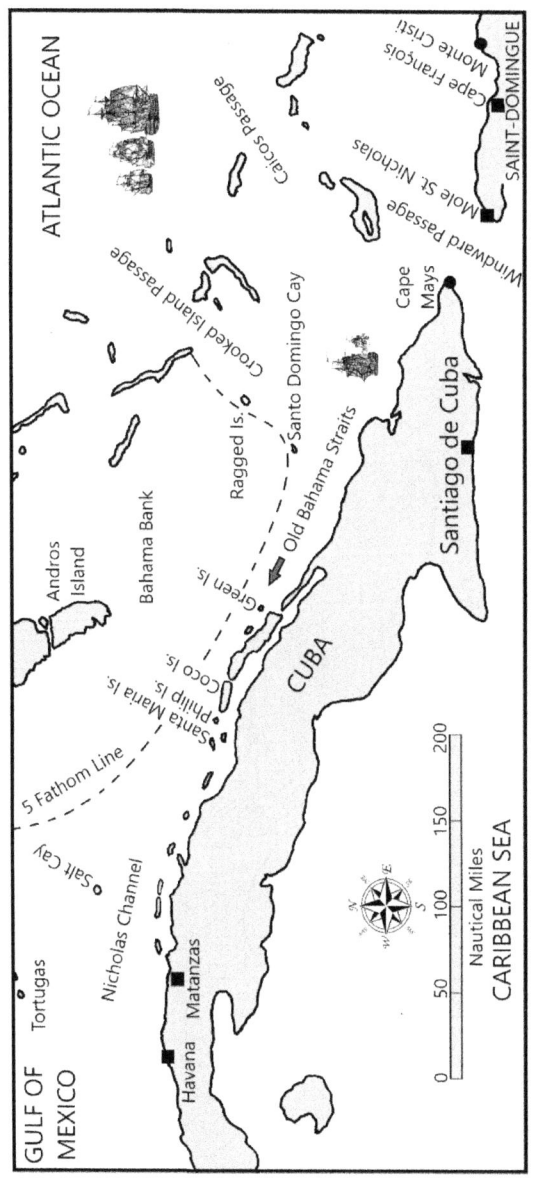

HAVANA

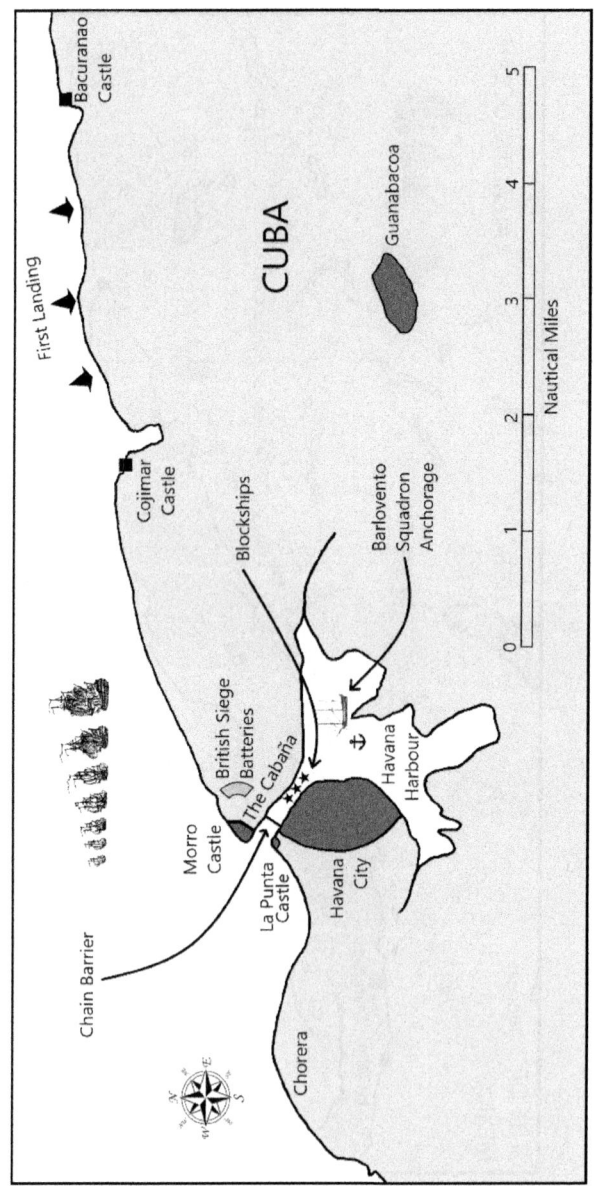

MIDDLE COLONIES

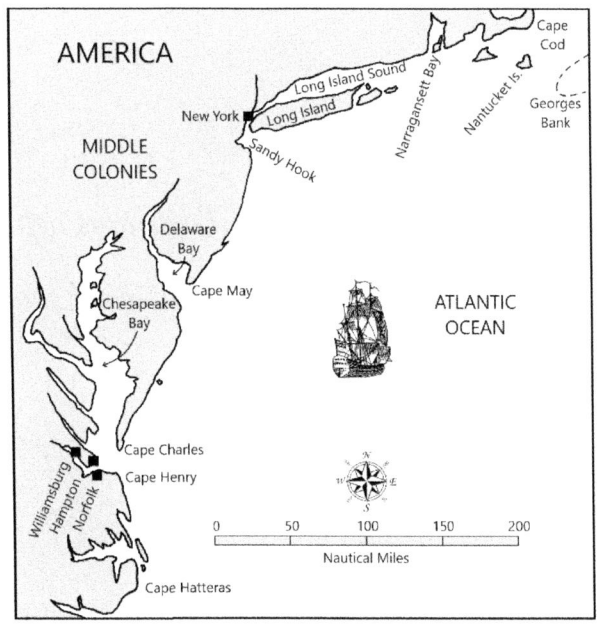

Chris Durbin

Then might I, with unrival'd strains deplore

Th' impervious horrors of a leeward shore!

The Shipwreck
An epic poem by William Falconer, 1762

INTRODUCTION

The Seven Years War in 1762

The war should have ended in early 1762. France had lost most of its overseas empire: Canada, the Caribbean sugar islands and the East Indies had all fallen to Britain's brilliant use of sea power. Even if France could make a final push against Prussia in Europe, it was becoming clear that George III didn't hold Hanover as close to his heart as his grandfather had, and it would not be the golden bargaining chip that it might have been. All the principal warring parties – France, Austria, Prussia and Russia, even Britain – were exhausted, and it was clear to King Louis that things could only get worse as the British navy ranged unchallenged across the oceans of the world.

However, there was a single ray of hope for France. In the August of 1761 King Charles III of Spain – King Carlos in his own language – was persuaded to honour his family ties; he signed a secret treaty in which he and King Louis formed a third Bourbon family pact against their common enemy, Britain. Deliberately or unintentionally, news of the treaty leaked out. When Britain heard of this, her ministers were withdrawn from the peace negotiations and the clouds of war gathered afresh.

France now staked everything on Spain's entry into the war and another hugely expensive push to take Hanover. However, Spain was slow to ready her navy for the coming conflict and her army was decaying and in no fit state to undertake even her own project, the planned invasion of Britain's ally, Portugal. In Germany, Prince Ferdinand was training more soldiers for the coming campaign season. Meanwhile, in the east, Prince Frederick was under pressure from the combined armies of Austria and Russia and was forced into a defensive strategy to preserve the very existence of Prussia.

Except for a single squadron that had been scraped together to protect the last substantial French possession in the Caribbean, Saint-Domingue, King Louis' ships were either destroyed, blockaded or sailing under British colours and it would take years to rebuild the French fleet.

Carlisle and Holbrooke

George Holbrooke recovered from his illness in time to take *Argonaut* back to the Caribbean during the winter of 1761. His timing was impeccable and he was ordered to escort a convoy from Antigua to the American colonies, with Lady Chiara and young Joshua Carlisle as passengers in his own ship. News of Spain's entry into the war had not reached the Leeward Islands Station, and he needed to use all his skill and imagination to repel an attack by a Spanish ship-of-the-line that heard the news before him. After another visit to Portsmouth, Holbrooke was sent to the blockade of Brest. His was the only ship on station when a French squadron – commanded by an old and wily adversary – escaped. He judged it best to follow them all the way to Newfoundland where they attacked and captured Saint Johns, destroying Britain's valuable cod fishery. Holbrooke joined the British force that ousted the French from Newfoundland and then followed them back across the Atlantic to a final confrontation off Brest in September 1762.

Edward Carlisle spent the later part of 1761 in the Caribbean, entangled in the web of diplomacy that preceded Spain's entry into the war. With his wife sailing as an interpreter and unofficial adviser, he visited Havana and met the governor-general of Cuba and the commander of the Barlovento Squadron, making personal contacts that would become useful later. He carried his old friend Don Alonso Fernández de Heredia, recently appointed as the governor-general of Guatemala, to his new domain, and he uncovered a plot to displace the British loggers on the Yucatan Peninsula. Ranging further afield, he carried the war against the French into the Gulf of Mexico and the mouths of the Mississippi. In early 1762 he bade farewell to his wife who was bound for their home in Virginia as a passenger in his friend Holbrooke's ship.

This book, *Old Bahama Straits,* starts in May 1762 as *Dartmouth* waits in the Windward Passage for the arrival of a vast British squadron and an invasion fleet, the objective of which is as yet unknown.

***

PROLOGUE

The King's Command

Wednesday, Sixth of January 1762.
Horse Guards, Whitehall, London.

The horses stamped and snorted as the white plumes of their breath soared lazily into the cold, clear air. Lord Anson eyed the distance from the door of the Admiralty building to the carriage. Only a month ago he would unhesitatingly have walked the couple of hundred yards from his office to the secret committee room at Horse Guards, taking the private route that avoided the public display on Whitehall. Now he was forced through infirmity to take a carriage and he was doubtful whether he could walk the twenty paces to its door without assistance. Twenty paltry paces, surely he could walk that distance unaided. With a determined clenching of his teeth he took a first tentative step onto the gravel. No, it was no good. If the Admiralty courtyard had been smooth flagstones he could have made it, but the shifting gravel defeated him. With an impatient gesture he beckoned to the two porters who had been waiting silently beside the door.

Anson's personal secretary showed the small ivory pass – a valuable and cherished token of his importance – that allowed the carriage to drive through the gates and into the courtyard. Horse Guards was prepared to receive him and, unlike the Admiralty, the headquarters of the British Army had any number of strong young officers at hand. His feet barely touched the ground as he was manoeuvred through the great doors and up to the committee room on the second floor. He was early, but that suited him, and he chose the most advantageous seat at the table and waited alone, for the only secretary allowed at these most confidential of cabinet meetings was Newcastle's own, and the great man had not yet arrived. This gave him a chance to order his thoughts without interruptions.

The Duke of Devonshire, who for the past few years had held the post of Lord Chamberlain, was the first to intrude upon Anson's thoughts, and he was closely followed by George Grenville, the leader of the commons. Anson had barely exchanged greetings with these first two when the Earl of Egremont, Secretary of State for the Southern Department, entered, rubbing his hands together and making for the fire.

Grenville was eager to speak because his duties in the Commons starved him of the company of the other members of the inner cabinet who saw each other daily in the House of Lords.

'I trust they're warmer in the Escorial. Bristol can tell us, if he's to be one of our number.'

The Earl of Bristol had been the ambassador to Spain for nearly four years and he'd certainly be able to offer wise council, but he'd been expelled from Spain as soon as Britain's ultimatum expired. Under normal circumstances he'd be home by now, but he'd decided to travel overland, using his diplomatic status to pass through France. His progress had been largely unknown until he arrived at a channel port where Anson's intelligence network had discovered him, and a report had arrived on the First Lord's desk moments before he left the Admiralty.

'His ship is being detained in Boulogne on some pretext or other. The French won't hold him for long, just enough to make their point, but he won't be at this meeting.'

Anson was secretly pleased that Bristol had been delayed, for his would have been an unpredictable voice at the meeting. The ambassador's views had only been revealed by his letters for these past years, and there was no telling what mad schemes he might propose. Anson smiled to himself; *mad* was an appropriate word. The Hervey family was known for its eccentricity, bordering on lunacy, and he'd had the devil's own job in keeping the Earl's younger brother, Captain the Honourable Augustus Hervey, in check.

Newcastle himself was the next to enter, deep in conversation with Ligonier, the head of the army, and they were followed a few moments later by Bute, holding the counterpart Northern Department to Egremont's Southern. Newcastle's personal secretary was the last man to enter the room, and he very deliberately confirmed that two soldiers were at their sentry posts beside the door. He nodded to the captain who was responsible for security – a young man from one of the guards regiments – who closed the door with a firm click of the latch.

***

'My lords, gentlemen. You'll be aware that the King has commanded that the inner cabinet and the military and naval chiefs should consider *the most effectual method of distressing and attacking the Spaniards,* his very own words. That is the sole purpose of this meeting although I'm willing to take other business if we have time. The elaborate security precautions are necessary for obvious reasons, as is the venue, away from the more public rooms in the Palace of Westminster. I'm sure you've all considered the matter privately over the past day, but I know the First Lord has thought of little else since it became evident that Spain was set on a course for war with our own country. It is useful to observe that His Majesty is not asking us *whether* an attack on Spanish interests is a wise course of action, he has already been persuaded of that, but is commanding us to propose the best means of doing so. The question, as I see it, is largely naval and military. What can we achieve with the forces at our disposal that will most hurt the Kingdom of Spain? We can all agree, I'm sure, that a direct attack on Spain itself, or on any of its European territories, risks entangling us in a long land campaign just at a time when we are attempting to bring this war to a close. However, we are fortunate that Spain is so dependent upon its empire, and the country would certainly be bankrupt without the silver coming across the Atlantic. They need to maintain their positions in the Caribbean in order to survive. We will therefore start with a consideration of Lord Anson's proposal for attacking Havana in the West Indies.'

Newcastle had a reputation for long-winded speeches but in this small, highly select group, he was positively succinct. Besides, he'd told nothing other than the truth when he said that Anson had been thinking of little else.

'Thank you, my Lord. Havana indeed, but we should first consider why Havana and not Cartagena or any of the other Spanish fortresses in the New World.'

Anson looked around at the other faces. He was sure of his men; he knew their motivations and their loyalties and he understood the limitations of their knowledge. Now that he was seated he felt at no disadvantage. His mind was as sharp as it had ever been, it was just his body that was betraying him, as surely as the sands of time slipped through the neck of an hour-glass. He had no illusions. This would in all probability be his last winter, and in any case, he couldn't stand the thought of another, not with his failing mobility. The coming campaign against Spain would be the last that he'd have a hand in directing.

He'd always doubted his country's ability to fight the combined arms of France and Spain, and his views were well known. Unlike France, Spain spent an almost equal amount on its navy as it did on its army. The Spanish navy, at least on paper, was far more dangerous than the French navy, more numerous and of better quality, ship-for-ship. It still smote upon his conscience that he'd been personally culpable in letting the Spanish spy Jorge Juan carry away the secrets of Britain's royal dockyards in 1749. The man had used his scientific credentials and his personal charm to probe deep into the mysteries of shipbuilding and then had persuaded some ninety of the best shipwrights – Catholics for the most part – to abscond to Spain. With that knowledge of shipyards and with French help in the design of new ships, Spain had transformed its fleet. And yet, and yet. The miracle had happened and the third Bourbon family pact had found the Spanish King's fleet still largely laid up. No rumour of war had stirred its laggard bureaucracy, and that superb fighting force was some six months away from being mobilised.

'All of the great Spanish ports lie to leeward of our own possessions. They're trapped in the Caribbean basin by our squadrons at Jamaica, Antigua and Barbados, and now by the French islands that have fallen to our arms. Their only way of bringing the wealth of the Indies out into the Atlantic is through the Florida Channel, and that way is dominated by Havana. Make no mistake, my lords, your navy commands the Windward Passage, the Mona Passage and the whole arc of the Lesser Antilles. If Spain can't command the Florida Channel, they might just as well leave the silver in the ground and the sugar on its canes, for they won't bring it back to Europe.'

Anson paused, looking for a reaction. He knew that these men had a good knowledge of the geography of the Caribbean Sea, but they'd probably never been exposed to such a concise explanation of how it could be used to sever the connection between Spain and its empire. This was geographical politics at its grandest, apportioning the wealth of the Indies in great sweeps of naval logic. Bute, cautious as ever, was the first to comment.

'The loss of Havana will distress King Charles more than any other action of ours, that's certain, but can it be done? These Spanish fortified ports are difficult to subdue, you only have to ask the shades of Admiral Vernon the truth of that, and General Wentworth. I'm sure it will require a considerable army as well as a vast number of ships, and meanwhile the Portuguese are asking for more regiments to be sent to repel the invasion that's certain to come. Is that not a better and less risky objective?'

Egremont looked sideways at Bute. He should have little to say, both the Caribbean and Portugal came within the Southern Department. Anson gazed at the wall, as though he had no opinion on the matter and it was left to Newcastle to press the point.

'Lord Ligonier, we've discussed this already, I know, but do you still believe the Portuguese can hold their border against Spain?'

Ligonier looked up for the first time in the meeting. His face always looked like a death-mask, but of late the skin had stretched even tighter across his skull, and now he had the timeless appearance of a man destined to live for ever, eking out the years in bloodless, cheerless, contemplation and scheming.

'With the seven thousand men, and the guns that we are already planning to send, yes, my Lord, I believe they can. There's a risk, for sure, but I don't believe it's a great one, and if it appears that the Spanish are overrunning our allies, then they can withdraw to the peninsula south of Torres Vedras and defend Lisbon until we can scrape together more men to send. If we adopt the First Lord's plan for Havana then I intend that most of the land force will come from the West Indies garrisons and the regiments that have been sent to Martinique. We'll also be raising militia regiments in the New England colonies and New York. Sure, I'll need to send some line regiments from England and Scotland and Ireland, to give the force some backbone, but not enough to prevent us reinforcing our army in Portugal.'

Newcastle nodded cautiously. He should have known that Anson and Ligonier would already have come to a common understanding, for it was certain that anything to be done against Spain would require a combined navy and army force. Ligonier probably thought this the last opportunity for glory for his army before the war came to an end.

'My Lord, if I may…'

Newcastle waved his hand at Anson with a resigned look on his face. He was a cautious man and for him this expedition looked like a reckless gamble, a colonial brawl that had no direct effect on Britain's position.

'As for the feasibility of taking Havana, can I assume that we are all aware of Admiral Knowles' report?'

Ligonier nodded emphatically while Newcastle and Egremont at least looked as though they were aware of the document's existence. Bute ignored the question, so perhaps he alone had no knowledge of it.

'When Knowles was governor of Jamaica he was invited to visit Havana, this would have been in 'fifty-six, during Ferdinand's reign and before King Charles raised the threat of Spain entering the war. It was a perfectly innocent visit but Knowles kept his eyes and ears open and wrote a report on Havana's defences. His conclusion is that it's perfectly feasible, either by landing to the east or to the west of the harbour entrance. The east is guarded by the Morro Castle and the west by the city walls. Either must be reduced by siege. In any case it's the navy's business to land the army and support it, but it's the army's business to take the place.'

Newcastle smiled through tight lips. Then Anson and Ligonier had come to an agreement, an unnatural alliance if ever there was one. He could see that Grenville wanted to speak.

'Excuse me, my Lord, but surely one of the objections to an attack on Havana has always been that a squadron has to approach from the west and beat up the coast past Cape San Antonio, thus giving the city days, perhaps weeks of notice of the attack. I think we all know how dangerous any delay can be in the tropics.'

Anson had to turn his head to face Grenville and the effort was evidently painful.

'That's true, and swift action is vital in the Caribbean. However, I've had a number of ships take the Old Bahama Straits in the past few years, the most recent only last month, and I expect a report daily. I'm satisfied that a squadron can make its way along the north coast of Cuba and that the trade wind will waft it on its way faster than any messenger can carry a warning to Havana.'

Grenville nodded towards Newcastle. It would be

untrue to say that the Speaker could sway the Commons, but he certainly understood its temperament better than anyone, and he appeared to be in favour. Newcastle caught the nod and smiled thinly.

'Well, gentlemen, our military and naval experts are convinced and I see no great practical objections to the project. I must say that I have personal reservations and would wish to see this war brought to a rapid conclusion rather than prolong the agony. However, we should put it to the vote. Lord Anson, perhaps you would go first.'

Anson said nothing but raised his finger and looked at the secretary to ensure that he'd seen it.

'Lord Ligonier?'

'Aye, my Lord.'

'Grenville?'

'It meets the King's demands. I say aye.'

Devonshire, Bute and Egremont all gave their assent, with greater or lesser enthusiasm.

'Well, I see that the Cabinet's will is for Havana and it appears that Lord Anson and Lord Ligonier are ready to let slip their dogs of war. I wouldn't want to present His Majesty with a divided opinion, so I'm content with the proposal. Let the record show a unanimous agreement.'

Newcastle waited while his secretary caught up.

'And now, Lord Egremont, you have another proposal to place before us. Manilla, is it not? An additional project, rather than an alternative, I understand.'

***

CHAPTER ONE

Guarda-Costa

Monday, Seventeenth of May 1762.
Dartmouth, at Sea, off Mole Saint Nicholas, Saint-Domingue.

'No sails in sight, sir, clear all around. I can see high land on the larboard beam.'

The tropical twilight was short and even after all these years it still caught Edward Carlisle by surprise. He'd been studying the sailing master's chart by the light of the lantern, and in the few minutes that he had his head down the sun had risen another degree or so and the horizon had become a hard, clear line separating the sea and the sky. That was the masthead lookout's cue to report what he saw. He heard the lookout's call but he still waited for the officer of the watch to make his report, for that was the correct way of things. The bell struck three times: ding-ding, ding, to signify that an hour-and-a-half of the morning watch had passed; it was half-past five and already the day was becoming warm.

David Wishart removed his hat and smiled happily, for it looked like turning into a brilliant day, and there was little formal restraint between him and his captain. Wishart had followed as a volunteer with benefit of neither rate nor rank when his uncle had been appointed first lieutenant into Carlisle's frigate *Fury*, and he'd been delighted when Carlisle rated him midshipman. After his uncle's death, he'd clung tightly to Carlisle as he moved from *Fury* into the larger frigate *Medina* and then to the glory of this fourth rate *Dartmouth*. At each move Wishart had improved his position until reaching his present commission as second lieutenant. Now he only had to hope that the war might last another few years and he could be promoted to master and commander and given his very own sloop.

'Good morning, sir. It's sunrise, the compass is correct

by observation, and the master's calculating the magnetic variation. We're under all plain sail steering sou'west-by-south with the high land behind Mole Saint Nicholas in sight east-sou'east three leagues. The trade wind's good and steady at east-by-north and there are no sails in sight. Oh, and the longboat's towing happily on a long painter on the larboard quarter.'

'Thank you, Mister Wishart. Keep a good lookout to the south and west, let me know the instant you sight anything.'

'Aye-aye sir.'

Carlisle glanced at the compass – more out of habit than through any need to check on Wishart's report – then he took the larboard ladder to the poop deck where he could walk in solitude and try to get one step ahead of the day. He spared a glance at the longboat to see that its mast was still rigged. He wouldn't normally have countenanced such a thing, but this steady, moderate trade wind offered few chances of the shrouds or the shroud plates being unduly strained, nor would it overrun the ship. He was still foggy from sleep, but after just a few paces his mind started to clear and he could think rationally. Something was afoot, that was for certain. The Jamaica Station had been unsettled since Admiral Holmes' untimely death in November; Captain Forrest had naturally stepped in but it was clear that it was only a temporary measure. Nobody was surprised when Commodore Sir Charles Douglas arrived from Antigua, bearing the King's commission as commander-in-chief, and news of a new campaign for the summer months. The pieces on the chess board were already in motion and *Dartmouth* was part of a strong squadron of eight ships-of-the-line commanded by Carlisle's old friend, Captain Augustus Hervey in the seventy-four-gun *Dragon*. Hervey's orders were to blockade Cape François where the Comte de Blénac's squadron had taken refuge. His squadron outnumbered the French, and it was an easy decision to keep his two frigates close at hand while dispatching *Dartmouth*, his smallest ship-of-the-line, to the west to watch the Windward Passage and the eastern end of the Old Bahama Straits.

Thus, *Dartmouth* was positioned at the crossroads of the Caribbean, and Mole Saint Nicholas had been designated as the rendezvous for the great mass of ships that were gathering for this secret expedition. Admiral Sir George Pocock had been sent from England, and Carlisle had heard that he'd touched at Barbados last month and he could be off Mole Saint Nicholas any day now. De Blénac at Cape François, the Spanish squadron at Havana and the potential for British battle squadrons, transports and storeships converging from Jamaica, Barbados and Martinique; it certainly warranted a good lookout.

Carlisle glanced at the commissioning pennant far above him at the main t'gallant masthead. With this quartering breeze his ship was being set to leeward, down into the Windward Passage from where he'd have a hard beat to regain his station. Well, they were still to the north of Cape François and he could wait until the change of the watch to wear ship and start beating to windward again. Hervey had given him scant directions as to where he should station himself, merely pointing out the obvious directions from where a Spanish or French squadron could arrive. The Spanish had a strong squadron at Havana, some twenty ships it was said, counting frigates and sloops as well as ships-of-the-line. It was a considerably greater force than Carlisle had seen when he visited that port back in December, before the rumours of war had become a reality. What would de Prado, the governor-general, do with that squadron? Carlisle remembered him as an indecisive man, more concerned with Spain's colonial politics than preparing for the coming war. The obvious use of twenty ships was to attempt an invasion of Jamaica, but if so, they had left it too late now that so much of Britain's naval and military might was converging on the Caribbean. And yet, if the Spanish fleet joined up with de Blénac's squadron, something could certainly be done. Hervey would

Old Bahama Straits

necessarily be keeping his ships to windward of Cape François, and he'd be cruising off Monte Cristi, leaving his two frigates to watch the French squadron. That was the correct disposition, but it did open the possibility of de Blénac escaping from the Cape and steering for the west towards Havana, before Hervey could be alerted. In that case, *Dartmouth* would have to stand in their way, to slow them down and allow Hervey to catch them, and for that he must be sure to stay to the north of Mole Saint Nicholas.

Carlisle walked to the poop deck rail and looked down to where Wishart was marking up his log.

'Mister Wishart. My compliments to the first lieutenant and the master, and I would like to wear ship on the change of the watch.'

'Aye-aye sir.'

It was clear then. The greatest risk was of the French escaping from Cape François and running to the west to meet the Spanish at Havana. They could take the Old Bahama Straits – although Carlisle thought that the navigational hazards made that unlikely – or they could run through the Windward Passage and follow the coast of Cuba to Cape San Antonio and thence to Havana. In either case he must stay to the north of Mole Saint Nicholas and not be set too far to the south or the west. Carlisle was content that he'd framed his ship's objectives for the day, and now he could smell his breakfast being prepared, its aroma wafting upwards through the air vents on the poop deck.

***

The sun had climbed far above the horizon when Carlisle came back on deck and the sticky heat was becoming oppressive. The sooner he brought the ship on to the wind to create a breeze across the deck, the sooner he'd feel comfortable, but he'd just heard seven bells struck and it was still half an hour to the change of the watch.

'What does the Mole bear now, Mister Wishart?'

'It's just become visible from the deck, sir, east three

leagues.'

Carlisle was growing anxious about his southing. He should have ordered the ship onto the wind half an hour ago, but he didn't want to bring the watch below on deck unnecessarily. He knew that most captains wouldn't have hesitated and in this instance they'd have been correct. He was already on the limit of his patrol area and another half an hour would take him two or three miles south. With this steady trade wind that would cost him four hours to recover. He could order Wishart to heave to, or to shorten sail, but either of those would betray his unease. No, he'd stand on until the watch changed.

He could see Mole Saint Nicholas for himself, and there wasn't a sail in sight. It seemed that the whole of the island of Hispaniola was holding its breath, waiting to see how Britain would deploy its naval might now that almost all of the island chain of the Lesser Antilles to windward had been taken. *Dartmouth* must be clearly visible from the shore and the fishermen and local traders were wisely choosing to stay in port.

Carlisle looked up again. The wind was steady, it hadn't shifted by a single point since the first light of dawn, and he could see a familiar figure standing precariously on the main t'gallant yard. Able Seaman Whittle, as ever was, fulfilling his self-appointed role of the ship's chief lookout. Carlisle and Whittle had both been raised on a plantation in Jamestown, Virginia, near the colonial capital of Williamsburg. Carlisle had been the elder by a good number of years and he was the plantation owner's second son. Whittle's father was an indentured servant who worked on the plantation, alongside the slaves. When the opportunity had arisen, Whittle had shaken the dust from his feet and followed Carlisle to sea. With that connection, he should have been rated petty officer by now, but Whittle could no more stick to a task than he could fly; he'd found a place where he was comfortable and he was determined to stick to it.

Whittle looked perfectly at ease there, with his arm wrapped around a halyard and his feet firmly on the yard. He was looking to leeward, across the ship's starboard quarter when Carlisle saw him stiffen.

'Sail ho! Sail on the starboard quarter. It looks like a schooner, sir.'

Whittle addressed himself directly to Carlisle, ignoring the officer of the watch. Only he could get away with that breach of the standing orders.

Carlisle picked up the speaking trumpet.

'What's its heading, Whittle?'

'Hard on the wind, larboard tack, sir. It's one of those Spanish schooners, I reckon, like we see off the coast sometimes. Main and fores'l, jib and stays'l, no tops'l.'

Whittle had good eyes, Carlisle knew, and if he thought it was a Spanish schooner then it probably was. It sounded like one of the Guarda-Costa vessels that had bedevilled relations with Spain for decades. They enforced the Spanish trading laws with vigour, although nowadays they rarely went to the lengths of cutting off a British master's ear, as it was alleged they had done to precipitate the last war. It must surely be heading for the north coast of Hispaniola; it would have hauled its wind by now if it was bound south through the Windward Passage. Most likely it was making for Cape François or the harbour at Mole Saint Nicholas. If it was the Cape, then the schooner would have to put in a tack soon, but it could just about fetch the Mole on its present course.

'Beat to quarters, Mister Wishart, we'll wear ship before we clear for action. I want to cut off that schooner before it can get to windward of us.'

'Hoist our colours, sir?'

'No, Mister Wishart, hoist a plain white flag if you please. Let's keep him guessing. A fourth rate here in the windward passage could easily be French, or Spanish for that matter, and perhaps we can lure him closer.'

Carlisle looked up briefly as the Bourbon white soared up to the mizzen masthead. French men-of-war flew white flags decorated with gold fleur-de-lis, but out at sea they typically flew a plain white flag to save the wear and tear on the gold thread, and in any case the gold embellishments could only be seen at close range.

The schooner certainly looked unconcerned and showed no signs of wanting to tack. Of course, being Spanish, it was more likely to make for the south side of the island, which was all in Spanish hands. Well they could whistle for it! *Dartmouth* was perfectly positioned to block that move, and also to block any attempt to make the Mole. What would that schooner's captain do when he realised that *Dartmouth* was British? The prudent thing would be to run back down to the Old Bahamas Straits, and hope that *Dartmouth* wouldn't follow. How to lure it closer?

'The ship is at quarters, sir, not yet cleared for action.'

That was Matthew Gresham, the first lieutenant, and Arthur Beazley the sailing master was at his side.

'Ready to wear ship whenever you like, sir, although I'd like to brail up the mizzen to favour that sprung mast.'

Carlisle ignored Beazley's concern about the mizzen mast; it was just one of those things that he had to bear in mind, like the creaking rudder and the garboard strakes that needed caulking and paying. *Dartmouth* was growing old before her time with so many years of hard campaigning. He stared at the schooner. How could he bring it close enough for *Dartmouth's* guns to settle the issue? The longboat gave him an idea.

'No, Mister Beazley. Heave to on the larboard tack, if you please. Mister Gresham, as soon as the ship is hove to, man the longboat with a boarding party; pistols and cutlasses and six of our best marksmen from among the marines, dressed as sailors. Mister Wishart is to command, and send him up here for a briefing. No guns to be run out, Mister Gresham, keep the gunports closed.'

Wishart had surrendered the deck to the sailing master and gone to his quarters on the lower gundeck, and it took half a minute for him to receive the message and appear again on the quarterdeck.

'Now, Mister Wishart. That schooner doesn't know who we are but the moment he suspects we're a British man-o'-war, my guess is that he'll tack and run for the west or maybe northwest to the Crooked Island Passage. As soon as you're underway you're to make sail towards him, looking as friendly as you can, so keep your weapons out of sight. Get to windward and when he tries to escape, hold him until I can come up. I expect he won't be able to tack or wear and man his guns at the same time, if he has any guns at all. Just pepper his decks, particularly the quarterdeck.'

Wishart grinned; this was just his kind of thing. He'd spent many a day in the longboat on duties of this kind, and he knew exactly what his captain needed.

Wishart and his crew tumbled into the longboat with the muskets passed quickly down, and in a matter of a couple of minutes the gaff mainsail had been hoisted and the boat shot out from under *Dartmouth's* stern. It must have looked innocent to the schooner, just a longboat from a friendly nation come to escort them into port; in any case, she stood on towards the Mole, with no sign of anxiety.

'Get underway on the starboard tack, Mister Beazley. Cross the schooner's bow, try to look as though you're on a regular patrol line.'

Carlisle watched the scene unfold, trying to imagine what the schooner captain was thinking. It looked as though he'd come from the north coast of Cuba, perhaps with dispatches, heading for Mole Saint Nicholas. Spain's entry into the war must seem unreal to a man who hadn't yet seen the enemy. He'd be expecting a French man-of-war off a French port, and that's exactly what he'd believe he'd found.

'Three miles now, sir, maybe two-and-a-half, and Mister Wishart is looking fair to getting to windward of him. Ah, he's tacking. He suspects us.'

'Bear away, Mister Beazley, after him! Never mind that mizzen.'

Wishart had seen the Spaniard's movements too. The

longboat was already on the starboard tack and on its present course it would intercept the schooner before it had run a mile. Carlisle drummed his fingers on the quarterdeck rail. All three ships were running towards the Old Bahama Straits now. There was no doubt that he'd come up with the schooner before the watch had ended, but that would take him too far to leeward, away from his designated patrol area. It all depended upon Wishart. Could he force the schooner off its course? The two vessels were close now, with barely a hundred yards between them and Carlisle could see that the marine muskets had started firing. It was too far and the longboat was too unstable a firing platform to expect any hits, but it might just deter the steersman. As Carlisle had hoped, the schooner was lying far over under the pressure of her sails and if she had any guns on deck they wouldn't be able to elevate far enough to fire at the longboat. There were puffs of smoke from the schooner now, some sort of resistance at least.

'Windward stuns'ls, do you think, Mister Beazley?'

Beazley looked aloft and glanced towards the quartermaster who gave an imperceptible nod.

'I was just thinking that sir. Yes, she'll carry them.'

'Then make it so, Mister Beazley. Let's come up with this gentleman before anyone gets hurt.'

The musketry was thick and fast now and there was a constant drift of powder smoke from both the schooner and the longboat. But Wishart was closing on the larger vessel and appeared to be drawing ahead. Suddenly, without any warning, the longboat's head came four points to windward. Wishart was using his greater speed to make a dash for the schooner. From *Dartmouth's* deck it all looked very serene. The longboat bumped against the schooner's side and held fast. As if by mutual consent and without any man of the longboats' crew setting foot on the schooner's deck, the firing ceased and the schooner's head flew up into the wind.

***

Old Bahama Straits

'Spanish guarda-costa *Santa Teresa* from Havana, sir, four three pounders and six swivels. I've examined her papers and her captain has what passes for a letter of marque from the governor-general, all regularly made out. As you guessed, she couldn't bring her guns to bear, not with the wind for'rard of her beam. No casualties on either side, sir.'

Wishart offered the ship's papers while he gazed at Carlisle with something like hero-worship; it had turned out just as his captain had predicted.

'They were carrying a Spanish sea officer, a lieutenant I believe, but I don't speak the language. He's in the boat now,' Wishart continued, gesturing over the side to where a uniformed figure sat rigid and self-conscious in the longboat's stern-sheets. There was something familiar about him, Carlisle thought.

'He was carrying dispatches but he cast them into the sea from the starboard side as I came on board to larboard, and they'd been well-weighted, I saw them sink.'

Carlisle looked disappointed. Dispatches from Havana would have made interesting reading.

'However, I looked into his cabin before I let him back in. I found a letter that looked as though it was an introduction to Monsieur de Blénac, and there was a map marked with the road from the Mole to Cape François. I'm sure that was his destination. He speaks passable French but very little English.'

Carlisle pondered for a moment. De Blénac could easily have sent a message to Havana from Cape François, and this was probably about the time that he'd expect a reply. He'd have warned that the British would likely be blockading the Cape, so an overland route from Mole Saint Nicholas would have appeared the safest way to send a reply. The best plan would be to send this man to Hervey and let him get what information he could. Hervey spoke fluent French and Spanish and had the imperious manner of one born to rule. If anyone could interrogate this Spaniard successfully, it was the Honourable Augustus

Hervey. Nevertheless, Carlisle knew that the first hours after capture were the most intimidating, and he was determined to ask a few questions himself.

'Very well, bring him on board. Mister Simmonds, meet us in my cabin and bring your notebook to record what passes between us, if you please. I know you don't speak Spanish, but just do your best. Mister Gresham, bring the other prisoners across, you can stow them in the hold for now, and put a prize crew into the schooner. When I've finished talking to our guest, Mister Wishart is to make all speed to Cape François, or to Monte Cristi, and deliver him to Captain Hervey.'

***

CHAPTER TWO

The Emissary

Monday, Seventeenth of May 1762.
Dartmouth, at Sea, off Mole Saint Nicholas, Saint-Domingue.

'You perhaps don't remember me, your Excellency. Capitán de Fragata Ramon de Laredo, on the staff of Almirante Gutierre de Hevia y Valdés, at your service.'

The Spanish commander – not a lieutenant as Wishart had assumed – bowed low with a gallant sweep of his plumed hat and looked expectantly at Carlisle. He was a tall man in his twenties, elegantly dressed in the blue and red Spanish naval uniform with his own black hair instead of an increasingly unfashionable white wig. He was trying to adopt the manner that he thought appropriate for the occasion, but succeeded only in looking anxious. He spoke in hesitant French and scanned Carlisle's face for some sign that he was understood. Carlisle paused a moment to assemble his reply in French, a language that he spoke well, then changed his mind. His Spanish had improved vastly in the previous year, under his wife's tutelage, and he decided to use that language instead; it would be a good opportunity to improve.

'Captain Edward Carlisle of His Britannic Majesty's Ship *Dartmouth*, at your service also. On the contrary, I remember you perfectly, we met at supper on board the admiral's flagship in Havana Bay last December.'

It was an inspired guess, but their visit to Havana had been short. There were only two entertainments, and just one of them was a naval affair. In any case the commander smiled, clearly pleased to have been remembered. He looked around with interest as though he expected to see someone else. It was Lady Chiara whom he sought, of course, all Spanish men looked for Chiara. It was her mediterranean looks, Carlisle supposed, and her aristocratic bearing. He was used to it, but he didn't choose to enlighten Laredo at the moment.

'May I present Lieutenant Gresham, my second-in-command?'

Gresham stepped forward and held out his hand in the English manner. They made an interesting contrast, the polished and patrician Spaniard and the rough-hewn English sea officer. Nobody could mistake the social gulf that separated the two men, and Laredo was clearly taken aback by Gresham's massive, intimidating presence. However, he was a Spanish nobleman, steeped in the traditions of courtesy, and he took Gresham's hand without any sign of reluctance.

'Now, would you accompany me to my cabin, Captain?'

Laredo had endured a week of rough company on board the guarda-costa. In fact the schooner's master had been not unlike Gresham: a competent seaman, but by Laredo's standards no gentleman. The cabin had boasted none of the comforts of a ship-of-the-line, and Laredo's servant had sweated blood to keep his uniform intact and presentable. The officers of the guarda-costa had little in common with those who held King Carlos' commission and it was no surprise to Laredo that he felt more at ease on board this enemy ship than he'd ever done on board the schooner.

***

Laredo visibly relaxed in the familiar surroundings of the great cabin of a man-of-war. He accepted a glass of wine and looked about with interest and appreciation. Carlisle's dining cabin was proportioned for a flag officer and indeed in times of peace the main purpose of these fifty-gun fourth rates was to accommodate a commander-in-chief on foreign stations. It was large, and the previous year Chiara had furnished it to suit her own tastes, and clearly it appealed to the Spanish sense of what was expected of a post-captain.

'I trust Lady Chiara is well, sir?'

'Certainly, but she has taken our son back to our home in Virginia, and sadly I must sail alone now. Are you married, Captain Laredo?'

Carlisle could see that Laredo very much appreciated being called *captain,* much as a British commander would.

'Yes sir, and my wife is in Havana; it suits her very well.'

There was an awkward pause. Both men knew that Carlisle could arrange for Laredo to be reunited with his wife by simply accepting his parole and landing him at Jamaica, from where he could take a passage back to Havana on a neutral ship, perhaps Dutch or Danish. If it took the easy route to the south of Cuba, he could be home in two weeks. Laredo glanced at Carlisle out of the corner of his eye. His captor looked as though he was inclined to be helpful; perhaps he could try for something even better.

'I wonder, sir, whether you might accept my parole until I am formally exchanged? You could send me in to the Mole under a flag of truce and I could look for a passage back to Havana. It would save you some inconvenience, I imagine.'

Carlisle had difficulty keeping a straight face. Laredo must take him for a fool to imagine that he'd land him at the very place that the guarda-costa was steering for. The dispatches may have gone over the side but it was certain that de Hevia hadn't sent a commander on this errand without telling him the content of those letters. It would be as good as delivering the dispatches to Cape François. Laredo had laid his cards on the table too soon, and he'd confirmed Carlisle's suspicions.

'I fear that's impossible without a better understanding of your mission, Captain. You were steering for the Mole and that is in the French part of Hispaniola, as you well know. My King, as you also know, has been at war with King Louis for some six years, and now we find that King Carlos has taken the side of his cousin. I would need to be certain that your errand to the Mole is not against Britain's interests.'

Another awkward pause. Carlisle could see that Laredo was considering how much he'd need to reveal in order to be granted parole. Surely he must realise that landing at the

Mole was out of the question, but he'd still prefer to go to Jamaica under parole than as a confined prisoner-of-war. There was nothing that he could do to salvage his mission, but he could still negotiate an early return to Havana. The alternative was to be sent to England to wait for the wheels of bureaucracy to turn sufficiently to match him against an equivalent British captive. Quite possibly – no, probably – that wouldn't happen until the war ended. That would be an important factor for Laredo but not the only one. Those dispatches would never reach de Blénac and with the difficulty of communicating between Havana and Cape François, it was almost certain that there was no duplicate being sent by another route. No, Laredo was de Hevia's only hope of coordinating his actions with the French squadron, so he must find a way of being put ashore. Carlisle waited patiently for the Spaniard to come to the same conclusion.

'Perhaps I could speak to you privately, sir?'

Laredo looked sideways towards Simmonds who was faithfully attempting to record the important points of the conversation, although he didn't understand one word in ten. His meaning was evident but Carlisle was determined that he'd have to ask explicitly for each concession.

'You would find it easier to speak without your words being recorded, I gather?'

Laredo looked uneasy for the first time since the interview started. Simmonds could see what Carlisle was trying to do and he stopped writing and rested his quill upon the inkpot. It was a clear signal that it was possible that the conversation could be unrecorded, but it also showed that Simmonds could start writing again at any moment. Laredo's face showed his emotions. As he hesitated a shaft of sunlight from the great stern windows caught the polished pewter inkpot and the ship's motion sent its reflection dancing across the cabin to rest momentarily upon the Spaniard's face. He jerked his head to the side in irritation, but that seemed to be the cue that he needed, and he shifted slightly so that he could look at Carlisle without being blinded.

'I believe, sir, that we can achieve a better understanding if we are alone.'

Carlisle studied Laredo as the seconds crept by. How much was the Spaniard prepared to reveal? Almost certainly it would be a mixture of truth and lies, but that was to be expected. He regretted speaking to Laredo in Spanish, it put him at a disadvantage and French might have been better, but what was done couldn't be undone, and at least it gave him an opportunity to ask the Spaniard to repeat himself. He'd reserve that tactic until he needed it.

'Very well. Mister Simmonds, would you leave us please?'

Simmonds gathered up his notebook, his inkpot and his quill and with a bow left the cabin. It was strangely quiet now they were alone. The usual shipboard sounds were muffled by the two bulkheads between this great cabin and the quarterdeck, and the poop deck above their heads was little frequented by the watch on deck. Carlisle leaned back in his chair as though he cared little for what Laredo had to say.

'My mission, sir, was to the commander of the French squadron at Cape François, the Comte de Blénac, to bring a letter from Admiral de Hevia…'

Laredo looked in vain for some sign that Carlisle was interested in this information, but Carlisle just watched his face impassively.

'…however, I regret that I have no knowledge of the contents of the letter.'

Carlisle could see that Laredo hardly expected to be believed, and he shook his head slowly.

'If that is all that you are prepared to tell me, Captain Laredo, then I'll recall my clerk and we can conclude this discussion. You can be my guest until I can find a means of sending you to Jamaica, or directly to England if we should be so fortunate as to meet a homeward bound convoy.'

Laredo pursed his lips and the fingers of his right hand

played nervously on the carved arm of his chair. He desperately wanted to be sent home to Havana; he had no desire to sit out this promising war in England, not when de Hevia's magnificent Barlovento Squadron was poised to sweep the British from the Caribbean. He knew all about Admiral Rodney and the fall of Martinique, but he also knew that the British had over-extended themselves and would find it difficult to concentrate their ships. Admiral de Hevia's squadron could scythe through the fragmented British force like a knife through butter, and if de Blénac could be persuaded to put his squadron under de Hevia's command, then there was no force on this side of the Atlantic that could stand before them. With Spain's entry into the war, the British fleet must surely concentrate in home waters to defend against a possible invasion, the admiral had been most positive on that point. Martinique would be the high point of British ambition in the Caribbean, and if they wanted to keep Jamaica they would have to bring what ships they had back to Port Royal. Yet, the Barlovento Squadron's first duty was to defend Havana, and Admiral de Hevia had no authority to use it in any other way until it was certain that Havana was safe. He'd therefore proposed a concentration of the Spanish and French squadrons at Havana, with the promise of opening up the superb Spanish shipyard facilities to de Blénac. Then, when it was clear that the British had no ambitions to attack the city, they would be free to choose their targets from among the enemy's possessions now scattered across the Caribbean. That was the message that he'd been carrying to de Blénac, and his own ambitions rested on it being properly understood. That was why he'd been sent and not a lieutenant, so that he could present his master's proposal in fluent French and with the force that it deserved. He thought rapidly for a plausible alternative story.

'You will grant my parole and send me to Saint-Domingue if I tell you the contents of the letter, sir?'

Carlisle resisted a smile. The Spaniard would certainly

not reveal his master's plan and then present that same plan to de Blénac, it would make no sense. Well, whatever he was about to hear could be discarded, and that at least would have some value.

'Oh, Captain Laredo,' he said shaking his head sadly, 'you surely don't believe that I'll give you parole to take your message to Monsieur de Blénac. No, I can't do that. What I can do is send you back to Port Royal with a recommendation to my own commander-in-chief that you be given parole to return to Havana, to await a formal exchange when your country is fortunate enough to be in possession of a British officer of equivalent rank. That is all that I can do.'

Laredo nodded in understanding. He'd expected nothing more, for it was generally accepted that parole to return to one's own territory could only be granted by the most senior officer on the station. Yet it was quite normally done, and a recommendation would almost guarantee it. He'd spin whatever tale this Captain Carlisle wanted to hear and then await events.

'Well, sir, I will tell you and trust that you will keep your side of the bargain. Admiral de Hevia proposes that he will take the Barlovento Squadron and meet de Blénac at Cape François. From there they will determine how best to meet Admiral Rodney's squadron and defeat it in battle. That will leave the rest of the British possessions defenceless: Jamaica was mentioned, and Barbados and Antigua. I was to impress upon Monsieur de Blénac the absolute necessity for combining our forces.'

Laredo watched Carlisle's face carefully. The plan was believable and in many ways it was superior to the real plan, except that no Spanish admiral could possibly remove his ships from Havana until it was clear that the city was not threatened. Did Carlisle know that? He'd spent years in the Caribbean, he'd been to Havana, so perhaps he had some ideas of the constraints upon the Barlovento Squadron's employment.

Carlisle showed no emotion but noted with interest that Laredo knew nothing of the great expedition that was underway.

'Forgive me, Captain Laredo, but how does Admiral de Hevia propose to reach Cape François?'

Laredo looked directly at Carlisle and answered quickly.

'Through the Florida Channel then hard on the wind into the Atlantic until he can weather the Caicos Islands on a single board.'

Carlisle nodded thoughtfully. The Spaniard was obviously lying, the question was how much of it he could discard. There wasn't the slightest question of de Hevia bringing his squadron out of the Caribbean entirely, even if he felt that he could leave Havana unprotected. And yet, the story about concentrating the Spanish and French squadrons sounded true, just not at Cape François.

'Is that all you have to tell me, Captain Laredo?'

'That is all, sir. There were some details about the facilities at Havana, but otherwise you have heard the whole plan.'

'Very well, then I'll keep my part of the bargain and recommend that you are granted parole...'

He was interrupted by a knock on the door.

'Yes, Mister Young,' he said to the midshipman who stood at the door.

'Mister Gresham's respects, sir. The lookout has sighted sails to the northeast. It looks like a substantial squadron.'

The clerk had slipped quietly into the cabin behind the midshipman. It was certain that Carlisle would want to go on deck and the confidential meeting with the Spaniard would have to be terminated.

'Very well. Ah, there's Mister Simmonds. Look after Captain Laredo, would you? He's probably hungry and we can think about a berth later.'

Carlisle bowed to Laredo and followed Young out of the cabin. The game of bluff with the Spaniard would have to wait until he knew whose ships these were. It could be de

Old Bahama Straits

Blénac having made his escape from Cape François, and in that case he'd likely be steering to pass Cuba south-about. If so, Hervey should be close on his heels, and *Dartmouth's* role was clear: he'd have to engage the French squadron, to delay them for as long as possible to allow Hervey to catch them. And yet, the one part of Laredo's story that he believed, was that he expected to find de Blénac still at Cape François. Perhaps it wasn't the French.

***

'Whittle's at the masthead. Last report was a pair of frigates with at least one of the line following. Beat to quarters, sir?'

The first lieutenant was eager for action, as always, but Carlisle was wary of turning the hands up so soon after they'd been dismissed, not unless it was necessary. Besides, he had a feeling about this squadron. Laredo certainly knew something that he wasn't revealing, and he wasn't expecting to find the French at sea.

'I think not, Mister Gresham. Let's see who these fellows are first.'

'Deck there! Two frigates for sure and it looks like a three-decker following. I can see sails beyond the three-decker, lots of them.'

Carlisle glanced at Gresham. A three-decker. De Blénac had nothing so large in his squadron. In fact, first and second rate ships rarely left home waters; they were kept in the main battle fleets to provide the heavyweight punch that shattered enemy lines of battle. Carlisle had heard that Admiral Pocock was flying his flag in the ninety-gun *Namur*, but he'd hardly believed it. Of course, Whittle could be wrong.

'Get underway, Mister Beazley, starboard tack, as close as she'll lie.'

They were closing at a furious rate now, perhaps a mile in every four minutes, and the reports came in thick and fast. A three-decker for certain, British probably.

'Deck there! She's flying a blue ensign at the main t'gallant masthead.'

Gresham rubbed his hands in anticipation.

'An admiral of the blue. Who can that be, and in a second rate to boot? In any case, that'll be seventeen guns, sir. I'll clear away the starboard twelve pounder battery.'

'Sir George Pocock, Mister Gresham, if I'm not mistaken. He was made a Knight Companion of the Bath earlier this year and he was moved up the flag list in the last general promotions.'

'Then Rodney must have been superseded on the Leeward Islands.'

'I think not. Pocock is commander of a special operation, to my understanding, although he's likely robbed Rodney of most of his ships. What that special operation is, I imagine we'll be told in proper time.'

'Well, it can't be Havana, that's for certain. The admiral would have carried the trade wind straight from Martinique to Jamaica if that was the case, and he'd be stretching away for Cape San Antonio by now.'

Carlisle made no comment. Gresham was right, of course, and it was an easy passage to the west corner of Cuba with the trade winds. From there it was a stiff beat along the Cuban coast to Havana, but at least the current would be in their favour. The problem was that it gave the garrison and fleet at Havana days or weeks of notice that an attack was on its way. That was why Havana had been secure from attack these past two centuries. The other way was to run along the north coast of Cuba, the Old Bahama Straits, but by common understanding it was no place for a great invasion fleet. *Dartmouth* had almost been lost on its treacherous reefs and shoals just five months before, and it was hard to imagine the difficulties of bringing a huge fleet – a battle squadron, transports and storeships – through those dangerous waters. And yet… Carlisle snapped out of his reverie. Probably they were bound for one of the places on the great island of Hispaniola; they were all legitimate targets now that Spain had joined the war.

'Mister Beazley, lay me under *Namur's* lee, if you please.'

***

CHAPTER THREE

Flagship

Monday, Seventeenth of May 1762.
Namur, at Sea, off Mole Saint Nicholas, Saint-Domingue.

Carlisle studied *Namur's* immense bulk – as vast as a Norman cathedral – while his boat's crew rowed him across. Massive, imposing, it was an unequivocal statement of Britain's power and prestige, a fortress fit for a great King, and armed and accoutred to impose the sovereign's will anywhere that salt water flowed. Pocock's flagship was a ship-of-the-line, as was *Dartmouth*, and when the broadsheet-reading public studied the balance of naval power, they saw only the headline figures with first, second, third and fourth rates all lumped together. That was the fundamental arithmetic of the line of battle. Yet, the most casual glance told a more complex story. *Namur* carried her guns on three decks, and the largest, her thirty-two pounders on the lower deck that fired a ball the size of a man's head, far eclipsed *Dartmouth's* twenty-fours. In a single broadside *Namur* could hurl eight hundred and forty-two pounds of solid cast iron shot at an enemy while *Dartmouth's* broadside weight was less than half of that. Furthermore, those three gun decks were supported by knees, frames and planking that were far heavier than *Dartmouth's*. *Namur* could give and receive punishment that would reduce a fifty-gun fourth rate to matchwood in minutes. That was why ships such as Carlisle's had been quietly excluded from the line of battle since the beginning of this war. *Namur* had fought at Rochefort, Louisbourg, Lagos, Quiberon Bay and Belle Isle while *Dartmouth* had been used as a cruiser, an oversize frigate in effect, destroying the enemy's commerce and protecting Britain's own, and the myriad of other tasks that could best be performed by something less than a third rate. Approaching Pocock's flagship was a humbling experience

Old Bahama Straits

for the captain of a fourth rate.

Carlisle was met at the entry-port by John Harrison who combined the duties of *Namur's* captain and Pocock's flag captain in one person. He hadn't expected that reception; Harrison's place was surely on the quarterdeck when this large mass of shipping was manoeuvering in a place such as the Windward Passage. Yet there was something different about *Namur* that Carlisle couldn't quite put his finger on. It was well-run, as one would expect of an admiral's flagship, but further than that it appeared to operate in an atmosphere of silence and calm. Carlisle had heard no bellowed orders, no cursing and no starting. He took pride in his own ship's quiet businesslike manner, but it was nothing compared with *Namur*.

'You have a guest, I see.'

Harrison replied in kind to Laredo's elaborate bow and made a courteous welcome in French while Carlisle made the introduction.

'Captain Laredo can be entertained by one of my lieutenants while you meet the admiral, he won't want a Spaniard to hear your conversation. Mister Melksham, if you please.'

The lieutenant took charge of Laredo and smoothly manoeuvred him away from the entry port. No further instructions were given, and evidently that was the way the ship worked. Harrison led the way aft along the middle gun deck towards the broad stairs that led up through the main hatch to the upper gun deck and thence to the quarterdeck.

'Do you know the admiral?'

'I regret I've never had the pleasure. I haven't been outside the Americas and the Mediterranean this whole war.'

'Ah, well you're not alone. He's been in the East Indies since the start of the war and has only come home now that the French have been hustled out of that part of the world. I was with him all that time and I like him, and now I find that I've grown unfamiliar with these waters. You know the

Caribbean well, I believe.'

'Yes, I've spent a fair amount of time on both the Leeward Islands and Jamaica stations.'

Carlisle didn't elaborate on that; he wanted to know more about this great expedition before he started offering advice that might not be appreciated.

'Well, you'll excuse our disarray, I trust; we have Lord Albemarle and his staff on board. Have you noticed how many people these soldiers need to plan a campaign? The same thing that would be done in the navy by a flag officer, his secretary and a captain requires cohorts of brigadier-generals, colonels and majors. All we have left is the secretary's office. By the way, you can expect the admiral to quiz you pretty hard. You've been as far west as the Gulf of Mexico and Havana, I'm told.'

Now was there something in Harrison's manner when he mentioned Havana? Carlisle noticed that he turned his face away as though he didn't want Carlisle to read anything in it.

'Yes, I went to Havana by way of the Old Bahama Straits in December then on to the Gulf of Mexico and Honduras. I believe I'm the last King's officer to be welcomed in the Spanish colonies before the Dons joined the war.'

Harrison nodded thoughtfully.

'You'll find the admiral easy-tempered I'm sure, but just don't bring Rodney into the conversation, if you can help it.'

Carlisle looked quizzically at Harrison. Admiral Rodney had just taken Martinique and was the man of the hour. In what way had he crossed swords with Pocock?

Harrison smiled grimly, correctly interpreting Carlisle's glance.

'You haven't heard? It appears that Rodney misunderstood – I think that's the most generous interpretation – Anson's letter that must have reached him at least a month ago. Instead of concentrating his forces to join this expedition he's scattered them to the four winds:

Douglas to Jamaica, Swanton to cruise the Spanish main and his frigates gone God knows where. The admiral has less than half the number of men-o'-war that he expected and barely sufficient for his needs. If de Blénac makes a rendezvous with the Spanish squadron based at Havana, we'll be hard pressed to meet them on an equal footing. It's little wonder that Rodney should have found himself too unwell – a fever he said – to make his report to Pocock in person. He sent his regrets and respects from Saint-Pierre where he's withdrawn to recuperate, but he unwisely left his flagship at the anchorage at Fort Royal; you'll see *Marlborough* in the rear of the squadron.'

Harrison waved airily towards the east where the rest of the squadron and the invasion fleet were all coming to the wind in obedience to *Namur's* movements. He realised that his expression was betraying his emotions and quickly turned the malicious grin, that accompanied the thought of Rodney's flagship being seized, into a benign smile. Evidently there was no love lost between Pocock's followers and Admiral Rodney.

'Well, be that as it may, here we are with a fine great gathering of His Majesty's sea and land forces, and I'll leave it to Sir George to tell you what's to be done with them, if he so chooses.'

Carlisle tried to slow their pace. He had questions that he urgently wanted to put to Harrison before he should be involved with the admiral. However, it was too late to ask as they were quickly before the door of the secretary's office. The marine sentry saluted and before Carlisle could utter another word they were in the presence of Sir George himself.

***

Harrison must have been told to bring Carlisle straight into the office, for they found the admiral standing beside the quarter gallery dictating a letter to his secretary. He stopped speaking abruptly when the door opened.

'Well, you can add the salutations. See that it's addressed

to Lord Anson himself and not to Clevland. He'll read it in any case but it's not for the eyes of any of the other commissioners.'

Carlisle wondered briefly what Pocock was writing that wasn't fit for the other members of the Admiralty Board to see. Did it concern Rodney and his alleged misinterpretation of his orders? Whatever it was, it was none of his business, but still…

'Ah, Captain Carlisle, it's good to meet you at last. I fell in with Hervey off Monte Christi and he told me that you were guarding the Windward Passage. Now I find that you have a prize. Coffee? We rarely serve anything stronger before dinner, isn't that right, Harrison? Ignore the noise from the other side of the partition, it's only the soldiers chewing over their disembarkation plans. It's extraordinary that they have anything to talk about as most of 'em don't know where in the world we're heading. Now what do you have to report?'

Sir George was an energetic man, it seemed, and Harrison made no attempt to answer the question that had been flung at him in the course of the monologue. However, Pocock evidently expected a reply from Carlisle.

'It's been quiet, Sir George. A few fishermen, but they keep close inshore and the usual traffic seems to be rather shy of coming out. All we've seen is this guarda-costa schooner that came through the Old Bahama Straits making for the Mole. There was a Spanish officer on board, Commander Laredo, one of Admiral de Hevia's staff. He was carrying dispatches for de Blénac at the Cape, but he threw them overboard as soon as it was evident that they'd otherwise be captured. I met the commander when I was in Havana last year, when I supped with Admiral de Hevia, so we were already acquainted.'

Pocock looked thoughtful as he stared out through the quarter gallery to the sparkling sea beyond.

'Yes, Havana, and you've met de Hevia, we'll talk more of that in a moment. Did this commander tell you anything?

He's rather too elevated for a mere courier, don't you think? Where is he now?'

'Lieutenant Melksham is entertaining him, Sir George,' Harrison replied before Carlisle could speak.

'Well I hope he's pouring wine down his throat. Now, Carlisle?'

'I've already questioned him, sir, as much as I could. He was to go overland to the Cape with his dispatches and then return to the Mole and take the Guarda-Costa back to Havana. He has a wife there, sir, and he's desperately keen to avoid spending what he sees as a promising war in England.'

'Did you offer him anything, Carlisle? Anything you can't retract?'

'I promised him that I would recommend to you that he be given parole to return to Havana in advance of a prisoner exchange, if he told me what he knew. He's intelligent enough, and he knows full well that you aren't bound by the agreement. It seems that he's reserved the best of his information for you, Sir George.'

Pocock smiled at that. It was perfectly normal for even the most incorruptible man to trade information for an easing of the conditions of his captivity. Any man in Laredo's position would judiciously dole out what he knew until he had a cast-iron commitment to his early release. He'd try to mislead his captors, of course, but Pocock's secretary was a master of interrogation, and by asking the same question in many forms he could usually smell a lie.

'According to Laredo, de Hevia proposes to bring his squadron from Havana, through the Florida Channel and thence down to Cape François to affect a combination with de Blénac. They would then descend upon the Leeward Islands, sweeping all before them and restore the French possessions.'

Pocock barked out a laugh and Harrison smiled in response.

'You believe that Carlisle?'

'Not in the slightest, sir. The Barlovento Squadron's overriding purpose is to protect Havana. The governor-general will never release it until he's certain that his city is not under threat. De Hevia might dream of one day descending upon the Antilles, but I've met him, and he's realistic enough to know that he won't be straying far from Havana this year.'

'Then we know what was not in those orders, that's a start. Captain Harrison, would you be so good as to tell my secretary that I'll want him to speak to the Spaniard? He has some French, I assume, Carlisle.'

'Yes, Sir George, he speaks good French but barely any English.'

'Excellent. Then the secretary is to finish that letter first; he can't entrust that to a clerk. Just check that the sentry is standing clear of the door, would you, and the servants can stay out of the cabin until I've finished with Captain Carlisle.'

Harrison bowed and withdrew. He was evidently used to his admiral's way of doing business and showed no resentment at being dismissed. Pocock paced a few steps to the office's tiny window. With *Namur* lying to the nor'easterly trade wind the whole of his command was out of sight, and the horizon was uninterrupted except for *Dartmouth* and the guarda-costa.

'I see you're keeping your prize tight under your lee, Captain Carlisle. Quite right too, you weren't under my orders when you took her and it's Sir James who'll benefit from the flag officer's eighth. Still, it's small beer compared with what I hope we'll take over the next few months.'

Pocock looked speculatively at Carlisle, as though he was trying to decide what his next words would be. He looked again at *Dartmouth* and her prize and at that moment *Namur's* head fell away from the wind, the great ship rolled alarmingly and a portion of Pocock's armada came into sight. That appeared to make up his mind.

'Tell me Captain Carlisle, what do you think is the

objective of this great armament?' He swept his hand in an arc to the forward part of the ship, where the bulk of his command was still invisible, 'What's brought these two hundred-odd ships and Lord Albemarle's army to this place?'

Pocock now looked more intently at Carlisle, as though he was trying to peer into his mind. Carlisle could see that it was important to Pocock that he knew whether his secrets had been kept, and he kept any expression from his face as he answered.

'When I left Port Royal the smart money was being placed on Saint-Domingue as a prelude to taking Santo Domingo from the Spanish and occupying the whole of Hispaniola. It appears that you're well positioned for a landing at the Mole or Port-au-Prince, Sir George…'

'Yes, yes, that's what everyone is saying. But you, Carlisle, what do *you* think?'

Carlisle paused for a moment. Why would an admiral of the blue be so interested in what a mere captain of a fourth rate had to say? He thought he knew the answer, and something that Harrison said about Havana came back to him.

'France would be pressing for peace now if it were not for Spain joining the war, and our own parliament must surely be hoping for an early resumption of talks. I expect King Louis has great hopes for his cousin's aid in taking back some of his lost territory before the negotiations. Invading Saint-Domingue will make little difference to the French, and Santo Domingo is not vital to Spain. I think – I believe – that a bolder blow against Spain alone would persuade Louis that there's no aid to be expected from that quarter.'

'Very good, Carlisle, but where? Where would you strike against Spain.'

'Havana, Sir George,' Carlisle looked for a reaction from the admiral and seeing none he plunged on, 'that's where their Barlovento Squadron is kept and it guards the route for the Flota to bring the wealth of the Indies back to Spain. If they can't pass through the Florida Channel then they must take the Windward Passage, the Mona Passage or any of the gaps through the Lesser Antilles, and we command all of those.'

'Then why, Captain Carlisle, have I not sailed straight from Martinique for the Yucatan Channel? Why have I taken this wild detour to the north?'

Pocock continued staring at Carlisle, trying to draw him out, as though in justification of some decision that he'd already made.

'The Old Bahama Straits, Sir George…'

'Exactly!'

Pocock smashed his palm down upon the table, and the office rang with the sound of it. There was a pause in the chatter from the great cabin, a silence of a half-dozen heartbeats, then it set off again, like a hive full of bees.

'And that's why I'm confiding in you, Carlisle. Only a handful of my closest staff know our destination, and even fewer know the route that we'll take to get there. Lord Anson told me that you navigated the Straits at the end of last year, and he gave me copies of your track with your soundings and sketches. I'd hoped to find you today and here you are. Oh, I'd have sent a frigate to scout the way if you weren't here, but now I can send *Dartmouth*. What do you think?'

Carlisle paused again, casting his mind back to that near-disastrous passage. If he hadn't been chasing a French convoy he'd have paid more heed to his ship's safety, and he'd never have come so close to grounding. Yes, this great fleet could make the passage, given the right preparation and a modest amount of luck.

'It could be done, Sir George, with markers to show the way past the worst obstructions. Once you've passed Salt Cay it's all plain sailing.'

'And that, Captain Carlisle, is where you come into my plans, unless this Commander Laredo tells my secretary something to alter my mind. I'll send *Namur's* carpenter and bosun across to your guarda-cost to do an initial survey and valuation, then I'll take her into service to be *Dartmouth's* tender. It'll save all that fuss with the prize court. Do you have a lieutenant that you can trust to command her for a few months?'

This was wonderful news, and evidently Pocock knew it as well. A condemned prize without the formality and expense of a prize court. He remembered Wishart's command of a schooner and a brig just a few months ago; he'd do the job admirably.

'Yes, Sir George. I'd like to keep my first lieutenant in *Dartmouth*, but my second has done this kind of thing before.'

'Good. He'll get no commission, you can just locally appoint him to the prize. Are you happy with that?'

This was an important point. The whole business of condemning prizes, buying them into the service and appointing a captain was bound up with naval custom and legal procedure. Pocock was imperiously setting aside the *Regulations and Instructions* and it carried a risk that their Lordships might not, in the end, approve. It was important that he obtained Carlisle's agreement because he was the nearest thing to an absolute owner of the guarda-costa. Nevertheless, Pocock's scheme cut through a whole raft of inconveniences. Carlisle nodded his assent.

'Then let's start this expedition in motion. Remember, you're to speak to nobody about this until Havana is in sight. Ah, here's my secretary.'

The secretary had opened the door noiselessly and glided across the office as though any sound at all would give away his master's secrets. It was absurd with the hubbub from the great cabin drowning out the ship's normal noises. He smiled through thin bloodless lips.

'Nothing of any value, Sir George. In my opinion, and based on the Spanish officer's insistence that de Hevia is offering to come to the Cape, the lost dispatches must propose the opposite. I believe Laredo's mission was to invite de Blénac to join de Hevia at Havana. There's nothing more to be got from him.'

'Then he's forfeited his chance of parole. You can consign him to the brig that's running down to Port Royal in a couple of days. What do you think of this story of his, Carlisle?'

'The Barlovento Squadron won't move from Havana until de Prado is convinced that there's no threat to the city. That was the sense that I had from my visit in December.'

Carlisle didn't add that much of that had come from his old friend Don Alonso, now the governor of Guatemala, who acknowledged no fealty to de Prado.

'Then you understand perfectly, Carlisle. Now, I want you gone before sunset, taking the schooner with you. Try to get as far as Salt Cay but not beyond, I don't want Havana to be warned that something's afoot. In any case you're to be back here by the twenty-eighth of this month to tell me if the Straits are passable.'

***

CHAPTER FOUR

A Shipless Sea

Tuesday, Eighteenth of May 1762.
Dartmouth, at Sea, off Ragged Island, The Old Bahama Straits.

Dartmouth and the prize schooner spread their wings to the blessed trade wind and with the current flowing strong and steady under their keels, they sped away to the nor'west, as though they were trying to race the sun to the horizon. All through that night they had no sight of another vessel and no sight of the shore; it was as though they were alone on a vast ocean rather than hurrying towards one of the narrowest and most dangerous straits in the world. When the sun rose on the Tuesday morning it hardly helped them. The high land of Cuba was in sight from the masthead, but nothing could be seen of the great Bahama Bank and its myriad of islands to starboard. Still, the traverse board showed the ship's speed through the water overnight, and Beazley had diligently recorded the current that they'd found when *Dartmouth* came this way in December. That gave them a good idea of their longitude and as the sun inched towards noon, Beazley was ready to fix their latitude. He stood on the poop deck, surrounded by a pack of young gentlemen, each clutching his octant and earnestly copying the sailing master's motions.

The sun's altitude increased, it paused at its zenith, then, before it started on its long journey back towards the horizon, the sailing master muttered '*noon it is,*' and lowered his octant to study the scale. He made some cryptic marks in his notebook then withdrew to his cabin abaft the wheel where he kept his precious charts. In five minutes he reappeared, and seeing Carlisle beside the binnacle, he removed his hat.

'Noon, sir. By dead reckoning and the meridian passage, Ragged Island's thirteen leagues on the starboard beam and the coast of Cuba is eight leagues to larboard. The nearest shoal water is Santo Domingo Cay five leagues to starboard and we've thirty-three leagues to run to Green Island where the true Straits start. The log's showing ten knots and we haven't had a cast of the lead line this four-and-twenty hours.'

'Very well, Mister Beazley. You may make it so.'

Beazley nodded to the mate of the watch. The marine sentry was already on the fo'c'sle with his hand on the bell-rope and at the first stroke of eight bells the watch below started pouring onto the deck to relieve their eager mates who were anxious for their dinner.

Carlisle waited for the last bell; it was always undignified to try to compete with the clamour.

'Just remind me, Mister Beazley, how far from Green Island to Santa Maria Island?'

'Twenty-eight leagues, sir.'

'And what speed over the ground are we making?'

Beazley scratched his head. This was always a difficult question and it exposed the fragility of his estimated position. His noon sight – the *meridian passage*, as it was known – told him how far the ship was off the coast of Cuba but it had nothing to say about their progress along this essentially east-west passage. He'd had a good departure fix from Cape Mays the previous evening but he couldn't directly measure the current, not without anchoring or putting down a boat. He had only his previous experience and the testimony of other sailing masters to help him. That was all very well, but the shoal water – the unmarked shoal water – was only five leagues to starboard, and from now the channel narrowed until at Green Island it was just three leagues broad with still no reliable marks to fix a ship's position.

'Well, sir, we found two knots here back in December but two-and-a-half in the Straits proper. I reckon we've made twelve knots. If this trade wind holds we'll be off Green Island at sunset.'

Old Bahama Straits

'Thank you, Mister Beazley. Heave to, if you please. I don't want to be off Green Island until sunrise tomorrow. We can employ that time by fixing the position of Santo Domingo Cay. Make the signal for Mister Wishart to come aboard, if you please; I fancy this is a task for something less than a ship-o'-the-line, don't you think?'

Beazley smiled broadly.

'Oh yes, sir, without a doubt. And it'll be of great assistance to know that cay's position, for future needs. Can I suggest that I go into the schooner, sir, if this is important?'

Carlisle kept a straight face. It was evident that Beazley was fishing for information. Carlisle had revealed nothing of Pocock's plans and had so far made no mention at all of Havana. As far as his officers were concerned *Dartmouth* could be heading for Florida or the Gulf of Mexico. Yet they were fast reaching the point where he could get the best from his senior officers if they knew why he was interested in this area. He knew that Beazley was quite competent to take the ship through the Straits at night in this fine weather, having done so only a few months ago, and it was only natural that he was wondering why they were apparently dawdling. He watched the workings of Beazley's face and out of the corner of his eye he saw the first lieutenant loitering within earshot, eager to pick up any crumbs of information. He made a snap decision and gestured to Gresham and Beazley.

'I see Mister Hooper has the watch. Would you join me in my cabin? Bring your chart of the Straits, if you please, Mister Beazley.'

***

Dartmouth lay easily to the nor'easterly trade wind, her bows rising and falling as she butted against the long swell. They were in deep water here but nevertheless they could hear, over the sounds of a working ship, the call of the leadsman.

'No bottom, sir, no bottom on this line.'

'He's a keen one, that Mister Hooper, he knows very well

that we're not in soundings.'

Beazley had a disapproving look on his face; he took it personally that anyone should so question his navigation as to cast the lead in water that he'd declared to be some five hundred fathoms deep. Gresham saw his opportunity.

'Oh, it does no harm and these waters are hardly well charted, Mister Beazley. I'm pleased to see that he's so diligent.'

'He'll be asking permission to cast the deep-sea lead if he's encouraged,' Beazley grumbled, 'and he won't find no bottom on that line neither.'

'I remember when the want of a cast of the lead nearly cost us the ship, and in these very waters too.'

Carlisle knew that Gresham was teasing the sailing master, but he had a good point. It was no great hardship to cast the lead even when it was almost certain to be fruitless, but Hooper should be more sensitive of Beazley's pride, which was of almost sinful proportions. Hooper had joined *Dartmouth* in Jamaica to replace Enrico, Carlisle's wife's cousin. Enrico had never held King George's commission, but had been appointed as a liaison officer from his home country, Sardinia. When his Sardinian naval commission had been withdrawn, there was no further justification for him taking a berth in *Dartmouth*, and he'd followed his cousin to Virginia to make a new life for himself. Hooper had held his lieutenant's commission for only a few months and considered himself fortunate to have been given a ship, with the present war apparently winding down. So far, Carlisle was pleased with his new third lieutenant.

'Let's leave Mister Hooper to his watch, gentlemen.'

Carlisle turned the chart around so that it was facing the three of them. It was a perfect chart for this occasion. It showed the whole of the island of Cuba from the Windward passage to the Florida Channel and the most cursory glance showed that *Dartmouth* must have some compelling reason to be hove to in such a tight spot, with the combination of wind and current setting them towards the horrors of the

Old Bahama Straits

Old Bahama Straits at a fast walking pace. He'd dismissed his servants, even Walker, and now he glanced around to be sure that nobody was watching or listening and placed his finger on the chart at *Dartmouth's* position.

'We're not here for our health and amusement, as you can imagine. I know that rumours are spreading around the ship, but we can do little about that for I can't reveal to the people where we're heading or our purpose. However, I can confide in you gentlemen, but before I do I must insist on absolute secrecy…'

He looked from Gresham to Beazley as both men nodded their understanding.

'…because I'm not exaggerating when I say that the success of Admiral Pocock's great armament relies upon it.'

His officers looked suitably impressed. Gresham had that look in his eye as though he was about to go into battle, while Beazley looked solemn and stared at his chart, perhaps hoping that the intensity of his gaze would reveal new information. Each man held his breath.

Carlisle disliked appearing dramatic, but having impressed the need for secrecy, it was impossible to disclose this momentous information without a metaphorical fanfare.

'It's Havana,' Carlisle announced, stabbing his finger at the indentation in the northwest corner of Cuba, 'and the admiral has it in mind to approach from the east, through the Old Bahama Straits. We're to scout ahead of the fleet and report if there is anything new since we last came this way.'

Gresham and Beazley exchanged glances. Had they been placing bets on Pocock's mission? Probably, and from their exchange of rueful looks it seemed that neither of them had guessed correctly, and it was no wonder. Taking a single ship-of-the-line through the Straits was dangerous enough, but bringing Pocock's massive invasion fleet, at least two hundred sail with everything from a ninety-gun ship to a two-masted victualler, looked positively foolhardy.

It took only a few minutes for Carlisle to tell them what he knew, and in truth there was little to say. His plan to pass through the narrowest part of the Straits in daytime made navigational sense and it also allowed them the opportunity to see with their own eyes whether the spring storms had changed the channel in any way. That still gave them time to reach Salt Cay, take a look at the Nicholas Channel, and make their way back to Pocock before the twenty-eighth of the month.

'Where we can, we should stay out of sight of the Cuban shore,' Gresham mused.

'Easier said than done, when we get deep into the Straits.'

Beazley traced his finger along the line of islands that hemmed in the Cuban side of the Straits. Coral cays mostly and they had the virtue – and the danger – of rising swiftly from deep water. There were no sandbanks to run aground upon but a lead line would offer scant warning of their proximity. It was quite the opposite of the situation on the north side where the expansive flats of the Bahama Bank guarded the far-distant islands.

'Well, be that as it may, that's our task. Now, Mister Beazley, I agree that you should go with the schooner to investigate Santo Domingo Cay. Its latitude is the most important thing, if you can set it down to some degree of accuracy then it'll be one hazard eliminated, at least. Mister Gresham and I will keep you in sight, in case you need assistance.'

'Aye-aye sir. I'm told that it can always be seen when there's a trade wind blowing, by the broken water over its top, even when the coral's not showing. We should have no trouble in this weather.'

***

The schooner returned late in the evening, just before sunset, and it was a deeply satisfied sailing master who was rowed across to *Dartmouth*.

'We found the Cay on the first pass, sir. It shows clear as

Old Bahama Straits

a bell with a strong surf pounding at it. I can see that it would be a danger if there's no wind, or on a black night, but not today. I'd need to stay there longer to fix it accurately, but I have its latitude to within a league and its longitude to within two or three leagues, enough for Sir George's ships to keep clear in any case.'

'Very well, Mister Beazley. Now, I want to be abreast Green Island at dawn, so get the ship underway, if you please, and then you can let Mister Hooper have the watch. I want to discuss the passage of the Straits before we're committed to it.

***

Carlisle paced the poop deck as the first light of the new day tinged the eastern horizon with orange and gold. At each turn at the taffrail the day advanced perceptibly. The upper edge of the sun became visible first as a slim crescent then as a gleaming lozenge, apparently detached from its main body. Then, in the twinkle of an eye, the lozenge was gone and a perfect section of the sun, a third of its mass or thereabouts, showed above the sea, so bright that it was no longer comfortable to observe it directly. The sphere grew and in another half-dozen turns its lower limb had tugged itself clear of the horizon with such speed that one almost expected to hear a *plop*, as it broke free, like the sound of an unseen trout rising to a fly. And with that dramatic start, the whole gleaming disc started its daily migration across the vault of the heavens.

He stopped at the poop deck rail and looked across the quarterdeck, the waist and the fo'c'sle, through the tracery of standing and running rigging, to the far western horizon. The rising sun had brightened the sky and now its vivid blue was clearly demarked from the grey of the sea. He swung his gaze to larboard where Cuba's high land showed clear and bright, but the low-lying shoreline was still invisible. Then to starboard, to the Bahamas side, where nothing whatsoever interrupted the pure line of the horizon. It was strange to think that it was the starboard side that posed the danger to *Dartmouth*. The chart clearly showed that the nearest sandbank was only six miles away, and it was deep enough that the sea above it wasn't disturbed in this weather. Yet that invisible sandbank could stop a ship dead and hold it in its grasp until the weather and the current broke it apart. That was what almost happened to *Dartmouth* just a few leagues from here, back in December, and it had only been by good seamanship and plain luck that they'd managed to kedge off before her stern struck the bank. It was strange to think that this apparently wide and benign sea held such dangers.

It was those dangers that he'd been thinking of ever since Pocock had given him this task. Even if *Dartmouth* led them through the Straits they could expect stragglers, and in these waters straggling carried the risk of striking on an unseen reef or sandbank. Taking the narrowest part – the thirty leagues from here to Santa Maria Island – in daylight would certainly be safer, but with the trade wind and this constant current, it would be courting disaster to have possibly a hundred ships backing and filling and waiting for daylight. No, that would never do, it was safer to keep them all moving to the west, even if their navigation was reduced to follow-my-leader like some childhood game. What loss rate would Pocock deem acceptable? One in twenty? One in ten? It was a fearful number that would be counted in sunken ships, lives cut short and stores lost. If the Straits had to be navigated by day and by night, how could the danger be reduced?

At one level the answer was obvious. Back in 'fifty-nine Carlisle had been responsible for buoying the channel that led up the Saint Lawrence River to Quebec. That had been a different scale of task, the dreaded Traverse was only a few miles long and narrow enough so that land could be seen on both sides. He'd laid buoys at each side of the channel, and where he couldn't lay buoys he'd anchored boats. Perhaps that was the answer. Flags and beacons on the cays, and boats where there were none. And at night? Well, he'd have a fire in each boat. Every ship carried at least one brazier for the armourer's use, and the storeships carried any number of them, for use of the soldiers once they'd been landed. With a couple of inches of water in the bilges and buckets to apply seawater, it would be safe enough. Sir George had told him to be back by the twenty-eighth. Carlisle hadn't asked, but he'd had the impression that the admiral intended to start on the passage as soon as *Dartmouth* returned. His plan for the boats needed at least a day to be organised, and he'd need to leave a day earlier than the fleet, to get all the boats and the parties for the cays in place. He calculated quickly. The trade wind had a good bit of north in it today. If that persisted he could make his way back to Mole Saint Nicholas on a single tack, just about. If he didn't delay off Salt Cay, he could be back amongst the squadron with a day to spare, two days possibly. He leaned over the rail to see Beazley in conversation with Gresham.

'Mister Beazley. Set all plain sail and stuns'ls alow and aloft. I want to be at Salt Cay by Thursday morning. Hang out a waft for Mister Wishart. He's to take station two miles astern and keep in sight of our lantern, I don't want him wandering off among the cays and the banks.'

***

Dartmouth sped through the narrows with a disregard for rocks and shoals that would have terrified anyone who hadn't been through before. There was no chance of casting a lead line but at each turn of the half-hour glass an exhilarated master's mate or midshipman reported the speed.

'Twelve knots, sir! Twelve knots and a fathom! Oh, if only Mister Angelini were here now, he did so love a good run with the wind on the quarter.'

Joseph Hooper, who had served his time in more sedate ships than *Dartmouth* and was as yet no fair replacement for Enrico, was open-mouthed in astonishment at this cavalier disregard for the safety of a King's ship. He reported the speeds to Carlisle with none of the relish with which they'd been given to him.

By sunrise on Wednesday they were close up with Santa Maria Island and by noon they were past the worst and into the broad and comfortable Nicholas Channel. Cuba was just a shadow on the horizon, visible only from the masthead. The sun set on a shipless sea as *Dartmouth* furled her stuns'ls and courses and settled down to a comfortable cruise to be off Salt Cay as the sun rose again. Barring some coasting and fishing canoes, seen far off on the banks and among the cays, the Old Bahama Straits and its eastern and western approaches had been innocent of traffic. It was as though the Cuban coast and the Bahama Banks were holding their breath, waiting in trepidation for some guessed-at cataclysmic event.

***

CHAPTER FIVE

The Picket

Wednesday, Nineteenth of May 1762.
Dartmouth, at Sea, off Salt Cay, The Nicholas Channel.

'Deck ho! I can see the schooner right astern, sir, about a mile. Nothing else in sight.'

Carlisle walked up to the poop deck. The morning watch had just been called and it was still over an hour to sunrise. As was to be expected this far west, the trade wind had dropped during the night, and the long swell created barely a ripple to diffuse any light. The sea was black and featureless except where the waxing, gibbous moon, a forearm's length above the horizon, cast its pale light over the silent sea, and the schooner sat in the centre of that gleaming silvery moon-glade. Probably all that Wishart could see of *Dartmouth* was the lantern on the taffrail, and it was a poor mark for judging distances, so he could be forgiven for being only a mile astern. Even as he watched, the eastern horizon started to lighten and by the time he turned away the moon's brilliance was being dimmed by the promise of a fresh dawn. He looked all around, from the stern, through the starboard beam, through the bow and the larboard side and back to the stern again. As Whittle had reported, there was nothing to be seen, but this was the time of day when the greatest vigilance was required. The rising sun could reveal a powerful Spanish squadron under *Dartmouth's* lee, or a fat and helpless French West Indiaman, hoping to make an undetected passage through the Florida Channel.

'Mister Gresham, the great guns are cleared away?'

'Aye sir, cleared away and there's a man in each division keeping the match alight.'

Carlisle made no reply. The question had been superfluous in any case, for the first lieutenant would chew off his own arm rather than be found wanting in his duty. At the beginning of this war, and indeed in his early months of commanding *Dartmouth*, he'd cleared for action and sent the hands to their quarters at each sunrise. He'd become more relaxed with greater experience, and had come to rely upon the ship's customary speed in making ready to fight. Now he only had the guns cleared away and he let the watch below sleep undisturbed, secure in the knowledge that he could deliver a devastating broadside in less than five minutes from the first alarm, and no enemy had ever been able to act within that time. Gresham really was near perfection as a second-in-command, and Carlisle hoped that he'd get his chance of promotion before this war was over. It caused him a pang of conscience. He'd given the schooner – what was her name? *Santa Teresa*, that was it – to Wishart, rather than to Gresham, and an independent command like that was the best way to be noticed and promoted to master and commander. He'd done it with barely a thought, for Wishart had the flexibility of mind to command a ship, while Gresham had spent most of his career in the rigid discipline of ships-of-the-line. It was unfair, of course, and Gresham would make a perfectly adequate commander of a sloop. Wishart, however, had that extra spark of independence, that quickness of thought and action that would make him an outstanding commander, when the chance came. Well, this war was certainly coming to an end and the chances were that neither Gresham nor Wishart would get their step-up before the awful reality of peacetime hit them. Gresham, he knew, would adapt easily to the life of a half-pay, unemployed lieutenant; he'd done it before in the last peace and now he had a comfortable cushion of prize money to rest upon. How would Wishart fare? He'd been just a boy the last time his country was without an acknowledged enemy.

'Deck there! There's a sail on the larboard bow, sir, at least there's something just starting to show. Perhaps three or four miles, sir, dead to leeward.'

Old Bahama Straits

Whittle made his report according to his own notions of how it should be done. It had always been thus and over the years Carlisle had attempted to impose a standard report upon him, but it had done no good. And Whittle was certainly the best lookout in the ship.

Carlisle thought rapidly. Commodore Douglas at Jamaica wouldn't have sent one of his ships here, and Pocock certainly hadn't sent any of his. It couldn't even be a British merchant ship; they were all firmly ordered to sail in convoys and every merchant master knew that his insurance would be invalidated if he chose a lone passage. It could be a British privateer hoping for a Havana prize now that Spain had joined the war. Nevertheless, the likelihood was that this was a Spanish ship, another guarda-costa or a King's ship acting as a picket to guard this northern route to Havana.

'Beat to quarters, Mister Gresham, clear for action. No drums in case he's still asleep, the sound will travel far in this light breeze. Where's the sailing master?'

'Here, sir.'

Beazley had tumbled from his cot at Whittle's first shout and now he was stuffing his shirt into his breeches and looking up at the sails.

'Set all plain sail, Mister Beazley, and hang out a waft for *Santa Teresa* to come within hail. Up helm, let's run down to this fellow and see how awake he is.'

***

Carlisle saw *Santa Teresa* set her tops'l and start to draw towards *Dartmouth*. Wishart must have been on deck when the signal was made for him to close for orders, but even so he was very prompt in obeying. Now the sleek schooner was showing her pace and moving fast, much faster than *Dartmouth*, and in ten minutes they'd be within hailing range. Taking up his telescope, he walked rapidly forward to the fo'c'sle, stepping over train tackles and sponges and rammers. Ah, now he could see it; a small ship perhaps, or a brig, and it was still snugged down for the night with its courses furled and only its tops'ls and heads'ls set. It didn't have the look of a British privateer, its tops'ls looked all wrong and the steeve of its bowsprit was too high, very old-fashioned to an eye used to the low bowsprits and big jibs and staysails of British privateers. He looked again. A brig, he was almost certain, and it was on the same course as *Dartmouth*, as though it was heading for Havana. So much the better, no lookout on this earth spent as much time searching astern as he did ahead, and *Dartmouth* was dead astern.

He closed his telescope with a snap and hastened back to the quarterdeck.

'The ship's cleared for action, sir, and the hands are at quarters.'

'Very well, Mister Gresham. Mister Beazley, I want every knot of speed that you can give me. Lay me on that brig's starboard beam, if you please.'

'Aye-aye sir. I'll set the stuns'ls if I may.'

'If you please, Master. Ah, I think we've been spotted.'

A bugle call came faintly back against the listless wind. It wasn't a full-throated call, as though the bugler was uncertain of his task. The second call was more strident. Perhaps the first was ordered by an officer of the watch who doubted his own authority. The second was probably ordered by the captain when he saw the awful reality of a ship-of-the-line creeping up astern of his brig.

The sun's upper limb had broken the horizon now, and the scene was starting to be bathed in a brighter light than the miserly moon had offered. Carlisle glanced over the larboard quarter to see *Santa Teresa* surging up, and there was Wishart at the end of the bowsprit with one foot on the jib-boom and his hand clutching the forestay, looking for all the world like one of those cheap prints that were sold in London, extolling the virtues of the British Tars. Wishart was evidently eager to hear his orders. Yes, it had been a good decision to give the younger, less experienced man the command.

'The brig's loosed her courses, sir and I can see men running out on her yards now, she'll be setting her stuns'ls soon.'

'Thank you, Mister Beazley.'

Carlisle ran up to the poop deck and climbed onto the hammock crane, steadying himself by the mizzen shrouds. *Santa Teresa's* fo'c'sle was right alongside *Dartmouth's* quarterdeck, and the distance hardly required raised voices.

'We must take her, Mister Wishart. You should have a knot or two over her, run down onto her larboard side and see what you can do to slow her down. Be careful, she probably has six pounders. Oh, and hoist your colours before you open fire.'

Wishart looked as though there was nowhere he'd rather be. His wide smile and his hair blowing in the wind reminded Carlisle more of an exuberant child than of a man holding the King's commission.

'British colours, sir?'

Carlisle was about to make an exasperated response when he saw that Wishart had let his high spirits get the better of him. He waved in reply as the schooner, yard-by-yard, overtook the lumbering great fourth rate.

***

'It'll be a short chase, sir. See how Mister Wishart is overhauling her.'

Carlisle could see that for himself, he didn't need his first lieutenant to tell him. The brig was less than two miles ahead of *Dartmouth*, but now they were both running dead before the wind, and they were of much the same speed.

Beazley was busy with his octant, taking a vertical angle of the brig's masthead. In ten minutes he'd be able to state definitively which of them was winning the race. He lowered his octant and stared at the brig for a moment.

'He should bear up three points and put the wind on his quarter, that would force us to approach him slantwise. What do you think, Mister Gresham?'

Carlisle had heard these discussions before. Gresham

couldn't help contradicting the sailing master, whether he disagreed with him or not. The first lieutenant looked up at the commissioning pennant but there was no help there, it just hung limply against the masthead with an occasional flutter as the lazy breeze caught it.

'I think not, Mister Beazley. Consider, to achieve its best speed a vessel of any kind must contrive that all its sails draw. With two masts,' he held up two fingers for clarity, 'a brig doesn't suffer the same blanketing effect that a three-masted ship does. He's probably fastest on a dead run and he'll know for certain that we'd prefer the wind on the quarter. No, I do believe he's on the right course, given the circumstances, and I name William Mountaine as my authority.'

Gresham tapped his coat pocket and smirked in triumph. He'd bought a copy of Mountaine's *Seaman's Vade Mecum* from an impoverished half-pay lieutenant in Jamaica, and was wont to quote from it as the one and only true authority on naval matters. If Mountaine said that the earth was flat and that the meridian lines were made of twenty-four inch cable, then as far as Gresham was concerned, there was no argument on the matter. The octavo book sat neatly in a uniform pocket, probably by design, and Gresham's increasing use of it drove the sailing master to distraction.

Beazley grimaced, snarled at the steersman to watch his course, and took up his octant again. Carlisle almost laughed outright. In this case the first lieutenant was correct, and not only because William Mountaine said so, and it had nothing to do with the chase being a brig and not ship-rigged. She was almost certainly making for Havana, and if she could outrun *Dartmouth*, she had a good chance of making it. Havana was some thirty-five leagues away and the current that ran from the Gulf of Mexico through the Florida Channel was stronger offshore than inshore. Unless the wind changed radically, the brig would have to keep its pursuer at arm's length until the friendly darkness enveloped them. Putting the wind on his quarter would only set the brig further into the stream, and delay the moment when it could seek safety under the Morro Castle's guns.

Beazley rested his octant again and studied the high trade wind clouds.

'We're almost matching her for speed, sir, perhaps we're a little slower, but not much. I fancy the wind is increasing a little, and that should be to our advantage.'

Carlisle followed the sailing master's gaze. Those clouds looked much more timid than they had yesterday; there was none of that trade wind boldness about them, and they were lower in the sky. Perhaps they'd get more wind, but he didn't believe it would be a great deal. His hopes rested with Wishart and even now the schooner had run clear of *Dartmouth's* jib-boom and was racing towards the brig. What would Wishart do? The man was irrepressible, and he'd know very well that *Dartmouth* was unlikely to catch the brig without the schooner's intervention. But *Santa Teresa* was so small. Her timbers would be no defence against six pound shot, and her own three pounders would hardly worry that brig. And there was another factor that only he and Gresham and Beazley knew. If he was to be back with Pocock in time to arrange his plan of beacons and boats to guide the fleet through the Straits, he must turn back today. What was more important, to ensure that the brig didn't take back to Havana a story of a British fourth rate loitering off Salt Cay, or to return to Pocock in time to arrange for the boats and beacons that would keep the fleet safe? He couldn't afford to chase through the night with the probability that in the morning the brig would be even further out of reach. He'd chase until the first dog watch, no later. At eight bells in the afternoon watch he'd turn back into the Straits unless he had the brig under his lee by that time.

***

Hewitt and Chips, that corruptible alliance of bosun and carpenter, studied the great girth of the mizzen mast. It was sprung, that much was for certain. It had been fished and woolded and its parlous state had been reported to the navy board before they left Jamaica. Normally they'd both have been happy to hide their problems and let the local authorities deal with it. However, in this case there were so many ships at Jamaica with similar problems that the yard at Port Royal was overwhelmed, and even if Pocock sympathised, there was nothing that he could do.

With the ship running fast in pursuit of the Spanish brig they could each feel the crepitus as the constituent parts of the mast worked against each other. They could hear it too, with the wind at the stern; a faint sound like a split willow on a riverbank, bending to the breeze. They were old campaigners, these two, and they hoped most fervently that their mizzen mast would be a ticket for an early departure from the Caribbean. Certainly the admiral wouldn't willingly send them home, but things looked different from Seething Lane, and a peremptory order to return could hardly be ignored even by a commander-in-chief. They were two minds acting as one, and no tales of prize money in the faraway future could divert them from their purpose. They agreed there and then that another written submission to the captain was required and meanwhile Hewitt would freshen the turns on the woolding. For even though they wanted to go home, they didn't want the mast to collapse this side of Portsmouth's Round Tower and condemn them to some other King's yard for repairs. They were Portsmouth born and bred and after this long commission their home port was calling.

***

CHAPTER SIX

Brave Fool

Wednesday, Nineteenth of May 1762.
Prize Schooner Santa Teresa, at Sea, off Salt Cay, The Nicholas Channel.

Wishart felt a fool as he stepped carefully back from the bowsprit. He'd let his tongue run away again, and in front of his captain! What foul demon had induced him to make that quip about the colours? He couldn't tell, but he'd made similar silly remarks all his life and he knew that they only tended to make him look immature and unready for the awesome responsibility of command. Well, he'd make up for it by bringing this damned Spaniard to heel, that would show Captain Carlisle his worth. Now, how to do that without having the schooner sunk beneath him? He snapped at his second-in-command.

'Mister Torrance, is the brig cleared for action? I haven't heard your report yet.'

Richard Torrance was the only other officer in the schooner. He'd been a midshipman and then a master's mate in *Dartmouth* and he knew Lieutenant Wishart very well. In fact, they'd messed together when Wishart was but a master's mate himself. Quarters! Cleared for action! Those phrases meant something in *Dartmouth*, but here in a prize schooner with three tiny three pounders a side and a handful of swivel guns it meant nothing. He had enough men to man one broadside, but that left none for the swivels, and if they had to trim the sails, the guns would be short-manned. The schooner had been manned for dispatch and scouting duties, not for a fleet action, for heaven's sake! But he knew David Wishart and had some idea of what caused him to speak so abruptly, and he knew that there was steel behind that youthful exterior.

'I beg your pardon, sir. The ship's cleared for action and

the hands are at their quarters. I can man one battery of the three pounders at a time but I've rigged the swivels and they have spare charges beside each one. The guns are charged but not loaded, awaiting your orders, sir.'

'Very well, Mister Torrance. Don't load the guns just yet. Stream the log, if you please.'

Wishart could see the crew looking at him from the waist. They knew the dangers; some of them had been in more engagements than he had, and they knew very well what six pound shot could do against these thin planks and frames. It would do no good to run up alongside the brig and fight it out broadside-to-broadside. If he did, there was an outside chance that he could slow the enemy down enough so that *Dartmouth* could come up and finish the job, but it would almost certainly be a victory won at the expense of the schooner and its crew. Most likely his men would be killed or wounded before he could fire a shot, and the effort, and all those lives, would be wasted.

'Five knots and a half, sir.'

Wishart could see that Torrance relayed the result of the log streaming as formally as he could, to make up for his tardiness in reporting quarters. That was good, but now it was time to win back his loyalty, to show that he was valued.

'Very well. What do you make of the brig's speed?'

Torrance looked forward over the starboard bow.

'Four knots at best, sir, and I can't see this wind changing much. The trade winds are failing now, as we should expect so close to the Florida Channel. That was what Mister Beazley told me.'

'Then we'll be alongside her in forty-five minutes.'

'That's so, sir.'

Now, was there a hint of reserve in that response. Torrance would be only human if he didn't relish the thought of a stand-up bare-knuckle fight against a vessel that was so far superior in every article. The entire crew was on deck manning the guns, and the after-most crews could hear every word that the officers said.

'Well, we must slow her down, Mister Torrance, and let Captain Carlisle come up. I've no intention of ranging up alongside her, but there's an alternative. Her captain daren't alter course because *Dartmouth* is too close and every yard that he loses is a yard closer to their capture. That gives us an opportunity. We have plenty of grape shot, I believe.'

'A tolerable amount, sir. Enough for ten broadsides for each battery, and there's canister for the swivels as well.'

Torrance was sounding enthusiastic now and the men at the guns were starting to smile as they ran to fetch the grape shot. They didn't know their captain's plan, but they knew that grape shot meant subtlety rather than an unequal contest.

***

'The guns are loaded with grape, sir. Being so short-handed, we might not get a chance to use the swivels, but they're loaded with canister in any case.'

'Very well, Mister Torrance. If it comes to it you and I can press a match to the priming as well as anyone else.'

The brig was closer now and they could clearly see the officers on the quarterdeck looking back at them.

'Quartermaster, steer as though you're going to range up on her larboard beam, but keep her on the starboard tack, I don't want to wear.'

'Aye-aye sir.'

The quartermaster pushed the tiller to starboard a little. Now the brig was two points on their starboard bow at about half a mile. *Santa Teresa* was almost sailing by the lee, but he needed those boomed mainsails over to larboard for his next manoeuvre.

'You see he's lining his taffrail with muskets, he means to pepper us as we draw up to him. As soon as we're in range you men are to crouch down behind the starboard gunwales. There's no value in giving him a target until we're ready to pay him back in kind.'

There was nothing much to do now but watch the wind and trim the sails to get the best speed out of the schooner.

She was fast, faster than Wishart had thought, and it wouldn't be long before those muskets were in range. Well, he could endure that for a while. Both ships were rising and falling on the long, lazy swell and it would only be by evil fortune that any musket ball found a target.

A puff of smoke rose from the brig's taffrail and an instant later a faint *pop!* confirmed that a musket had been fired. There was no telling where the ball had gone, and Wishart shook his head at the waste of powder and shot. Nevertheless, it suggested that *Santa Teresa* would soon be within range of harassing fire.

'Lie down, men,' Wishart shouted. 'Mister Torrance, you must be ready if I fall, so take your place abaft the mainmast, if you please.'

Torrance looked as though he'd object but saw the determination in Wishart's eyes. Only the captain and the quartermaster-cum-steersman needed to expose themselves at this stage.

A larger puff of smoke, and a louder bang. The brig had rigged a swivel on the taffrail and its half pound ball whirred menacingly as it passed down the schooner's side. The swivel was useful when ships were yardarm-to-yardarm, but it was ineffective at more than fifty yards. At this distance it was little better than a musket, except for the greater weight of its ball. Neither vessel could use its great guns, as none of them could traverse far enough to reach the target. Given more time, the brig could have moved a six pounder aft, but that would have taken an hour at least, even if they already had eye bolts in place. And it would be a gun lost if it came to a broadside battle, and from the brig's perspective, the schooner looked very much as though that was the plan.

Closer and closer. The swivels and the muskets were causing damage now and small holes were starting to appear in the sails, but the rise of the schooner's foredeck offered an unexpected protection for the gun crews.

'Mister Torrance. I'll call for the larboard battery in a moment, but keep the crews to starboard until we start our turn,' he gestured with his hand held low to keep it out of the brig's sight, 'I'm going to bear up across her stern.'

The gun crews were nodding in understanding.

Santa Teresa's jib-boom was perhaps fifty yards from the brig's stern. Just a little further. Wishart winced as a musket ball struck his hat and sent it whirling into the sea. Now or never!

'Helm a-lee,' he shouted. 'Larboard battery fire as you bear.'

The schooner swung across the brig's stern and rushed slantwise upon her quarter. Wishart hauled on the mainsheet himself as two of the gun's crews handled the foresheets and the heads'ls. The tops'l flapped as it lost its wind but the manoeuvre was working. Wishart heard the first of the guns fire and saw the brig's taffrail disappear as the nine balls of the grape shot spread out like a giant shotgun. The second and third followed and now there was nobody looking down at them from the brig's quarterdeck. The next manoeuvre had to be timed to perfection. If the schooner came too far onto the brig's quarter, her captain would surely be tempted to yaw a couple of points so that his six pounders could bear.

'Stand by to wear ship! Mister Torrance, leave one man to reload each of the larboard guns and then standby the starboard battery!'

The brig had swivels on each quarter, but the schooner's grape shot had destroyed the taffrail and the starboard swivel hung at a drunken angle. It was strangely quiet for a few moments as though both vessels were gathering their thoughts.

'Muskets at their stern windows, sir!'

The quartermaster was keeping cool and he'd seen the danger as three musket barrels emerged through the shattered glass of the brig's cabin.

Pop, Pop, Pop!

One of the musket balls ricocheted off the binnacle leaving a bright scar in the weathered wood.

'Up helm! Wear ship!'

'Excuse me sir.'

Wishart stepped to the side. The seaman who'd been sent into the prize as a cook was running from swivel to swivel, aiming quickly and pressing the slow match to the priming, not waiting to see the result before moving to the next. He was aiming high; that was good, and the brig's mainsail and rigging were being shredded. Torrance was among the guns, heaving on train tackles and swabbing and reloading.

'Starboard battery, Mister Torrance. Fire when your guns bear.'

The schooner pitched heavily as it turned into the brig's wake and the booms swung dangerously across the deck as her stern came through the wind. They were crossing the brig's stern again and Wishart heard the explosions of the three pounders. The cook looked like a fiend from the nether regions of hell as he leapt from swivel to swivel, firing their charge of musket balls at the helpless enemy. The brig's stern had lost all of its windows and the taffrail had disappeared, but none of that was slowing her. Wishart could see that the rudder was still operating, still keeping the brig on its resolute course towards safety. Chains were rigged on either side to allow the brig to be steered if the wheel or the tiller were shot away, but there was little chance of that happening, not when the schooner was firing from so much lower than the brig's quarterdeck.

'She's yawing to larboard, sir!'

The quartermaster was watching the brig as well as his own steering and the trim of his sails. Yawing to starboard! The Spanish captain must have tired of this terrier snapping at his heels and was going to risk slowing his progress in order to fire a broadside and deal with the schooner once and for all.

'Up helm. Wear ship.'

The quartermaster needed no encouraging, he could see the danger as well as Wishart. The sail trimmers weren't

Old Bahama Straits

ready and this time the sheets hadn't been hauled in. The booms crashed across and the schooner rolled hard to starboard as she swung again under the brig's stern. They were further away now as the schooner had lost distance with these manoeuvres, but at least she hadn't needed to tack, that would have left her far in the enemy's wake.

Wishart saw the brig's side as the Spanish captain brought her around. It was a race now between the brig turning far enough for her larboard battery to bear, and the schooner gathering way and following her stern around. God, her side looked enormous, and those six pounders might as well have been thirty-twos as far as the schooner was concerned.

'Fire as you bear, Mister Torrance.'

The brig's guns were hard against the sides of her ports, and Wishart could almost see down the barrel of the aftermost one.

Bang! Bang! Bang! The schooner's three pounders fired. The cook was frantically trying to reload the swivels, ripping the expended mugs out of the breeches and dropping in the fresh ones, complete with their charges of powder and their canisters of musket balls. But it was hopeless, it would have taken three trained gunners to keep up that rate of fire. He fumbled and dropped a mug, and bent down to collect it.

At that moment the brig's aftermost gun fired. It was at the very extreme of its traverse and it looked as though the Spanish captain had decided that his brig could be yawed thus far and no further. The six pound ball smashed into the gunwale above the cook's head, destroying the iron bracket and dropping the heavy swivel gun onto the cook's back.

Wishart had no time to spare, for his schooner was moving rapidly across the brig's stern. The brig's other five guns of the battery saved their ammunition, they had no hope of traversing far enough to reach the schooner. The cook was painfully struggling from under the broken swivel and looking wildly about him.

'Her rudder's jammed, Mister Wishart, look!'

The quartermaster was pointing with one hand while leaning his body against the tiller to keep the schooner on course.

Wishart stared at the brig's rudder. It should be over to starboard now, to bring the brig back onto its course; that was the sensible thing to do, but it was nearly fore-and-aft. He grabbed his telescope. Ah, one of the grape shot had hit the retaining chain where it left the brig through a small hawse, and it had jammed the chain fast. The rudder could be moved to larboard but not to starboard, and even as he watched he saw that they were trying to dislodge the ball by vigorous movements of the tiller.

'Hold this course, Quartermaster. Mister Torrance, we'll fire again from the larboard battery.'

A quick look astern showed that *Dartmouth* was still nearly two miles away. Would they see that the brig's steering had been damaged? Yes, *Dartmouth's* bows swung fractionally to larboard, half a point, no more.

'There's a man climbing through the stern windows sir. They're handing him a crow.'

The quartermaster spoke softly. He was an older seaman, more thoughtful than most, and he knew what was to happen next. The gun captains were still reloading, but soon their hands would go up and that man would be blown away by a hail of grape and cannister.

Wishart watched in fascination. They were so close that they could see the expressions on the enemy's faces. Someone, it looked like the captain, was leaning over the taffrail and gesturing angrily for the brave man to come back through the window. He looked anxiously at the schooner that was now within easy range and leaned far over to shout at the man. But he wasn't listening. He had hold of the crow and was wedging himself beside the rudder head and trying to get the right angle to force the crow under the jammed chain.

The Spanish captain waved frantically at Wishart then his head disappeared below the remains of the taffrail.

'Hold your fire, Mister Torrance.'

Bang! The cook fired the forward swivel and its load of musket balls spattered around the vulnerable Spanish seaman. Probably the cook's hearing had been shattered, or perhaps he just didn't understand. The nearest gun captain grabbed his arm and pulled him down.

Wishart looked up again just in time to see the Bourbon white emblazoned with the red and gold of Spain come floating down from the peak of the gaff yard.

***

'It was the captain's younger brother-in-law, you know. He had high notions of his honour and courage and wouldn't be stopped. Apparently the captain didn't relish returning to Havana and telling his wife that he'd lost her only brother, and his body was somewhere on the Atlantic Drift, passing Florida and on its way to Europe. I can sympathise with him; I wake up in a cold sweat imagining what Lady Chiara would have done to me if I'd lost Enrico.'

Carlisle could use the Christian names of old shipmates when talking to Wishart; they'd sailed together for seven years now. He looked out of the stern window to where the brig was lying to under his lee. Even from here he could see his own carpenter's crew working on the stern and a gaggle of seamen under the bosun's direction clambering all over the masts and rigging. They were to be underway before noon, and there was not a moment to lose.

Wishart looked too. He was hoping that the next thing that Carlisle would say was to offer him command of the brig, to bring it back to Admiral Pocock in triumph, and to have his name known, with all the opportunities that would open as a consequence.

'Well, it was our good fortune, sir. The way they were slamming that tiller over, that grape shot would have dislodged in a moment, according to Chips. Then we could have hung under his stern all day without bringing him to.'

'Yes, courage and honour are all very well, but they need to be moderated by a good serving of common sense. The master-at-arms has had to separate the captain and his brother-in-law, so that there's no bloodshed in the hold. As we thought, the brig was a picket to watch this approach to Havana. They'd only just come on station, victualled for a month, and they weren't expecting to be relieved for at least two weeks, so in all probability the governor-general knows nothing of our reconnaissance.'

There was no value in hiding their destination any longer. It was obvious to the lowliest ship's boy, and it had been Wishart's working assumption from the moment that he'd been sent to stop the brig.

'Now, you'll take command of the brig. *San Leon* is her name, incidentally, another damned guarda-costa, a privateer really and little better than a pirate; we'll have a whole collection of them soon. Follow me back up the Old Bahama Straits as best you can, but if you can't keep up then meet me off Mole Saint Nicholas. How did young Torrance behave? Is he ready to take the schooner, with the same crew?'

Wishart gulped. He'd hoped for the brig, expected it even, but to be asked his opinion of Torrance and his fitness for this temporary command, that was a compliment indeed. This was not the moment for flippant remarks.

'Thank you, sir, and I'm honoured by your confidence. Mister Torrance performed to my best expectations, and he's in all respects fit to take the schooner.'

Carlisle looked sadly at Wishart, and held him with his gaze.

'You can't expect your step from this, you know. If it was a King's ship then there'd have been a good chance that the admiral would make you master and commander and give you a temporary commission, but not a guarda-costa, I regret.'

***

CHAPTER SEVEN

The Step

Friday, Twenty-Eighth of May 1762.
Dartmouth, at Sea, off Mole Saint Nicholas.

Pocock's fleet looked much as Carlisle had left it eleven days before. There had been a strong blow from the south just the previous day and some of the ships were somewhat worse for wear, with hands aloft bending on spare tops'ls. A brig under the flagship's lee had fared particularly badly and was having the utmost difficulty keeping its station with its jib-boom and its fore-topmast missing. Carlisle brought *Dartmouth* into station as close to *Namur* as he dared, and at the signal from the flagship had himself rowed across, with his boat's crew dressed in their finery for a call on the commander-in-chief.

'Carlisle, you may have come in the nick of time, and for two reasons. First because I plan to start on the passage of the Straits on Sunday, and I hope you have some good news for me, but second, I see you've taken a brig. Is she fit for a passage back to England, an urgent passage?'

Carlisle was almost rocked back on his heels by Sir George's manner. There had been no preamble and it was clear that his great expedition was on the wing.

'The brig's ready, Sir George. She was handled roughly by our prize schooner, her stern windows are all boarded up and she has a jury-rigged taffrail. Otherwise, she floats and she moves and she can fight if need be, but she doesn't look her best.'

'The schooner, you say, that little thing?' Pocock pointed out of the window to where *Santa Teresa* lay hove to beside *San Leon*, looking very tiny indeed. 'Did your lieutenant – I regret I don't recall his name – take her alone?'

'Lieutenant Wishart, a most gallant and deserving officer, Sir George. *Dartmouth* was in sight for the capture but we expended not an ounce of powder nor suffered a scratch to our paintwork. Mister Wishart took her alone by wearing to and fro under her stern and peppering her with grapeshot and cannister. One of the grape lodged in her rudder chains and rather than suffer more insults, she struck. She's the *San Leon* of six guns, another guarda-costa out of Havana. She'd been sent out as a picket to watch the Straits.'

Pocock looked appraisingly at Carlisle. There was clearly a story to tell here.

'Rudder chains? That's rather putting on airs and graces for a little brig. Did they alert Havana to your presence?'

'No, Sir George. We carried out the business off Salt Cay and out of sight of land. There were no other sails in sight and the brig isn't expected back at Havana until the second of June.'

'Excellent, well I see we're setting out none too soon. We should be off Havana before de Hevia realises that anything is amiss with his arrangements for watching the Straits. No details now, but can I bring this fleet through the Straits without losing too many of them?'

Carlisle drew a breath. This was not the time for temporising.

'Yes, Sir George and I have some ideas to make it safer…'

Pocock held up his hand.

'That's all I need to know for the present, I'll hear about your ideas later. Now and most immediately, I need to send dispatches back to Lord Anson to tell him this great endeavour is underway. You see that sad-looking brig,' he waved to the shattered vessel that Carlisle had seen as he approached, 'that was to carry them, but clearly not now, after she was so badly handled in the heavy weather. If you think this Lieutenant Wishart is a fit and proper person, I'll give him a commission as master and commander and he can carry the dispatches in that prize of his. It's a suitable reward for his efforts, don't you think? And this might be his last chance this war. I'll give you another lieutenant, God knows I have enough of 'em. Anson can confirm Wishart's commission while he still doesn't know whether Spain is capable of defying us in the West Indies and prolonging this war. Once we've taken Havana it'll look quite different and he won't be able to confirm promotions, not with a clear conscience and a due regard for the public purse. What do you think?'

'I hardly have words, Sir George,' he thought fast and silently thanked Wishart who had given him a full account of the brig's material state and stores. '*San Leon* will need provisions and water, she only has a month's worth, but that can easily be made good today and she can sail before sunset. It might be prudent to give her a carpenter or a good carpenter's mate, just in case.'

'Yes, through the Crooked Island Passage and on to England. Send Mister Wishart to me and I'll brief him in person. There's another matter. I'd planned to send a sloop to Port Royal and that seemed a good opportunity to dispose of your Spanish friend Laredo. The storm has left me somewhat embarrassed for sloops, so I'll be sending him back to you. He has a great regard for you, and particularly for Lady Chiara. I've never met her, of course, but she made quite an impression on him.'

Pocock raised an eyebrow and grinned covertly. Carlisle was used to this by now, and it was amazing how sea officers who had never seen his wife had heard all about her. For a lady who had only once set foot in England, and then only for a few days as an unmarried maid, her reputation had spread far and wide, and he was universally envied.

'I'll hang out a signal for mail and send a boat around the men-o'-war. The last thing Mister Wishart will want is to have two hundred-odd boats calling on him while he's trying to get away, and I'll pass the word around that they're not to try. Mail through the flagship or not at all, and they can like it or lump it. Now, about this scheme of yours to ease the dangers of the Straits.'

***

Carlisle was in his cabin with Beazley, surrounded by charts of the Old Bahama Straits and long columns of soundings and bearings. He'd said his goodbyes to Wishart, sent his mail across and now he was turning his attention to the next phase of this campaign. There was a knock and a midshipman stepped into the cabin, removed his hat and bowed low quickly.

'Beg your pardon, sir. Mister Gresham's respects and there's a boat from *Dragon* coming alongside with Captain Hervey on board.'

Carlisle grimaced. He really was too busy to entertain the Honourable Augustus Hervey even though he was one of his oldest naval acquaintances. They'd been in the Mediterranean together before the start of the war, Hervey in *Phoenix* and he in *Fury*, two aged little frigates enjoying the peacetime round of port visits with their inevitable entertainments. It all seemed so long ago, in a time of innocence and gaiety.

'Very well, I'll come.'

Hervey ran lightly up the few steps of the ladder and through the entry port. *Dartmouth* must seem tiny to him after his own vast third rate. For *Dragon* was a mighty seventy-four, and a substantial step up from a mere fifty-gun ship.

'I hope you don't mind the intrusion, Carlisle, but I have a favour to ask.'

Carlisle smiled at that. Hervey was the younger brother to the Earl of Bristol, and as the elder brother was unmarried and showed no signs of a desire for a wife, there was every chance that he'd succeed to the title. Added to that, Hervey was the member for Bury St. Edmunds and despite being of an age with Carlisle, he was eight or nine years his senior on the post-captains list. Augustus Hervey carried around him an air of hereditary entitlement and was

Old Bahama Straits

known better for assuming the compliance of commoners than for requesting favours. Still, Carlisle liked Hervey and knew that underneath that rather carefree exterior there beat the heart of a true fighting sea officer, and he was, after all, that rarest of things, a good friend.

'Shall we step into the cabin, sir?'

'Now, don't mistake me, Carlisle, I have every respect for our commander-in-chief, but he closed the mail while I was half way through a particularly well-phrased letter to Elizabeth. Well, you know the situation, I can't expect much but it's as well that we don't disagree in public, and the women do like a good letter.'

Hervey spoke in staccato phrases, chopping up his sentences at random and leaving Carlisle to join them together to make sense. As a young man he'd embarked upon an ill-conceived and secret marriage, one that he quickly regretted but could find no way of dissolving. Long ago he'd subjected Carlisle to his views on the married state and there were few secrets left.

'Well, now I find that I'm forbidden to communicate with your man Wishart. I remember him by-the-bye. He was nephew to your lieutenant in *Fury*, the one who died in his moment of glory as he hauled down the French colours on that frigate you captured. I'm pleased that he has his step, and not a moment too soon with this ghastly talk of peace. I daren't even send a boat to the brig, but you could. Sir George could easily believe that Wishart left his chest behind, or his sword, or something. In any case, here's the letter, and I'd be obliged.'

Carlisle grinned. Hervey's good nature made it impossible to deny a favour, and he was correct that Pocock wouldn't even raise an eyebrow at a boat from *Dartmouth* going to the brig. In any case, there were any number of boats containing carpenters and bosuns helping with the last-minute repairs. One more from *Dartmouth* wouldn't be noticed.

'Of course, sir. One moment, if you please. Walker, pass

the word for Mister Simmonds. Ah, there you are.'

Simmonds had been waiting in his tiny office across the lobby from the captain's day cabin, and he'd heard his name mentioned.

'A boat, Mister Simmonds. Place this letter in a sealed bag and take it to Mister Wishart before he gets underway. Take a case of Madeira too. I'd meant to give him something for his voyage but it slipped my mind. If you have to explain yourself, then you can say just that, but I don't imagine there'll be any trouble. Oh, and I'd be obliged if the brig could pass close under our lee before he bears up for the Crooked Island Passage.'

Hervey had already moved on from the conversation and his attention had been caught by Carlisle's charts.

'Is this how you intend to guide us through the Straits?'

'Yes. Bonfires on the dry cays and anchored boats with braziers on the sunken reefs. The admiral will be sending out orders before sunset to gather in firewood and braziers, and boats. I'll sail a day ahead with that little prize schooner and I hope to have every significant cay and reef between Green Island and Santa Maria Island marked, both day and night, before the fleet sets out.'

Hervey studied the chart again. He could see where Carlisle had positioned the bonfires and also where the boats were to anchor. He looked up with a frown.

'Is this all really necessary, Carlisle? I mean, the Straits are wide enough. It looks like the narrowest part is here, just west of Green Island, and even there it's at least three leagues wide. I admit that I've never been there, but even so, isn't the danger exaggerated? You went through easily enough in December, didn't you?'

Carlisle smiled again. He'd explained this to Pocock and to Albemarle, it would do no harm to convince Hervey.

'Oh, it's wide enough and any competent seaman should be able to find his way through a three league passage. The problem here is that there are no points of reference to the north, and you'd be aground between two casts of the lead,

Old Bahama Straits

even if the fleet had leisure for sounding its way through. Even the south shore is treacherous. There's deep water up to a mile from most of the cays, but they're so low-lying that they can't be seen at night nor if there's thick weather. By the time you're in soundings it's too late. And then there's the current, two knots and more in places, and the unrelenting trade wind. Make no mistake, once the fleet is underway there'll be no turning back and no anchoring. You'll appreciate those beacons, I can assure you.'

Hervey looked more closely at the chart and followed the lines of soundings with his index finger. Now he could see what Carlisle meant, and he nodded in understanding.

Carlisle leaned across the chart and stabbed his finger at the well-remembered reef.

'You say that I passed through easily enough, but this is where I so nearly came to grief. I had to kedge off against the wind and current with my rudder bouncing up and down within feet of disaster. The admiral asked for my opinion of how many ships he'll lose if we go through without these preparations…'

Hervey cocked his head and waited with interest.

'…One in ten if we're lucky. There are no pilots you know. Port Royal was scoured but all that could be found was a very old man who was nearly blind.'

Hervey was intrigued and they spent a half hour poring over the chart together. It was well into the dog watches when the same midshipman appeared again at the cabin door.

'Beg your pardon, sir. *San Leon* is getting underway. Mister Gresham begs to inform you that both watches are on deck.'

'Very well, tell mister Gresham that I'll be up directly. Captain Hervey, would you like to join me?'

***

The sun was still far above the western horizon as Carlisle and Hervey strode up to the poop deck, and it was a glorious sight that awaited them, one that a King's officer couldn't fail to appreciate. *Dartmouth* lay hove to on the starboard tack just a few cables under the flagship's lee, and to windward of Pocock's vast invasion fleet. In a great arc to the west and south, all that could be seen was a solid mass of masts and sails where the battle squadron and the fleet of storeships and transports and all the variety of other vessels awaited the order to start upon their great endeavour. The little *San Leon* had filled her sails and was stretching across towards *Dartmouth*, the only vessel in that huge armada that was making way with a purpose.

Carlisle heard Gresham give the orders and watched as the topmen ran lightly up the rigging, spreading out on the upper yards where they clung precariously to breast lines that had been rigged for the purpose, with their feet upon the good pine of the yards. There was no clinging to the yards with their feet on the horses, not when Mister Wishart was about to pass by in all his promoted splendour. Below them, every man able to go aloft was crowding the lower yards and on deck those who couldn't climb the ratlines, manned the hammock railings, clinging to whatever support was available.

'Silence on deck!'

Gresham's stentorian bellow hushed the hundreds of excited men, and the ship waited with bated breath. It was clear that Wishart understood the purpose of the request to pass *Dartmouth* on his way to the Crooked Island Passage, and he was going to make the most of this. The brig would pass *Dartmouth* at pistol shot distance, close enough for men to recognise their friends. There was nobody in the brig's rigging, Wishart couldn't spare them from the sheets and braces, but they were all on deck waiting expectantly.

'Three cheers for Captain Wishart!'

The men cheered with gusto. Wishart had been a popular officer and they knew how to show their appreciation. The noise was loud on *Dartmouth's* deck, but on the brig, where all the voices were directed, it must have been like a solid wall of sound. *San Leon* was moving fast and by the time its crew replied they were already past *Dartmouth's* jib-boom, and it was a mere echo of the full-throated roar of the *Dartmouths*. They watched as the brig hauled its wind, leaning majestically to the breeze.

Hervey could see that Carlisle was visibly moved and they stood quietly for a few moments as the crew noisily descended from the rigging, eagerly anticipating their supper and their second issue of the grog ration.

'You'll be sorry to lose him, I gather.'

'I will. He's my last officer from *Fury* you know, the last who remembers Byng's battle off Minorca. I took him on as a volunteer and he stayed with me after his uncle died. He has no home at all in England, and knows absolutely nobody except some distant relatives in Scotland. Oh, he'll make his way and he has plenty of prize money, but I do hope his promotion is confirmed.'

'It will be. When he reaches the Admiralty with his dispatches, Anson will still be wondering whether this expedition will succeed. If it does it'll mean the end of the war, I expect, but if it doesn't, well, it could go on for years and we'll need all the young commanders we can get. Lord Anson will be worried when he reads those dispatches. I'm sure that Sir George has made the most of Rodney's ill-considered dispositions. He has only just over half the ships he expected you know. And then there are the American regiments; where are they? They should have been here in April but the only word that Albemarle has heard is that they'll be here in June or July. No, Anson won't have the luxury of believing that the war's won, not until he hears news that Havana has fallen.'

'The Americans, my countrymen of course. I fear for our reputation if they don't appear.'

'Don't take it personally, Carlisle. You're a King's officer, whatever the place of your birth.'

Carlisle didn't reply. It was easy for a man like Hervey to reassure him, but he'd heard the whispers behind his back. Whether justified or not, there was a perception that

Americans hadn't done enough in this war to ensure the survival of their own colonies, and he felt it most acutely.

They watched until the brig disappeared to the nor'west, until the short tropical twilight descended and Hervey departed in his boat for *Dragon*. Carlisle couldn't shake off the feeling of depression and it was as well that he had to present his final plan for the passage of the Straits to Pocock in the morning, otherwise Wishart's departure would have gnawed at him all night.

***

Down on the quarterdeck, as the sun dropped below the horizon, Laredo was in halting conversation with Hooper; neither knew enough of the other's language to make it easy. He too had watched the brig departing and breathed a sigh of relief. He still hoped that he could find a way to be returned to his countrymen and his wife in Havana. He understood enough to know that Wishart had been promoted and that Hooper had moved up to be the second lieutenant of *Dartmouth*, and that a new third lieutenant was expected. Even as he struggled with Hooper's ridiculous mangling of his language, he was considering how this new alignment could work to his advantage. For he was quite certain that the admiral would have forgotten his existence by now. If he was to influence anyone, it was Captain Carlisle and his officers, and he bent his mind to that sole purpose.

***

CHAPTER EIGHT

Dire Straits

Sunday, Thirtieth of May 1762.
Dartmouth, at Sea, The Old Bahama Straits.

'By the deep, thirty.'

Carlisle glanced at Beazley who nodded warily and pointed to the broken water half a mile to the north, with a gleaming patch of sand showing in the intervals between the waves.

'That'll be Santo Domingo Cay, sir.'

'Bring her to then, Mister Beazley, and send the boat coxswain up to me.'

It was late in the dog watches, the trade wind was blowing no more than a pleasant breeze and the sun was still hot as it beat down out of a cloudless sky. That tiny patch of land breaking the northern horizon about half a mile away was just one of those uninhabited – and uninhabitable – islands that dotted this vast expanse of treacherous water known as the Bahama Bank. The only firm and permanent land was out of sight below the horizon some nine leagues to the north where Ragged Island maintained a precarious existence among the reefs and shallows.

'Jordan sir, Coxswain of *Centaur*.'

Carlisle had briefed him before and he'd seemed competent enough. All he had to do was take a yawl and its crew over to that tiny wave-swept island, set up a flagpole and his brazier and fly a flag by day and burn a fire by night. Simple, and yet so many things could go wrong. It was too early for a hurricane, but a strong storm could easily sweep away his boat and leave he and his crew fighting for their survival on a patch of sand with no food and no water. A lot rested on this man's shoulders. If the fleet ever saw his marker they'd be five leagues too far to the north and must immediately steer to the southwest to find the entrance to the Straits. If the fleet should be so far astray in its latitude, and if the beacon wasn't spotted, then the cumulative navigational errors would have them all aground before ever they passed Green Island. And of course, if Beazley had set down the cay's position inaccurately, or mistaken it for another cay, they could be among the reefs before they knew they had left deep water.

'Well, Jordan, you have a vital task...'

The seaman gazed steadily back at Carlisle. It wasn't an insolent stare, but the reassuring look of a competent man ready to carry out his duty.

'...now repeat your orders, if you please.'

Jordan squared his shoulders. He was tall, as tall as Carlisle, and with a broader chest and massive arms and thighs.

'I'm to take the boat to that island over there, sir, Santo Domingo Cay, and beach the boat with an anchor carried ashore. I'm to set up a flagpole and brazier...'

Carlisle listened as Jordan repeated his orders. The man clearly understood, and he'd grasped the importance of the square of sailcloth to protect his men from the sun, of the need to husband the stock of wood that towered over the oarsmen in the boat, and of the importance of the brazier at night. Pocock's ships would be looking out for it. If all went well they'd sail past twenty miles to the south and Jordan would never know that they had passed. His was a thankless task, but a vital one, and he at least appeared to understand that.

'You've enough provisions for a week, but the schooner will come back for you once the fleet has passed through. It's Sunday today, you can expect to be brought off on Wednesday or Thursday. If you see nothing by Friday, make your own way to the west and follow the Cuban coast until you find the fleet.'

'Aye-aye sir. Friday it is.'

Carlisle watched as the yawl pulled for Santo Domingo Cay. It couldn't hoist a sail, being too overburdened with firewood, food and water, but it wasn't long before it was drawn up on the cay's gleaming sandy shore. Through his telescope, Carlisle could see the flagpole being erected and a blue flag broke out at its head. Blue meant all was well. If it had been a red flag, *Dartmouth* would have had to wait while whatever problem Jordan had was resolved. The last that he saw of Jordan and his party was the mountain of firewood being carried ashore above the high tide mark.

'Get the ship underway, Mister Beazley. We've another dozen of these to do before the fleet comes through.'

***

The breeze increased as *Dartmouth* stood away for the west. It would be Monday morning before they came to the next mark, the tail of the bank where the true Straits started. There they'd anchor *Namur's* longboat, being the largest in the fleet, with a brazier and a mountain of firewood. Every mark was vital in this transit of the Straits, but the first two were by far the most important. Unless they were sadly astray, the fleet would never sight Santo Domingo Cay, but it was a wise precaution, nevertheless.

This next one was different. Here the Straits came to their narrowest point and the beacon must be sighted before the fleet could continue. A master's mate from *Culloden* was in charge of the longboat and after running some lines of soundings he found the tail of the bank and anchored in ten fathoms, sending up a blue flag to announce that all was well. From here it was easy, and the gaggle of boats towing behind *Dartmouth* reduced steadily as each mark was established and manned. There was no time to lose, for Carlisle secretly planned to drop off the last party – a boat anchored off Santa Maria Island – in time to beat back up the Straits and meet Pocock before he came to Green Island. It would be tight, and he might have to entrust the final mark to Torrance in the schooner, but it would be one more step towards assuring the safe passage of the fleet.

***

'I regret that you didn't get noticed by Sir George, Mister Gresham.'

Carlisle and his first lieutenant had fallen into step on the poop deck and had been pacing side by side for some minutes, speaking of the weather and tomorrow's marks to be laid. Gresham didn't immediately answer, he appeared to be choosing his words carefully.

'I didn't expect to, sir. Young David has a gift for imaginative action that I lack. Oh, I consider myself bold enough, but he can see the opportunity to slip around to the enemy's scullery window while I just keep bludgeoning away at the front door. No, I think the admiral has made a good decision and I only hope that their Lordships see fit to confirm the rank, for he'll make a fine frigate captain after a short spell in a sloop. If I could prolong this war to give him the time to be made post, I'd do so in an instant.'

Carlisle risked a sideways glance at Gresham. He'd never heard a sea officer speak with such candour about his prospects, nor with such brutal realism. Every brother officer that he knew lived and breathed for the opportunity for promotion. It was the principal topic of conversation in every wardroom and gunroom that he'd ever inhabited, and it was almost the sole topic when post-captains dined together. Yet his first lieutenant was in deadly earnest, one look at his face showed that. Certainly Gresham was old, he'd been commissioned a lieutenant in the last war, he'd stayed a lieutenant right through the peace, and it looked like he'd still be a lieutenant at the end of this present war. Carlisle opened his mouth to speak, to offer sympathy, then thought better of it and just asked the obvious question.

'You've no wish for promotion then?'

At that Gresham stopped dead and turned towards his captain.

'Oh, I hope I haven't given that impression, sir. If promotion was offered I'd accept it with the greatest good will. It's just that I have a realistic view of my prospects. I have no friends to argue my case and I don't know a soul at the Admiralty or at Seething Lane. Begging your pardon, sir, but you know so few people in England that even your interest can hardly help me. I'd have to do something spectacular to be noticed, and that just hasn't happened. Yes, I yearn for the glory of post rank, but I know that there's as much chance of a seat in the Lords as there is of being made master and commander, let alone being gazetted.'

Carlisle couldn't respond to that. Considered objectively, Gresham was absolutely correct, and with a general feeling abroad that the war was ending, it would indeed take a miracle.

'But I tell you what, sir, I might wish for promotion but I'm perfectly content that it should never happen. Before you took command I'd hardly made a penny in prize money and head money, but I had a letter from Hawkins & Hammond back in Jamaica and lo and behold, I have enough to see me in genteel comfort for the rest of my days. It's all due to you, sir. If you don't mind me saying, you have a rare talent for prizes.'

Carlisle let out a deep laugh. Of course, Gresham was right. They had the same prize agent – that was the normal arrangement – and Carlisle had also received a very encouraging statement of his account in Jamaica. Gresham had no home in England to be maintained, no widowed mother to support, no unmarried sisters, no wife and no children, natural or otherwise. Hawkins & Hammond would have invested Gresham's money and it must be growing vigorously, with next to nothing being drawn. Three years ago, shortly after taking command of *Dartmouth*, he'd smiled to hear from Gresham that all he desired from the blessings of the land was a cottage and a wife, in that order. At the time he'd taken it as an amusing bit of repartee, and he'd repeated it to Chiara in a letter, in just that spirit. It was beginning to appear that Gresham spoke no more or less than the literal truth.

'Yes, a cottage and a wife, you once told me.'

'Aye, that's right. A cottage first, to attract the wife, you understand. A good solid cottage with space for two and some help, perhaps some nippers. I doubt whether I'll go to sea again after *Dartmouth* pays off. Those clerks of the cheque in Portsmouth can stop my half pay if they like, and I can laugh at them, if my prize account is halfway true. Somewhere within a short ride of Portsmouth will suit me, in case I have a yearning to talk over old times. A place with a bit of land for a kitchen garden and some shooting or fishing nearby. Captain Holbrooke lives in Wickham doesn't he? Perhaps I'll speak to him about the best place. Wickham or Petersfield, either will do nicely, and then if I can't find a neat wife, well, there's more wrong with me than I'd guessed. Now, sir, don't take that to mean that I wouldn't appreciate any opportunities that arise, it's just that I don't expect them, and I stand by what I said, Mister Wishart is a better choice for command.'

They talked long into the first watch, perhaps the most open conversation they'd ever had. It was difficult to be completely frank when the unbridgeable gulf between a lieutenant and a post-captain lay between them, and each man knew that such an opportunity would probably never come again. The sailing master, the other lieutenants, Hooper and the new third, Francis Pentland, saw them and marvelled, and the old and wise quartermasters nodded their greying heads in a knowing way.

***

Carlisle steadied himself against the binnacle as the schooner leaned far over to the strong trade wind. He'd taken Beazley with him and left Gresham in command of *Dartmouth*, with orders to anchor the last of the marker boats off Santa Maria Island and then return through the Straits to rejoin Pocock's squadron.

'What do you think, Mister Beazley, will we make Green Island on this tack?'

Beazley studied the compass for a moment, squinting to see the markings in the fading light.

Old Bahama Straits

'Aye sir, we'll make it, if the wind doesn't come any further easterly. We'd never have done it in *Dartmouth*, mind, she'd never lie close enough.'

It was true. The schooner could lie at least a point closer to the wind than the fourth rate, and that would make the difference between meeting the fleet before it committed to the passage, and meeting them some way into the Straits. Carlisle knew that *Namur's* sailing master was competent, and Beazley had spent hours with him, going over the route, but only *Dartmouth's* officers had sailed through the Straits recently and had any pretensions to a full knowledge of its dangers.

'There's the first beacon, sir.'

Carlisle hadn't noticed it, but there on the starboard was a pinpoint of orange light. It was the wrong colour for a star and in any case it was too low in the sky to be visible this soon after sunset.

'That's Philip Island, sir. *Orford's* longboat is anchored five cables into the Straits. Their brazier seems to be working well enough.'

Carlisle had to think hard. It was difficult to remember all the boats that they'd sent on their way, all the islands and all the submerged banks that should now be marked by a similar orange point of light. Yes, *Orford* had sent a midshipman with the longboat, a squat, hairy man in his late twenties. He didn't look very promising but he seemed to have his crew under control and that light in the darkness proved that all was well, for the moment. He remembered his last discussion with Sir George. The admiral had hoped, but hardly expected, that Carlisle would be able to meet him on Tuesday morning, not only for his pilotage skills but also so that he could check that the beacons were alight. The fleet would make slow progress through the Straits, and night would certainly fall before they were all through.

'We won't see the next for a couple of hours. You take some rest, sir, I'm happy enough up here.'

Carlisle looked sideways at Beazley. The sailing master

already had his head in his charts, mentally marking off the schooner's progress through the Straits. If ever there was a man who was happy in his work it was Arthur Beazley. As Carlisle watched, Beazley looked up to check that the steersman was keeping his course then quickly back down to his charts. In a flash of intuition Carlisle realised that this was one of the high points of his life, to be responsible for bringing this vast fleet through waters that were supposed to be impassable for great ships. The Straits had been marked and now it only remained for the fleet to be led through, and Beazley wanted to be the man to do it. Well, it looked as though he'd have his wish, and he'd be on *Namur's* quarterdeck before the great fleet entered the Straits.

***

CHAPTER NINE

The Chase

Wednesday, Second of June 1762.
Dartmouth, at Sea, off Salt Cay, The Old Bahama Straits.

Carlisle had learned the whole, tedious meaning of the word *slow*. With a convoy of two hundred ships in a place as dangerous as the Old Bahama Straits, nothing at all happened quickly. So measured was the pace that he'd needed to send additional rations and firewood to the parties in the boats and on the cays, and reassure them that they hadn't been forgotten. He'd borrowed two more longboats from Pocock's battle squadron, and a midshipman for each boat. Yet however much the men-of-war, the transports and the storeships spilled their wind and even backed their tops'ls, the steady trade wind and the inexorable current swept them through the Straits at a pace that no messenger on land could match. For the north coast of Cuba, as far west as Matanzas, was devoid of cities or even respectable towns. The few rustics that saw their tops'ls on the far northern horizon rubbed their eyes and went back to their tilling and fishing. No matter how slow the progress of the fleet, no word of it could come to the governor-general at Havana.

After Pocock passed Santa Maria Island, he sent *Dartmouth* ahead to the west of Salt Cay, to *put a stopper on the Florida Channel*, as he said. Thus, as day dawned on the second of June, Carlisle found himself cruising slowly sou'west with only the t'gallants of the frigates *Alarm* and *Echo* in sight. Beazley was back, and that was a relief. Carlisle hadn't realised how much he relied upon his sailing master. It had only been a few days, but Carlisle had fretted over his ship's navigation and had resorted to keeping his own private reckoning of their position. There was nothing else in sight, nothing to suggest that this was a grand meeting point of the oceans, where three great and ancient highways met and through which the wealth of the Indies flowed to enrich the King of Spain's coffers.

Carlisle was enjoying a pre-breakfast stroll on the poop deck, free from the tensions of leading the invasion fleet through the Straits, and with nothing more than the everyday cares of a King's ship to concern him. At least on the poop deck – where no man dared disturb him – he was safe from the constant game of hide-and-seek with Laredo, who sought him out as the only man on board with enough mastery of Spanish to hold a conversation. For the commander was a talkative man. Simmonds did his best to protect his captain and even now he was walking the quarterdeck with the Spaniard, discussing something that seemed to interest Laredo and conveying their meaning with elaborate hand gestures. Carlisle could smell his breakfast and in a few moments Walker would appear and announce that it was ready. That would mean an hour of Spanish conversation, for it had become accepted that his guest would breakfast with the captain and take dinner and supper in the wardroom. He was no burden over a meal, being a charming man with a great store of anecdotes about life in Havana; it was the remainder of the day when Carlisle endeavoured to keep him at arm's length. And here was Walker now. Laredo had obviously noticed him because he glanced expectantly up at the poop deck rail, where he saw that Carlisle was already striding towards the ladder that led to the quarterdeck.

'Would you care to join me for breakfast, Captain Laredo?'

Carlisle was proud of his progress in Spanish and he framed the question with care, to be as nearly correct as he was able. There was no doubt that Laredo's presence was helping immensely, and he looked forward to surprising Chiara with his new-found fluency.

'With the greatest of pleasure, sir.'

Laredo couldn't help bowing every time he spoke to

Carlisle, and it amused the young gentlemen and the quartermaster and steersmen, who covertly mimicked him when they thought their captain wasn't watching.

Carlisle moved aside to let Laredo follow Walker. Breakfast in the great cabin was a sumptuous affair – as far as two-week old bread and his dwindling cabin provisions would allow – and today he'd invited Hooper and Young to make a table for four. He could see that Walker had laid out some of the potted meats and fish that he so loved and he felt a rumbling in his stomach to remind him that it had been many hours since supper.

'Sail ho! Sail two points for'rard of the larboard beam, just showing over the horizon.'

The lookout's hail could be heard clearly through the cabin skylight. Carlisle paused, waiting for more information. He expected Pocock's battle squadron and invasion fleet to appear from somewhere to the south of east, but this sighting was in the south-southwest and it was too early. Even if Pocock had decided to pick up the pace now that the dangerous part of the Straits was behind him, he'd still be far to the east-southeast.

'Is that the fleet?'

The officer of the watch's hail was muffled by the two sets of doors that separated the cabin from the quarterdeck. It was Pentland, showing his inexperience. He'd come to *Dartmouth* from the flagship, just one of those supernumerary, newly-promoted and thoroughly unwanted lieutenants that plagued every commander-in-chief, until a berth could be found for him. Whittle – for it was inevitable that he was at the masthead to make the sighting – paused long enough to show what he thought of the question and the questioner.

'No sir, too far to the west.'

Hooper and Young exchanged glances. They'd both suffered Whittle's insolence, and both knew that it was a delicate matter. Their captain didn't have favourites and in general he treated all of the crew alike. All, that is, except

Whittle. Pentland's silence showed that he'd taken their advice to heart.

'Deck ho! There could be more than one of them, on the starboard tack, hard on the wind.'

Carlisle was entirely absorbed in Whittle's reports, and he was frozen in place with one hand on his chair and his ear cocked to the skylight. If those ships were hard on the wind then they must have come from Havana. What would they do when they saw *Dartmouth*? At all costs they mustn't be allowed to run back to Havana carrying a tale of an unknown ship-of-the-line lurking in the Florida Channel. It took a discreet cough from Walker to recall him to his duties as a host.

'Mister Hooper, carry on with breakfast, if you please.'

Carlisle had turned for the cabin door before he remembered his guest. It took a moment to form the Spanish phrase.

'Forgive me Captain Laredo, but I find that I'm needed on deck.'

Laredo rose and bowed, but Carlisle was already through the door and striding for the quarterdeck.

***

'Deck there! I can see t'gallants on the larboard quarter now. It looks like *Alarm* and *Echo*. And those sails on the larboard bow look like a frigate and a sloop.'

Carlisle had barely caught his breath as the new reports came down from the masthead. *Alarm* and *Echo* were the two frigates that Sir George had put in the vanguard of his battle squadron. They should be some two leagues ahead of *Namur*. Things were looking distinctly busy in this crossroads of the oceans.

'Where's the master? Ah, there you are, Mister Beazley. Strike the t'gallants, furl the tops'ls and the jib.'

There was a chance that the ships to the southwest hadn't yet seen *Dartmouth*, and in that case it was better to make his ship as invisible as possible. Bare poles on the horizon were much less easy to spot than t'gallants and tops'ls. Carlisle tried to imagine what the enemy could see. If they glimpsed *Dartmouth's* masts at all, it would be a reasonable assumption that they were looking at the brig that had been sent to patrol Salt Cay, the brig that was now on its way to Portsmouth with Wishart in command. They wouldn't be able to see *Alarm* and *Echo*, not yet, but they soon would.

But what could those sails belong to? Scouts for the Barlovento Squadron, sallying forth to bring Pocock's squadron to battle? If news of the invasion fleet had come to Havana, then it would be an obvious move for Admiral de Hevia to get his squadron to sea before it was bottled up in Havana. Yet it seemed unlikely, they'd seen no vessels in the Straits and even if *Dartmouth* had been sighted from the Cuban shore, any messenger would take many days to struggle across the wild north coast of Cuba to warn Havana. Could it be a relief for the brig that should still be on station? The timing was a little early, but not much.

'Captain, sir,' Whittle had shinned up the fragile t'gallant pole mast and was holding on with one hand while he leaned out to call the quarterdeck, 'there are three or four sails beyond the frigate and the sloop. It looks like a small convoy of merchantmen.'

Ah, then it was neither the Barlovento Squadron nor a relief for the brig. Yet still, if they saw *Dartmouth* or the frigates and recognised them as British, they'd surely run back to Havana with the news.

'Mister Beazley, I want every knot of speed we can make without a scrap of sail above the peak of the mizzen. Come three points to starboard, if you please.'

Beazley nodded. He could see that Carlisle wanted to get behind the enemy convoy before they were aware of the British presence.

'Courses and mizzen, lower stuns'ls, fore stays'l, sprits'l, and sprits'l tops'l. That should give us a good six knots sailing large, and we should strike the pennant.'

Beazley looked up at the mizzen.

'Once we've set the lower stuns'ls the mizzen will be doing no good, and I still don't like the feel of that woolding.'

'Very well, Mister Beazley, furl the mizzen and drop the peak.'

Gresham came hurrying up from where he'd been checking the upper deck guns.

'Beat to quarters, sir?'

'Not just yet, Mister Gresham. Let Captain Laredo have his breakfast in peace.'

Gresham smiled. He knew very well that Carlisle didn't want the Spaniard on deck while he was thinking through his next move.

Carlisle watched as the t'gallant yards were lowered and their sails furled, then the tops'ls and the mizzen. The ship looked odd with no canvas above the tops, and even odder when the additional sails started to be set. The lower stuns'ls and the sprits'ls took longer than he'd hoped, but then they hadn't been used for months and the bosun had to resort to loud encouragement to get the job done.

'Whittle, what do you see now?'

'A frigate and a sloop for sure, sir. Four brigs and schooners beyond them. Coming along peaceably enough. *Alert* and *Echo* are still under easy sail, I don't believe they've seen the convoy.'

'A cast of the log if you please Mister Pentland. Ah Captain Laredo. I believe we have sighted some of your countrymen.'

Laredo looked confused for a moment and studied the empty horizon. Carlisle pointed up to the masthead and he nodded his head and looked around. There were no signs of clearing for action and the guns lay idle behind their closed ports.

'A small convoy, I believe, Captain Laredo. Two small men-o'-war as an escort.'

Laredo shrugged.

'A timber convoy for Saint Augustine, perhaps. The

Old Bahama Straits

dockyard is always in need of timber and the Florida forests are Havana's main source of supply.'

Carlisle looked at the chart. If that was true then they'd be taking advantage of the slack current near the north coast of Cuba before they picked up the main stream running from the Old Bahama Straits and turning north to run past Florida into the Atlantic. Then *Dartmouth* was in the wrong place to cut them off from Havana, too far north. The Spaniards could bear away at any moment and then they'd be heading straight for *Dartmouth*, and that would never do. One sight of an unknown two-decker and they'd run for Havana without a second thought.

'Mister Beazley, come two more points to starboard. Any change in their course, Whittle?'

Shouting up to the masthead was easy when *Dartmouth* had the wind on her stern.

'No, sir. They're still hard on the wind.'

'What do you think, Mister Beazley?'

Beazley looked up to where the commissioning pennant should be. It was an instinctive gesture and he quickly looked down to the dog-vanes on the quarterdeck.

'If they don't see us then they must be half blind. Of course they might take us for that brig, it'll be difficult to see our mizzen at that range. Any moment now they'll see the frigates and then they'll run for sure. We'll do best to keep the hands on deck, sir.'

'You're right Master. Mister Gresham, beat to quarters but don't clear for action, not yet.'

***

The minutes passed as the sun rose higher in the sky. Four bells was struck, and still the little convoy came on. *Dartmouth* was now somewhat to the west of them, but not enough to start working into a position between them and Havana.

'Deck there. I've lost sight of the frigates now. The last I saw they were backing their tops'ls. Oh, the chase is wearing, sir.'

'Damn! They must have seen *Alarm* and *Echo*. Make all sail, Mister Beazley. Come to larboard and put the wind on your beam.'

There was a rush of hands to loose the upper sails and *Dartmouth's* speed noticeably increased.

'Whittle, give me a bearing of the chase when we're steady, and report the frigates as soon as they come back into sight.'

Gresham was rubbing his hands together in anticipation of a promising action.

'If the Dons saw the frigates then you can bet that the frigates saw the convoy, or at least the escorts, sir. *Alarm* and *Echo* will be piling on sail now.'

'Deck there. The chase is right on the beam.'

Carlisle scanned the southerly horizon but from the deck it appeared as innocent of any vessels as at the day of creation. He slung his telescope over his shoulder and scrambled over the hammock nettings to the windward main ratlines. It seemed further than when he last went aloft and he realised with a pang of conscience that he couldn't remember when that was. Out over the futtock shrouds and onto the maintop, a moment to catch his breath and then on to the topmast tressle-trees.

Whittle had come down from the t'gallant masthead and was pointing over the larboard beam. Carlisle saw them immediately, a group of pale patches breaking the pure line of the horizon. How Whittle could tell what they were with only the naked eye was more than he could understand. He waited for his breathing to steady then brought the telescope up. It took a moment to synchronise with the rhythm of the moving ship, but eventually he brought the whole group of sails into his arc of vision. He could see now that there was a decent-sized frigate to the left, then what looked very much like a small frigate or a sloop, perhaps a privateer even, then four more vessels, clearly merchantmen. It was just an impression and Carlisle couldn't be sure, but they appeared to have a livelier motion than the escorting ships, suggesting that they were lightly laden. It corroborated Laredo's identification as timber ships, outward bound in ballast for Florida.

'They're in a much greater hurry now, sir, they were just taking their time when I first saw them.'

'Thank you, Whittle.'

Carlisle watched them for ten minutes. *Dartmouth* was head-reaching on them, that much was certain, and at this rate had at least a chance of getting between them and Havana before night. What would he do if he was in their position? Matanzas was under their lee and they could run for that much smaller port. The fact that they hadn't perhaps suggested that the frigate was a King's ship with a proper sense of responsibility to report to Havana. There was another factor too. If they ran for Matanzas they'd arrive there before dark, and it was a big, deep bay that couldn't be properly covered by batteries. If they sought refuge there they must assume that the frigates that they'd spotted would follow them, and then there would be no escape.

'I can just make out our frigates now, sir.'

Carlisle followed Whittle's pointing finger. He could see nothing until he trained his telescope in the direction that the able seaman was indicating. Ah yes. Two sets of t'gallants stretching out under the nor'easterly breeze. John Lendrick had *Echo*, the smaller of the two. He'd heard somewhere that *Alarm* had a temporary commander, a man called Alms, and that *Alarm* had been coppered in the same fit of experimentation that had seen Holbrooke's frigate sheathed below the waterline. It would be interesting to see how it did in a chase. Lendrick was the senior frigate captain by some years, but still junior to Carlisle. He was almost certainly aware of *Dartmouth* moving purposefully to cut off the convoy's escape, otherwise he'd probably have held back and let them go. Without *Dartmouth* they'd probably make Havana unharmed, and if they couldn't positively state that they'd been chased by British frigates, the governor-general wouldn't be too alarmed. There were a hundred reasons why the convoy should have sighted some unidentified sails in that position, and even if he believed that they were British frigates, that didn't mean Havana was under threat. Lendrick must have concluded that with *Dartmouth* likely to cut them off, it was worth the chase.

'Keep me informed Whittle.'

Carlisle made his measured progress back down to the deck, moving slowly so that he could think it through. In an hour he'd be able to signal *Echo* and tell Lendrick whether he wanted him to continue chasing or haul his wind and return to his proper station on the battle squadron. Sir George would have seen them go, would know they were chasing, but he'd do nothing to split up his battle squadron. A frigate or two more-or-less was of no consequence, but with the threat of the Barlovento squadron ahead and de Blénac astern, he must keep his ships-of-the-line together. By the time Carlisle reached the deck he was certain that he was acting correctly. He must spare no effort in preventing those Spanish frigates reporting to the admiral in Havana. With luck he could intercept them before they came within sight of the Morro Castle, and with Lendrick's two frigates coming up fast to cut them off from the shore, there was every chance of making a clean sweep of the escorts and the merchantmen.

'Mister Beazley, make our course west-sou'west, directly for Havana. Let's see if we can get around that convoy.'

'Aye-aye sir.'

***

CHAPTER TEN

Timber Convoy

Wednesday, Second of June 1762.
Dartmouth, at Sea, off Salt Cay, The Old Bahama Straits.

Dartmouth stretched away to the west-southwest with the tail of the trade wind under her stern. Carlisle didn't interfere; this was work that could be left to the sailing master and the bosun in the certain knowledge that they'd get every knot of speed that it was possible for an old fourth rate to achieve. Noon, and dinner was served from the galley that had been left alight despite the ship being at quarters. The men ate in haste, for they all knew what this chase meant to them. There were six enemy ships under their lee, all ripe for the taking, and they were probably worth six month's pay to every able seaman.

'We're walking up to them now, sir. We'll be alongside that frigate before the last dog watch, and *Alarm* and *Echo* won't be far behind.'

Beazley had been on the poop deck, taking a vertical angle of the Spanish frigate's masthead. It showed the altitude increasing, minute by minute, and unless something could be done to slow down *Dartmouth* and the two British frigates it spelled the convoy's inevitable doom. He stowed his octant in its case and placed it in the binnacle, under the compass; it was not an instrument to be subjected to the rough-and-tumble of life on a quarterdeck.

Carlisle raised his telescope. He could see the Spanish convoy clearly from the quarterdeck. A tall frigate – almost certainly a King's ship – brought up the rear, then a slim, predatory sloop that could be a privateer, and then the timber ships in the lead – two brigs and two schooners – with all sails set to the languid breeze. Beazley was right, although perhaps a little pessimistic. *Dartmouth* was far faster than the merchantmen and would certainly catch them during the first dog watch, but it wasn't the merchantmen that concerned him. He swung around to look at the British frigates. They were hunting in a pack with stuns'ls aloft and alow, and they were making at least a knot better than *Dartmouth*. It was a simple calculation. If the Spanish kept their formation, *Dartmouth* would be first on the scene and would deal with the escorts out of hand. *Alarm* and *Echo* would bypass the action and gather up the merchantmen. It would all be accomplished out of sight of land, easy as you like, as long as the two escorts stayed with the convoy.

'What would you do, Mister Gresham, say you were the commander of that convoy escort?'

Gresham looked thoughtful. He'd just come from an earnest discussion on a moderately honeycombed twenty-four pound cannon and was still mulling over whether he'd declare it unfit for use. The gunner thought it should be condemned but like all gunners he was born cautious, that was how they lived long enough to draw their superannuation. He took a quick look through the quarterdeck telescope and seemed satisfied. Gresham had been at sea almost all of his life, with just a few years on half pay between the wars, and he could tell more about a ship from a glance at two leagues than most could tell from walking its decks.

'A King's ship for certain, sir, and a private ship…'

'Not a guarda-costa then.'

'No, sir. This one's far too lean and hungry. It may have a guarda-costa captain, or even a King's officer on board for this trip, but her regular business is privateering. The governor-general must be issuing letters as fast as his secretary can write 'em. I'll bet that ship was on the Guinea run until a month ago, but there's more money to be made privateering now that Spain's at war. I'd send the privateer ahead at all speed to take the news to Havana, and I'd use the frigate to try to slow us down and allow the convoy to escape at night.'

Carlisle was aware of Laredo hovering on the edge of the conversation. He'd been given the freedom of the quarterdeck deliberately, in case he felt the need to help his captors. He still hoped to be paroled to Havana, and could see that his best chance lay in making himself useful to Carlisle, with judiciously offered snippets of information. Nothing to change the course of the campaign, of course, but enough to create a feeling that he'd earned a reward. Laredo couldn't understand two words of the conversation, but he could tell that the Englishmen were interested in the identities of the escort. Well, he'd already told them about the timber-ships, it would do no harm to give them the escort's names. He spoke slowly in Spanish so that Carlisle wouldn't have to ask him to repeat himself. It was foolish of course, but he felt that if he volunteered the information rather than responding to a question, and if he only said it once, it didn't count as aiding the enemy.

'The frigate is *Thetis*, sir, a King's ship of thirty-two nine pound guns. She's been at Havana for many years, longer than I've been on the station. The other one's *Fenix*. She was a slaver until a month ago, but his Excellency gave the master a letter of marque as soon as he came in from his last voyage.'

Carlisle didn't look directly at Laredo but brought his telescope up to his eye again as though he didn't value the Spaniard's information at all. He replied in a casual a tone.

'Ah, then I expect Admiral de Hevia is using *Fenix* as another frigate. How very sensible. He can take the news back to Havana, no doubt.'

'Oh no, sir, not at all. The master of *Fenix* is nothing but a merchant captain. He has no knowledge of naval matters. The admiral would hardly agree to see him.'

'Hmmm.'

Carlisle continued to act as though this was just a casual conversation but privately he was analysing this new information. If the admiral would ignore – or at best treat with suspicion – anything the privateer told him, then the captain of that Frigate must either leave the convoy to fend for itself and run for Havana, or he must place a King's officer on the privateer and send it off instead, while he protected the convoy. There'd been no boat traffic between the frigate and the privateer and there could be none now that they were in a deadly race with their reputations and their liberties at stake. What then?

'*Thetis* will fight, sir, I'm sure of that. The captain's honour won't allow anything less, not with this war just starting…'

Carlisle nodded, but didn't reply.

'…and *Fenix* will have been contracted to protect the convoy. He'll at least fire his guns before he runs for Havana, otherwise his contract will be void.'

Laredo wanted to talk, he desperately wanted to please his captor without giving away anything that could be of real use. He'd already guessed that Havana was the objective of this vast expedition and had determined that his own personal line would be drawn at revealing anything about El Morro's defences. Those were secrets too deep to be divulged, and they could too easily be traced back to him. This squabble between a little fourth rate and the Florida timber convoy had no bearing on the greater matter.

'The timber ships of course have no guns, sir.'

Carlisle had already decided that he'd heard enough. Laredo's intentions were perfectly clear and he'd decided to raise the subject of parole when he thought Pocock might be in a receptive mood. Now was the time to shut Laredo out, to make him more desperate the next time.

'No, certainly not, Captain Laredo, there will be no room for them once they're loaded.'

It was a relief to return to English.

'Mister Beazley. D'you see that the privateer is somewhat to windward of the frigate? Unless something changes I'll engage the privateer first and leave the frigate to *Alarm* and *Echo*. We can sweep up the timber ships at leisure. Mister Gresham, draw the ball and load with chain shot if you please. I expect our first broadside will be at long range, so your quarter gunners are to have a care for their training and elevation.'

***

Laredo haunted the quarterdeck as *Dartmouth* ran down towards the convoy. The frigate and the privateer were some five cables apart and still holding their position between the convoy and its pursuers.

Carlisle heard one bell struck. Half an hour into the first dog watch and they were already within long cannon shot of the two convoy escorts. The two British frigates were just a mile astern now. There was no possible escape for the convoy. By all the logic of war the Spanish escort should have abandoned them long ago and run fast for Havana. Even now they'd have a decent chance of at least one of them making it. Perhaps they didn't understand the gravity of the situation, they hadn't guessed that Pocock's battle squadron and invasion fleet was just over the horizon. However, Carlisle had met Admiral de Hevia and he had some notion of what he'd say to a frigate captain who abandoned a convoy merely to report an old fourth rate and two frigates.

He looked through his telescope again. The Spanish frigate was cleared for action with its guns run out. He could see right over the taffrail onto the length of the quarterdeck, and at this distance it appeared a model of calm and readiness. The privateer was another matter entirely. Carlisle was used to seeing British privateers; they were a constant presence in the Caribbean, and on the whole they were well manned and efficient. Not so this *Fenix*. It must have set out with the same crew that had sailed on its slaving expeditions, where all that was required was to keep control of a hundred or so humans, most of them confined in chains. They must have thought this an easy contract, to escort the timber ships to Saint Augustine and back; a sure way to make a profit without the uncertainty of hunting for English prizes. They were discovering that any passage in time of war was fraught with unforeseen dangers. Their deck was in turmoil with the crew clearly being exercised at loading and running out the handful of what looked like three pound guns.

'They'll be off as soon as they hear our guns, sir.'

'Just so, Mister Gresham, just so. In that case we must make our first broadside count. He'll be expecting us to close to about two or three cables and pound him with round shot, but as you say, he'll be off at the first shot and we'll never see him again.'

Gresham smiled, he could see what his captain planned.

'Then we should hammer his sails with chain shot at five or six cables, sir.'

'Exactly. I see your starboard guns are already elevated. We only need to knock away one spar to slow him down, then he's ours. Don't bother about the frigate, leave him to *Alarm* and *Echo* and keep your gunports closed to larboard. Keep the gun crews below the gunwales and they'll be safe enough from nine pound shot. He can fire at us all he likes, just so long as he sees his duty in protecting the convoy.'

***

Bang!

The sound of the gun was muted and distorted as it fought against the following wind. Carlisle looked up in time to see the puff of smoke over the Spanish frigate and a splash as a nine pound ball fell into the sea close on *Dartmouth's* starboard bow.

'Good shooting for the Dons. What do you think to the distance, Mister Beazley, a mile?'

The sailing master was one of the few men on board who had fought the Spanish in the previous war. Carlisle was another, and Gresham, but most of *Dartmouth's* crew were too young to have been engaged.

'Barely eight cables, and I've seen the Gosport ferry make better practice than that…'

Bang!

Beazley was interrupted by another gun, but this time the

Old Bahama Straits

ball fell so close alongside that the men on the fo'c'sle were wetted by the spray.

'A mile if it's a yard,' said Gresham, taking advantage of the pause. 'he'll be away in a moment, you mark my words.'

Carlisle shut out the continual bickering between the first lieutenant and the sailing master. It had been going on all commission, mostly in a good natured way, but just occasionally it had caused bad blood. Strangely, it was better when they had a wager on their disagreement. Neither man seemed to resent losing money and in a strange way the transaction capped the argument and stopped it becoming bitter. Hundreds of guineas must have changed hands in the past three years.

'Hold your fire, Mister Gresham. Mister Beazley, make it obvious to the frigate that we're not interested in him; come two points to starboard.'

The frigate's broadside was starting to be visible, and her long row of guns were thrusting through their ports seeking out the British ship. Carlisle could see their muzzles trained as far aft as it was possible to go. He even heard the whistle that the frigate's captain blew to signal the broadside. There was a loud and prolonged crash, the frigate's side disappeared in a cloud of powder smoke, and *Dartmouth* flinched as half a dozen nine pound balls smashed into her sides. It was as well that the larboard ports were closed and only one ball caused any substantial damage. It smashed into an iron band on the mainmast and ricocheted down to destroy a swivel gun, taking its marine aimer's arm with it into the deeps of the sea. The man looked uncomprehendingly at the remains of his limb then slowly crumpled down to the deck as his legs lost their strength.

Gresham peered over to larboard. If ever a ship could look nervous it was that little privateer. It wasn't actually shaking, but the people on deck were moving in jerky motions and stopping randomly, not knowing what to do. The men on the quarterdeck were shuffling towards whatever shelter they could find, behind the mizzen mast and low down under the gunwales. This wasn't what they'd signed up for and the crew evidently was not charmed to be standing up to an enemy ship-of-the-line.

'Two minutes and we'll be able to reach him, sir.'

Gresham was standing on the hammock netting, judging the distance. He knew they probably only had one chance.

'Stand by the starboard battery, Mister Gresham.'

Carlisle eyed the privateer narrowly. One chance and then he was sure the logic of war would reassert itself and the Spaniard would be off, weaving between the timber ships and carrying its tale of English men-of-war in the Florida Channel. One chance. He looked down at the upper deck gun crews. Every gun captain was squinting along his barrel, using short, abrupt motions of his hand to direct the men, some with hand spikes under the trunnions and others with hammers for the quoins. He glanced at the privateer. Ah, her captain had had enough and he was off. Carlisle could see the men running to the halyards and sheets and braces, to make every sail draw. Now or never.

Carlisle brought his whistle to his lips and blew a single blast.

'Fire!'

Gresham's bellow could waken the dead and there was no need for the midshipman to relay the order to the lower gun deck. *Dartmouth* staggered as the broadside roared out, the recoil of her great guns was far more dangerous to the ship's timbers than those puny nine pounders that had hit her a few minutes earlier.

The privateer took the full blast of the chain shot in her upper works and rigging. Splinters flew from her light gunwales and in an instant her sails were shredded.

'There goes her mizzen yard.'

Beazley showed no emotion whatsoever at the success of the broadside. Certainly the privateer could run downwind without the lateen mizzen and in fact her speed would be little diminished, but it would take time to clear away the wreckage and trim her sails on the mainmast and foremast, and time was a luxury that she didn't have.

'Reload with ball, Mister Gresham. Close her, Mister Beazley, put me alongside at pistol shot range.'

Slowly, inexorably, the great two-decker ran down to the little privateer. Carlisle looked over his shoulder at the frigate. He could see that her captain was having second thoughts about protecting the convoy and was sending men aloft to set the t'gallants. Already she was starting to draw ahead of *Dartmouth*.

'Mister Gresham. You see the frigate? Is the larboard battery ready?'

Gresham was caught unprepared. All his gun crews were to starboard reloading to finish the privateer, and only one man, the second gun captain, was at each of the larboard guns.

'One moment, sir.'

Carlisle fumed as the confusion at the guns resolved itself. It took only a few minutes but in that time the frigate had surged ahead and the privateer was fast clearing her wrecked mizzen.

As the starboard guns were reloaded, the crews rushed as a body to the larboard battery. Carlisle heard the report from the lower gun deck and saw Gresham look quickly at the long row of black, menacing cannons.

'Larboard battery ready, sir.'

One blast on the whistle and the larboard battery fired. Carlisle had forgotten that it was loaded with chain and the banshee howl startled him. It was longer range than the broadside that the privateer had endured, and it had a less dramatic effect. Some holes in the sails, a few loose sheets and halyards, but no important spars were shot away. Well, the frigates would have to earn their keep after all.

'Starboard battery, Mister Gresham. Sailing Master, lay me close alongside that privateer. Let's deal with him before he slips away.'

***

It was all over bar the shouting. *Alarm* and *Echo* swept

past *Dartmouth* in hot pursuit of the frigate. Carlisle could see that it wouldn't get far as the two superb British frigates flew after it, one on each quarter like hounds coursing a hare. The privateer took one look at *Dartmouth's* wicked starboard broadside, saw that it would be delivered at much shorter range than the last, and its captain struck his colours with his own hand before disaster overtook them. Joseph Hooper had his first experience of the glory of taking a private man-of-war's surrender. From there it was just a matter of sending a boat to each of the timber ships with a midshipman or master's mate to accept the surrender. Before sunset the three frigates – with *Fenix* flying Pocock's blue ensign over the white and red and gold of Spain – tacked back towards *Dartmouth*, rejoicing that they'd been in sight at the moment that each of the timber ships had struck.

***

CHAPTER ELEVEN

Denial

Sunday, Sixth of June 1762.
Castillo de los Tres Reyes del Morro, Havana.

It was cold on the water and the pre-dawn mist seeped through the governor-general's cloak, sending a chill to his chest. It had been many years since he'd been soldiering and he'd forgotten the sheer discomfort of it all – the damp, the cold, the hard seats and the constant need to be hurrying away on foolish errands – and he very much suspected that he was on one now. The message from Cojimar was ominous enough, and it was signed by the commandant of the castle, Gabriel Subiera. *A large fleet approaching from the east*, it said, *close inshore*. Well, when Subiera wrote that he couldn't possibly have seen anything other than the lights that the ships were using to keep in company through the night. It might have looked like a large fleet, but really, it could be anything.

De Prado grumbled as he was helped out of his boat under the great walls of El Morro. He could see that the garrison had stood to, and the guns were mostly run out, with lanterns casting an unearthly glow and slow matches sputtering in their tubs. If Subiera was right, this fleet should have passed Cojimar by now and be close to the harbour entrance, in sight from El Morro. He saw another boat approaching out of the gloom and recognised Admiral de Hevia's barge. He stamped his foot in exasperation. There was no evidence of a threat to the city and harbour, and yet the alarm was spreading. Soon some fools would be blowing trumpets and beating drums in the city, and then there would be no stopping the panic. And this was an important day. The new grand church of Saint Ignatius – Havana wasn't the seat of a Bishopric and had no cathedral – hadn't been finished but the Jesuits had declared it fit to celebrate

Pentecost, and a great procession had been arranged. He certainly must be there. There'd be doves, for heaven's sake, live white doves released from some sort of contraption in the cupola, and who knew what conclusions would be drawn if he was nowhere to be seen? De Prado frowned at the thought of the Jesuits. They'd been a thorn in his side since he'd arrived at Havana. They thought they were above the law, a separate government owing no allegiance to him, the King's own representative. Something would have to be done about them, but it was a problem for King Carlos, not for him; they were too powerful to be sanctioned by a mere governor-general.

El Castillo de los Tres Reyes del Morro – The Castle of the Three Kings of the Rock in English – was an impressive fortification. It rose high above the sea on a natural outcrop, dominating the entrance to Havana Harbour. In principle, no enemy force could enter the harbour without first silencing El Morro's guns. It was both the harbour's principal defence and the symbol of the proud city's strength and pride. And it was tall; de Prado kept himself fit, but he was feeling his age when he reached the ultimate pinnacle of the castle.

'Over there, your Excellency.'

De Prado could see the lights with his naked eye. They were still far to the east, perhaps even to the east of Cojimar, and somewhat offshore. He took the telescope that was offered, but it didn't help. Certainly there were a lot of lights out there, but there was no telling what they belonged to or which direction they were heading.

'What do you make of it, Admiral? They're ships after all; your business, not mine.'

De Hevia was attuned to Havana's politics. He knew the pressures on de Prado, but he also had a more realistic – more pessimistic, some would say – opinion of the dangers to the city since Britain had declared war. The Pentecost procession was important, certainly, but if what he was seeing was a British invasion fleet, then the procession would have to take second place. Still, it was unlikely.

'The French perhaps, your Excellency. It's sooner than I would have expected but if Commander Laredo made a fast passage and found de Blénac receptive, it's just possible.'

De Prado grunted in reply. Yes, it could be the French and that would bring problems of its own. He'd agreed that de Hevia should send that invitation for de Blénac to bring his squadron to Havana, but only because he was certain that it would be rejected. He'd had this conversation – this argument – with de Hevia time and time again. Until he, the governor-general, had certain knowledge that Havana was not under threat, the Barlovento Squadron was going nowhere. If de Blénac imagined otherwise he'd be disappointed, and he could guess at the diplomatic furore that would follow if a letter from him – the governor-general – lured one of the last remaining French squadrons to the far ends of the Caribbean for no good purpose.

'I thought you told me that Captain Laredo hadn't returned yet.'

'He hasn't your Excellency, but there could be many reasons for that. The message could have been passed and then Laredo found himself unable to return to Havana.'

'With that wife of his waiting for him? You are surely jesting, Admiral.'

De Hevia smiled covertly. Laredo's wife was celebrated throughout the squadron and she had more opportunities for liaisons than any other naval wife in the city, and God new, they all had opportunity enough with the general dearth of women.

'Or perhaps a trade convoy, your Excellency, a British convoy that has rounded Cape San Antonio and is steering for the Florida Channel. They'd plan to pass here in the night, for certain.'

De Prado nodded. Subiera must have imagined that he'd seen them steering west, it was an easy mistake to make when all he could see was a mass of lights. Perhaps they'd even been set to the west a little by the combination of the current running through the Old Bahama Straits and the trade wind. Havana, he knew, had been established here at the junction of three wind systems and three ocean currents, at least partly to take advantage of those aids and constraints to navigation. Strange things could happen offshore as the trade wind's last gasp coincided with the start of the Atlantic Drift.

De Hevia moved closer to de Prado, looked furtively around, and whispered in his ear.

'However, your Excellency, it's my duty to point out that this could be a British squadron…,'

He looked again at the group of lights as de Prado recoiled with a sour look.

'…it could even be an invasion fleet.'

'I'll thank you, Admiral de Hevia, to keep such thoughts to yourself until we know more.'

De Prado snapped out his retort in a low but savage voice to avoid being overheard. He picked up the telescope and rested it on the cold stone of the embrasure. Dawn was approaching. It was an unfortunate moment as the lights at sea were fading but the ships that they belonged to were not yet visible.

'A convoy, as you suggested, Admiral,' he said in a clear voice. 'It's standing away to the northeast, for the Florida Channel.'

De Hevia pursed his lips. He couldn't even see the ships now, more less determine what they were and where they were heading.

'Now, I must return to the city for the procession. I would be grateful, Admiral, if you would stay here to keep a seaman's eye on affairs. We spoke about the quality of the commandants of the forts, and nothing I've seen today has changed my mind. They must be replaced, all of them. Pray present me with a list of sea officers that would be more suitable; just until your squadron should need to go to sea again, of course.'

Old Bahama Straits

'Very well, your Excellency.'

'And send a message to Subiera at Cojimar, tell him what we've decided. Perhaps he'll learn a little moderation when he chooses to drag his commander-in-chief out of bed before dawn.'

De Prado turned towards the steps, glad to be free of this distraction. It couldn't be the British, they would never dare bring a great squadron through the Old Bahama Straits, it was unheard of. And yet, there was that fourth rate in December, what was its name? *Dartmouth*, that was it. The captain had a most charming wife, far too good for a British officer. He hadn't admitted it, but he must have brought his ship through the Straits. That meant the British had a pilot to hand with recent knowledge of Havana's weak spot. Just for a moment he felt uneasy.

***

Admiral de Hevia paced the open space behind the gun embrasures. He could see de Prado's boat pulling fast across the harbour entrance for the city. It was difficult to put himself in the governor-general's shoes; the man had so many conflicting cares that it was a wonder that he could make any coherent decisions. In this case it was because of the long-running power struggle between successive governors-general and the Jesuits, in its essence a conflict between state and church, or a faction of the church in any case. Yet he couldn't help feeling that in this matter de Prado was mistaken. He looked again to the northeast. The ships' lights had been extinguished by the rising sun and its brilliance made it difficult to see anything in that direction, but he just had the impression that they were heading west, not northeast. There was certainly a great number of them but then, the British trade convoys often had over a hundred ships. It was no use staring through the telescope, he'd blind himself in an instant and even below his shading palm his eyes watered so much that he could barely see.

Nevertheless, bit-by-bit, the daily miracle of dawn was consummated. The sun's lower limb pulled itself clear of the horizon and suddenly he could see them, a vast armada of ships all under sail. He couldn't tell which way they were heading, not yet, but he'd know in thirty minutes or so. Certainly, it *could* be a trade convoy...

It was a good road to Cojimar, some four miles, and a mounted man could be there and back in an hour. Subiera would certainly have a better view of the ships and might already have read the message telling him that it was nothing more than a homebound British convoy. He considered commandeering a horse and going himself to Cojimar, but instantly rejected the idea. From here he could see the city, the harbour and the wide ocean with the unknown ships sitting like paper toys on the very rim of the horizon. Coming or going? He still couldn't tell.

***

De Hevia looked to the east, towards Cojimar. The castle was hidden by a wooded outcrop of the hills, but he could see the road that skirted the blue ocean, and what he saw on the road worried him. A rider – he could swear it was the same man that had been sent with the message to Subiera – was whipping his horse mercilessly so that its hooves raised a cloud of dust on the road. He waited patiently, looking occasionally at the ships that to his eye were growing larger, not smaller.

'Your Excellency, a message from Captain Subiera.'

The man was gasping for breath and his clothes that had looked neat and fresh an hour ago were covered in dust, as though he'd ridden far through a long hot day, not less than ten miles in the cool of the morning.

The wax seal looked as though it had been applied in haste, and the address, to de Hevia personally, had been scrawled by a soldier, and an inadequately educated one at that. Subiera was clearly terrified. The governor-general had stated his firmly held opinion and this rather junior captain of artillery was placed in the position of having to contradict him. Subiera was certain – certain enough to openly disagree with the King's own representative – that the ships were heading west. They were moving slowly, certainly, but their heads were all towards the western horizon, and there were more than a hundred of them!

De Hevia kept his face immobile and ran through the alternatives again. As he did so he heard the bells of all the churches in the city and the great bells of the almost-completed Saint Ignatius, ring out for the feast of Pentecost.

Not a British trade convoy, that was certain. No convoy commander would risk the wealth of a West Indies convoy in the Old Bahama Straits, it was a giant step beyond the risk of bringing a battle squadron through. It couldn't be de Blénac either, not unless he'd miraculously multiplied his fleet at least tenfold. A French trade convoy? There wasn't that much trade left in the French West Indies and in any case they'd make straight for the open Atlantic from their mustering port at Cape François. De Hevia's heart pounded as he excluded all the possibilities, leaving just one certainty. It was the British, come in force to wrest Havana from the King of Spain and add this jewel of his crown to King George's growing Empire of the Indies!

***

The church was packed and de Hevia felt out of place in his dusty undress uniform. He could have sent an aide, but he knew how difficult it would be to get to de Prado. He must do it himself or wait for Mass to end – and it would be a long Mass, for certain. The air was heavy with incense and the choir had just started on the *Veni Sancte Spiritus*. The doves were to be released at the conclusion of the sequence; he knew that because he'd lent a party of his flagship's topmen to release them from the specially constructed circular vent in the cupola. Nobody else would risk clambering around in the partly-built void below the roof. It would form a punctuation in the solemn Mass, a break before the Alleluia and the gospel reading, and all eyes would be on the doves, not on the altar and with luck not on the governor-general.

'Da virtutis meritum, da salutis exitum, da perenne gaudium, Amen, Alleluia.'

Grant us in life Thy grace that we in peace may die and ever be in joy before Thy face.

There was a breathless hush as the choir's final notes faded away. De Hevia shivered involuntarily. If he was right – and he'd never been more certain of anything in his life – there would be many here today who would die in a far from peaceful manner as Havana's castles and walls were battered by the British artillery.

The doves were released to a collective gasp. Twelve of them, to represent the closest followers of Christ who had waited in the upper room for the Holy Spirit to descend. They wheeled and swooped around the nave, searching in vain for a way out of the church and yet appearing to the upturned faces of the worshipers like messengers from God, like angels on the wing. De Hevia crossed himself and hurried forward, squeezing through the gaps in the crowd until he was so close to de Prado that the great man became aware of his presence.

'It's the British, your Excellency, I'm certain. A battle squadron and a fleet of transports and storeships. They're off Cojimar still, but they're advancing on the harbour. Two hundred ships, at least.'

De Prado showed no emotion at all and gave no indication that he'd heard. Everyone knew that a war with Britain carried the risk of Havana coming under attack, and an urgent discussion at this of all times between the governor-general and the commander of the Barlovento Squadron would certainly raise questions. This was neither the time nor the place to incite a panic. He stared ahead and could have been speaking to himself.

'I will come to El Morro after Mass, Admiral, and we will see what we will see.'

'Very well, Your Excellency,' de Hevia was nettled at the

governor-general's response, 'but at least allow me to set the chain across the harbour mouth.'

De Prado considered for a moment. He still thought that a British invasion was unlikely, although he recognised that de Hevia was not an excitable man prone to rash conclusions. If it was an invasion, then without the chain the harbour mouth could be forced by determined captains, even under El Morro's guns. It would cause terrible losses in the first ships to come through, but he knew that the British were quite capable of trying it as a nautical version of a *coup de main*. The chain could be deployed in a couple of hours and it was often done as an exercise, although never on a Sunday, and certainly not on Pentecost Sunday. On balance, it was a sensible precaution, proportionate to the threat.

'As you wish, Admiral, although I'll believe it when I see it. Now leave quietly, if you please.'

De Hevia retreated the way he'd come, but he was troubled. De Prado's attitude reminded him of the strange tales he'd heard of *El Draco* insisting on finishing his game of bowls before sending his fleet to face the grand armada nearly two hundred years ago. That was all very good, but Drake commanded a fleet that could take to the sea and contest the passage. With the squadron bottled up in the harbour, de Prado had nothing and was left with a strategy of craven defence. All that he could do was shelter behind Havana's walls and towers and wait … for what, exactly? Yellow fever? A hurricane? An act of God?

***

De Prado set his face in a reverential expression through Mass, and he broke his fast with the vicar general without letting any of his anxiety show. It was only after the coffee had been drunk that he made his apologies and had himself rowed back to El Morro. What he saw settled the question. A vast fleet – a veritable armada – was sailing serenely past the harbour entrance just out of long cannon range of the castle. It was a majestic sight in the bright sunshine. A battle squadron led the way followed by rank upon rank of storeships and transports, and the rear was defended by yet more ships-of-the line. Two hundred was certainly not an exaggeration. Majestic, yes, but also menacing and the artillerymen around him were stripped for action rather than dressed for a parade as they usually would be for a visit from the governor-general. The guns were run out, the slow match was to hand and the spare roundshot was stacked between each embrasure. El Morro was ready at a moment's notice to contest the passage into Havana harbour. He walked slowly to the west side of the platform and looked out over the harbour mouth where he could see the massive iron chain slung across the channel. He had to admit that de Hevia had done well. The British showed no immediate intention of attacking but if they did they would pay in blood for attempting to force a way through.

'An admiral of the blue, your Excellency.' De Hevia lowered his telescope. 'Perhaps it's this Sir George Pocock that we've heard of, fresh from the East Indies. Oh for de Blénac to appear now; the British don't have enough ships-of-the-line to withstand our combined force.'

'De Blénac won't follow, Admiral. The British would never have come through the Straits if they weren't certain of their rear, you know that.'

De Hevia nodded sadly. He knew what was coming next, and he knew that de Prado had the force of law and the King's authority behind him.

'Well Admiral, it seems that Captain Subiera was correct. I'll call a council of war for this afternoon. Meanwhile, prepare your three blockships, if you please. You can choose whichever are most suitable, they'll be of no use as men-of-war now, and I'll see that list of your officers who are to take command of the castles. Your best officers, if you please, and I'll want to know the reason if you choose not to offer Captain Velasco for El Morro.'

***

CHAPTER TWELVE

Three Brothers

Sunday, Sixth of June 1762.
Namur, at Sea, off Cojímar, Cuba.

Cuba's green shores slid by as though in a dream. It felt novel to be in sight of land, where the ship's progress could be measured against fixed, definite points and its distance from danger could be assessed by something other than a lead line. The wind contributed to the feeling of peace as it blew at nothing more than a whispering zephyr, nudging the ship westerly at barely walking pace. The people were all on deck, even those who weren't on watch, each man entranced by the sight as though they'd just raised the land after a long ocean passage, rather than a short run through the Straits.

Carlisle too was watching the shore, but he was at the same time deep in conversation with Laredo and their pointing and gesturing suggested an exchange of information that was more than just casual gossip. It was wonderful how Carlisle's Spanish had improved in the past three weeks. It had already been passable, thanks to Chiara's efforts, but he'd set himself to talk to the Spanish commander as much as his duties as a captain would allow, and they naturally spoke Spanish, in the high dialect of Castille. There was no point in hiding their destination now, and in any case it must have been obvious since this great armada had started moving into the Old Bahama Straits.

He'd learned a lot about Laredo in these conversations, as well as a great deal about the Barlovento Squadron, but less of Havana's defences. At first he'd been surprised at the commander's willingness – nay, his eagerness – to indulge his captor's curiosity, until he'd started to understand why he was prepared to risk his career for the chance of early parole and a return to Havana. He knew at their first meeting that Laredo was a worried man, and now he knew why. A year ago he'd married a rare Sicilian beauty of exquisite grace and impeccable breeding and brought her out to Havana. So far, so good, but it turned out that the Señora had fixed ideas about the balance of power in a marriage. Carlisle thought ruefully that she sounded not unlike his own wife. However, Señora Laredo was flirtatious, even by Havana's lax, tropical standards. Perhaps she was too young to understand the effect that she had on men, but anyhow she was actively pursued by half of Havana's land officers and almost all of the squadron's sea officers, some with amazing persistence. Laredo suspected that he'd been chosen for the errand to de Blénac not for his diplomatic skills, but in order to get him out of the way, to clear the firing arcs for one of his wife's more ardent admirers.

There was little that Laredo wouldn't discuss, and Carlisle was certain that he was telling the truth, but not the whole truth. The number of ships in the Barlovento Squadron – less than he'd thought – the guns on the city's walls, the number and quality of the regiments, all were open topics. However, when the conversation turned to the Morro Castle, Laredo's face turned blank and he feigned ignorance. Perhaps that was his own personal line that he wouldn't cross, his salve for his honour, and his defence should he be called to account by his Spanish masters. There was something about that fortress, some secret that it was assumed that foreigners didn't share. Yet even that knowledge was useful to Carlisle, for it established a positive gap in his intelligence and set a defined boundary: *here* is what I do know, and *here*, beyond this line, is what I don't. It also gave Carlisle confidence that everything else that Laredo told him was the truth, as far as he knew it. For he'd already tested the commander by asking about matters that he'd seen with his own eyes six months ago.

'Captain, sir. The flagship's hung out a signal for *Dartmouth's* captain to repair on board.'

Old Bahama Straits

'Very well, Mister Gresham. Call away the longboat and my boat's crew. Ah, Mister Simmonds. You'll come with me.'

***

Namur's side looked massive and daunting as Souter steered the longboat towards the entry port. Everything was on a different scale in this vast second rate and even the smallest detail was a novel experience. The bowman couldn't even reach the main chains with his boathook, but had to take hold of a line that was seized to an eyebolt fixed to the ship's side. He and Souter held the longboat in close so that Carlisle could ascend the ladder to the entry port without having to jump. They heard the wail of the pipes and then at an abrupt wave from a midshipman, they let go, the oarsmen shipped their oars and they steered back for *Dartmouth* and their supper.

'It's good to see you again, Captain Carlisle. You haven't met Lord Albemarle, I believe. My Lord, this is the officer that guided us through the Straits and indeed is the last King's officer to visit Havana.'

Carlisle bowed. Albemarle came from an old and profoundly protestant Dutch family, the Keppels, who had come over with King William in the last century and, through faithful but unspecified services, had produced the first Earl. Since then the family had infiltrated the very heart of the British establishment. George was a privy councillor, one of the King's closest advisers. His two younger brothers, having prospered in the navy and the army, had joined him on this expedition. Augustus Keppel was Pocock's deputy flying a commodore's pennant and William Keppel was a major general of infantry. They were a dynasty to be treated with respect, if one wanted to prosper in Georgian England. Rumour had it that when the second Earl had died, he'd left the family with a mountain of debt, and these three sons, George, Augustus and William, were determined that this expedition against Havana would repair the family's finances. They were all here in the room, all called to hear Carlisle's opinions on the task at hand, and significantly there were only two others. This then wasn't a council of war, but more a sort of private audience.

Albemarle extended his hand and introduced his brothers. Carlisle already knew Augustus Keppel, and he wasn't surprised to see him here. He'd commanded the naval forces at Belle Isle and could be expected to have a good working knowledge of combined operations against an enemy shore. Holbrooke's letters had spoken well of him, even betraying a certain warmth in their relationship. There were old friends from the Quebec campaign too. Colonel Guy Carleton who'd been Wolfe's quartermaster-general and William Howe who'd been the adjutant-general. Both greeted Carlisle with enthusiasm as well they may, for Carlisle had landed them both on hostile shores in difficult circumstances. They were specialists in opposed landings, both of them, and if this was the quality of Albemarle's staff, then there was little to fear for the conduct of this expedition.

Pocock straightened the chart that he was studying and beckoned to Carlisle.

'Now that we're here, Carlisle, all theorising must end and we have to decide where the main thrust will be delivered against the city, and that will determine where we land. Now, you have the most recent knowledge of the place and I know that you've been pumping your Spaniard for information. Perhaps you could favour us with your thoughts.'

Carlisle winced at the mention of his Spaniard. The fewer people who knew that Laredo was singing like a caged bird, the better, and not only for the security of the expedition, but for Laredo's own safety when he was returned to his countrymen. For Carlisle had a great deal of sympathy for Laredo, and was determined to secure his release on parole as soon as the time seemed right. What he didn't want to do was send the man back to a hangman's noose or a public garrotting.

Pocock tilted his head to one side in an odd gesture, rather like a crow testing the ground before deciding which worm to attack. Carlisle cleared his throat and leaned over the chart.

'I saw only the harbour side of the city, Sir George, and I wasn't able to walk the walls on the western side, nor did I see the landward side of the Morro Castle. However, the walls were spoken of as being strong and well maintained. What the Spaniards really fear is an enemy gaining control of the Cabaña, this ridge of high land on the eastern side of the channel. A few heavy batteries on those heights could dominate the city and make it impossible to defend.'

'They've fortified it, no doubt. The ridge, I mean.'

Albemarle had produced a pair of spectacles from his pocket and was studying the chart with great care. It was evident from the way he turned his head from his fellows, that he was embarrassed about his need for them.

'In December, my Lord, the batteries on the Cabaña were in a poor state of repair and the ridge was overgrown. I heard that the King had ordered them to be repaired, but I understand that they've done nothing to rectify the situation. You'd think they didn't believe an attack was possible.'

'Then a landing somewhere on this eastern coast would allow us to advance on the Cabaña. What of the fortress here, the Morro Castle? Surely that will need to be taken.'

Carlisle realised he was being addressed again.

'Certainly, my Lord. The castle can be resupplied from the city with the greatest ease; the channel is only some two hundred yards wide. Again, I didn't visit the castle, but I understand that its guns can cover its landward approach and make life very uncomfortable on the Cabaña. In my opinion, the Morro Castle is the key to the city. If our forces hold it then the city is defenceless. The Cabaña is important, certainly, but its value is contingent on taking the castle.'

'Can the castle be taken from the sea?'

Carlisle glanced at Pocock who it appeared was ready for

this question.

'An act of desperation, I fear, my Lord. You can see the height of the embrasures from here. There's no room to manoeuvre, so my ships would have to anchor, and the sea bed drops off so near the shore that they'd be anchored right under the Morro's guns, and their own guns wouldn't be able to elevate far enough for the shot to do any damage. I'll try it if necessary, of course, but I have a low expectation of success. Carlisle, did you learn anything about the landward side of the castle, beyond what Admiral Knowles told us?'

'Very little, sir. The Spanish won't let foreigners near the place or allow them to view it from the east. There's something they're hiding, some feature of its defences, but I haven't been able to determine whether it's a strength or a weakness.'

Nobody spoke for a moment or two as they studied the chart. Carleton looked up with a wry smile.

'Then it's a landing and a siege. Well, at least we know what's needed.'

Albemarle nodded and took up Carleton's thread of thought.

'I don't like the west side. It looks like it could be a long siege to reduce those walls, and the fever season's upon us. We could lose half our army while we're waiting for the engineers to dig their saps and the gunners to make a practicable breach. What do you think, Admiral?'

'It looks like prime yellow jack territory to me, my Lord, and of course the hurricane season's already started. Whatever we do must be done swiftly. I'd have attempted to sail straight into the harbour and damn the Morro's guns if they hadn't got that chain in place already. I expect there will be block ships in there soon. I agree, a landing to the east and a march upon the Cabaña and the Morro Castle appears our best option. There's a good beach here, between Cojimar and... what's this place further east, Bacuranao?'

Old Bahama Straits

'We'll need to protect our left flank, my Lord. A position here at Guanabacoa should do it, although it'll split our force.'

Howe pointed to an inland town to the southeast of the harbour. It dominated the city's eastern approaches and certainly must be held to prevent a flanking counter attack.

'How long is that beach,' Albemarle asked.

Pocock stepped it off with a pair of dividers.

'If this chart's to be believed then it's three miles. It certainly appeared that long as we passed it. The sea looked relatively calm too. A good beach for the flatboats.'

'And it's wide enough to get the whole army ashore in one day. I like it; what do you say, Sir George?'

'I'll place a few ships to suppress these forts at either end, but they didn't look like they can offer much resistance.'

Silence again as each man considered the landing, imagining the scene as the grenadiers and the light infantry waded ashore and faced any opposition that might have been moved into place.

'I believe, my Lord, that there's little risk of the landing being opposed by a large force. Nevertheless, a diversion would be useful. Here, to the west, at Chorera, it'll at least be believable. It seems that we have enough ships to both cover the real landing and make a credible display on the other side of the city.'

Carleton seemed to be the agent for decision making, the voice that spoke first and forced everyone to state their opinion. Pocock glanced again at the chart.

'I can send a respectable force of ships-of-the-line to the west and still have enough to cover the landing in the east. If I send all the storeships west as well, it'll have the appearance of a determined invasion. I can make a show of loading the marines into the ships' boats, that should persuade them that we're in earnest. You won't need the storeships until your force is landed from the transports, and from the shore they look much the same.'

'Then are we agreed, Sir George?'

'Aye, my Lord, I agree. But for the love of God let's make it quick, before the yellow jack lays us all low or a hurricane destroys us.'

***

'How much are you getting from your Spaniard, Carlisle, is he singing?'

They'd retired to Pocock's cabin, leaving the soldiers to make their plans in the great cabin. Albemarle and his staff had to finalise the loading of the flatboats and ensure that the correct units found their boats in the first light of dawn the next day. The naval planning was easier and Commodore Keppel was already issuing the orders that would move all the ships into the right places.

'He's desperate to be paroled, sir. I gather his wife is something of a beauty and half of the garrison and all the fleet is guilty under the tenth commandment. He fears what might happen in the turmoil of a city under siege, and even more if we should take the place. Oh, he won't directly reveal secrets that he considers vital, but he's prepared to offer collateral information, and that covers a surprising number of topics.'

'You don't suspect he's lying to you then? Is your Spanish good enough for that?'

'It's improving every day, sir. I cured him of dissembling very early on by asking him a few questions where I already knew the answer.'

'Have you promised anything?'

'Only that I'll consider recommending parole to you, sir. He knows that he'll get nothing better, and he's prepared to continue on that basis. In truth, he's past the point where he can recant, and he must now fear that we could expose him to his masters.'

'Well, I'll leave the decision on parole in your hands. You may send him ashore with all the usual fanfare when you believe his usefulness is over, or when you get sick of his company. Just send a note to my secretary and he'll give you the appropriate letter.'

'There's one thing you should know, Sir George. I mentioned that there's some secret about the Morro Castle's landward defences, and that Laredo won't speak of it. Well, I caught a hint when I was in Havana that there might be an obstacle, a deep ditch or something of that nature on the eastern side that will make a land assault difficult or impossible. I've probed on that, but he won't talk, and I didn't want to alarm the soldiers. Perhaps you could mention it.'

Pocock gazed out of the window with his hands behind his back, evidently thinking. He turned suddenly, catching Carlisle unawares.

'It wouldn't surprise me, but I want the army to discover that for themselves, otherwise they'll expect an immediate seaborne bombardment, and you've heard my views on that. You know, I'm prepared to shed the squadron's blood to take the Morro Castle, but only after the army has tried its best. There'll be little enough for us to do once the army's ashore and I know I'll come under pressure to contribute, and that can be my bargaining counter. I'll give Lord Albemarle any number of sailors to shift his gun batteries, I'll even man the batteries and fire the damned guns if need be, but between you and me the thought of placing valuable ships-of-the-line under the Morro Castle's walls doesn't appeal at all. That's a step that I'll only take *in extremis*.'

***

CHAPTER THIRTEEN

The Landing

Monday, Seventh of June 1762.
Dartmouth, at Sea, off Cojimar, Cuba.

'No bottom, no bottom on this line!'

Carlisle turned to Beazley with an unspoken question. It was hard to look unconcerned when your ship was less than half a mile from the shore and the lead-line could find no bottom.

'It's the current, sir. It's been sweeping past here since old Noah's time, since the Flood you understand, and it's carved the channel deep and steep. There's a sort of underwater escarpment here, according to what charts we have, and we won't strike twenty fathoms until we're maybe three or four cables from the shore.'

'Very well Mister Beazley, heave to and keep the lead going. What do you think of this wind?'

Beazley stared up at the pennant then wet his finger and held it aloft. He spent an infuriating few seconds studying the clouds, turning to view every point of the compass.

'Fading, sir, fading. It's the trade wind still, but weak and unreliable. A good day for those flatboats and I reckon the soldiers will be thankful.'

'Well, they're not our concern today. Mister Gresham! do you see anything?'

Carlisle shouted up to the maintop where the first lieutenant's massive figure could be seen scanning the shore through his telescope.

'The beach looks deserted, sir. I can see a road from here, a few hundred yards behind the trees, but there's nothing moving. It branches off to the castle and away again parallel to the beach.'

Carlisle looked at his watch just as eight bells were struck, but there was no urgent rush of men changing the watch. They'd all taken their breakfast before dawn and had been standing beside their guns since the first sliver of sun had appeared in the east-northeast. It looked like Pocock's plan was working. The admiral had taken thirteen ships-of-the-line and nearly a hundred storeships to Chorera, to the west of the harbour entrance, and should now be entertaining the Spaniards by moving his marines around in the boats, feigning preparations for landing. At that distance from the shore, the defenders wouldn't be able to distinguish a marine uniform from those of the regular line regiments. The dull booming of Pocock's guns could just be heard as he pounded the castle and the shoreline at Chorera. It was a good plan. Even if the Spaniards had a force large enough to contest a landing, they'd have to split it between the two sites, and not only were they some six miles apart, but the great city and harbour of Havana lay between. De Prado would have to decide which potential landing site he'd defend, or as seemed likely, he'd have to hold his army close to Havana until the invader's intention was clear.

'There's smoke coming from the castle, sir.'

Carlisle turned to look to the west. Cojimar Castle was a modest affair of dressed coral limestone blocks on a low stony outcrop. Its walls were perhaps the height of *Dartmouth's* maintop where Gresham was now standing, and Laredo had said that it mounted ten guns of eighteen and twenty-four pounds. In true Spanish fashion it had a small, circular, roofed watchtower at each corner, probably only large enough for one man. Carlisle had never really understood their purpose; it would be baking hot in there during the day and the tiny observation slits were of little use. There was a small battery to the left of the castle and an earthwork, and behind that a body of soldiers could be seen by the twinkling of the rising sun reflecting from their bayonets. Laredo had been dismissive of the fort's quality, remarking that it was garrisoned by men that none of the line regiments or the artillery batteries wanted. It marked the western end of this three-mile beach, and *Dartmouth* was keeping a respectful distance from it.

'Heated shot, sir?'

'I think not, Mister Beazley. The air is still cool and if those were braziers, we'd see a heat haze by now. Breakfast, I suspect, nothing more.'

Beazley stared through his own telescope and nodded his head. The captain was right. He'd seen shot being heated and the intense heat would have created distortions above the firing platforms. That flag of Spain would appear to be dancing by now, instead of drooping listlessly to the fitful breeze.

So far the gunners at Cojimar had observed an unspoken truce with *Dartmouth*, and it wasn't surprising. *Dartmouth* was the nearest ship but beyond the fourth rate there were seven other ships-of-the-line, a handful of frigates, sloops and bomb ketches, and a hundred-and-fifty-odd transports. It would have been foolish to start a battle when none may be necessary. Captain Subiera was still smarting at his report of yesterday being disbelieved and he wasn't inclined to stick his neck out any further. Besides, he'd seen that ship before when *Dartmouth* sailed into Havana in December. Despite the generally-held opinion that ships couldn't stand against fortresses, he knew that the result of a duel was not pre-determined.

'Deep twenty!'

'There, we're on the ledge now, sir, and drifting in.'

'Very well, Mister Beazley. Put her on the starboard tack. I think this is close enough.'

Dartmouth's crew was well drilled after all this time together. At a shout from the bosun a man from each gun ran for the braces and sheets and in five minute the great ship's stern had been swung through the wind. Now her bows were pointing to seaward but her larboard battery covered the western corner of the beach and the castle.

Dartmouth had been given perhaps the most technically difficult station of all. The northeasterly wind and the west-flowing current combined to carry all the ships westwards towards Cojimar Castle, but it was *Dartmouth* that would first have to deal with the Spanish guns. Keppel had foreseen this and had deliberately placed his only fourth rate in that position. He'd also manoeuvred his squadron so that they had approached from the west, keeping clear of Cojimar and reaching the twenty-fathom ledge well to the east of their stations to allow for drift before they anchored. Only the men-of-war were underway now, and the transports had already anchored some five cables from the beach.

'Captain, sir. There's a band of cavalry coming down the road from the castle. A small squadron it looks like.'

Carlisle turned his telescope on the shore. He could just make out the bright flashes as the sun reflected off lances and swords. This would be the famous Spanish light cavalry. They had no breastplates or bright helmets, and were mounted on the small, hardy horses that were all that could survive in the tropics. A scouting party, he guessed, to assess whether this was a landing in earnest, or just a demonstration to disguise the real point of main effort.

'Mister Gresham, come down and attend to your guns. I think we can give them a couple of broadsides before we must come about.'

Despite his size, Gresham would have made an excellent topman and he came down the ratlines like an oversized version of the black, long-armed apes that were reported to live in the forests of the Spanish Main. He was issuing his orders before his boots had even touched the deck.

'D'ye see the target, quarter gunners? Lever those guns around then.'

Carlisle could see that it was all in hand. One broadside certainly, and another if he ordered *Dartmouth* to bear away a point. That would bring her within range of the castle's guns of course, but it would be worth it.

'Fire when you're ready, Mister Gresham.'

A quarter mile from the castle the road dipped down towards the beach, leaving the cover of the trees, and now the cavalry was clearly visible. Carlisle could sense their nervousness and saw them set their spurs and urge their horses into a canter, to reach the trees again some half mile away.

Carlisle loved this moment. True, he hated the slaughter that the broadside would cause, but there was something satisfying about that row of guns, all pointing in the same direction with their crews poised like statues and their gun captains with one arm raised and the other outstretched ready to have the slow match thrust into their hands. It was the culmination of all the months and years of effort to bring *Dartmouth* to her present peak of efficiency. It was why parliament had voted the money to build the ship, to equip it and store it and send it on its way to do the King's bidding. He had a feeling that he'd never know such professional fulfilment again.

'Fire!'

Gresham's shouted word brought all those slow matches down on the guns in almost the same instant. There was a second's delay while the fire raced down the priming tube, and then twenty-five guns roared in unison. When the smoke cleared, Carlisle could see the results. The cavalry had been thrown into confusion. He could only see three horses and their riders on the ground, perhaps four, but that was all he'd expected at that distance. Yet it wasn't the casualties, but the effect on the morale of those that survived. The tight, regular formation had been shattered and now horses and men were racing along the road to the shelter of the trees. A group at the rear had turned back towards the castle, splitting the squadron in two.

'Fire!'

The second broadside caught Carlisle unawares and he had to clutch the hammock netting to avoid falling. Only one horse down this time and he could see there would be no third opportunity, for as he watched the last of the riders disappeared into the trees. Four or five in total then. The harsh arithmetic of war would suggest that the Spaniards had the best of the encounter, for the cost in treasure of deploying that light cavalry squadron was infinitesimal compared with the cost of bringing *Dartmouth* to this place. Yet it was the morale factor that mattered most. Those Spanish horsemen had been defeated and they knew it, but looking down at his own gun crews urgently reloading, with their smiles gleaming out of powder-stained faces, he knew that they were ready to fight again, and would do so with a will.

'Seven cables off the fort, sir, and we're in sixteen fathoms of water, shoaling.'

Beazley had been attending to the navigation while the guns had been firing. Seven cables was too close. Keppel had wanted *Dartmouth* to leave the castle alone unless they were fired upon. There was a separate fate planned for the defenders of Cojimar.

'Stand out to sea, Mister Beazley. You may tack when you estimate the castle at ten cables.'

'Aye-aye sir. We'll be fighting this wind and current all day, I reckon.'

Carlisle nodded and glanced at the fort. He could see activity on its walls and then twin puffs of smoke appeared, followed by the dull booms of heavy guns.

Gresham's head popped up from the waist at the first sound of the guns. Carlisle couldn't help thinking that his timing was just about right to be decapitated if the Spanish guns had been pointed better.

'Short and wide of our stern, sir. Those gunners aren't used to firing at moving targets. Will you reply?'

'I think not, Mister Gresham. Keep your course, Mister Beazley.'

***

Two bells rang out from the fo'c'sle, and right on time the vast union flag at *Valiant's* masthead came down and a single gun bellowed out its imperative command.

'There they go, sir.'

Gresham had caught the excitement of the moment, and despite his long-standing contempt for the army and all its works, he was as anxious for their success as anyone.

Fifty flatboats, as though steered by a single hand, pulled away from the gaggle of transports and organised themselves into two parallel lines, just as George Holbrooke had described. Carlisle's friend had been one of the first commanders of a flatboat division back in '58 on the Brittany coast, and he had a fund of stories about these most interesting craft.

Carlisle could see Colonel Howe in the centre of the first line, his boat adorned with a variety of gaily coloured flags. The frigates had moved close into the shore an hour before, at the turn of the watch, and had been steadily peppering the tree line with grapeshot and roundshot, but with little obvious effect. Now they redoubled their efforts and a positive storm of shot smashed into the innocent beach. To Carlisle's eye, it appeared deserted and even the cavalry had withdrawn towards Havana, taking the exposed stretch at a gallop until they were in the shelter of the trees again.

A pause, and then, with a wild waving of flags, the first line started pulling steadily for the shore as the second line rested on its oars. Carlisle was transfixed by the sight and watched carefully through his telescope. *Dartmouth* was a mere observer this morning. It was deemed too dangerous to put the ships-of-the-line close enough to help with the bombardment; Keppel was holding them in reserve until they might be needed, and until the threat of the landing failing was great enough to warrant the risk.

The tall mitre hats of the grenadiers showed clearly as they were rowed towards the centre of the beach, and a battalion's worth of light infantry were in the boats nearest to *Dartmouth* on the right of the line. Keppel had ordered that each boat be commanded by at least a midshipman, and Carlisle could see them now, standing to drop their grapnels as they felt the first surge of the steepening waves lifting their sterns. The grapnels would perform the twin roles of keeping the boats' sterns to the sea and assisting in hauling them off once they'd landed their soldiers. The boats powered through the moderate surf and in a few moments the first were crashing onto the hard sand. Carlisle could see two seamen on each boat jumping into the water in an attempt to hold the bows steady as the long planks were deployed for the soldiers. He saw Howe step ashore and stride up the undefended beach.

'There's the second line, sir. Regular musketeers by the look of them. Ah, the first line of boats are starting to haul off now.'

It was a wonderful sight. Under the bright tropical sun the grenadiers and light infantry were skirmishing forward towards the trees. As the line infantry arrived they were quickly organised into their companies and formed up in defensive lines on the beach. It all proceeded in regular fashion, as if it was a demonstration under the King's eye. There was some sporadic firing from the smaller Bacuranao Castle at the east end of the beach, but otherwise nothing to disturb the orderly landing. The first wave was to secure the beach then wait for the second wave before moving inland. Carlisle guessed that Howe must be sorely tempted to seize the moment and push forward immediately, but yet he waited for the overwhelming force that Albemarle wanted.

***

It was midday before the second wave started to disembark onto the shore. The beach was becoming a mass of red coats with the brightly coloured facings that distinguished one regiment from another adding a touch of variety to the scene. Albemarle was ashore now and things were starting to move. It was difficult to see what was happening once the companies left the beach, but there was certainly a move to the west, towards the Cojimar Castle and Havana. The castle was starting to fire its guns at the advancing soldiers and the breastwork to its left was shrouded in smoke. It looked like the little castle would be an obstacle for that part of the landing force that was to follow the coast road west.

***

CHAPTER FOURTEEN

Marines and Seamen

Monday, Seventh of June 1762.
Dartmouth, at Sea, off Cojimar, Cuba.

'From the Flag, sir. It's one of the special signals, to *Dragon*, *Dartmouth*, *Bonetta*, *Basilisk* and *Thunderer*. Commence action against Cojimar Castle.'

'Very well, Mister Young, look out for signals from *Dragon*.'

Hervey was the senior and would have been expecting this signal. Carlisle could see *Dragon* clearly but didn't expect much, for Hervey had already given written orders to the ships addressed and would expect them to know what to do.

'Mister Beazley. Take us towards the castle under tops'ls. Bring her to a single anchor at three cables distance but in no less than five fathoms of water. *Dragon* will be to seaward of us and we must leave room for the sloop and the bomb ketches to come inshore.'

There was a flurry of activity and then *Dartmouth* started moving into position. The gunners on the castle's walls must have known what was coming next and they immediately shifted their target from the advancing landing force to these menacing ships.

'By the deep, nine.'

The current was negligible here but the weak nor'easterly was still pushing the ship towards the shore.

'By the mark, seven.'

Beazley studied the castle with narrowed eyes.

'Four cables, sir. I'll anchor at three.'

Carlisle nodded.

'Stand by to anchor!'

Beazley was generally a quiet man but when he needed to be heard his voice was powerful and wonderfully clear.

Old Bahama Straits

Hewlett, the bosun, raised his hand from the fo'c'sle where he was watching the activities on the cathead.

'Mark six!'

'Slip!'

At Beazley's command the anchor was released and it dragged its cable the few fathoms to the sea bed. At the same time the tops'ls were furled and *Dartmouth* swung around gently to face the sea breeze, with her bows to the north. Water spouts were starting to rise around the ship and Carlisle felt the hammer blows as Spanish balls struck his ship's hull somewhere forward, but without causing any appreciable damage. They'd be the first of many, for he had no illusions about the dangers of trading shots with a regular stone fortress, small though this one was.

'Mister Gresham, will your larboard battery bear?'

'Aye sir, it will, but I'll set a spring to starboard in case the wind shifts.'

'Very well, commence firing at the castle.'

***

Ah, the joy of having good subordinate officers. Beazley had brought the ship to this position with the minimum of delay and without the risk of grounding. Hewlett had anchored the ship and was now ensuring that all was ready to weigh anchor and set sail at a moment's notice. The boats were being brought close in on the starboard side and the yawl was already rowing out to secure the spring to the cable to turn the ship. Gresham could be left to do what he did best, to pound the castle and the breastwork with his beloved twenty-four pounders. Now he could turn his mind to the next phase.

'Mister Pontneuf, if you please.'

The marine lieutenant had been studying the shore through his own small campaign telescope. He was dressed for fighting on land and his second lieutenant, Francis Kemp, was at his side.

'You see the situation, Mister Pontneuf?'

'I do, sir. I'll start moving my marines into the boats

immediately.'

'I can't tell if you'll be needed, but it's best to be prepared.'

'Oh, we'll be needed, sir. Lord Albemarle won't want to divert his marching regiments to take that little castle, it'll break up his momentum. Those Spaniards just need a nudge to get them moving. They'll see their flank being turned and when we come at 'em they'll spike their guns and withdraw towards the Morro Castle. The sooner Captain Hervey gives the word the better; I wouldn't want my marines to miss out on the fighting.'

'Then get into your boat Mister Pontneuf and let me know when you're ready. I see *Dragon* and *Bonetta* have their boats alongside.'

Carlisle winced as a shot smashed into the hammocks surrounding the poop deck over his head, and showered him with scraps of cloth and rope ends. The ships were taking damage. Well, they could take it, but the castle was being hit by some sixty or so heavy guns every few minutes, and there was a constant roar of cannon fire punctuated by the deeper bellowing of the ten and thirteen inch mortars mounted in *Basilisk* and *Thunderer*. All of Hervey's ships had anchored; they were no longer moving targets and they were pitted against the castle's dozen guns sheltered behind coral limestone slabs. *Dartmouth* had been hit around the forward end of the lower gun deck and the mainmast bitts had been shattered by a shot that had missed one of the fo'c'sle gun crews by a hair's breadth. A scribbled note from the surgeon told Carlisle that one man was dead and there were two wounded in the sick bay, yet he could see that they were prevailing. The breastwork on the landward side of the castle had been *Dartmouth's* particular responsibility and it was badly hit. There were no more muskets in sight behind it and Carlisle had seen them withdrawing in haste to new positions behind the castle. *Dragon's* thirty-two pounders were ripping the castle's masonry apart and the mortars had found their range and were raining down their bombs on

Old Bahama Straits

the flimsy roof.

'Their fire's slackening, sir.'

'I do believe it is Mister Beazley, they appear to have only six guns in action now. Look, the grenadiers are moving up the road to turn their flank. If they delay much longer they'll be trapped.'

Horace Young touched his hat.

'From *Dragon*, sir. Special signal, send away the marines.'

Carlisle looked at the huge third rate. He could see that it too had been damaged but its frames and planking were more substantial than *Dartmouth's* and it all looked superficial. Hervey was standing on the poop deck waving towards the castle. His meaning was clear without the signal.

'Away boats!' Carlisle shouted.

***

Almost before the words had left Carlisle's mouth, Pontneuf ordered the boats to row for the shore.

'The jetty, Mister Pentland, if you please.'

The defenders had omitted to destroy the jetty on this eastern side of the castle, and Pontneuf could see that it was the best place to put his men ashore. It should have been covered by fire from the breastwork but that had been abandoned when the bombardment started. It wasn't even adequately covered by the castle's guns and those that could send shot in that direction were busy exchanging blows with the ships.

Pentland pounded Souter's shoulder and pointed to the stone jetty. Souter nodded and leaned on the tiller. He looked over his shoulder to see the pinnace, the yawl and the cutter following him.

A Spanish shot – one only – landed among the boats, sending a spout of water over the longboat and the yawl. Then they were so close to the castle that its guns couldn't depress far enough. Fifty yards and *Dartmouth's* longboat was in the lead. Pontneuf would be damned if he'd let *Dragon's* marine captain take the honour of being first ashore.

It looked like the boats would arrive unopposed. Then Pontneuf saw a band of Spaniards coming from the southern side of the castle, running towards the breastwork. There must have been a hundred of them, almost as many as the combined force of marines from *Dragon* and *Dartmouth*. They were forming a double line behind the partly destroyed breastwork with the sergeants and corporals urging the men into their places. A junior officer at the right of the line was diverting a dozen men to form a flank guard against the expected arrival of the grenadiers.

Pontneuf took it all in with a single glance. The grenadiers were already influencing the shape of this battle by their menacing approach on the enemy's flank, but they'd be too late to take part. Yet that was the weak part of the enemy's line and it was unprotected by the castle's walls. Once that flank was turned the Spaniards must retire or be overwhelmed.

Meanwhile the marines were in a perilous position. With no protection against the Spanish fire from the breastwork, there was no alternative to an immediate assault, and there was no time to wait for orders from *Dragon's* marine captain.

'Mister Kemp,' he shouted to the pinnace that was threatening to overtake the longboat, 'We'll take the left flank, leave the centre for the *Dragons*. Don't delay, go straight at 'em.'

Kemp waved his hat in reply. He could see what Pontneuf intended.

'Toss your oars.'

Souter had left it to the last moment and the larboard oarsmen barely had time to swing their oars upright before the longboat hit the jetty a glancing blow. He kept the tiller hard to starboard and the longboat scraped along the hard coral limestone blocks until it came to a shuddering halt in the angle between the sea wall and the jetty. The two bow oarsmen leapt ashore with the painter while Souter took a turn around a handy wooden bollard.

The marines poured over the gunwale following

Pontneuf and without waiting to form a line they raced for the left of the breastwork at its furthest end from the castle.

***

Pentland looked quickly around him. The longboat's marines had all gone and now *Dartmouth's* other boats were crashing into the jetty and *Dragon's* boats were only a few yards behind. He knew what he was meant to do: wait for the marines to finish their business then carry them back to *Dartmouth*. He knew that, but he had an overpowering feeling that this was his chance. It had been difficult joining a ship with *Dartmouth's* high reputation, one that had already fought through more than three years of war and where the other officers were well known and trusted. If he could do something today, make some impact on the unfolding battle, then he could stake a claim for membership of this brotherhood. He heard Souter shouting at the quarter gunner in the bows. He'd had no opportunity to fire his swivel gun, and now it was masked below the lip of the jetty, unable to train on the enemy position. For a moment he didn't know what was happening, then he saw a powerful man – Davies was his name – wrench the swivel bodily from its mounting and hand it up to the quarter gunner who had jumped up onto the jetty and was looking for a suitable crack in the masonry to insert the spigot. If he wasn't careful, his boat's crew was going to take a part in the battle whether he liked it or not. He could see the oarsmen looking questioningly at him; some were easing their cutlasses out of their scabbards while others just looked uncertain.

'Souter, get the men on the jetty, make sure they remember their cutlasses and pistols.'

That was an important point. Most of them had laid their weapons below the thwarts, both to prevent them impeding their rowing and to keep them out of the marines' hands.

'Quarter gunner!' he'd forgotten the man's name, 'fire at the centre of the breastwork.'

Pentland didn't wait to see his orders carried out but hauled himself quickly onto the stone of the jetty. He had nineteen of a crew including Souter and himself, and every man had a sword or cutlass and a pistol. Surely he could do something. Pontneuf and Kemp were almost at the far end of the breastwork now and he could see their swords rising and falling as they hacked at the defenders. The marines were thrusting their bayonets at anything that moved, but none had yet managed to clamber over the breastwork. They were locked into a brawl for a thirty-yard section of wall, and it was anyone's guess who would prevail. At that moment *Dragon's* marines charged past the boat's crew heading for the centre of the breastwork. He could see that his seamen couldn't help either group, they were engaged in a frontal fight against a strongly defended obstacle in which cutlasses and pistols had no place. The flanks then.

Pentland waved his sword as he supposed one should.

'Follow me men. The flank.'

He heard the swivel gun's first shot then the clatter as the cast iron mug dropped onto the stone path making way for the next load. Then he launched himself off to the left, running slantwise across the path that the marines had taken. He felt drunk as he ran on the hard, unyielding ground; he'd been used to *Dartmouth's* deck for these past weeks and his feet still felt for a ship's movement. His little band seemed to be ignored as they ran for the enemy's right flank. He could hear the pinnace's crew following him, and all the others, but he didn't risk a look over his shoulder. It was all happening quickly now. He passed twenty yards behind the red coats of the marines and felt the wind of a stray musket shot pass close to his face. There was the end of the breastwork and it looked undefended. Of course, that flank guard would have seen the present danger of the attacking marines and rushed to help. He veered right, keeping a healthy distance from the fight at the breastwork and led his seamen in a wide sweep around the ragged end of the stone wall.

He skidded to a halt and held up his hand. He had a moment to get this right, just a few seconds before the

Spaniards reacted to this new attack. He could see a junior officer frantically trying to extricate a few men to face the flank attack, but with the marines' bayonets thrusting over the wall and the obvious threat of the attackers exploiting a gap in the line of defenders, he was being ignored.

Pentland looked to his right and left. He had over thirty men now and each had some sort of weapon. They were blowing hard having pulled a boat at full speed then raced over uneven ground to reach this point, but they looked eager enough.

Well, it worked last time, perhaps they'd follow him again. Pentland waved his sword and started running towards the enraged junior officer. He felt a surge of pride as he realised that his seamen were following him, all screaming like maniacs and waving their cutlasses and pistols. Two or three Spanish soldiers realised their danger and turned to obey their officer, but they had all fired their muskets and they faced the onrush with nothing but their bayonets and their courage. Neither was enough and the tide of British seamen swept over them and started hacking its way into the surprised men at the breastwork. Pentland tried to get to the Spanish officer. He'd been brought up to believe that personal combat with the enemy's commander was the pinnacle of his gentlemanly code of conduct, and his father had paid good money for his fencing lessons before he'd found a patron to take his son to sea. But there was no fancy swordsmanship here, just the hack and slash of the cutlasses, the popping of the pistols and the bitter hand-to-hand fighting once they were so close to the enemy that nothing else would work.

Pentland burst through into the clear. He could see anxious Spanish faces glancing in his direction as they held their places at the breastwork, and a few of them were breaking away to face him. Pontneuf scrambled over the breastwork and grinned at him; that was the first real warmth he'd ever felt from the austere marine first lieutenant. There was no time for words and his seamen were looking around wondering what to do next. Pontneuf motioned with a wide sweep of his left arm. That was it, continue the outflanking movement and menace the enemy's line of retreat. Pentland was vaguely aware of these principles of land warfare, but had never really believed that he'd have to employ them. He looked around him. Souter was there looking truly fearful with blood running from a scalp wound, and behind him Davies was cradling the swivel gun in his massive arms, using a piece of canvas to protect himself from the heat of its barrel, and the quarter gunner was close behind with a basket of mugs and half pound shot.

'Souter. Take command of the gun and fire into the enemy's rear. The rest of you follow me.'

Another wave of his sword – it was wonderful how that gesture was so expressive, so imperative – and he sprinted slantwise across the enemy's rear. He had time to look around as he ran. He saw Davies raise the swivel above his head – it must have burned his hands terribly – and with a great shout thrust its spigot into the hard earth. The gun was almost touching the ground, but its very presence and the sound of its shot would worry the enemy even if it did no direct damage.

Pentland was thinking fast now. He mustn't go too far and leave a gap between his men and the marines, and he didn't have a strong enough force to prevent the Spaniards escaping. That would take muskets and bayonets and military discipline, and his seamen possessed none of those. No, his task was to shape the battlefield, to force the Spaniards back towards the castle and to narrow their avenue for escape. There was a small wall here, nothing more than a boundary marker for the castle's premises, he imagined, but it was good enough for his purpose. A quick look told him that the marines were over the breastwork in half a dozen places and the Spaniards were withdrawing towards the castle. Ah, *Dragon's* marines were pouring over the breastwork close to the castle's wall. They were blocking the postern that the Spaniards had emerged from and now there was a sense of panic in the defending force. One by one, the Spanish soldiers started turning away from their posts. They could see that their avenue of retreat was closing and they had no faith in the castle's ability to withstand the sort of impetuous attack that had carried the breastwork. They started to withdraw slowly, then one started to run and soon the whole force was rushing towards the narrowing gap between the seamen and the castle. Then the castle's great landward gates swung open and the garrison followed. Pentland leaned on the low wall, content to watch as the marines hunted the fleeing Spaniards across the hard-packed earth and through the strip of dense forest until they found the road to the Morro Castle.

***

It was evening and the sun had already slipped below the gaunt embrasures and towers of Cojimar Castle, silhouetting the union flag that flew proudly from its flagpole. *Dartmouth* lay peacefully to her anchor with the gentle breeze bringing the exotic scents from the land. Carlisle could hear the noise from the wardroom even as he paced the poop deck; it easily pierced through the decks and brought the sounds of laughter that rivalled those that came from the men's messes further forward. For it had been a great day for *Dartmouth,* and Hervey had been kind enough to give the credit for taking the castle to *Dartmouth's* marines and seamen. *Dragon's* marines had been essential, of course, but they'd arrived that crucial few minutes too late to claim the laurels.

Amazingly, there'd been no dangerous wounds among the boats' crews. The marines were a different matter and Pontneuf had sent back a boat load of wounded and a report naming two of his men who'd died in that brutal little action. Nevertheless, he too had praised Pentland's initiative and the courage of the seamen. Now they had a few hours to celebrate until they had to man the boats in the morning to get the vast mass of stores ashore that would support Albemarle's army. He heard Pentland's voice rise and fall as he recounted the action. He'd never heard his new third lieutenant venture an opinion before, nor expose himself in any way. Yes, it had been a good action and despite the losses, *Dartmouth* had come out of the day stronger than she'd started it.

***

Old Bahama Straits

CHAPTER FIFTEEN

Misgivings

Wednesday, Thirtieth of June 1762.
Dragon, at Sea, off the Morro Castle, Havana.

Carlisle looked back at his ship as his longboat rowed slowly and steadily towards *Dragon*. It had been three weeks since the army had been put ashore at Cojimar and three weeks since he'd reduced the castle there. He was pleased with the performance of his new officer, Pentland, and it was a joy to see how he'd gained the men's respect by that short but furious fifteen minutes of action against the Spanish infantry. He still missed Wishart, but he couldn't complain about the newcomers and he could see that both Hooper and Pentland would soon grow into their positions.

It wasn't his officers that worried him right now, it was the uncertainty of this whole expedition. If there was one thing that the navy had learned from its frequent wars in the Caribbean, it was that speed was of the essence. Whole armies had been destroyed by the inevitable tropical diseases and although the ships' companies were usually only affected when they anchored close to the shore, they too would fall sick eventually. There seemed to be no sense of urgency to this campaign. The army controlled all of the immediate area to the east of Havana Bay, including Guanabacoa, a small town that could threaten the invader's flank. Only the Morro Castle still stood to prevent the British setting up batteries on the Cabaña to fire down upon the city and the Spanish squadron and merchant ships in the harbour. Batteries had been established to reduce the castle, but its walls were strong and there seemed to be no enthusiasm for a coup de main to cut short the siege.

There was another unknown too. Pocock's ships had been robbed of guns, powder and shot to set up the batteries facing the Morro Castle, and each had sent a band of sailors to drag the guns into position and to serve them whenever they should start their bombardment. The only ships that had avoided the depletion of their armament were the five that had been entrusted to Hervey, and it wasn't at all clear why that should be. The informal squadron had done little except cruise to the east in case the French under de Blénac should arrive, or a fresh squadron from Spain, but nobody really believed that either was likely. What were they being reserved for then? Perhaps he was about to find out.

***

It was the strangest dinner party that Carlisle had ever known. Apart from the sheer improbability of it all – *Dragon* was lying to a soft breeze less than a mile off the fearsome guns of the Morro Castle – the party was not of one mind and its members weren't inclined to agree. Hervey of *Dragon* presided and beside him were the captains of four other ships-of-the-line: James Campbell of *Stirling Castle*, Thomas Burnett of *Marlborough*, William Goostrey of *Cambridge* and Carlisle himself. All commanded third rates except Carlisle with his little fifty-gun fourth rate, and all except *Stirling Castle* and *Dartmouth* mounted massive thirty-two pounders on their lower deck.

'Surely it's an affair for the soldiers. We've brought 'em here, we've landed 'em in safety and we feed 'em with stores and munitions as fast as they demand. They've taken our guns and our men, our water and our wine and now they want us to reduce the Morro Castle for them. Good God, we've all seen that castle. We'll be lucky if our guns can even reach their embrasures, much less do any damage. Let them do their job while we do ours, I say.'

Campbell sat back with his arms folded and a dissatisfied scowl on his face. He was the oldest of the five; he had fully ten years on the others who were all in their late thirties, and he looked it. His was the first voice to make comment after Hervey had outlined the plan for a naval bombardment of the Morro Castle, and if he spoke for the majority then it spelled disaster for this attempt at shortening the campaign.

Old Bahama Straits

Carlisle looked around; the other two captains seemed to be reserving their judgement and it wasn't clear just what they thought. However, he knew Hervey well and he was surprised by the mildness of his reply.

'I understand your concern, Campbell and I agree that it's an enterprise with a high level of risk…'

Campbell looked mollified, but surely he didn't expect the attempt to be abandoned merely because of his misgivings.

'… and the admiral made that quite clear to Lord Albemarle, as did Mister Keppel. They considered the risk but it weighed little against the overriding need to have this siege completed at the very earliest time possible. Yellow jack is already creeping into the ranks as you all well know. I believe we've each had sailors returned to our ships in a high fever, haven't we?'

'Aye, we have,' said Goostrey. 'I had six men sent back to *Cambridge* from the batteries just yesterday. My surgeon assures me that the disease can't be passed from man-to-man, but I'm not so sure. They're isolated in the for'rard end of the lower gun deck, in any case, and no visiting allowed. I agree, this campaign must be brought to a successful conclusion soon, before the disease or the hurricanes do for us all. If the end can be brought forward by putting my ship under the Morro Castle's guns, then so be it.'

Carlisle noticed that Goostrey avoided Campbell's eyes. It was an awkward situation and however Campbell dressed it up, it did look as though he might have personal reasons for not wanting to take his ship within range of the enemy's guns. Nevertheless, it was unfair, and in an age where honour was defended by duelling, it was dangerous to even hint at cowardly motives. After all, Campbell had made some sound arguments.

'Does Lord Albemarle believe that we of the sea service have not bled enough, is that it? An equal effusion of vital fluids from all. I do trust that we make decisions on better arguments than that! Yet still, he has a point and I dread to think what an epidemic of putrid fevers will do to us all, and my sailing master keeps muttering about the immutable laws of probability and the inevitability of a hurricane before the season is much older.'

Burnett was an eloquent man with a good brain, and he could see as well as anyone that something must soon be done to break the dangerous deadlock that was developing ashore.

Carlisle was perfectly positioned to observe the other four, and to make an educated guess at their motivations. Burnett and Goostrey had developed the appearance of a lofty disregard for their own safety, as any captain of a ship-of-the-line must surely do, or be driven stark mad. It was one of the most perilous positions to be placed in. His whole job, his very reason for existence while in command, was to bring his ship close enough to the enemy to engage with its heavy guns. That meant a range of fifty yards or less, and at that distance a man in a captain's uniform on the quarterdeck was both an easy target for a marksman and in the most likely and exposed position to be struck down by the awful randomness of a broadside. They all knew that, and yet each man had called in every favour, had greased every palm that had a chance of influencing their fate, just so that they could be placed in that position. Burnett and Goostrey appeared to understand and accept that, but Campbell had a nervous, hunted look about him as his eyes cast around the cabin looking for support.

'Carlisle, surely you agree with me. Your frames and planks won't stand very many of the Morro's shot, less even than my own ship, and your twenty-four pounders can do no more than mine.'

Then that was it. *Dragon*, *Marlborough* and *Cambridge* were all proper third rates and not only did they carry thirty-two pounders, but they were built to carry the heavier armament and to withstand the battering of enemy shot of the same size. *Cambridge*, in fact, was a three-decked third rate, the last of a derided type of ship that had proved to be crank in any kind of wind, yet she was strongly built and powerfully armed. In contrast, *Stirling Castle* carried only twenty-fours and was built accordingly. She was smaller and lighter and her frames and planking were not very much better than *Dartmouth's*. It was a fair consideration and questions of personal bravery aside, neither of the two smaller ships had any business being subjected to the Morro Castle's guns at short range.

Hervey smiled and fiddled with his wine glass, twirling the expensive spiral stem between his fingers. He'd been criticised quite publicly for his abrasive manner and it looked like he'd taken it to heart. Certainly Carlisle had never seen him so calm in the face of such intransigence.

'I take all these points and there's truth in each of them. However,' he replaced his wine glass and caught each man's eye in turn, 'the imperative is to take the Morro Castle as swiftly as possible. If the castle falls the city can't last out much longer and then our duty will have been fulfilled. As for the choice of ships, I'm surprised it's not obvious to you all. Ours are the last that haven't given some of our guns to the siege batteries. We four third rates are the only truly battle-worthy ships left, with reasonably full complements of men and guns. I'll come to Carlisle's part in this plan in a moment.'

Carlisle could tell that Hervey was taking no more discussion on the matter, now it was down to business.

'*Dragon*, *Marlborough* and *Cambridge* will be the assaulting force...'

Carlisle glanced at Campbell, was that a hint of relief that passed across his face?

'...and will anchor under the castle's walls. The distance will be determined when Carlisle and I have run a line of soundings; that will be after twilight this evening. I'm certain that we can anchor, but if we have to go so close that our guns can't elevate to reach the castle's embrasures, then I shall advise Mister Keppel and the admiral accordingly.

However, I have every confidence that the survey will prove that it can be done. We can expect a sea breeze from about seven o'clock tomorrow. As soon as there's enough wind *Stirling Castle* will pass along the north face of the castle and back and fill, engaging the enemy's guns while the three of us,' he looked at Goostrey and Burnett, 'anchor under the western walls and commence battering. Once we are anchored *Stirling Castle* will remain underway to annoy the enemy to the north.'

Campbell couldn't keep the appalled expression from his face. His ship would be first into action and would remain engaged throughout, albeit as a moving target rather than a stationary one. He noticed Carlisle's appraising gaze and with an effort controlled his emotions.

'*Dartmouth* will stand by to assist any of us that find ourselves in difficulty. To that end, Carlisle, I'd be obliged if you'll have two sets of towing hawsers made ready and all your boats in the water. I don't anticipate calling *Dartmouth* in to bombard the Morro Castle, but you'll see there is a special signal to the effect, just in case.'

Carlisle looked down at the sheet of paper that he'd found at his seat. It had two columns of coloured flags with brief descriptions of where they were to be flown and what they meant. It was becoming quite the fashion for admirals and commodores and senior captains to issue these for specific operations. Carlisle imagined that it was only a matter of time before their Lordships gathered them all together and issued a comprehensive set of signals for all occasions. One particular flag caught his attention, because at first glance it had no business being there. It was a normal red ensign, a red rectangle with the union flag quartered at the top nearest the halyard. It was the insignia of the red squadrons of the fleet, and Pocock was an admiral of the blue, so all of the ships carried his blue ensign. The description beside the red ensign was short and to the point. *When flown in the mizzen shrouds, the captain of this ship is dead or incapacitated.*

A thin smile crossed Hervey's lips.

'I see you've spotted the red ensign, Carlisle.'

Hervey paused while the other three captains consulted their lists. Burnett and Goostrey nodded thoughtfully but Carlisle could have sworn that Campbell's face lost a shade of its colour. Is this what happens with age? Does ones youthful assurance of invincibility fade with the passing years?

'If I should fall then Captain Campbell, as the next in seniority, will take my place in command of the action and will fly a plain red square at *Stirling Castle's* main to mark his elevation, the same flag that *Dragon* will fly to initiate the action. If any of the four of us should fall then our second is immediately to fly a red ensign at the fore masthead or where it can best be seen. I deem it essential that a post-captain assumes command without delay and that, Carlisle, is your task. If you see the red ensign you are to take command of that ship without further orders.'

It was a sobering thought and Carlisle had to ask the obvious question.

'And if I should fall?'

Hervey smiled broadly at that.

'I hope you take this in the spirit that it's given Carlisle. I know Mister Gresham – your first lieutenant – both personally and by reputation and I know your sailing master too. Between them they can fulfil *Dartmouth's* task of pulling any of us out of action just as well as you can. I won't say that your absence won't be missed, but, well, you know as well as I that our ships won't fall apart for want of our presence. However, I'm sure I don't need to remind any of you that it takes more than technical mastery of our trade to keep a ship in the line of battle when the shot starts flying. That's our prerogative, gentlemen, and it's what sets us apart from our lieutenants and our warrant officers, excellent fellows though they are. Every minute that one of our ships lies under the Morro Castle's guns without a post-captain walking the quarterdeck is a minute when the ship won't be hammering the enemy as hard as it should. That's why I need you to be prepared for the worst, Captain Carlisle, and God forbid that the need should come to pass.

***

They'd decided to use *Dartmouth's* yawl for the soundings, principally so that *Dragon's* crew could be rested before what they all knew would be an exhausting day, but also so that Hervey could keep a close hold on the information about the ground below the castle. It seemed to Carlisle that Hervey was determined to make the attempt on the Morro Castle, even if it meant his three third rates would have to anchor so close that their great guns would be unable to elevate far enough to sweep the castle's embrasures. If the soundings suggested that was the case, then Carlisle guessed that Hervey wanted that information isolated in *Dartmouth*, and not spread to *Dragon*, *Marlborough* and *Cambridge,* and certainly not to *Stirling Castle.*

After a light supper in *Dartmouth's* great cabin, Carlisle and Hervey watched from the poop deck as the sun slipped below the horizon and the tropical night fell with an unseemly rush. Yet the night wasn't dark and the moon, just past its first quarter, hung over the Morro Castle like some sort of celestial beacon to guide seafarers into a safe haven. It was a peaceful scene, one that the modern romantic painters would catch in an intricacy of shades of silver and grey.

'Well, they can see us from the castle, that's for sure. What did you call it Carlisle, this shaft of light illuminating the sea?'

'A moon-glade. It has a lyrical ring to it, don't you think?'

'Lyrical, yes, but unless the clouds come in soon we'll have to wait until half past one when the moon sets, and that'll only give us a pair of hours before morning twilight. I do worry what excuses Campbell will dream up before then; it'll be much better if I can report that the plan is feasible before midnight.'

Carlisle nodded, but he was shocked at hearing Hervey

speak of Campbell in those terms. The man certainly had misgivings and an ungenerous interpretation could be that he was afraid to take his ship into action. Nevertheless, it wasn't a subject to be discussed except between close friends. Was Hervey truly a friend? It was difficult to view him in those terms when it was well known that he was likely to inherit the Earldom of Bristol from his sickly brother before many more years had passed. He'd become famous, a statesman if he chose or a candidate for the admiralty board; First Lord even. Meanwhile Carlisle would slide gratefully into anonymity once this war was over, and their paths would likely never cross again. Yet despite that, the two men were close, for each in his own way had cut himself off from the society of his fellows. Hervey because of his acerbic nature, his unwise marriage and his continued and voluble support of the long dead Admiral Byng. Carlisle, however, was a naturally solitary person made more so by his hatred of the constant barbs of criticism against his fellow Americans. It was commonplace to decry their military prowess and to pour scorn on them for a perceived lacklustre performance in this war. Not friends then, not exactly, but in this navy in conflict with half of Europe and at war within itself, they were the next best thing. Carlisle was considering just this situation as they silently watched the world grow dark.

'It's a shame, what's happening to your Americans. I understand Amherst wasn't informed of the need to support this campaign until sometime in April, after the first letter went astray and the second was late. It's no fault of his that they haven't arrived yet.'

Carlisle looked sideways at him. Had Hervey been reading his thoughts?

'Yes. I understand they're on their way, mostly from New England, I've heard. They'll have to run the gauntlet of de Blénac's squadron as they pass through the Windward Passage, though, and that won't be easy with all our men-o'-war here off Havana.'

'Well, let's hope they come soon, before Albemarle's army's laid low by disease. That's why tomorrow's so important, not just to demonstrate our commitment to the army, but there's a real chance of battering the Morro Castle into submission. Ah, do you see? The cloud's thickening before the moon, just as it has every night this past week.'

It surely was and as if to confirm it, Beazley's shadowy form could be seen approaching.

'It's that same bank of cloud, sir. I can't say for certain that it's here for the night, but that appears to have been the pattern. Shall I call away the boat's crew, sir?'

Carlisle glanced at Hervey who nodded in the darkness.

'Then let us be away, Captain Carlisle, and see what our old and trusted friend the lead line has to tell us.'

***

CHAPTER SIXTEEN

Soundings

Wednesday, Thirtieth of June 1762.
Dartmouth's Yawl, at Sea, off the Morro Castle, Havana.

The oars made barely a sound as they levered against the canvas-wrapped thole pins and there wasn't a single light in the boat, not even a dark lantern. The yawl passed through the night with something between a sigh and a whisper and the few stars to the north where the sky was clear of clouds showed nothing but a vague grey shadow that shared little with the hard oak and elm of a yawl belonging to one of His Britannic Majesty's ships-of-the-line. Only a faint luminescence stirred up by its passage through the water betrayed that something moved over the vastness of the ocean, and that was minimised by the yawl's slow and steady pace. Nobody spoke and even the laboured breathing of the oarsmen seemed like an affront to the profound silence.

Souter, eight brawny oarsmen and *Dartmouth's* two best leadsmen manned the boat, while Hervey, Carlisle and Beazley went about the business of determining whether tomorrow's expedition had any chance of success.

'This should do, we're about three cables off. You can start soundings here, Mister Beazley.'

Carlisle's whisper sounded like a shout on this still night and the stroke oar winced and instinctively looked over his shoulder towards the castle, sending the whole crew off their timing. It was a miracle that they didn't make more noise and Souter leaned forward and rapped the guilty man's ear with his knuckle.

'It won't happen again, sir,' he hissed savagely, 'stroke oar will keep his eyes in the boat from now.'

This was an old, old story. If the oarsmen could be persuaded to ignore everything that was going on around them they could keep to a perfect stroke, but one distraction, one change in the tempo and the effect rippled through both banks of oars in a flash. Before anything could be done there would be oars flailing in the air, raising splashes and retarding the boat's progress, possibly with fatal consequences.

'They can rest on their oars for a spell now, Souter.'

A whispered word and suddenly all eight oars were parallel to the water with the oarsmen leaning their forearms on the inboard ends while they rested before the next spell of rowing.

'No bottom at twenty fathoms.'

Carlisle realised that he hadn't heard the splash of the first lead line entering the water. Beazley must have had the leadsman lower it through the first half fathom before letting the line run through his fingers. That would never do for a ship underway because the depth must be measured when the line is vertical. To achieve that the lead line is cast well in front of the ship so that it becomes up-and-down as it reaches the sea bed. It wasn't an exact art, but a good leadsman who knew roughly what depths to expect could achieve that vertical reading more often than not. Tonight, with the boat almost stationary, no such skill was required.

'By the mark, twenty.'

That was the second leadsman, on the larboard side of the yawl. Then his guess had been right and they'd struck twenty fathoms just about three cables off the castle.

Souter nudged Carlisle and pointed out across the starboard bow. At first Carlisle could see nothing and he hissed a query at the coxswain.

'It's the lighthouse, sir. You can just see its peak now and again.'

Hervey pointed. He'd seen the unlit tower, but it was still invisible to Carlisle.

'There's our mark then,' said Hervey. 'Keep the lighthouse four points on the starboard bow and we should slant in to the northern part of the water that we're interested in.'

Carlisle could hear Beazley's chalk scratching on his slate. He couldn't possibly see what he was writing but he might just be able to decipher it back in *Dartmouth*. Twenty fathoms with the Morro Castle lighthouse bearing *about* east-southeast and *about* three cables distant. It was no good wishing they had a lighted compass for the bearing and a moon to give them a better idea of the distance; either would bring down the fury of the Morro's guns upon them in an instant.

'Ready your oars.'

Souter's orders were a little louder now that he knew for certain how far away the enemy was.

'Give way.'

Souter saw the stroke oarsman haul his oar against the thole pin and could see that the rest were following him. He leaned against the tiller and the yawl's head swung slowly towards the northeast.

Carlisle could see a little better now. The night was no less dark, but his eyes were becoming accustomed to this profound blackness. He could even persuade himself that he could see the top of the darkened lighthouse. He could certainly see the oarsmen's faces, although he couldn't distinguish their features.

'Ten strokes and we'll take another cast of the lead lines.'

Carlisle could hear Souter counting quietly.

'…seven, eight, one more stroke then rest on your oars, Nobby.'

The yawl came quietly to a halt again and at a soft word from Beazley the two lead lines were lowered into the black water. Carlisle looked over the side and by some occult trick of the sea's glowing nighttime creatures, he could follow the course of the starboard line as it descended into the depths.

'By the mark fifteen.'

'By the deep fourteen.'

Those differences were to be expected as no two lead lines were exactly alike and neither responded the same as the other to the currents that swept below the yawl. It was a little past slack water at the bottom of the tide according to Beazley, and the waters would be rushing from the sea, through the channel and into Havana Harbour. Whatever course Souter steered, they were being set to the south and east and if they did nothing they'd fetch up against the defensive chain before the sun poked over the horizon again.

Beazley looked towards the lighthouse. It was further away now but evidently he could see something and Carlisle again heard the sound of his chalk scratching on the slate.

'Two-and-a-half cables off, sir, and I reckon that lighthouse is southeast-by-south. Fourteen fathoms, I would say, the starboard line was dragging somewhat astern.'

Fourteen fathoms. Carlisle knew that they needed to find five fathoms. Anything more than that and in the light winds that were forecast the ships would swing too much for accurate gunnery. He felt Hervey's head close to his own.

'Steer straight for the lighthouse, Carlisle. Let's find that five cable sounding. I don't like the look of that cloud cover.'

Carlisle looked across to the south. Hervey was right, and what was once a solid bank of cloud had started to break up. The moon hadn't peeped through yet, but it was only a matter of time.

'Can you see the lighthouse, Souter?'

'Aye sir.'

Souter pointed just forward of the starboard beam. Carlisle peered into the darkness but could see nothing.

'Very well, get underway and steer for it. I'll tell you when to rest again.'

Ten strokes, twenty strokes, and even Carlisle could see the lighthouse now, with its smooth, pale coral limestone pinnacle catching the diffused glow from the hidden moon.

'That looks like two cables, sir.'

Beazley had a good eye for distances and Carlisle knew that he couldn't do better.

Old Bahama Straits

'Rest here, Souter.'

Aye-aye sir. One more stroke, Nobby.'

The yawl slowed again and the two lead lines snaked over the side. Now Carlisle thought he could see them reach the bottom, certainly much less line was paid out than before.

'By the deep, six.'

A pause. The larboard leadsman seemed to be lifting his lead off the bottom and letting it swing to the vertical.

'Deep, six.'

'Two cables, sir. Maybe a mite less.'

Beazley was whispering again. They were only four hundred yards from an alert and dangerous enemy and caution was essential.

'Bring us in to three hundred yards, Carlisle.'

Carlisle had never heard Hervey's voice sounding tense before, but then, they'd never been in quite this situation. Another hundred yards! Carlisle would have withdrawn now, content with the information that he'd gleaned. What was it that drove Hervey? A fear that others would say that his success was due to the accident of his birth, perhaps. Whatever it was, it was bringing everyone in the yawl that much closer to death or imprisonment.

Souter ordered ten more strokes then the yawl fell silent again.

'Mark, five.'

'Deep, four.'

Beazley sounded tense too. There was no excuse now for not seeing the lighthouse; it loomed over them like a giant gleaming needle, menacing in its austere solitude.

'A cable-and-a-half, sir, and the lighthouse must bear a little south of east.'

That far south! Then the yawl was being set towards the harbour faster than Carlisle had thought. And was the moon starting to penetrate the clouds? He exchanged a glance with Hervey, who nodded and gestured towards the open sea.

'Strech out now, Souter. We've seen enough. Put the

lighthouse on your starboard quarter and let's find *Dartmouth*.'

There was a real sense of urgency. The stroke oar's first pull was long and deep and as soon as the yawl started moving he picked up the pace until it was racing through the still water. Carlisle looked astern. He could see the whole of the Morro Castle, silhouetted against the gibbous moon. The yawl must be visible to the sentries by now, and at this range they were a good honest target for twelve and eighteen pound guns. As if the Spanish could hear his thoughts, the darkness was split by a tongue of flame and a deep boom rang out from the castle. The ball fell twenty yards off the yawl's starboard beam and a luminescent column of water leaped into the air and fell from sight as swiftly as it came.

'Pull!' shouted Souter. 'Pull for all you're worth!'

'Eighteen pounders. I'd have thought they'd be saving their ammunition instead of wasting it on a little yawl.'

Carlisle was feeling light-headed with fatigue and stress, otherwise he'd never have made such a pointless comment.

'Perhaps they guess what we've been about,' Hervey replied. 'These soundings are worth a whole magazine of powder and shot.'

Flash-boom! Another shot. This one landed to larboard but closer.

The yawl raced through the lightening night pursued by the glowing water spouts that came close but never close enough. By the time that they saw *Dartmouth's* top light it was clear that the Spanish gunners were wasting their ammunition. In another twenty minutes they were alongside and clambering back aboard.

'Well Carlisle, if that's how you fifty-gun ships spend your nights, I'll stay with the line of battle, if you don't mind.'

Hervey always knew the right thing to say; it was part of his breeding, Carlisle imagined, and for the yawl's crew it was all the reward they needed for their efforts. They'd

Old Bahama Straits

repeat the words of an Earl's brother for years to come as they took their beer and grog around the mess table.

***

Carlisle was dog-tired and all he wanted was to surrender to sleep and let his body replenish its vital spark for the exertions that would be required in the morning. He saw Hervey rowed over to *Dragon* then turned for his cabin, already relaxing in anticipation of the cool sheets. But here was his clerk blocking his path looking apologetic. It couldn't be the ship's books, not at this time of night, and any other problems were likely to be brought to him by the first lieutenant or the sailing master.

'I beg your pardon sir. Captain Laredo requests a moment of your time. He says that it's urgent and concerning tomorrow's action.'

Carlisle stopped dead. How did a Spaniard know about the planned bombardment? Then he relaxed. The word had passed around the ship like fire in a hayfield and Laredo had learned enough English to pick up the essentials of the conversations that went on around him. And then, he messed in the wardroom, and he could hardly expect his officers to ignore the most important event in weeks. Probably, in their generous manner, they'd told him the outlines, safe in the knowledge that he was incarcerated on board *Dartmouth* and couldn't take the information to the castle's defenders.

'Oh, show him in Simmonds. Let's hear what he has to say, and you can stay to listen.'

Carlisle took a savage delight in detaining his secretary. Simmonds hadn't spent a harrowing few hours drifting around in a boat under the enemy's guns, he could afford to lose a few hours of sleep.

Laredo looked fresh and rested. Carlisle noticed that he was wearing a clean shirt, not the one he'd had when he was captured, and it looked very much like it belonged to one of *Dartmouth's* officers. That was the extent of his acceptance into the wardroom, and it was hardly surprising that he knew all that was going on in the ship. He accepted a glass of wine and sat in silence for a moment as though at a loss for how to start.

'You asked to see me, Captain Laredo,' Carlisle prompted. He spoke in Spanish as the most certain way of avoiding misunderstandings.

'Yes, sir...'

Another pause while the Spaniard toyed with his glass. He looked at Carlisle and seemed to come to a decision, then he dropped his eyes again.

'I understand, sir, that you have been surveying the anchorage off El Morro.'

Laredo looked up as though waiting for a response. Carlisle chose not to reply but returned the gaze until the Spaniard grew uncomfortable.

'If that is true, sir, then I could have saved you some trouble, and in fact I can still offer some information that you might not have been able to glean in such a short time.'

Carlisle knew that he should be interested, but he was so very tired and he wasn't in the mood for this verbal fencing. He exchanged a look with Simmonds who shifted in his seat, ready to escort Laredo back to the wardroom.

'Captain Laredo. You must know that I can't offer you parole while this siege is in progress. I've already said that I'll plead your case before the commander-in-chief at the appropriate time, but that time is likely to be after Havana has capitulated. If you have some useful information then it's in your interests to reveal it now. You know the alternative; your case won't be included in the terms of the surrender and whatever happens to the garrison and to the officers of the ships, you'll be sent back to England to await an exchange. We both know that could take a very long time with so few British officers in Spanish hands. I'll be your advocate in recognition of the help you've already given, but I don't know Admiral Pocock's mind and he's likely to have more pressing matters to concern him when the siege is over. Positive information that materially shortens the siege is your best hope of being repatriated. But you know this, we've had this conversation already.'

Carlisle deliberately set his face in a harsh, unyielding expression. He'd long ago decided that Laredo would be freed on the day that Havana surrendered, and Pocock had said that he'd leave the decision in Carlisle's hands. Even if the siege should fail, he'd send Laredo ashore under a flag of truce, just out of a sense of fairness. No new revelations would change that, but he didn't want Laredo to know that his parole was already assured.

Laredo looked visibly moved by Carlisle's speech delivered in such good Spanish, and the English captain was right, he did know all of those conditions that attended his hopes of parole, and he knew the consequences of his parole not being accepted. He stiffened his shoulders and replied in a formal voice.

'I wouldn't want this fine ship to run aground, sir, not after all your hospitality.'

He reached in his coat pocket and handed over a quarto sheet of paper. Carlisle looked at it briefly. It was a rough rendering of the anchorage off El Morro, showing depths out to twenty fathoms and curved arrows to show the run of the tide. It was nothing that he hadn't already discovered and it wasn't worth sending over to Hervey. It was, however, an indication of the lengths that Laredo would go to in order to achieve his parole. He placed the little chart on his table and looked hard at the Spaniard.

'Is that all, Captain Laredo?'

Laredo suddenly looked unsure of himself, very much like the desperate, discouraged captive that he was.

'It is all, sir.'

'Very well, then I wish you a good night, Captain, and I hope that I'll have the opportunity to recommend your case to the admiral in the near future. Stay for a moment, if you please, Mister Simmonds.'

***

'A desperate man, Mister Simmonds.'

'Indeed so, sir. I have his parole letter ready for the appropriate moment. The admiral's secretary has approved the wording and in his opinion you can issue it whenever you see fit. Today even.'

Carlisle could see that Laredo had become a favourite among his officers. He was willing to bet that everyone from Gresham down to the lowliest young gentleman would send the Spaniard ashore with the greatest good will. Yet there was something more for Laredo to do, Carlisle could feel it, and he wasn't prepared to part with him until that something had revealed itself.

'Then keep that letter safe, Mister Simmonds, and I hope that we can use it before many more weeks have passed.'

***

CHAPTER SEVENTEEN

Red Ensign

Thursday, First of July 1762.
Dragon, at Sea, off the Morro Castle, Havana.

'Will this breeze suffice, Mister Roberts?'

Hervey's sailing master was older than most and over his many years at sea in His Majesty's ships he'd learned how to deal with imperious captains like the Honourable Augustus Hervey. He economised on his words and only told Hervey what he thought his captain needed to know, and when he did open his mouth he made sure that he spoke plainly. He made his colleague Beazley seem positively talkative.

'A light breeze from the north, sir. It'll suffice, but I fancy it might fade through the forenoon.'

'Very well. Make the signal for the squadron to proceed.'

Like the sailing master, Hervey's young officers knew what was expected of them. They were used to their captain's habit of throwing out orders without specifying who was to carry them out, and the most likely recipients made certain that they were always in hearing range. The signal midshipman, a tall man who must have been at least old enough to take the lieutenant's examination, answered promptly.

'Aye-aye sir.'

He didn't need to look at the list of special signals, this one was easy. A red square at the main masthead. The flag was already bent on and it took just a few seconds for the quartermaster's mate to run it up on its halyard. The midshipman was very careful to make his report using the exact words that Hervey had used when making the list of special signals.

'Signal made, sir. The squadron is to proceed with the action.'

Hervey gave no indication that he'd heard the report.

That also was what his officers expected.

'The ship's cleared for action, sir, and the hands are at their quarters.'

At thirty-seven Peter Foulkes was older than the general run of first lieutenants, and most of his contemporaries had been made commander long ago. He'd been Hervey's first lieutenant in *Phoenix*, before the war, and Hervey had sought him out again when he'd been given command of *Dragon*. It wasn't that Foulkes was a particularly good first lieutenant, there were many better, but he was a man utterly without ambition and although he ruled the ship with a rod of iron, he was entirely submissive to his captain's whims. When *Phoenix* was cruising the Mediterranean in the halcyon days of peace, Hervey could leave the ship for extended periods in whatever port they were visiting, secure in the knowledge that when he returned he'd find things just as he'd left them. He'd considered using some of his considerable influence to get Foulkes promoted to commander, but every time that it crossed his mind he rebelled at the idea of losing him. In any case, unless this campaign was a complete failure, the war would be over in a year and Foulkes would have to endure another spell on half pay, whatever his rank.

'Watch *Stirling Castle's* movements, Mister Roberts, and set your tops'ls when they do.'

Hervey looked astern at the three ships to seaward. *Cambridge* was the closest, looking huge, majestic and dangerous in the glory of her three decks. He could see that Goostrey had his men aloft ready to set sail and his gun ports were all open with the muzzles of the great guns thrusting out on each side of the ship. Further north again he could see *Marlborough* in a similar state but with only two rows of guns. Little *Dartmouth* was abreast of *Marlborough* and her gun ports were closed. Even from here he could see the two cables leading out of the stern gun ports and onto the poop deck, ready to be sent across to any of his ships in difficulty, and the gaggle of boats alongside told their story of a ship ready for any emergency. He turned and looked ahead. The Morro Castle was over a mile away but even from here it looked vast and intimidating. Its sheer walls appeared at this distance to rise straight from the blue sea, and their smooth faces were innocent of windows or embrasures. For the Morro Castle carried its guns on fighting platforms at the very top of the walls and there, far above the sea, the embrasures stood like a row of teeth, snarling towards the enemy. A tough nut indeed, and Hervey had no illusions about the dangers of this day.

Hervey had left a last letter to his mother with Carlisle – he cared nothing for his wife – and was ready now to do his utmost to reduce the Morro Castle's defences. He heard the first rumble of the batteries to landward of the castle, for this was to be a combined operation. If the plan worked, if the castle's guns should be silenced and a practicable breach made in its walls, then Albemarle's line regiments were ready to sweep across the rubble and take ownership of this vital part of the city's defences. That was the plan, but like Keppel and Pocock himself, he had severe reservations. The Morro Castle's walls were just too high and too thick. Even if he could anchor his squadron close enough for his guns to be effective, they'd hardly be able to elevate far enough to reach the embrasures at the top of those walls. At best he could engage enough of the Spanish gunners to give the landward guns a chance. The Grand Battery had been finished only yesterday and its eight twenty-four pound guns – all borrowed from Pocock's ships – and two fifteen-inch mortars were just two hundred yards from the castle's walls. Two other batteries were also due to unmask today, William's and Dixon's. The Morro Castle would be faced by nearly two hundred assorted guns and mortars, but still the odds lay with the defenders. Given time the walls would be breached, but a single day, in Hervey's opinion, was unlikely to produce the result that the army so desperately needed. Whatever happened it would be hot work in those siege batteries and any diversion from the sea would help.

Hervey's gaze swept across *Stirling Castle*. He stared for a moment then raised his telescope. There was a good deal of activity on the deck, but the upper yards were innocent of the men that would be needed to set the tops'ls.

'What's happening on *Stirling Castle*?' he asked of the quarterdeck. 'Why isn't that damned ship underway?'

None of his officers dared to reply. They all affected a deep interest in their duties, for it was clear to each of them that *Stirling Castle* was not at all ready to lead the squadron into the attack.

'Mister Foulkes. Take the yawl over there and find out what's going on. My compliments to Captain Campbell and he's to get underway immediately and take his position on the north face of the castle.'

Hervey fumed as he waited for his first lieutenant to return. He had nobody to share his feelings of frustration; he kept his officers at arm's length and discussed nothing with them beside the business of the ship. The only person that he felt comfortable with was Carlisle, and he recognised a misfit like himself when he saw one. Not that Carlisle and he shared much in common, beyond the command of a ship-of-the-line, but he had a fellow-feeling for the Virginian. How he wished Carlisle was here now so that he could tell him what he thought of James Campbell.

The yawl was only alongside *Stirling Castle* for a few moments and then he saw Foulkes drop down from the entry port and the boat sped back towards *Dragon*.

'Captain Campbell sends his respects, sir, and he says that his sails are stowed for protection from the weather and he'll need some more time before he can get underway.'

Hervey rarely looked astonished, but it was hard to hide his feelings in the face of such an outrageous report. He mastered himself before replying.

'I can see from here that his tops'ls and sprits'l are bent on, what more does he need?'

'He was reluctant to speak to me, sir. He just bade me bring this message and then insisted that I leave his quarterdeck before I could speak to his own first lieutenant.'

'Could you see any reason why he's not making way towards the castle?'

'No, sir. It was just an impression, but I felt that his officers were frustrated by it all. The ship was cleared for action and the hands were all at the guns, as far as I could see; it merely wanted a word and the topmen would be on the yards in a moment.'

Hervey stared at Foulkes. There was no value in losing his temper now and he must make the best job of it that he could. *Stirling Castle* was supposed to draw the castle's fire while the other three third rates anchored on the west and northwest sides. Perhaps if he started moving it would recall Campbell to his duty.

'Mister Roberts, let fall the tops'ls and the sprits'l. Your anchor berth is off the northwest corner of the castle in five fathoms of water. You may start heaving the lead immediately. Mister Foulkes, tell the bosun to stand by to come to a single anchor and prepare a spring on the larboard side.'

***

The breeze caught *Dragon's* tops'ls and she started to move towards the castle, stemming the ebb tide and moving at a snail's pace over the ground. Hervey trained his telescope at the fighting platforms at the top of the walls. He could see people moving there, presumably gunners brought over from the landward side as soon as this fresh attack became apparent. The curtain walls and bastions gleamed in the light of the new day but over and beyond the castle the blue sky was stained dark by clouds of powder smoke and dust from smashed masonry, while the dull rumble and thud of siege artillery filled the ears.

'Beg your pardon, sir, *Stirling Castle's* set her fore tops'l now, she's starting to move.'

'Too late, too late. She'll have to cross our hawse to get into position now. Hold your course, Mister Roberts.'

'Captain, sir. There's a boat pulling towards us from *Dartmouth*.'

The tall midshipman's station was on the poop deck and he had a better overall view than anyone. Hervey leaned out over the starboard hammock netting and looked aft. Sure enough there was the boat with Carlisle himself standing in the stern sheets. A glance told him that *Stirling Castle* was falling further behind and was now well out to seaward. Hervey was incredulous at what he was seeing, but it was becoming obvious that Campbell had no intention of placing his ship under the Morro Castle's guns.

Carlisle's boat came swiftly up on *Dragon's* quarter. Hervey knew his own reputation for imperturbability, and tried now to look as though he was unconcerned by the evil turn of events.

'Captain Carlisle, good morning to you, and a fine one it is for a fight, don't you think.'

Carlisle glanced over at *Stirling Castle* as if for a final confirmation of the situation before committing himself.

'That it is, sir. I've come to offer my services as it appears that Captain Campbell is having difficulties.'

'Ha! Difficulties indeed. We'll speak more of that another day, Carlisle. For now, I'm grateful for your offer and pleased to see an officer ready to do his duty, but I'd rather have you prepare to haul us off if we get stuck. I expect *Stirling Castle* will join me in his own good time. Take a message to Captain Campbell on your way back, if you'd be so kind. Tell him I'm expecting him to take his station against the north face of the Morro Castle without further delay. Those exact words, Carlisle, without further delay, if you please.'

Carlisle waved in reply; there was really nothing else to be said. He knew he'd be making an enemy of Campbell by delivering that message, but then it was hardly likely that he'd be in command much longer, for if he knew anything about Hervey, it was that he would certainly demand a court martial for this inaction. *Stirling Castle* had the look of a ship that would find any reason to avoid coming into action. He wondered what on earth Campbell's officers thought of it, because they'd certainly be tainted by association when the story came out.

***

Hervey watched Carlisle's boat round to alongside *Stirling Castle's* quarterdeck. He thought he could see Campbell gesticulating, the actions of a man explaining that he was the victim of circumstances, that it wasn't his fault that he couldn't carry out his orders. He turned away in disgust, dismissing *Stirling Castle* from his mind. He had no doubt that Campbell would back and fill on the seaward side of the squadron, safe from the Morro Castle's artillery but close enough so that he could claim to have remained at the scene of the action. Well, there would be a reckoning, but for today he had business to attend.

'Mister Foulkes. Hold your fire until we're at anchor.'

Dragon crept slowly south with the castle's walls seemingly growing higher and higher as they approached. Hervey noticed the first guns firing from the north wall and remembered that *Stirling Castle* should be there, suppressing that fire to allow the battering force to get into position. He didn't notice at first that his ship had been hit, but he saw a sad figure slumped between the arms of two loblolly boys being carried below. The reports from the lead line were of more interest at the moment. Ten fathoms, eight. The castle seemed much closer than it did last night, in the dark. Five fathoms. They were just at the northwest angle now, in the perfect position.

'Anchor here, Mister Roberts. Let me know when the springs are rigged.'

Hervey took no further interest in the operation. Goostrey was bringing *Cambridge* up on his starboard side now, steering for his station to the southeast of *Dragon*, and it was time for *Dragon's* guns to start pounding the Morro Castle. He looked up at the tall castle walls. Foulkes would have to fire as the ship rolled on the lazy swell to have any chance of hitting the embrasures, but that was what he was good at.

'Mister Foulkes, you may start firing.'

Hervey looked over the side to see the bosun in the yawl attaching the spring to the hawser. It was a perilous task as he was exposed to not only the castle's great guns but to long musket fire from the loopholes that he could now see across the face of the walls. That yawl was the only boat he had today; he'd left all of his others with the transports to clear the decks for the guns, and to preserve them from what promised to be great danger.

With an almighty crash, *Dragon's* larboard broadside opened the account. Every shot hit the castle, they could hardly miss at this range, but if any reached high enough to sweep the embrasures, it wasn't evident. Hervey could see that *Cambridge* was coming to her anchor and rigging springs and a glance astern showed that *Marlborough* was doing the same. To his disgust, Hervey saw that *Stirling Castle* still stood aloof, some half a mile to the northwest of the action. Now all he had to do was walk his quarterdeck and see that his guns kept firing. His ship was being hard hit, he could see. Luckily the same geometry which meant that his own guns couldn't reach the castle's fighting platforms meant that the Morro Castle's guns had difficulty depressing far enough to sweep *Dragon's* deck. Most of the Spanish balls passed through the masts and the rigging, damaging spars and sails and parting sheets and halyards. A quick look showed him that *Cambridge* and *Marlborough* were suffering the same punishment, and still Campbell's ship played the spectator.

It was impossible to see how the landward batteries were faring. In fact with the incessant noise of the cannonade from three ships-of-the line, and the castle's reply, it wasn't evident that the Grand Battery, William's and Dixon's were still firing at all.

'My telescope, if you please.'

The tall midshipman passed Hervey's telescope to him, treating it with the reverence that was normally associated with a religious relic or some regalia associated with a coronation.

Hervey trained first on Keppel's flagship and then on Pocock's. As he thought, there was no recall signal. Then it was likely that the army's batteries were still in action.

A large piece of timber from the mizzen top fell through a gap in the splinter net and missed Hervey by a yard. He looked around to take stock. The few Spanish balls that reached the deck were causing mayhem as their trajectory took them over the protective hammock nets and right into the waist where the upper deck guns were being served. Two of them were out of action, and by the look of the wounded men being carried below and the dead that had been dragged into the scuppers, Foulkes had made the right decision to concentrate on keeping the lower deck guns firing by redirecting the crews from the damaged guns. As he watched, a shot came arcing in over the hammock nets, narrowly missing a file of marines who were firing their muskets at extreme range. It struck the deck and ricocheted into a seaman who had been taking a drink from a fire bucket. In an instant the living human being was transformed into a mess of twitching, bloody limbs and a torso torn into two parts. Hervey saw this but didn't register it as a man's life, to him it was just one less seaman to man the guns, one tiny diminution of his ability to keep firing at the Morro Castle.

'The spring's parted, sir. Shot away by the look of it. I'll get the bosun to rig a new one.'

Hervey nodded in reply to the sailing master. There was nothing he could do, and he knew that the bosun could handle it. He'd need the yawl of course and a quick look told him that it was still afloat on the disengaged side of the ship.

'The stern's swinging towards the shore sir, must be slack water.'

'Very well, Mister Roberts, tell the bosun to rig the spring as fast as he can.'

'*Cambridge* is hoisting a flag to her fore masthead, sir.'

The tall signal midshipman had his telescope to his eye.

It wasn't really necessary as they could both see that it was a red ensign. Then Goostrey was dead or incapacitated. It crossed Hervey's mind that this was the moment for Campbell to redeem himself, to prove that whatever the reason for *Stirling Castle* keeping clear of the action, it wasn't her captain's lack of personal courage. He was nearer to *Cambridge* than Carlisle was, and he could be on deck taking command before *Dartmouth's* yawl had made half the distance between the two ships. He looked in vain.

'*Dartmouth's* yawl's on the way, sir.'

Yes, there was Carlisle standing in the stern sheets, clearly eager to take command of the leaderless ship. Hervey watched as the yawl raced towards *Cambridge*, he saw it swing neatly alongside and he saw Carlisle and another man, perhaps his clerk, run up the treads and through the entry port. A minute passed, a minute in which *Cambridge's* guns were noticeably slower in firing than they had been before.

The tall midshipman watched the ship intently, waiting for what he knew was coming.

'*Cambridge* has struck her red ensign sir.'

Hervey hadn't realised that he was holding his breath, and he let it out now in a long sigh. Carlisle had taken command; he just hoped with all his heart that he didn't suffer the same fate as poor Goostrey.

He felt a shudder run through the ship and saw Roberts looking over the side.

'Captain, sir. I do believe we're aground by the stern.'

Hervey looked over the side and beckoned to his clerk.

'Take down this note for Commodore Keppel. '*I am unluckily aground but my guns bear. I cannot perceive the enemy's fire to slacken…*'

The note went on to describe the action so far, the circumstances of the ships' shot not reaching the Spanish guns, but stopped short of requesting that they withdraw.

'Now, send that by the yawl as soon as the spring's been rigged afresh.'

***

CHAPTER EIGHTEEN

Gresham's Day

Thursday, First of July 1762.
Dartmouth, at Sea, off the Morro Castle, Havana.

Gresham watched the yawl pull hastily over towards *Cambridge* and saw Carlisle and Simmonds disappear through the entry port. Well, he was in command of *Dartmouth* now, but there was little for him to do but watch for signals. He could see that *Cambridge's* fire had slackened after the red ensign was hoisted. Perhaps it was his imagination, but it appeared that the rate increased again soon after Carlisle arrived; he'd show them how it was done. Goostrey had a fine reputation as a fighting captain, but Gresham was convinced that nobody could command a ship-of-the-line like Carlisle. He only regretted that he wasn't there with his captain. What a joy to command three decks of great guns under enemy fire! He could just imagine the heave under his feet as the thirty-two pounders fired, the powder smoke and the wall of noise that would envelop him at each broadside. He was letting his imagination run riot when he was interrupted by Midshipman Young leaping into his path.

'Mister Gresham, sir.'

Horace Young removed his hat all the way, not the half-hearted performance that he usually used to greet the first lieutenant, but the full obeisance for the captain of a King's ship. He waited hat in hand until he was acknowledged, his eyes wide at the awesome responsibility of delivering this particular message. For he knew what it meant for *Dartmouth*, as did everyone else who had seen the signal.

'From *Dragon*, sir. A blue square at the foremast head. It's the special signal to say that they're aground and need assistance.'

Gresham didn't need a telescope, not at that distance, and a quick look confirmed the report. He could already see a stream of water from *Dragon's* scuppers where the butts had been staved, and the precious liquid was being pumped over the side. That in itself spoke volumes about the ship's situation, and it was quick work; it suggested that Hervey had no doubt about his predicament. Another look revealed a party around a gun just forward of the quarterdeck; they weren't loading and running out, but hauling the thing towards the fo'c'sle. Then *Dragon* must be aground by the stern.

Beazley was looking at the stricken ship too.

'*Dragon's* yawl's in the water, it looks like they're rigging another spring.'

In a flash Gresham realised what had happened. The spring must have parted allowing the stern to swing to the sea breeze and ground in the shallows below the castle's walls. A new spring would do them no good now, the lead would be too acute and it wouldn't provide enough leverage; they must be hauled bodily off.

'Where's the wind, Mister Beazley?'

'Nor'-nor'east, Mister Gresham, and the tide's still ebbing perhaps a knot, maybe less.'

No power on earth would persuade Beazley to refer to his old sparring partner Gresham as *sir*, or *captain*, they'd served together too long for that. It was Beazley's not-so-subtle protest, but in all else he'd obey Gresham's orders as though he was the legally commissioned captain.

Gresham glanced at the compass and then at the three ships lying off the fort. If he tried to pass a line to *Dragon* the wind would bring him down upon the grounded ship before ever he could secure the tow, and the ebb tide was too weak to help. It would have to be a kedge anchor. A lifetime's experience told him what must be done.

'Mister Beazley. We'll come to anchor to seaward of *Dragon* using the second bower. Then we'll haul up short and drop the best bower and pass the cable back to her fo'c'sle. You've sounded the anchorage, can it be done?'

Beazley looked up at the commissioning pennant hanging limply but with a decided lean to the sou'west, then he glanced over to *Dragon*.

'It could work, Mister Gresham. The bottom drops off fast there and we'll only need to be half a cable to seaward to be in safe water. Yes, it can be done.'

'Mister Hewitt?'

The bosun scratched his chin as he thought through the problem.

'Aye sir. I can run the cable back from the best bower outboard of everything, in through the larboard chaser port, and seize it to the cable that we laid out yesterday. I can send a messenger line over in the longboat.'

'Very well, let's get started then. Standby the second bower for anchoring, Mister Hewitt. Mister Beazley, tops'ls and fore stays'l.'

Dartmouth came sluggishly off the wind with a maddening reluctance to move decisively in these light airs.

'Does she need the mizzen, Mister Beazley?'

'I think not, Mister Gresham, I don't fancy showing too much sail aft.'

Beazley considered for a moment then ordered the fore tops'l to be backed. It took the way off the ship but it brought her head around to the southwest and soon they were moving slowly down towards the stricken *Dragon*. Beazley was watching the set of the sails and the stranded ship. This was what he did best, balancing the wind against tide to bring a great two-decker into a precise position on a lee shore. A rapid volley of orders trimmed the sails just so and the quartermaster adjusted the helm for every tiny movement of the ship's head.

'She's leaning further every minute.'

Gresham was watching *Dragon's* masts as they heeled a little more to each heave of the sea. He wasn't used to standing back and orchestrating all this. He itched to be doing something, but he could tell that it was all under control and he tried to stand as Carlisle did, watching impassively until he needed to intervene. Beazley would bring the ship to anchor, Hewitt would have the anchors and cables ready in time, and Hooper would run the messenger over to *Dragon* the instant the best bower touched ground. All was well, so far.

'Two cables, Mister Gresham.'

'Very well, Mister Beazley.'

Gresham leaned back and raised his chin with his hands cupped either side of his mouth.

'Stand by to anchor,' he roared.

Hewitt waved in reply from the fo'c'sle.

'One cable.'

Dragon seemed close enough to touch and yet it was important not to come too close. If *Dartmouth* should fall afoul of the larger ship there'd be no dragging them clear and the falling tide would leave two ships to be battered into ruin by the castle's guns.

'*Dragon's* main topmast is going sir.'

Midshipman Young had spotted the way that Hervey's upper masts were losing their regular shape. The main topmast with the t'gallant mast above it were waving like willow wands in a breeze. It was professionally fascinating to note the moment when the shrouds and stays could no longer support the moving mass and the whole lot would come crashing down, probably bringing the fore t'gallant with it. Gresham dragged his eyes away, it had no bearing on the task at hand.

'Bring her to, Mister Beazley. Furl the tops'ls and fore stays'l. Show a corner of the mizzen to bring her around.'

Dartmouth's bows swung to starboard as Gresham watched for the right moment. The flotsam over the side was moving more slowly as the great ship's way came off. Any moment now…

'Slip!'

Gresham's voice must have been heard in the castle and in an instant the second bower plunged into the shallow

Old Bahama Straits

water. *Dartmouth's* head swung to the sou'west, into the fading ebb tide, and she lay back upon her anchor with her stern waving indecisively as the wind and tidal stream contested for primacy.

'Hold at that! Stand by the best bower! Away yawl.'

The yawl crawled away from *Dartmouth's* stern. It was dragging the heavy messenger from the stern port under Pentland's direction. He had to let out just enough so that the yawl wasn't retarded by the strain, but not so much that it was dragging a great bight of rope through the water. The further the yawl pulled the slower it went and it appeared to the anxious Gresham that it reached *Dragon* with the very last of the oarsmen's energy. There was a flurry of activity around *Dragon's* bowsprit and hawse and then an arm came up on her fo'c'sle: the messenger had been brought to the capstan.

'Slip the best bower! Stand by the seizings.'

The best bower followed the second and Hewitt leaped along *Dartmouth's* gunwale from forward to aft slashing at the light cords that held the huge seventeen-and-a-half inch circumference cable fast to *Dartmouth's* side. The last seizing was cut and the cable dropped into the sea with a dull splash. That was *Dartmouth's* task complete. Gresham could see the messenger running into *Dragon's* hawse hole, dripping water as it ran over the lip. Soon the massive cable itself followed, two lengths of a hundred and twenty fathoms each, seized end-to-end. *Dragon's* guns were almost silenced now, as so many of their crews had been sent to the capstan. It needed over two hundred men to heave in and stow a cable, and *Dragon's* gun crews had already been reduced by deaths and injuries.

'Ah, there goes the bitter end,' Hewitt announced; then more softly 'and I'll have a ticket for it from *Dragon's* bosun before the day's out; he won't profit by a best bower and a pair of cables at my expense.'

The sound of the capstan's pawls came cheerily over the water and in a few minutes the cable would be seized to the capstan messenger and it would be mere backbreaking routine to haul *Dragon* off the ground, if she wasn't stuck fast.

***

Gresham scanned the castle's embrasures. It seemed that the Spanish guns were firing with renewed fury now that they could see that this stricken third rate might slip through their fingers. *Dragon's* bows started to move sideways as the anchor cable tightened, exposing her stern to the castle's raking fire. Her main topmast and t'gallant mast were hanging over the ship's starboard side, but it was clear that Hervey couldn't spare enough people to deal with that, not until *Dartmouth's* anchor had been brought home and catted. Every few seconds a shot passed through *Dragon's* masts and sails, and every minute one smashed into her hull.

'They're using short charges, sir. That way they can drop them onto *Dragon's* hull, but they won't have the force of a ball fired with a full charge.'

Gresham nodded at the gunner who'd come up from his magazine for want of any need for cartridges. *Dartmouth's* line of fire was entirely obscured by *Dragon* but if all went well she'd be afloat and underway in a matter of minutes, and Hervey would surely take his ship out of the battle.

'Mister Beazley. The minute *Dragon* floats free we'll get the second bower in and take her place in the firing line.'

'Will you slip the cable?'

'No, Mister Beazley, not with *Dragon* having our best bower. I can't risk losing both of them. We'll weigh anchor in a regular fashion. Where's the bosun?'

'Here sir. You want to weigh anchor, I gather.'

'Yes, Mister Hewitt. Man the capstan and the tiers, if you please.'

'Blue square hauled down on *Dragon*, sir.'

Amidst all the frenzied efforts Young had stuck to his duties as Signals Midshipman and he was the only one to see *Dragon's* signal come down.

'I take that to mean that she's afloat. Weigh anchor, Mister Beazley.'

Gresham turned away to study Hervey's ship. It was a wreck and the Spanish guns with their light charges were sweeping its deck with almost every shot. Men were falling before Gresham's eyes and the sooner Hervey got his ship out of range the better. However, there was something odd. The cable to *Dragon's* best bower was hanging slack, it was no longer being hauled in. Now Gresham could see that while everyone else was focussed on getting *Dragon* clear of the shoal ground, Pentland, presumably directed by Hervey, had quietly replaced the spring to *Dartmouth's* cable. Even now it was being hauled taut and inch by inch *Dragon's* broadside turned back to the enemy.

Beazley looked shocked.

'Good God, I do believe he intends to stay there. Here comes the yawl now. Mister Pentland will have something to tell us, no doubt.'

The yawl hooked onto the main chains and Pentland hurried up to the quarterdeck, quite forgetting to put on his coat that he'd removed under the hot tropical sun. Beazley looked disapproving, but Gresham hardly cared.

'From Captain Hervey, sir. He thanks you for coming to his aid and requests that *Dartmouth* gets underway and stands by in case of need.'

'Then he intends to return to the fight, Mister Pentland?'

'Yes sir. He does.'

'What are his casualties?'

'I don't know, sir, but they're considerable.'

Gresham looked over at *Dragon*. Hervey's guns were firing again but still very few of them managed to reach the castle's embrasures. Should he send his gun crews to *Dragon*? Hervey hadn't asked for them and probably he felt it more important that *Dartmouth* should be properly manned to offer assistance if it was needed again. Still, it seemed wrong to stand back while those three gallant ships were pounded by the Spaniards.

'He didn't ask for any of *Dartmouth's* men, Mister Pentland?'

Pentland was starting to feel nervous under this scrutiny, as though he should have asked all these questions. But Hervey wasn't a man to be quizzed by a mere lieutenant, and Pentland was sure that Hervey would have asked if he wanted men.

'No sir, not as far as I could tell. If I might say, sir, Captain Hervey wouldn't be shy of asking if he needed anything.'

Gresham barked out a laugh. Pentland was right of course. Hervey had been brought up to demand whatever he wanted, and if he hadn't asked it was best to leave well enough alone.

'When the anchor's aweigh, Mister Beazley, take us five cables to seaward of the castle and heave to. I'll be on the poop deck.'

***

Gresham had a better view from here. He could see the three ships-of-the-line pounding away, and if he squinted, he could see the castle's half-charged lazy roundshot in their slow, drooping trajectory towards their targets. It was a clever idea but really the Spanish should have thought of it earlier. Tearing apart the British masts and spars and sails was all well and good, but it had no bearing on the outcome of this battle. The Morro Castle's commander must know that those three ships would stay there and fight it out until ordered to withdraw even if they were totally dismasted.

He looked over to the nor'west to see *Stirling Castle* hove to at a distance that seemed to suggest that she was part of the action without actually risking the Spanish castle's fire. There would be a reckoning after this was all over, Gresham was sure of that. From all he knew of Hervey, it was certain that he'd demand that Campbell be brought before a court martial.

He felt a thud. Then one at least of the castle's guns had been directed against *Dartmouth*. Well, it didn't matter, they'd be out of range in a few minutes and they could start getting another cable ready at the stern, in case of need.

***

CHAPTER NINETEEN

Three Decker

Thursday, First of July 1762.
Cambridge, at Sea, off the Morro Castle, Havana.

Carlisle bounded up through *Cambridge's* entry port followed by Simmonds and was led up to the quarterdeck by a white-faced lieutenant who he didn't know. There was no sign of Goostrey but it was clear that everyone was in shock, although outwardly all was in order. The sailing master stood beside the wheel with a young-looking quartermaster beside him. A man dressed as a lieutenant, older than the one that had met him at the entry port, was shouting down to the upper deck guns to keep firing, but the ship had lost its vital spark. The guns were being served, sure, but it was as though they were manned by automatons going through the drill but without any conviction. The first lieutenant, for that was who the older man was, didn't greet him nor did he acknowledge Carlisle's presence. It was as though he couldn't function beyond the routines that he knew so well. Carlisle took this all in with a glance and strode over to the binnacle. He swept his eye over the officers standing around, compelling them to pay attention, to look at him. He had no time for the fulsome speech that was normally required on taking command.

'I'm Captain Carlisle of *Dartmouth* and I have command of this ship.'

The words were like a bolt of lightning, and officers and petty officers shook themselves into motion as though a puppet show had been brought to life by the pulling of strings.

'Mainwaring, sir. First of *Cambridge*...'

Carlisle cut him short, there would be time for introductions later.

'Get down below, Mister Mainwaring, and inject some

enthusiasm into the guns. Tell them what's happened and that I've taken command. We have a castle to reduce.'

Carlisle swung away from the first lieutenant to face a portly man in a plain blue suit.

'Your name, sir?'

'Shardlake, sir, sailing master.'

'First thing's first, Mister Shardlake. Are you ready to get underway? How much water is under your keel?'

'I just need to drop the tops'ls, let go the spring and heave in the anchor, sir. The capstan's not been hit, our head's to seaward, as you can see and we can be away on the starboard tack in no time at all. We had two fathoms under our keel half an hour ago.'

The sailing master was indecently keen to be away from this ghastly place. Well, he'd be disappointed. *Stirling Castle's* example left no room for any eagerness to withdraw.

'A cast of the lead then, Mister Shardlake, and what happened to Captain Goostrey?'

'A musket ball in the chest, sir, from one of those loopholes, I suppose. He was still breathing when they took him below, but...'

Shardlake shook his head and looked stricken. Carlisle had heard that *Cambridge* was a happy ship and that Goostrey was well loved by all; evidently it was true.

'My compliments to the surgeon and I'd be grateful to hear Captain Goostrey's condition. Now, pass the word for the bosun and the carpenter. I want reports on the ship's state, starting with anything that will prevent us floating, moving or fighting. Mister Simmonds, take notes if you please, and for pity's sake somebody strike that damned red ensign before we frighten the whole squadron.'

***

Goostrey was dead; he hadn't survived being carried down to the cockpit. Carlisle could imagine the scene and just hoped that Goostrey hadn't been conscious. He knew that if he was to die, he'd far rather do so on the quarterdeck under God's own sun than in the gloom and stink of the orlop deck. Goostrey would have been carried through the upper, the middle and the lower gun decks and would have been seen by the crews nearest to the ladders. The news would have spread like wildfire from gun to gun, even in the heat of the action. No wonder the pace of firing had slackened so much. He spotted the first lieutenant coming back up to the quarterdeck.

'They're back at it now, sir. We've lost one gun on the upper deck and one on the middle, but the lower deck thirty-two pounders are all still firing. Problem is, sir, that the castle's guns are all right up on the top and we can't reach them, we're just raising dust from the walls.'

Carlisle turned and skidded in a slick of blood. Perhaps that was poor Goostrey's; it almost certainly was, in fact. Strangely it didn't worry him to be standing at the exact spot where his predecessor had been brought down, the heat of an action allowed little time to brood upon its dangers.

Mainwaring was right. *Cambridge's* guns were firing in a constant barrage as each was loaded and run out, rather than waiting for full broadsides. He could see that the gun captains were waiting for the ship to roll to starboard on the swell in an attempt to reach the Spanish defenders. There were noticeably more shots as the ship rolled away from the castle than there were when she was on an even keel or leaning landward. Nevertheless, as he watched not a single ball reached as high as the embrasures. From a few feet below the enemy's guns to some twenty feet above the rock upon which the castle sat, its walls were pitted and cracked where the squadron's roundshot had struck. But the coral limestone blocks were absorbing the impact and the combined gunnery of three ships-of-the-line was doing no good at all. The ship needed to be heeled away from the castle. The conventional way of doing that was to shift the ballast or stores or guns or to swing the largest boats outboard, for good measure filling them with water from the washdeck pump. There wasn't time to shift either the ballast or the stores and the boats had all been left with the squadron, except for the little yawl, and that was just too small to make any difference. That left the guns, but if they stopped firing there was no point in *Cambridge* being here at all. But perhaps he could do something. Carlisle started to do the calculations in his head but it was too complicated. *Cambridge* had thirty-two pounders on the lower deck, eighteens on the middle deck and nines on the upper, and the permutations were far too numerous. To hell with it, a guess would have to do.

'Mister Mainwaring, keep the lower deck guns firing. I want all the upper deck guns – the nine pounders – and half the middle deck guns hauled over to starboard, and all the starboard guns run out on every deck, tight up to the port-sills. That should give us a heel and it might just be enough. Where's the gunner? Get him up here, he's doing no good in the magazine.'

Mainwaring had a quick mind and he instantly knew what Carlisle intended.

Shardlake interrupted Carlisle's calculations.

'Captain, sir. *Dragon's* aground and signalling for *Dartmouth* to assist. We have a fathom and a half under us.'

'Then man the capstan – don't use any more of the gun crews than necessary – and haul in a quarter cable. It's a steep bed here and that should keep us clear. Is *Dartmouth* underway?'

'She's just letting fall her tops'ls and stays'l, sir.'

Carlisle felt a pang of regret that he wasn't on *Dartmouth's* quarterdeck. It would be a nice piece of work to haul a third rate off the ground under the Morro's guns, but he knew that Gresham would rise to the occasion; that was partly the reason that *Dartmouth* had been selected for this task. So much to do! Men were running everywhere now as the guns started to move. Only the heaviest guns – the thirty-two pounders on the lower deck – were firing as all the other crews laboured to give *Cambridge* a heel to starboard. He could see that it was working and now the occasional shot was reaching the embrasures. That would give the Spanish gunners something to think about, and the ship was still capable of heeling further.

'Chips, sir.'

The man was so obviously a ship's carpenter that it was almost laughable. Even in the middle of a hot action he had a pencil behind his ear, a boxwood rule in his waistcoat pocket and a softwood wedge in his hand.

'Nothing much to worry about. We've no holes below the water and nothing to stop us fighting, though the gunwales and hammock nets will need some work once we're clear. Bosun begs to be excused reporting, sir. He's splicing the starboard main tops'l yard brace and he'll come down as soon as he can leave it to his mates, but he says it's all in hand, sir.'

The first lieutenant was next to report.

'That's all the starboard guns run out, sir, and all the larboard nine pounders and half of the eighteens lashed alongside their mates, with their muzzles as far outboard as they'll go. I'll have the men back at the remaining larboard eighteens soon. My word, but it's working, sir. Just look at those shots on the embrasures!'

Fully half of the lower deck guns were reaching their target now. If the thirty-twos could do it then the eighteens would surely add to the destruction as soon as their crews could get back to them.

'Well done, Mister Mainwaring.'

It must have been difficult apportioning the gun crews to shift the unwieldy brutes across the encumbered deck while at the same time finding enough muscle power to turn the capstan and keep the lower deck guns in action. And it wasn't just his imagination that everyone was working with more purpose. They could see that their shots were having an effect on the castle's defences, and it was boosting their morale like nothing else could.

A shout from Simmonds caught his attention and he saw that one at least of the Spanish guns had been put out of action. The coral limestone blocks of the merlons on the left side of its embrasure were shattered and the gun's muzzle was tilted far above its natural range. That was one less gun to maim and kill the ship's crew. Another advantage was also making itself felt. As *Cambridge* heeled to starboard the upper deck gun crews and the people on the quarterdeck and fo'c'sle were less exposed to those Spanish balls that managed to fall into the ship rather than pass through its masts and spars. Ah, some of the eighteen pounders were firing now and they were reaching the embrasures too. The Morro Castle wasn't having it all its own way.

The sailing master had regained his enthusiasm too. It was wonderful to see the effect of just a modest success. He drew Carlisle's attention to the third rate at the far left of the bombardment line.

'It looks like *Marlborough's* copying us, sir. Look, you can see them busy as bees on the quarterdeck and fo'c'sle. *Dragon's* fire has slackened though, she's too busy trying to get afloat again.'

Yes, that was all good, but Carlisle could see that more of the Spanish balls were landing on *Cambridge's* deck than before. Partly that was due to the ship being hauled further away to keep clear of the shoal, but also he guessed that the Spanish gunners were using short charges. A ball – a twenty-four pounder by the look of it – hit the quarterdeck forward of the wheel and bounced clear above the gunwale and into the sea alongside. That would never happen with a full charge of powder but it did mean that they could expect more hits on the deck and the hull, and a twenty-four pound shot at slow speed could maim a man as readily as it could with a full charge, even though it wouldn't penetrate a good thickness of solid oak.

***

Carlisle had never known such a hot action. The surgeon reported thirty men under his care, and another eleven dead. Every moment, it seemed, another man was being dragged or supported off the upper deck. The only comfort was that barely a single Spanish shot pitched low enough to reach the middle or lower gun decks, so the casualties were confined to the upper deck, the quarter deck, the fo'c'sle and the poop deck, and even there they were lighter due to the deck's angle of heel. As for the siege batteries on the other side of the fort, the landward side, they might have been on the moon for all that Carlisle could tell. Theirs was a wholly separate action, remote and unknowable; whether they were succeeding or not, all that Hervey's ships could do was keep firing, keep firing, keep firing.

***

Carlisle was being swept up in the action. The minutes passed like hours and his perception of what was happening outside this borrowed ship narrowed with each strike of the bell. He felt every shot that hit *Cambridge* and he saw every man that was struck down on the upper deck as though it happened in half real time. There was some truth in that because the course of the slow balls could almost be observed. He was reminded of an account that he'd heard from one of the land battles in Germany, how the enemy's shot had bounced across the summer-hardened ground and eventually, with their momentum largely spent, rolled and skipped towards the lines of infantry. The young soldiers thought they could stop the rolling shot with their feet, but the solid cast iron balls still had enough speed and weight to take a foot clean off at the ankle.

Four bells. The tide had turned and now the three ships were starting to turn so far that the springs on the anchor cables were ineffective. The wind was picking up from the north too and soon the three ships would be close to a dangerous lee shore.

'There's a boat coming from *Valiant*, sir, Commodore Keppel's flagship. It's steering for *Dragon*.'

'Very well, Mister Shardlake.'

Carlisle felt he knew what message that boat was bringing. This bombardment from the sea had failed. Despite the heroic efforts and the sacrifices, only three of the castle's guns on this seaward side had been put out of action, and the cost to the ships was simply too high. Another hour and these three third rates would be rendered useless for any further service until they'd had the attentions of a King's yard, and the nearest of those was two-hundred-and-fifty leagues away in Jamaica. Pocock couldn't afford to lose his fighting ships at that rate. He watched the boat come alongside and saw the officer run up through *Dragon's* entry port and reappear on the quarterdeck. There was a pause while he spoke to Hervey, then Hervey turned and said something to a lieutenant. A few moments later the red square that flew at *Dragon's* truncated main masthead came down with a rush. There was a pause as a new flag was bent on in its place and then a plain yellow square of bunting soared aloft.

Shardlake removed his hat to make his report.

'*Dragon's* signalling for all ships to withdraw…'

Shardlake never did finish his report. In an explosion of canvas and oak, a shot burst through the hammock nets and with its last ounce of energy glanced across the sailing master's chest, killing him instantly. It was travelling so slowly that it knocked the sailing master down without drawing any blood, but his chest was stove in. Carlisle just stared in shocked amazement.

***

CHAPTER TWENTY

Malaga Wine

Friday, Twenty-Third of July 1762.
Dartmouth, at Sea, off the Morro Castle, Havana.

The morning's news had all been bad. The army was falling sick, as anyone who knew the tropics could have predicted, and now many of the sailors that had been sent ashore to establish and man the siege batteries were returning to their ships with dangerous fevers, if they returned at all. He'd read a report from the artillery commander, and it made depressing reading:

> *Fluxes and intermittent fevers is the general disorder, occasioned chiefly by violent heats and great damps in the night.*

It was very noticeable that sailors who didn't venture ashore were rarely sick, but the army needed men desperately and some were already talking about abandoning the enterprise through want of soldiers fit to meet the enemy. And that led to the next matter that so exercised Carlisle, the whereabouts of the American regiments. It was well known that some four thousand men had been recruited in the New England colonies specifically for the campaign against Havana, but none had arrived yet. By some perverse logic his brother officers blamed him for the Americans' absence, and he was thin-skinned enough to allow it to worry him. Now, to cap it all, his presence was demanded in the flagship. Curiously his summons came under the joint signatures of Pocock and Albemarle, and he was to bring Commander Laredo with him. It was lucky that the letter hadn't come a few days later because Carlisle had been considering offering Laredo his parole and sending him ashore without consulting either admiral or general. How he'd have explained that away was beyond his guessing, and reminding Pocock that he'd given him just that authority would do no good at all. Of course, the weather had turned bad and despite Souter's judicious use of a tarpaulin, he and Laredo were being soaked by salt spray as the longboat butted its way under sail towards the flagship.

***

'We'll talk to Captain Laredo later, I hope, but I want to test this on you first, as you know both of the gentlemen concerned.'

Pocock had the use of the great cabin again and now, on the occasions that Albemarle visited from his shore headquarters, the general had only the dining cabin for his own use. Carlisle could hear the general, for he wasn't a quiet man, and the cabin partitions were merely a single layer of panelling. Laredo was being entertained by a lieutenant on the admiral's staff who knew some Spanish, so Carlisle and Pocock were alone for now.

'You'll be aware, Carlisle, that something must be done to take the Morro Castle. That was a brave attempt of Hervey's and incidentally he mentioned you particularly for taking poor Goostrey's place, and for your first lieutenant's seamanship in laying out a kedge for *Dragon*. However, I won't talk about it anymore today.'

Pocock looked disturbed and stared out of the window at the browns and greens of the Cuban shore.

'You can imagine that I'll have to convene a court martial board to investigate certain allegations against Captain Campbell, and I don't want to pre-judge the matter. Now, where was I? Ah yes. The Morro Castle still holds out and until we take it we can't expect the city to surrender, not with any shred of honour. Everything I know about the Spanish suggests that de Prado will have to answer to King Charles when we send him home, and I wouldn't be surprised if the King takes the same stand that the old King George did in Byng's case. If we want Havana to capitulate without the bloody business of storming its walls, we must give the governor-general a plausible way out, a staged process that leads naturally from the Morro Castle to the city. If he digs his heels in the miners are preparing to blow the glacis and redoubt at the castle's seaward end and I hope that the soldiers will consider that a practicable breach, but I've agreed with Lord Albemarle that we'll offer decent terms if they'll give up the castle immediately.'

Carlisle could do no more than nod. He thought he knew where this was leading.

'Now, the Morro Castle's commandant was replaced as soon as we arrived. It was regarded as a sinecure and the old soldier who had the command could hardly walk unaided, let alone resist a siege. The present commandant is a post-captain from one of the Barlovento Squadron ships. You know him, I believe?'

It was clear that Pocock required an answer and Carlisle's heart sank as the awful extent of his involvement in this started to dawn upon him.

'Yes, Sir George. I met him at dinner last December when I visited Havana, Luis Vicente de Velasco. He has a long string of other names and titles of course, but that's his everyday name. A most impressive and active officer as I remember.'

'Good, and you speak excellent Spanish; then you're just the man for the job. Now, does Captain Laredo also know Captain Velasco?'

There was no point in dissembling and it was a dangerous thing to attempt with a man wielding the awesome powers of a commander-in-chief.

'It would be strange if he didn't, Sir George, with Laredo on de Hevia's staff and Velasco commanding one of his ships-of-the-line. We've spoken about him often.'

'Do you know, Carlisle, it makes me so happy when a plan falls into place. Lord Albemarle and I have put together an offer to this Velasco, a generous offer including the usual flags and arms and a free passage to the city, rather than the Thames and Portsmouth hulks, if he'll surrender the Morro

Castle entire and undamaged. I doubt whether they have enough powder to destroy it in any case. That will allow them to hold out behind the city's walls for a week or two until it becomes obvious that they must surrender that also or face an indecent effusion of blood for no good end. The initial offer won't say anything about the city's fate, but I want them to understand that the same offer will be made a week or two later, with repatriation to Spain under parole. It's a better offer than they'll get once those mines are set. I want you and Laredo to deliver this letter and the verbal message that goes with it. Now, you know these people, what's your honest opinion of the odds on success?'

Carlisle thought for a moment.

'The terms are generous, Sir George, and in a rational world Velasco should seize on this opportunity…'

'But you don't believe he will, is that it, Carlisle?'

'Just so, sir. I said that I was impressed with Velasco, and I'll explain why. We had a long conversation over coffee while the other Spanish officers were diverted by my wife.'

Pocock smiled at that. Carlisle's wife was a topic of much gentlemanly conversation in the Jamaica and Leeward Island squadrons.

'He's a man of old-world virtues, with a single-minded desire to distinguish himself. If you've ever read Don Quixote and can set aside the humour and parody, you'll recognise what I mean. This command of the Morro Castle was openly mooted for months before your squadron arrived, and Laredo had heard Velasco talk about how it would be the only post of honour for a sea officer if Havana is under siege. He knew even then that the Barlovento Squadron wouldn't be allowed to leave Havana while it was threatened. Laredo has told me that he doesn't believe that Velasco will surrender the Morro Castle while one stone stands upon another and while he has a sword in his hand.'

Pocock fiddled with an unopened letter on his desk, probably the actual letter that was to be delivered to Velasco.

'I understand Carlisle, and I thank you for your candour. Nevertheless, it must be attempted and I've no doubt that you're the man for the job. What I won't do is hold up any offensive operations for a substantial time while you deliver the letter, because if you're right, then the mines mustn't be delayed by a day, no, not by a dog watch with this yellow jack sweeping through the camps. I can prevail upon Lord Albemarle to hold the batteries' fire for an hour to show good will, but that will be all. If you get a chance to see the northeast corner of the Morro Castle, where the walls reach the sea cliffs, he'd be very interested in your observations. It appears that there's some sort of obstruction there, a deep ditch perhaps, that we haven't yet seen. I expect they'll keep you away from there, but still, if you have the opportunity. Now, let's set a time then I want to speak to your man Laredo, just to be sure that he understands the situation and the implied extension of the offer to cover the city. He has a wife in Havana, so he has every incentive to help us.'

***

Dartmouth lay hove to just beyond the effective range of the castle's great guns. The wind had died away in the late afternoon leaving a long, languid swell from the nor'west and a sticky heat that soaked a man's shirt and left it clinging like glue to his body. The only thing on the wide ocean that was moving with a distinct purpose was *Dartmouth's* longboat as it rowed slowly towards the harbour entrance, rising and falling through a fathom-and-a-half between each peak and trough of the swell. So still was the air that it was only the boat's motion that gave life to the two flags that drooped listlessly from tall spars lashed to the transom: the union flag that could decently represent both the navy and the army, and a plain white flag as a sign of truce.

Carlisle was in his best frock coat over a woollen waistcoat, and it felt like death after so many months in the more relaxed rig that was appropriate for a bitterly fought campaign in the tropics. Laredo was beside him, Pentland commanded the boat and Souter was steering. The whole

Old Bahama Straits

boat's crew were in their best outfits for the occasion, each man wearing a straw hat emblazoned with the ship's name, a striped shirt, a red silk scarf and a blue jacket over blue trousers and shoes, actual leather shoes, not list slippers. To a man they all felt it was right and proper that they should suffer so when their captain was being rowed into the enemy camp in the glorious role of *parlementaire*.

'Here sir?'

'Yes Mister Pentland, just here.'

Pentland nodded at Souter who gave the orders for the oarsmen to rest on their oars. When the boat came to a complete stop he stood in the stern sheets and directed his voice to the bows.

'Drummer!'

The marine drummer had joined *Dartmouth* as a boy, barely past his tenth birthday, but he was almost a grown man now and a veteran of many campaigns. He'd beaten his drum for quarters and to clear for action more times than he could possibly remember and looked reassuringly competent as he raised his drumsticks. At a further nod from Pentland the drummer brought his sticks down forcefully and the stirring sound of the *Chamade* broke the stillness. He played for a full minute by Pentland's pocket watch and then the trumpeter took over. Like all rated ships, *Dartmouth's* establishment included a trumpeter. He was one of the complement of seamen, not a marine, but he was far more useful as a fore-topman in the starboard watch and he hadn't touched his trumpet for months. The drummer looked scornful as the faltering notes tumbled uncertainly from the trumpet's mouth.

Pentland looked at Carlisle and made a helpless gesture.

'It doesn't matter, Mister Pentland, but perhaps a little practice once a week would avoid embarrassment in the future. Get underway, if you please and we'll repeat this twice more before we come to the harbour mouth.'

Soon they were under the castle's guns and only a cable from the wharf at the castle's western side.

'Stop here, Mister Pentland. Can you see any movement?'

There was a certain dignity to be observed in these affairs, and it wouldn't do for Carlisle – a post-captain and a parlementaire – to be seen anxiously looking for a reception party. Pentland, however, as the officer in charge of the boat had no such conventional restrictions, and he studied the stone wharf under the shade of his hand.

'There are two Spanish boats alongside, sir, both look empty, and there's a field gun – a six pounder by the look of it – drawn up with its crew behind a makeshift breastwork. It looks like sand-filled sacks, sir. I can see a postern door in the castle walls, but it's closed.'

'Very well. Let me know if anything changes.'

Carlisle shifted his position on the seat. Souter always brought a cushion for his captain but it seemed very thin today. Probably it was the wasting of his muscles that came as a natural companion to that great leveller, advancing age. He had a sack at his feet, the mail taken from a Spanish packet boat bound for Havana, a gesture of friendship that Albemarle had thought might encourage Velasco to consider the offer. He'd already decided that he'd wait here for thirty minutes, and if nothing happened in that time he'd abandon the attempt. What he hadn't considered was that with the certainty of half a dozen Spanish telescopes trained upon the boat, he couldn't possibly show his impatience by looking at his watch, not even for a moment. He saw Pentland reach for his own watch.

'No, Mister Pentland. We must be like the stoics of ancient Greece. Leave your watch in your pocket if you please.'

A breeze started to play across the face of the sea and very faintly it brought the sound of two bells from *Dartmouth's* fo'c'sle. He remembered one bell in the first dog watch when he'd given his final instructions to Gresham. It must have been ten minutes later that the boat cast off from the ship's side and another fifteen to row this far, what with the stops for announcing their approach. Then they'd been here five minutes or thereabouts. Well, he'd wait another ten by his own reckoning, that should give time for Velasco to hunt out his best coat and sword.

'The postern's opening, sir. There's a guard coming out, a dozen men with muskets and an officer. They're forming two ranks outside the door. A drummer and a trumpeter are coming out now, and another officer, a lean man in a blue coat and a red waistcoat, leaning on a stick.'

Carlisle nodded. Velasco was obeying the conventions, and that at least was encouraging. He was matching his guard to the number of seamen in the longboat and it looked like he was going to answer drum-for-drum and trumpet-for-trumpet. Had he recognised Laredo? It seemed likely, and in that case the numbers were exact, a Spaniard to match every Englishman, just as he'd have expected. He could see for himself now. The Spanish drummer raised his sticks and beat a leisurely tattoo, then the trumpeter followed with a rather more creditable performance than *Dartmouth's* topman.

'Return the compliment Mister Pentland, then take me alongside the wharf.'

***

Carlisle stepped carefully out of the longboat, standing tall and dignified. He was followed by Laredo, who was looking far less assured of his reception.

'Capitán de Navío Luis Vicente de Velasco e Isla, at your service, sir, but I see that we have already met.'

'Captain Edward Carlisle, sir, at your service. Yes, I had the honour of being introduced to you in December. You know Capitán de Fragata Ramon de Laredo, I'm sure. Capitan Laredo has given his parole that he will return to the British squadron this afternoon. I'm sure you understand the situation.'

Velasco and Laredo bowed politely to each other, but there was a definite restraint on Velasco's part. He'd have been less than human if he didn't glance at the sack that

Pentland carried.

'Ah, this is a quantity of personal mail for the squadron and garrison at Havana. It fell into our hands when we took a packet off Cape San Antonio. Lord Albemarle and Sir George Pocock hope that you will accept it as an earnest of goodwill between gentlemen who unfortunately find themselves on opposing sides of a national disagreement.'

Carlisle had practiced this difficult Spanish phrase with Laredo's help and he was proud of his fluency; he bowed and Velasco returned the compliment.

'Of course, that is not the reason for my visit, Captain, and I hope that there is somewhere that we can talk.'

***

Velasco led the way into the castle through the postern door. Carlisle noticed that it was made of some dark tropical wood and was immensely thick and studded with stout iron bolts. The approach to the door was covered by a dozen loopholes for muskets and four embrasures that looked ideal places for mounting wall pieces. Evidently this was no soft underbelly of the castle. Velasco was limping and his lieutenant stayed close, evidently in case he stumbled, but he set up a fine pace on what must have been a familiar route.

They passed through a maze of passages and chambers and climbed so many stairs that it was certain that they were being taken to the very highest point of the castle. Eventually they burst into the open onto a platform that looked over the castle's walls to the southwest, where the whole of the city, the harbour and the approach channel were open to their view.

'When I saw that it was you, Captain Carlisle, I had a table placed here for our meeting. You will understand, I'm sure, that your mortars have rendered this place too dangerous for everyday use, but they seem to have ceased, at least for the time being, and my lieutenants tell me that your miners have laid down their tools too. We must take advantage of this while we can and take our wine in as

Old Bahama Straits

civilised a way as possible.'

Velasco motioned for Carlisle and Laredo to sit and he took a chair for himself. A Spanish marine brought wine, a tough looking man with a bandaged arm.

'You will see, sir, that few of us are undamaged, and I have a piece of one of Lord Albemarle's mortars in my leg. The physician says I must come to terms with it, for it will be with me to my grave. Now, before we start, I must tell Captain Laredo his family news.'

Laredo started at that. He'd heard nothing of his wife since he left Havana on his errand to de Blénac.

'I, of course, have not left the castle for some weeks, but I was told a few days ago that your wife is well and that she knows that you are a guest of Captain Carlisle. I regret that is all I know.'

Laredo bowed. He knew that he could expect nothing more. His wife couldn't have guessed that he'd meet Velasco today.

'Now, Captain Velasco, our time is short so I must deliver the message from Lord Albemarle and Admiral Pocock.'

Carlisle reached into his coat pocket and passed the letter to Velasco. The Spaniard turned it over and examined the seal. He looked satisfied.

'El Morro, as I'm sure you are aware, is becoming indefensible. That letter offers you terms for an honourable withdrawal to Havana, with personal arms and colours flying, if you will undertake to leave the castle as it is now. Clearly his Lordship and the admiral are eager to progress the siege and I'm authorised to wait for an hour for your reply, no more. I should add that at this moment both of the commanders are minded to offer similar terms to the city when the time comes, and that would include repatriation to Spain under parole for the entire garrison. That would be a much more satisfactory conclusion than imprisonment until the end of the war, I'm sure you'll agree. Nevertheless, this letter only addresses El Morro, and Lord

Albemarle ventures to suggest that King Carlos himself would be the first to order you to capitulate, to preserve the life of such an illustrious and distinguished officer.'

Velasco didn't immediately reply but gazed across at the beautiful city that lay before him. In a moment of clairvoyance Carlisle guessed that Velasco foresaw his own death in this place. It was as though he was savouring a last vision of the beauty of the world in this stolen hour of peace before he was pitched back into this unequal struggle. It was clear that there was little chance of Velasco accepting, but Carlisle had never expected him to.

'Would you permit me a moment alone with Captain Laredo?'

'Certainly, sir. The captain has given his parole and knows that he must return to my ship with me.'

Laredo rose and followed Velasco, leaving Carlisle with his glass of wine and the company of the lieutenant. Carlisle spent the time, perhaps ten minutes, looking across at Havana. There was nothing in the conventions of war that prevented him taking advantage of this moment to imprint upon his memory those parts of the defences that he didn't already know, but he looked in vain, for there was nothing new to see from this vantage point except the chain across the harbour and the sunken ships blocking the channel. Pocock knew all about them already, and perhaps that was why Velasco was prepared to offer him this view.

They returned after ten minutes with Velasco looking as determined as ever and Laredo wearing an expression of resignation.

'I would be grateful if you would pass my thanks to Lord Albemarle and Sir George Pocock but I find that I cannot with honour accept this proposal. If they expect this castle to fall easily they will be sadly disappointed and they will find that my soldiers will imitate the constancy of their captain and will not easily be moved. There is still much to expect of fortune. Now, I have sent a case of Malaga to your boat and I hope that you will accept it in return for the most handsome gesture of returning our mail. May God go with you, Captain Carlisle.'

***

CHAPTER TWENTY-ONE

A Contrast in Characters

Sunday, Twenty-Fifth July 1762.
Dartmouth, at Sea, off Santa Maria Island, Cuba.

Albemarle had just shrugged; he hadn't imagined that Velasco would so easily give up the Morro Castle. Pocock had at least shown an interest in the man and what drove him to stay in such a hopeless position but within ten minutes it was out of their minds. In half an hour, as far as they were concerned, the attempt to persuade the Spanish to give up Havana's principal defensive work might never have happened. For Carlisle too, it had been a short and intense episode, and now he had a new mission to claim his attention. Pocock had given him his orders at the same meeting where the admiral had learned of Carlisle's failure to tempt Velasco; he was to proceed to the Old Bahama Straits and discover what had happened to the troop convoys from America. Carlisle couldn't help thinking that it was a single punishment for two separate sins. First he was a colonial American himself and must, apparently, bear part of the fault for their late arrival, and second, for all the low expectations of his embassy to Velasco, it had come to nothing, and he was the only senior officer who could be blamed. Still, he was away from the squadron and free from the pestilence that was striking down one in three of the men who had contact with the shore. In fact, it was a pleasure to be underway with a purpose and this refreshing northerly breeze had hurried them through the Nicholas Channel on a beam reach, so that at dawn on the Sunday, just thirty-six hours after being dispatched, Beazley was able to fix the ship's position off Santa Maria Island. There was a sail too, and Horace Young was there to report.

'*Richmond*, sir, thirty-eight, Captain John Elphinstone.'

Young was becoming a good signal midshipman and he

Old Bahama Straits

had a keen enough eye to pick out not just the type of vessel, but the exact ship by name, as long as he'd seen it before. His identification of *Richmond* had been made with assurance and Pocock's squadron list named its captain.

'Very well, Mister Young. Make the squadron signal for *Richmond's* captain to come on board *Dartmouth*.'

Carlisle had only briefly met Elphinstone, but they had a mutual friend in George Holbrooke. Elphinstone and Holbrooke had both been captured on the beach at Saint-Cast in 'fifty-eight and both had lost their ships as a result. Elphinstone had been lucky to be gazetted and given a frigate with only four months on half pay, while Holbrooke had been sent to the North American wilderness to join the expedition against Fort Niagara, and he hadn't been promoted until nearly a year had passed.

'Heave to Mister Beazley, let *Richmond* stay to windward. It'll be a good opportunity to test the strength of the current against those cays over there.'

Beazley sniffed. He'd tested the current many times already. This was where the Old Bahama Straits opened into the Nicholas Channel and naturally the current slackened as it escaped the confining waters of the narrower passage. He was irritated that Carlisle should remind him of his duty but still, after bringing the ship to on the larboard tack, he took a boat compass, his octant and a deeply reluctant young gentleman to the poop deck, leaving Hooper on watch on the quarterdeck.

'Now then young man, the captain wants to know the strength of the current, so how will you go about measuring it? What, you don't know? And you two years at sea already and badgering the captain to be made a midshipman?'

In truth, this was what Beazley enjoyed more than anything, the opportunity to make a youngster's life a misery while indulging himself in the more arcane parts of his profession.

***

Richmond's yawl hooked onto the main chains and John Elphinstone came bounding up through the entry port, pausing only to remove his hat as the bosun's mate's pipes twittered their greeting.

'How good to see you, Captain Elphinstone. Will you come below? I'd welcome your opinion on a Malaga wine that's come straight from the castle of El Morro.'

Elphinstone stopped in his tracks.

'They've taken the Morro Castle, sir?'

'Oh no, I just visited to try to persuade the commandant to surrender the place to us. It was no use, of course, but he's a gentlemanly fellow and sent me on my way with a case of wine, perhaps you'd like to try it.'

Elphinstone looked relieved. There was a rumour going around that ships that were detached from the squadron at the time that the Spaniards capitulated would forfeit their share of the prize money, and as Havana was one of the wealthiest cities in the Spanish empire, his loss would be considerable. Elphinstone wasn't a close enough friend to discuss such things with, but Carlisle recognised the signs. Elphinstone had no family money and he was relying upon this war – in fact this very campaign – to make his fortune.

The Malaga was good and Elphinstone particularly appreciated it as he was down to the last derided anonymous bottles in his own cabin stores. Sometimes he wondered whether what he was sold was wine at all, and not cheap grape juice rounded out with even cheaper brandy or arrack.

'I've been ordered to take your ship under command and see that the American convoys arrive off Havana as quickly as possible. It's conceivable that the whole enterprise will fail otherwise, you know, for lack of soldiers fit to stand in the line. You may read my orders if you wish.'

'Oh, there's no need for that, sir. The admiral warned me that he might send reinforcements and insisted that I stay to the west of Santa Maria Island so that I can be found. I've had examples of his orders myself, I'll hardly learn anything that you can't tell me.'

Old Bahama Straits

Carlisle smiled. He was starting to like Elphinstone. Many junior post-captains would have refused to give an inch until they'd seen their ship's name in black and white above an admiral's signature. Some would have stood their ground merely as a point of principle. It appeared that they'd work well together.

'Have you heard anything of them yet? Lord Albemarle is at his wit's end for men, what with the yellow jack decimating his army. He's already furious that they're coming in two separate convoys. It seems like the second group only left New York three weeks ago.'

'The convoys? No, nothing at all, and I'm hamstrung by my orders. I've been stemming the wind and current for the past week and haven't seen a sail. It seems that even the fishermen have taken fright.'

'Of course, they might not even come through these Straits. The admiral gave them the option of coming through the Florida Channel or south of Cuba, but of course he's had no reply. There's a frigate waiting off Grand Bahama in case they come that way, another off Cape San Antonio and Commodore Douglas at Jamaica should be guarding de Blénac's squadron at Cape François.'

'You know this area better than anybody now, sir. What would you do? Which way would you come?'

Carlisle considered for a moment.

'The Florida Channel is a more direct route and there's far less chance of meeting the enemy in force, but if they can't catch a fair wind they could take weeks battling the current. At least the Caicos Passage and the Old Bahama Straits have mostly following winds and currents. It's de Blénac's squadron and the cays and reefs that worry me most about that route. They could come straight through the Windward Passage and round Cuba to the south, but the admiral warned them that there's a Spanish squadron at Santiago de Cuba. On balance, with no covering battle squadron, I'd take the Florida Channel, but who knows what they'll do? If proof was ever needed that the Spanish chose well in establishing Havana, this is it. Three important ocean passages, three currents and three winds all meeting at one point, and Havana standing guard.'

Carlisle stopped abruptly. He was preaching, and Elphinstone was not an inexperienced captain who needed paternal guidance.

'Well, my orders allow me to send you down the Straits if I see fit…'

A knock at the door stopped Carlisle in mid-sentence. It was Horace Young, suitably overawed in the presence of two post-captains.

'I beg your pardon, sir. *Richmond* is signalling, sail in sight to windward.'

Carlisle and Elphinstone glanced at each other. *Dartmouth* had been drifting westward, testing the current, so *Richmond* must be at least a mile to windward. That would account for her seeing the sail first despite *Dartmouth's* taller masts.

'Sail ho! Sail to windward, just to the right of *Richmond*. It looks like a man-o'-war, a third rate, perhaps.'

Whittle's voice passed easily through the skylight and into the cabin. The anticipated convoy or de Blénac's squadron, or just a passing ship on its lawful occasions; whatever it was they must be prepared.

'You'd better get back to your ship, Captain Elphinstone, and I hope you'll accept a couple of this fine Malaga. Mister Young, my compliments to Lieutenant Hooper and he's to make sail and close *Richmond*. Pass the word to *Richmond's* boat.'

***

Carlisle watched the yawl pull slowly across from the third rate. Was there a hint of reluctance in its sluggish progress? No, that was just Carlisle's imagination. He could see John Hale sitting in the stern sheets with what looked like a mail sack beside him. He'd been posted a mere month after Carlisle, but that month made him the subordinate as long as they were both on the post-captain's list. They'd

Old Bahama Straits

never met but Carlisle knew that Hale was an older man and some hinted that he resented the late age of his promotion. Hale said nothing until they were in the great cabin.

'We left New York on the ninth of June: *Intrepid*, *Chesterfield*, John Scaife in command, and sixteen transports with the Forty-Sixth of Foot and something approaching two thousand soldiers from the northern colonies embarked. God, we've had a torrid time of it! Foul winds at Sandy Hook and *Intrepid* dragged her anchor and took the ground, I couldn't haul her off for two days on account of the gales. Contrary winds all the way to the Caicos Passage, then four days ago one of the transports ran aground near Green Island at the entrance to the Straits. She was stuck fast so I left another to stand by and take her men off if it becomes necessary. I've heard nothing more of them. Then, yesterday just as I thought we were clear, *Chesterfield* strayed to the south and was brought up on a little reef off Coco Island, some twelve or thirteen leagues from here. She took another four of the transports with her when they followed in her wake. The current was strong there, and the trade wind was relentless, and I could do nothing but keep moving to the west. So here you see us, just ten of my sixteen transports left and *Chesterfield* aground. On my last sight of her, all her masts were gone by the board and she was heaving further onto the reef at each minute.'

The contrast between Elphinstone's breezy cheerfulness and Hale's dour pessimism could hardly have been more marked. Carlisle wanted to quiz the man, to ask whether nothing could have been done for the nine hundred odd desperately needed soldiers that he'd left behind to fend for themselves, but he knew that he'd get no more. And really, he probably couldn't have done any better if he'd been there himself. The current was at its strongest just where *Chesterfield* and the four transports had come to grief, and the wind had a lot of easterly in it yesterday. Probably Hale did the right thing in pressing on with the transports that he still had. Nevertheless, something should be done, but not by Hale. Another glance proved that the man had been unnerved by his experience, and he was waiting to be told what to do. The sooner he took *Intrepid* out of these dangerous waters the better.

'Do you have any news of the second convoy?'

'Only that they were expected to leave in two or three weeks after the first convoy. It was the New York Provincials that were the problem, they were tardy in mustering and slow in raising the extra men. I do have a vast quantity of mail for the squadron and I took the liberty of extracting yours and *Richmond's* before coming over here.'

That was a dangerous thing to do and directly contrary to the instructions; it showed Hale's desperation to appear obliging. Still it would be good to have his letters early, it could be another week before they passed through the admiral's secretary's hands and were distributed to the other ships.

'Mister Simmonds, pass the word for Mister Beazley and tell him to bring his chart of the Straits. My compliments to Mister Hooper and he's to hang out a signal for *Richmond's* captain to come on board *Dartmouth*. Then you may address yourself to our letters.'

Elphinstone would just have to suffer two boat trips in one day, but he'd be pleased to receive the mail.

Beazley arrived before Hale had finished his first glass of wine. He asked a few questions then made some light pencil marks on his chart.

'Thirteen leagues to where *Chesterfield* is aground with the four transports, sir, and thirty leagues to the other two, and there's a good bit of northerly in the wind now.'

'If we leave within the hour, how soon can we make *Chesterfield's* position?'

'Not before sunset, sir, and we'll have to back and fill until dawn tomorrow with the current against us.'

Carlisle strode to the window and looked out at the sparkling sea and the ranks of trade wind waves. Yes, they were coming almost from the north, and Beazley's answer was just what he wanted to hear.

'If we leave just after eight bells with three transports, how long?'

Beazley scratched his head and stared at the chart.

'They're not very weatherly, those transports, but they go well enough on a reach. We'll be there at dawn tomorrow if the wind holds.'

Carlisle strode over and looked at the chart for no more than ten seconds. It was quite clear now.

'We'll take all of the soldiers out of three of the transports and pack them into the remaining seven. They'll survive, they'll be ashore in three days and wishing they were back on board, however hard the deck planks. Captain Hale, I'd be obliged if you'll continue to Havana with the remaining seven as soon as they've disembarked their soldiers. I'll follow as soon as I've seen the situation at Coco Island. I'll take *Richmond* with the three empty transports to rescue *Chesterfield's* men and embark the soldiers from the three grounded transports. We'll keep a lookout for the transport that you left behind at Green Island, what was her name?'

'*Falls*, and the grounded transport is *Juno*; she won't get off that reef after yesterday's blow, her back will be broken for sure. Then you can look for four transports coming out of the Straits in the next few days.'

'That's my reckoning, Captain Hale, *Dartmouth*, *Richmond* and four transports. They're valuable, sure, but right now it's the nine hundred soldiers that will make the difference.'

Hale looked embarrassed, his eyes shifting from the chart to Beazley. Carlisle took the hint.

'Thank you, Mister Beazley.'

The sailing master gathered up his chart and left the cabin with a covert backward glance at Hale. He thought he knew why he was being dismissed. He'd sailed with *Intrepid's* master many years ago and the man had no backbone. He was good enough in the open ocean but he insisted on taking a pilot within sight of land, whenever one was available. He was infamous for demanding a pilot to come to anchor at Spithead, for heaven's sake! Beazley could imagine how he'd have fared in the Old Bahama Straits. It was a spell in *Intrepid* for Mister Beazley, no doubt about it, and to back up his hunch he went straight to his cabin and started packing what he'd need. He smiled slyly; he could at least demand a pilot's pay for the time he was on board *Intrepid*, and the clerks at Seething Lane would never notice that he'd been paid twice.

Never had men moved so fast. *Dartmouth's* officers rowed from ship to ship detailing those that would disgorge their soldiers and those that would take on the additional bodies. They passed the word that the relief squadron would start its journey eastward at exactly two bells in the afternoon watch, and any soldiers that were still onboard would be heading back up the Straits, and that applied equally to their kit. The three transports were cleared in record time and exactly at the stroke of two bells the little flotilla filled its sails on the larboard tack towards Coco Island.

***

CHAPTER TWENTY-TWO

The Convoy

Monday, Twenty-Sixth July 1762.
Dartmouth, at Sea, Old Bahama Straits.

'Mister Simmonds, be so good as to bring the letters into my cabin.'

Simmonds would already have skimmed all the letters from the Navy Board and, if there were any, from the Admiralty. The latter was unlikely as *Dartmouth* was under Pocock's orders and as a commander-in-chief, their Lordships would generally address all letters regarding the ships in his squadron to the admiral himself. Nevertheless there would be a good few from his *affectionate friends* in Seething Lane.

'There's nothing that requires your immediate attention, sir. The navy board has asked for a survey on the sprung mizzen, but Mister Hewlett is already considering how he can muster three other bosuns or carpenters to make a quorum.'

Simmonds laid Carlisle's personal letters on his writing desk and departed silently. Walker, diligent as always, brought coffee. There were letters from a few brother officers, one from George Holbrooke, he noticed, and an intriguing package from Ann Holbrooke; and there were six letters from Chiara. Usually he had enough self-discipline to start reading from the oldest letter, but today he was desperate for news, and opened the most recent first. He saw that it was dated the thirtieth of May from Williamsburg; that must have been the last possible date for a letter to reach the New York convoy before it sailed on the ninth of June.

My Dear Edward,
You will be delighted to know that my confinement is

proceeding well and the doctor is confident that it will be an October baby, or possibly November.

Carlisle sat back in shock. That was the danger of reading the latest letter first. Chiara would have broken the news much more gently at first, but for this most recent letter she was writing under the assumption that he knew that he was to be a father for the second time. He did a quick calculation. Ah yes, the final few days in Port Royal back in January, before Chiara embarked in *Argonaut* bound for Antigua and then Hampton. Well, it wasn't unusual. He read on:

I've engaged the same midwife who attended me for Joshua's birth, and she is quite sure that we will be blessed with a baby girl. I won't trouble you with the details but there are signs that she swears are positive indicators. I'm not so certain and am prepared for either eventuality. In any case, the baby appears to be growing well and I feel much more comfortable than I did at this stage with Joshua.

Now for less pleasant news. We buried your father last Wednesday in the parish church.

Never, never again would he read his letters out of order. He hung his head for a moment in remorse that he couldn't have attended his father in his final days. At least they parted on good terms, even though it hadn't always been so. His affairs were in order too, he'd seen to that with the help of his friend George Wythe.

I won't repeat all the circumstances of his death but the funeral was a dignified affair and Mister Fauquier honoured you by making an appearance. It does seem that your reputation grows even without your presence. Little Joshua is quite lost without his grandfather but the summer is upon us and he'll soon find other distractions.

Old Bahama Straits

The remainder of the letter was just news of the doings of the great and good in Williamsburg. He should have read it with interest but his mind was on the two greater items, his father's death and his imminent second child. Would he be home for the birth? It was possible, but only if Albemarle's army moved with more urgency than they'd shown so far. That made him think of the American reinforcements. The gossip in the flagship was all about the danger of Albemarle simply running out of soldiers fit enough for the rigours of a siege. That made it all the more imperative that he should rescue the nine-hundred soldiers stranded on a cay in the Old Bahama Straits, and find that second convoy.

***

Carlisle set aside George Holbrooke's letter and picked up Ann's package. It was the size of an octavo book, like Gresham's *Vade Mecum* and there was a short letter to accompany it.

> *I know George won't mind me writing to you while he is away, he sailed for the Brest blockade last week and I don't know when I'll see him again. I enclose a book of poetry that might interest you. Last year I was persuaded against my better judgement to subscribe to its publishing and had completely forgotten about it. It was only when a large box arrived yesterday at Mulberry House that I realised that my subscription entitled me to six copies of the book! It's an epic poem, rather long, about a merchant ship that founders on a rocky coast, and as I'm confident that such a fate won't befall your fine Dartmouth, I felt that you should have a copy.*

Carlisle unwrapped the book. It was finely bound in calfskin and mustered some hundred-and-sixty-odd pages with engravings. He turned to the title page and saw the author's name, William Falconer. He'd seen that name before, attached to some shorter poems in the Gentleman's Magazine. It was an expensive item and it was no wonder that it had needed subscriptions to be published. This Falconer must have some useful connections to have interested enough people with money to spare. He flicked idly through the pages and his eyes rested on an engraving of a ship cast ashore on an iron-bound coast, dismasted and at the mercy of the wind and waves. The author had described the chilling scene at length – at great length – but one couplet caught his attention:

Then might I, with unrival'd strains deplore
Th' impervious horrors of a leeward shore!

Amen to that, Carlisle thought, Amen.

***

Monday's dawn revealed a dismal scene. *Chesterfield* had driven far up the reef and her back was broken. The four transports were stationed in a regular line of bearing on the frigate's beam, each with its bows firmly in the coral's grip. Carlisle was reminded of the book that he'd received from Ann. They must have struck one after the other without ever being aware that they were standing into danger. It was a sparkling day with only a light wind to ruffle the sea, and on a day like this it was hard to see how five well-found, well-manned ships could go so badly astray. However, Carlisle had been this way several times, and he could imagine the fatal confusion on a dark night with a strong breeze and current running under the keel. *Chesterfield* should have done better, but the transports following the frigate's stern light didn't stand a chance. Well, the next blow would see the end of them.

'There they are, sir, on that little island over there.'

Gresham had been searching the islands with his telescope. He knew that shipwrecked mariners would always try to find dry land rather than stay in their stricken ships, and sure enough a village of sailcloth tents had sprouted up on a small cay just a quarter mile from the scene of the grounding. Half a dozen boats had been pulled up beyond the reach of the tide and a union flag was flying from a salvaged spar.

'We'll feel our way into ten fathoms with the lead, Mister Torrance, and lay out the best and second bower anchors. Mister Young, make the signal for all ships to follow my motions.'

Torrance had risen to the occasion. He wasn't as experienced as Beazley and he didn't carry the same authority, but he was better than some fully-fledged sailing masters that Carlisle had known. He confidently conned *Dartmouth* towards the shore until he heard the leadsman's call.

'By the mark, ten.'

At a nod from Carlisle, Torrance raised his chin and shouted to the fo'c'sle.

'Slip the larboard bower.'

***

'I'd have been underway in one of the transport's boats before the end of the day, sir, my own were all lost when *Chesterfield* drove up onto the reef.'

Carlisle had taken a boat to the little island. It really was a pathetic affair and would certainly be inundated in a hurricane. John Scaife seemed almost resentful that he'd been rescued. He was even older than Hale, somewhere in his mid-fifties, Carlisle thought, and he had the slower mental processes to match. It was terrifying to imagine this man in command when his ship touched ground on a dark, windy night in the Old Bahama Straits, but perhaps he was being unfair.

'I'd have left my first lieutenant in command at the island with orders to burn lights at night while I sailed for Havana to fetch help.'

And that was it. Scaife knew that the inevitable court martial could easily find him guilty of hazarding his ship and the transports, and he'd determined on a course of action that would at least show that he was doing something to remedy the situation. He could even have achieved some renown for a long passage in an open boat in these notorious waters. Now, because of this damned colonial, he'd be known as the man who was rescued from an island off Cuba. Yet he must be careful, for Carlisle was quite likely to sit on the board that tried him.

'Well, I'm here now and we must be away. Be so kind as to embark *Chesterfield's* people in *Dartmouth* and *Richmond*, the soldiers and the transport crews can all go in the three transports that I brought. I can offer you my day cabin in *Dartmouth*.'

Carlisle wanted to keep Scaife under his eye until he could be delivered to Pocock. The more he saw, the more certain he was that a court martial wouldn't be sympathetic to Scaife, and it was important that he should be able to say that the man had been under his supervision since he was rescued.

'I want to be underway in the afternoon, without fail, and I fancy the wind will pick up in the dog watches. Have you seen anything of the two transports that ran aground off Green Island?'

'Nothing, sir.'

Scaife looked like a defeated man and he excused himself to make his arrangements.

Carlisle looked around the island; it didn't take long. There was a grove of stunted palm trees in the middle but otherwise it was bare, with no water and a beating sun overhead. He paused for a moment beside two rustic crosses that showed where men had been buried. Whether they'd drowned or died of disease or natural causes, Carlisle would never know. It was right and proper to bury the men on dry land whenever possible, but the next blow would sweep away the crosses and the thin covering of sand, and the land crabs would deal with what was left. We are but dust, and to dust we return.

'Beg your pardon, sir…'

Souter had come from his boat at a slow run.

'*Dartmouth's* signalling, sir. I think it's the same as *Richmond* made yesterday. Here's your telescope, sir.'

Souter couldn't be expected to know the contents of the signal book, but Carlisle had become used to having a full report from Young. Yes, it was the signal for a sail in sight to windward. He trained the telescope to the right and saw it immediately, a transport, as alike to the four that were aground and the three at anchor, as were peas in a pod. That must be *Falls*, in which case all his ducklings had been gathered in, or at least all those that could still swim.

***

It was a fair wind for Havana and by the time he arrived Hale had delivered his fifteen-hundred soldiers and *Intrepid* was anchored close to the shore off Cojimar. Pocock had wasted no time in showing his displeasure, and Hale's great guns were being systematically loaded into boats for the army's siege batteries. Carlisle had a moment of misgiving, but quickly dismissed it. Pocock must have read the sealed report that he'd sent in with Hale, and he'd already judged and condemned the hapless captain on Carlisle's evidence. Hale's case might never come to a court martial – after all, he hadn't lost his ship – but the whole of the navy would know his commander-in-chief's opinion of his conduct in the Old Bahama Straits.

Two-and-a-half-thousand soldiers, that's what the first convoy had brought in. There were provincial companies from Rhode Island, Connecticut, New York and New Jersey, as well as a complete battalion of the Forty-Sixth of Foot. Albemarle and his staff were delighted, but Carlisle couldn't help wondering how long it would be before these men who had never served in the tropics succumbed to its diseases. Well, there was still another convoy to come, but that was to be left to Elphinstone, who was condemned to his lonely vigil in the Straits waiting for them to be sighted.

There was one man at least with a reason to be cheerful. Beazley strode back on board *Dartmouth* patting his pockets and winking broadly at Gresham. He had a ticket for his time as pilot in *Intrepid*, and he didn't care who knew it.

***

CHAPTER TWENTY-THREE

The Batteries

Thursday, 29 July 1762.
Durnford and Valiant Batteries, the Morro Castle, Havana.

Boom!

The ground shook as the thirty-two pound naval gun fired and its recoil sent it backward up the inclined ramp of timbers. It was immediately seized upon by its crew who wedged the front trucks to stop it rolling forward again; there were no campaign carriages for thirty-two pounders. They wielded the screw, the sponge and the rammers just as they'd have done in the more confined spaces of a gun deck. The man with the rammer jumped back smartly as soon as the wad was firmly in place to prevent the ball rolling back down the barrel. It wasn't strictly necessary when the guns were on dry ground instead of their usual place on a ship's deck that pitched and swayed at the sea's whim. However, it was a drill that they understood and the master gunner thought it might help to keep the ball firmly in contact with the powder cartridge. The front wedges were knocked out with the maul and an encouraging heft of a hand spike had the gun rolling back into position between the merlons. The gun captain squinted along the barrel and waved to the men with the hand spikes to train the gun exactly on the part of the castle's walls that this battery was responsible for destroying.

A few moments work with a quill and a powder horn, and the gun was loaded, primed and run out.

'Ready!' he shouted.

The quarter gunner had been waiting for this moment. He leaned out and quickly rested the long arm of his quadrant in the gun's barrel; it was too dangerous to be exposed for more than a second or two with the Morro Castle's marksmen ready for such an opportunity. He waited for the pendulum to come to rest, then thrust a pole with a polished piece of silvered brass fastened to its end between the barrel and the side of the merlon until he could see the reflection of the quadrant's scale. The gun barrel was hot and the quadrant scale was difficult to see through the shimmering air and the distorted reflection. He wiped a bead of sweat from his eye.

'A gnat's whisker on the quoin, Jimmy.'

The gun captain tapped the quoin with his maul and the barrel fell a degree.

The quarter gunner watched carefully as the pendulum came to rest again. All that a Spanish marksman would see was this strange pole and perhaps a reflection from the sun; the quarter gunner was safe behind the merlon.

'That'll do.'

He hastily retrieved his quadrant and moved on to the next gun. In all his years at sea he'd never used a gunner's quadrant. *Dartmouth* had four of them and the master gunner religiously mustered them every month, checked them off in his account book, polished them and returned them to their resting place deep in his storeroom. They had no place on board a ship that was never steady enough for that kind of shooting, but now their true value showed through. The mirror-on-a-stick was a gift from the armourer who had previously served in an artillery regiment and knew the dangers of exposing oneself in a battery this close to an active enemy.

The gun captain took a last look to confirm that his crew were all standing back and that there was nothing to prevent the gun's recoil, then he reached behind and pulled the linstock out of its socket and pressed the glowing end of the slow match to the priming powder.

Boom!

The smoke was whipped away by the breeze and through his telescope Carlisle saw the impact of the shot on the coral limestone. It raised a small plume of dust and a little cascade of debris ran down the walls some three hundred yards distant, and then nothing. In a few seconds there was nought to show that a thirty-two pound shot had been delivered against its target. The gun, its carriage, the tools to load and point it, the powder, the ball and the very men of the gun's crew who had sweated under the tropical sun had been brought from England at vast expense to make that shot. Yet, to the casual observer, for all the damage that it did, King George might have been better advised to save his treasure for a more fruitful purpose.

The gun crews threw themselves at the frightfully hot monster and started the whole process again. Their rate of fire was perhaps half as fast as they were used to on board *Dartmouth*, but still it was faster than the other batteries where the professional gunners of the Royal Artillery were much more particular about their point of aim. Speed against accuracy, which was the more important? In this case, with the castle's walls apparently impervious to the largest of solid shot, Carlisle suspected that speed held primacy. This was a psychological battle, and the purpose of this battering was to persuade the castle's garrison that there was no hope. Well, he'd met Captain Velasco, and he had his own views of the likelihood of that man being frightened into surrender.

Carlisle considered all this ruefully as the three guns of the Durnford Battery pounded away at the castle's walls under Hooper's direction. There had been four guns, but one of them lay on its side where a Spanish ball had struck its carriage, and there it would stay until a spare carriage could be brought from *Intrepid*. Just a few yards to his left the Valiant battery was similarly pounding away under the direction of a lieutenant from *Stirling Castle*, an earnest young man named Farndale who was desperate to show his courage and zeal after his captain's behaviour at the naval bombardment of the castle.

It was inevitable, of course. As soon as he'd delivered the first American convoy to Lord Albemarle he'd received a short letter from Sir George informing him that he was to send a hundred of his seamen ashore to man the Durnford Battery, and that he was to take personal command of it and the neighbouring Valiant battery. All ammunition, victuals, water and stores were to be provided by *Dartmouth* and should replacements be needed for the crews of either battery they were to be found from his own ship. Only his guns were saved from the insatiable demands of the siege. There was not a word of congratulations for saving the convoy, not even an acknowledgement that those two-and-a-half-thousand soldiers quite probably made the difference between continuing the siege and admitting that this vast expedition had achieved nothing. *Dartmouth* had been lucky to be spared the army's insatiable demand for men and guns until now, but with the arrival of the first American convoy, his fourth rate was surplus to the navy's requirements. It couldn't even be kept in reserve as part of the battle squadron, because of its light build and meagre firepower.

Now his biggest problem was to keep his hundred seamen healthy. The common opinion was that the fevers that brought down so many men came from the damp night air, the heat and unhealthy miasmas from swampy ground. He could do something about that and already the first canvas for tents had started to arrive from the ships. Old t'gallants, made of the lightest canvas that had been further thinned by constant use, were ideal for the job and the sailmaker had half a dozen of them waiting to be condemned when they next visited a King's yard. Carlisle would have to countersign the bosun's accounts, of course, to prove that they hadn't been sold or otherwise appropriated, but at least he knew that they'd be expended in a good cause.

Crash!

A Spanish shot hit the protective fascines that made up one of the merlons. The ball didn't penetrate to the battery, but instantly a wisp of smoke formed and grew where the hot ball came into contact with the tinder-dry canes and reeds. A party of seamen who had been resting in the shade of a t'gallant awning rushed forward with buckets of water to prevent a fire breaking out. That water had been brought from the sea by hand, bucket-by-bucket, and Carlisle was desperate that it wasn't squandered. Providing salt water for fires was difficult enough but fresh water for drinking was unobtainable on this arid plateau, and every drop had to be brought in barrels from *Dartmouth*. Water – or lack of it – had been the undoing of the Grand Battery whose remains were just to the left of Valiant. It was supposed to pound the castle with its eight guns and mortars and make a practicable breach, it was the chief hope for reducing the Morro Castle and it had been built at enormous labour and cost the lives of dozens of soldiers who had fallen ill with exposure to the feverish air. However, they'd been too eager and hadn't brought up enough water, expecting that they'd find some to hand. When the fascines that made up the Grand Battery's merlons caught fire there wasn't enough within reach and the whole thing, breastworks, ramps, and gun carriages, was burned through. Finally and most spectacularly, the ready-use magazine caught a spark and exploded, completing the destruction. Now it was a mere musket line with just enough protection to allow the infantry to fire at anyone seen moving on the enemy's walls.

It had come to this: the reduction of the Morro Castle was in the hands of a half-dozen small batteries, two of them manned by sailors, and the mining operation against the counterscarp and the seaward bastion.

***

Carlisle walked the thirty yards to the Valiant battery; it was just a little dangerous because he was only three hundred yards from the castle. Occasionally, when there was a worthwhile target, a Spanish marksman – it appeared to be just one man – braved the volleys of musketry from what was left of the Grand Battery and sent a few aimed shots into the British lines. Carlisle had already lost a valuable topman that way, but it was unseemly for a post-captain to run on the field of battle and it would inevitably worry the men. More dangerous than the marksman was the less frequent volley of musketry that was aimed at a single target. Where one man could hardly be expected to hit a target at two hundred yards, twenty musketeers had a much better chance. Luckily the volleys were rare, probably because Velasco's men had more important things to do, preparing for an attack that must surely come soon.

So Carlisle walked a little faster than normal, you could even call it a brisk walk, calculating that he'd only be exposed for twenty seconds; in that time no volley could be organised and the unknown Spanish marksman could hardly be expected to make a carefully aimed shot. He tried to look unconcerned but wasn't sure that he was fooling anyone. Ten yards, so far so good. Twenty yards and he felt his hat plucked from his head to spin away into the coarse scrub beside the path. It was a musket ball, and he neither saw the puff of smoke from the Morro Castle nor heard the shot above the thunder of the great guns. It had a sense of unreality, like a dream. He steeled himself to walk the last ten yards but was conscious that his faster gait – almost a trot – wasn't quite the thing. The safety of the Valiant battery came as a relief and he looked with positive affection at the rude breastwork and the sweating sailors stripped to their waists.

'Beg your pardon, sir.'

A nimble midshipman, barely more than a boy, squeezed past Carlisle and ran out to retrieve his hat and officiously dusted it off before presenting it. The bullet had clipped the turned-up brim and passed through the crown, leaving a neat hole about the same diameter as an index finger. It must have missed his scalp by less than an inch. He studied the midshipman. It was a brave but foolish thing to do, no hat was worth a man's life, and yet Carlisle couldn't bring himself to berate the youngster who was grinning inanely at him. He'd suffered the shame of *Stirling Castle's* tardiness and probably he'd cheerfully have run out in front of an entire company of enemy musketeers to restore his ship's honour.

Old Bahama Straits

For it was certainly true that at some future promotion board the fact that he'd served in *Stirling Castle* at Havana would be used to compare him against other candidates.

'Thank you, Mister…'

'Carmichael, your honour, Joseph Carmichael and I'm very pleased to meet you, sir.'

Just briefly Carlisle wondered whether he was seeing a future Anson or a Hawke, or a Howe, a Benbow or a Vernon. Acts of heroism were everyday occurrences, but there was something about this man's attitude to danger that set him apart.

There were smiles all around and a cheer. The gun crews had seen what happened and so had the lieutenant; they were *Stirling Castle's* to a man, and they knew the situation and thoroughly approved of Mister Carmichael's action. The notion that a post-captain's hat wasn't worth a midshipman's life was not one that any of them would have subscribed to.

***

All four of the Valiant battery's guns were firing and with Durnford's three they made a near-continuous sound as the well-practiced naval gunners loaded and fired at a furious rate. They resented deeply the time that it took to confirm the gun's training and elevation and the quarter gunners with their quadrants were subjected to a steady stream of abuse. In their normal duties at their shipboard guns, aiming was almost an afterthought because every captain's objective was to bring his broadside so close to the enemy that his guns simply couldn't miss. Even if they fired from a greater distance, the movement of the ship made accuracy almost impossible, and it was the rate of fire that won the day. That prodigious expenditure of shot and powder needed a logistic effort to match, and two-thirds of Carlisle's men were employed in the long chain of supply that led from *Dartmouth* to the shore and eventually to the batteries. Campbell should have been commanding the batteries, but he was under a cloud – not exactly under arrest, but the next best thing – and awaiting court martial. Nothing was expected of him now and he was presumably spending his time preparing his defence and brooding on his uncertain future. Carlisle didn't know the specific charges that he faced, but if cowardice was one of them and if he was found guilty, then it was entirely possible that he'd suffer the penalty of death for his shameful inaction. After all, Admiral Byng had been shot after being specifically cleared of the charge of cowardice; his crime was merely failing to do his utmost. Yes, John Campbell must have a lot on his mind at the moment and Pocock no doubt was right to keep him confined to his ship. Yet Carlisle would have been quite happy to have been spared this onerous duty.

'Are you making any impression, Mister Farndale?'

The lieutenant started as though he was surprised to be addressed. Carlisle had heard that *Stirling Castle's* officers and men were being ostracised by the rest of the squadron, and it was certainly true that there was little mixing between the Durnford and Valiant batteries. He'd only had a brief word with Farndale that morning and evidently he'd assumed that was the extent of Carlisle's condescension. Well, Carlisle knew a thing or two about being the outsider.

'Very little, sir. I've been here twelve days now, since the battery was established, and we've been pounding away at the same spot day in, day out, with nothing more than a few scars on that curtain wall to show for our troubles. The artillery commander comes around each day and sometimes tells us to fire at the embrasures, but mostly it's the curtain. I don't know how thick those walls are, sir, but without the grand battery I can see that we have a labour of weeks ahead of us.'

'How are your men holding up?'

'Well, that's another thing, sir. We've buried six of them already and only one of those was due to the enemy. I've sent another… how many have we sent back, Mister Carmichael?'

'Nineteen, sir and there's another two that really should

go, to give them a chance.'

'It's mostly yellow jack, but also some putrid fevers. They've been sleeping under canvas after the first two days, but still they're falling sick. I know what to look out for now; when they complain of a headache, that's when it starts.'

Carlisle looked around at the gun crews. They all looked vigorous enough but he knew that the yellow fever struck quickly and a man who could run out a thirty-two pounder in the forenoon could be on his back in the afternoon and buried the next day.

'Keep at it, Mister Farndale and let me know if you need anything to keep the guns in action.'

It was all he could say, really, but he had a deep sense of the futility of this siege. It needed something to break through this long, slow, battle of attrition.

***

Carlisle's inspection of the batteries was interrupted by Horace Young, coming breathlessly from the beach and bearing a letter.

'From Admiral Pocock, sir, and he bade me tell you that the contents are urgent and are not to fall into the enemy's hands under any circumstances.'

Carlisle walked to the rear of the battery, to a protected spot behind the magazine where he could open the letter without being watched by curious eyes. The thirty-two pounders continued to roar and the occasional returning fire thudded into the fascines, but this had already become an accompaniment to his life, a mere inconvenience that continued in the background whatever he did.

The letter was indeed from Sir George.

…Lord Albemarle intends that the mines at the seaward bastion will be blown tomorrow afternoon and he will send his instructions for the batteries under your command by separate letter.

There was more about the need to support the army to

the best of his ability, but it was the last paragraph that was most intriguing.

It is by no means certain that the mines will make a practicable breach, largely because of the extraordinary depth of the ditch and the strength of the scarp and counterscarp, all of which became apparent when the mining commenced…

Carlisle remembered now, that was one of the few things that Laredo wasn't prepared to discuss, probably because he feared being held accountable by his own people. Then again, every man has a line that he won't cross, and not only for self-serving reasons.

…in that case another attempt will be made to offer terms to Captain Velasco. It will be useful to have Commander Laredo with you if you should need to meet the captain, and therefore you are directed to bring Commander Laredo ashore before noon tomorrow and hold yourself and him ready at the battery beside the glacis at the seaward bastion. You are to wait upon your orders from either Lord Albemarle or Major General Keppel, who will be commanding at the breach.

So that was it, that was how the stalemate would be broken, and he was to be close up with the forlorn hope, the band of soldiers who would rush through whatever breach was made by the mines. Out of the frying pan and into the fire; he could guess that by comparison with the seaward bastion, the batteries would seem like a peaceful refuge.

***

CHAPTER TWENTY-FOUR

Shot in the Dark

Friday, 30 July 1762.
Seaward Bastion, the Morro Castle, Havana.

'Elias Durnford, sir, Corps of Engineers.'

Carlisle could just make out the young man's shape in the darkness, as the waxing, gibbous moon slipped quietly below the low land over beyond Chorera. He appeared young, of medium height and slim. His whispered introduction betrayed either an earnest or nervous manner, it was hard to tell which. Durnford had assisted in laying out and building the batteries, and although a mere ensign, he'd apparently made such a good job of it that one of them had been named for him.

'I recommend we wait another half an hour, sir, until it's truly dark.'

Carlisle nodded; it was best to keep speech to a minimum so close to the castle's walls. They were crouched behind the fascines of the tiny battery that had been set up where the castle's glacis ended and a low wall rose to protect the last few yards to the sea cliffs. This was the furthest forward of all the army's positions except for the miners who were tunnelling under the covered way and counterscarp. The shadowy shapes of naval guns gave some comfort but the squat, ugly coehorn mortars always looked sinister. Carlisle could remember embarking one in a longboat at Louisbourg, but that had been only for signalling purposes. These eighteen coehorns were intended to soften up the defenders before the forlorn hope was sent into the breach that might or might not be produced when the mines were exploded.

The minutes crept by. It was certainly darker, but with no clouds the stars gave a ghastly, unearthly illumination that seemed to mock the night. It almost appeared to be growing lighter, but that was an illusion caused by Carlisle's rapidly improving night vision; he knew it well from long hours on the deck of a ship during the night watches. He tried to orientate himself. The battery had been constructed in the dead ground below the glacis in front of the seaward bastion. This was determined to be the castle's weak point because all of the remainder of the landward face was protected by a truly terrifying ditch. It stretched along the entire eastern face of the castle from landward bastion to seaward bastion and here at the seaward end it was sixty-three feet deep and fifty-six feet wide. It was the secret that Laredo was not prepared to divulge, and no foreigners had ever been allowed to see it. Carlisle had been entirely unaware of its existence, and he was the last King's officer to visit Havana before Spain joined in the war against Britain. It was too wide to bridge and too deep to fill and it was the cause of most of the despair in Albemarle's headquarters. Yet even this formidable obstacle had its weakness. Here at the seaward end there was a narrow projection of rock that had been left to protect the ditch from inundation during hurricanes. It was extended by this little wall that swept around to join with the glacis. That gave a starting point for the miners to tunnel below the covered way, the counterscarp and the bastion with the hope of both filling the ditch and creating a breach when the mines were blown. Carlisle therefore had the wall of the glacis in front of him, the sea cliffs to his right and the cleared ground before the glacis to his left. It seemed a precarious place to find a post-captain and Carlisle silently cursed his own readiness to volunteer for this kind of escapade. It had come from a casual comment thrown out by a colonel on General Keppel's staff, an observation that it might be useful if Carlisle saw the proposed site of the breach before he and his Spanish officer followed close behind the forlorn hope.

Old Bahama Straits

The same colonel had made some slighting comment about the late arrival of the provincials from New York, and that was all that Carlisle needed to commit himself to this mad adventure in the middle of the night.

Now that he could see better, he became aware of the half company of infantry that had been posted to cover the battery and the entrance to the mine. They were from the Forty-Sixth of Foot, the very men that he'd brought out of the Straits only a few days before. The Forty-Sixth was a regular line regiment but they suffered from having come to Havana in the same convoy as the provincial regiments, and whether they liked it or not they were classed by the rest of Albemarle's army as colonials.

Their captain recognised Carlisle; he removed his hat and bowed low, which was quite an achievement as nobody was standing straight in this dangerous place. The musketeers were lined up along the bottom of the glacis. By rights there should have been no cover there, but the peculiar arrangement of this seaward bastion gave them four feet of masonry to crouch behind. Their numbers had not yet been reduced by the deadly diseases that had swept through Albemarle's force, and they looked fresh and keen.

***

Carlisle could see the top of the glacis now and the ridge of rock that protected the ditch. He tapped Durnford on the shoulder and pointed forward. It was strange that the Spaniards had neglected this part of their defences. It was at the angle of the two faces of the bastion and to cover it with musket fire would require a defender to lean far out between the merlons and expose himself to the massed musketry below. Normally the one-man lookout post at the angle of the bastion would offer a fine view of the end of the glacis, but that had fallen a victim to the siege batteries many days ago, and its ruins were now lapped by the waves. It wasn't an entirely safe position, but it was less dangerous than anywhere else this close to the castle.

The rough coral limestone tore at Carlisle's waistcoat as

he crawled stealthily up the thirty feet of the glacis behind Durnford. They were in the defenders' dead ground, but he was astonished that the Spanish weren't doing more to suppress the mining. They'd sent out two sorties that he knew of, but both had been thrown back with great loss of life. Yet it was evident that if they did nothing the mines would eventually be blown. Perhaps they thought that such a great ditch with such a high scarp and counterscarp would be unaffected by the mines. Still, it seemed strange.

Durnford came to a stop and Carlisle crawled up beside him. They were on the very lip of the glacis and below them the monstrous ditch looked black and forbidding in the starlight, with the high scarp and the bastion rising tall and proud at the other side. A volley of musketry rang out from the Forty-Sixth behind them, suppressive fire to keep the Spanish from showing themselves. Carlisle pressed himself lower into the glacis, wishing they'd save their volleys until he was safely back in the battery. He had an insane urge to giggle as he realised the absurdity of the notion that a battery right under the Morro Castle's walls could be regarded as safe.

The musketry stopped as abruptly as it had started and there were no answering shots from the Spanish. Carlisle started to relax and study the fortifications; after all, that was why he was here.

Durnford soundlessly pointed to the scarp and swung his hand down to the covered way below them and beyond to the counterscarp, then made a motion for an explosion. Carlisle nodded encouragingly. Then the engineer pointed to the spur of rock at their right. It was narrow and jagged but passable by a man who wasn't too particular about his safety. Unlike their position on the glacis, the spur was covered by the northern face of the bastion and by the extension to the bastion a little way further along. It looked like an act of self-murder to step out onto that precarious path under the Spanish guns, but the miners had been using it for a week now to reach one of the entrances to the mine, and they had only lost three or four men. One of those was a seaman from *Dartmouth*, a Cornishman who'd volunteered when the call had been put out to the squadron for experienced miners. Some seventy men had answered the call, tempted by the promise of a cash bonus and perhaps by a sense of duty.

Carlisle felt a tap on his shoulder again and Durnford pointed at the face of the bastion before them and made a downward motion with his arms. Carlisle looked at him and shook his head, he didn't understand. Durnford leaned his head close and cupped his hand between his mouth and Carlisle's ear.

'The charge should produce a breach just there, sir. It's impossible to be certain but I hope that the covered way and the counterscarp will fall into the ditch and a portion of the scarp and bastion too. The assault force will be able to scramble down into the ditch and up again. You see how they can be covered by musketeers along this glacis?'

He swept his arm to the left where the lip of the glacis disappeared into the night.

Carlisle tried to imagine it. The awful explosion, the crash of falling masonry and the towering columns of smoke and dust. The coehorns and the covering muskets would start firing immediately, even before General Keppel had decided there was a practicable breach and made the final decision that would release the forlorn hope. That would be the moment for Velasco to commit his reserve, to do anything to throw back the attack. *Les Enfants Perdus*, The Lost Children, that was what the French called the attacking force that was first into the breach, and never was there a more appropriate phrase.

'Have you seen enough, sir.'

Carlisle had seen more than enough, yet he was pleased that it wasn't he that suggested the withdrawal.

'Yes, thank you, Mister Durnford.'

He turned awkwardly around and crawled back down towards the battery. Another volley of musketry crashed out and briefly lit up the glacis. A single shot rang out from the bastion but if it was aimed at the two officers, it missed its mark.

***

The battery felt like a safe haven after the appallingly exposed position on the glacis. Carlisle paused to catch his breath and took an offered mug of water. They'd whispered before but now that seemed unnecessary.

'You see the situation, sir. I expect General Keppel will want the mines blown tomorrow, today rather, when it's light, so although it looks impossible now, if we can take down both faces of the ditch, it should make a useful breach.'

'And if it doesn't, Mister Durnford, what then?'

The young man looked thoughtful.

'Well, sir, it'll be more of the same, battering and mining, unless Lord Albemarle decides to try a direct assault on the city walls to the west. In either case the army and the artillery are in a race against the yellow fever. That's why your Americans are so important, sir. Oh, I do beg your pardon, but everyone considers that they belong to you, sir.'

Carlisle just stared at Durnford. So it had come to that, even the subalterns associated him with the provincial troops. Well, he just hoped that nobody was disappointed. Still, it was interesting that Durnford made a distinction between the army and the artillery and the engineers, for strictly speaking both of the latter came under the authority of the Board of Ordnance and not the War Office. The difference had never seemed important to Carlisle but clearly to the Corps of Engineers at least, it was significant.

***

Carlisle had a word with the captain in command of the half company of the Forty-Sixth then turned to follow Durnford back towards the main batteries. They were just about to leave the battery when the blackness of the night sky was rent asunder by a succession of flashes, the crack of small cannon and the dreadful sound of iron balls smashing into fascines and gabions. There was immediate consternation. The attack hadn't come from the castle walls but from the friendly sea, and the infantry didn't immediately understand what was happening. Carlisle reacted swiftly.

'Captain, you're being attacked from the sea. Get your musketeers over there. Where are the gunners? Move that twelve pounder to cover the cliffs. Do you have grapeshot? Very well, shout when you're loaded.'

There was no need for silence now and the near-continuous flashes lit up the scene so that it was clear what was happening. Only a hundred yards offshore two small schooners had sailed slowly past the Morro Castle's seaward bastion and now they were coming abreast the British battery. Carlisle could see them clearly; they carried four guns apiece, possibly six pounders but certainly no larger. That was an awful lot of flashes from only eight guns. He looked hard at the second of the two and saw that it was towing a substantial raft that itself was firing what looked like half a dozen guns. A hail of grapeshot hit the battery every dozen seconds.

Carlisle waved urgently. The attack looked dangerous but he knew better. The schooners' guns were all on the upper deck and their crews were exposed to counter-fire, and the floating battery had simple fascines to protect the gun crews.

'Volley fire, Captain. Leave the leading one, he'll be out of range soon and he'll have to tack. Fire at the second schooner.'

It wasn't clear that the captain of the Forty-Sixth really understood, but he knew when he was being given direct orders and this was outside his experience. He wasn't to know that the schooner couldn't halt its own progress but must stand on until it was past and clear before tacking and re-passing the battery. He hadn't considered that there were only nine balls in each round of grapeshot and however much more destructive they were than the smaller musket balls, they just couldn't hit enough targets. Nevertheless, three of his men had already fallen and few survived a grapeshot wound. There was a low wall to the seaward side of the battery and his fifty men were soon lined up along it. Now he could see what the naval captain meant. The first schooner was already past the point where it could do the most damage and was still sailing on.

'Volley fire!' he shouted.

The sergeants used their half-pikes to move the men into position and at a command the first volley rang out. The schooner was only a hundred yards away and of fifty musket balls at that range certainly half should find their target, lit up as it was by its own musket flashes. And muskets could be reloaded in thirty seconds by the soldiers of a regular infantry company.

'Keep at it, Captain. Don't worry about the raft.'

The company of the Forty-Sixth poured volley after volley into the schooner. In just a few minutes its decks were clear, every one of the crew were dead, wounded or driven below, and her guns fell silent. With nobody at the tiller her head swung to the south, into the ragged land breeze, and the raft swung alongside, grinding its guns against the schooner's hull. In less than a minute the two vessels were hopelessly entangled and the schooner was masking the floating battery's guns.

'Now Captain. Fire at the lead schooner. The tide will take care of those two.'

The Forty-Sixth turned its fury onto the first schooner that had now tacked and was about to come back into range. One, two, three volleys. Probably no more than half a dozen balls had reached the target but the Spanish captain had seen all too clearly what had happened to his consort, and he wanted none of it. It was too dark to see any details but Carlisle could imagine what was happening. The helm was being put up and the schooner's bows turned seaward to circle around out of range of the musket fire. The second schooner and the floating battery were now unmanageable and were drifting westward on the tide; they were already too far off to either engage the battery or be engaged by it.

'Twelve pounder ready, sir!'

That was quick work, considering that the gun crew had been happily asleep under their gun until the Spanish schooners had started firing.

Carlisle stared to seaward. The lead schooner was just visible as a dark shadow on the sea with its sails reflecting the starlight.

'You see your target? Very well, fire as fast as you can reload.'

Boom!

After the schooners' tiny cannons and the musket fire, a twelve pounder sounded indecently loud, as impolite as a shout in church.

There was no chance of seeing the effect of the shot, but a twelve pounder charge of grapeshot was a very different matter to a four or six pounder. They both carried nine balls but the former had a vastly greater destructive power and any one of them could disable one of the schooner's small cannon or tear down a gunwale. One way or another the schooner kept going, heading west for the harbour entrance.

'Beg your pardon, sir, but I can see other sails out beyond the schooner.'

Durnford was pointing to the right of the lead schooner, the one that was scurrying away as fast as wind and tide could take it.

Carlisle looked carefully. A frigate or a sloop. He knew how unlikely it was that the Spanish would risk sending out such a vessel into the teeth of Pocock's squadron with its overwhelming numbers. Half a minute and he was convinced. One of the sloops, *Bonetta*, *Cygnet* or *Lurcher*, fourteen or sixteen guns. God help the Spanish schooners if they didn't get behind the chain boom before they were caught.

***

Carlisle waited at the battery for he knew that the sound

of gunfire would soon bring one of General Keppel's staff officers, or even Keppel himself. Evidently the captain of the Forty-Sixth was deferring to his orders because he had the definite look of a man waiting to be directed.

'What were your losses, Captain?'

'Three dead and one wounded. He might survive, no bones are broken, but those grape shot don't leave many wounded. But I beg your pardon, sir, you must know all about that.'

The man clearly wanted to talk. Carlisle noted that he'd set an extra guard on the glacis and lookouts over the sea. He'd even pointed out the sloop, so that there was less chance of it being fired upon if it strayed too close to the battery.

'I want to thank you, sir. That's our first engagement here after arriving late, and all things considered it was successful. I'm afraid that I'd have fired at that first schooner, being the one that was hurting us, and ignored the one following. Still, the rest of the army won't be putting the mock upon us anymore.'

'I'm pleased to hear it, Captain. I do hope they weren't calling you *colonials*.'

The captain looked wary. He knew all about Carlisle and even knew that he could be a bit prickly about his origins, but he took comfort from the intimacy of the soft, dark, anonymous night.

'I regret they were, sir. Still, I guess we'll have done some good for all the real colonials too. You know, the Forty-Sixth was at Fort Carillon, Fort Niagara and Montreal, sir, and that's more than most of those fellows can claim, and we fought side by side with Provincials and Militia, aye, and the savages too, and we're proud of it. Your people have nothing to be ashamed of, sir, and I hope they'll have the chance to prove themselves before this campaign is over.'

Carlisle looked at the captain more closely. He appeared a little old for his rank and surely such extensive service in the Americas would have propelled him to field rank. But of course he'd have to wait for a vacancy in his regiment and then muster the cash to purchase the next rank; it wasn't like promotion in the navy at all.

'You were at Fort Niagara? Did you by any chance meet Captain Holbrooke, George Holbrooke?'

The captain smiled broadly, his teeth showing white in the starlight.

'I did that, sir. Is he a friend of yours?'

'Oh yes, he was my first lieutenant in a frigate in just these waters five years ago. He told me about the Niagara campaign.'

'Well, sir. I wouldn't say this to just anyone, but if it wasn't for Captain Holbrooke I dare say we'd have had to abandon the siege. When Colonel Massey fell wounded at La Belle Famille, it was Captain Holbrooke who gave the example by standing to receive the French charge. Oh, if I live a hundred years I won't see another day like that.'

***

CHAPTER TWENTY-FIVE

Les Enfants Perdus

Friday, 30 July 1762.
Seaward Bastion, the Morro Castle, Havana.

Carlisle staggered back to the Durnford Battery, pushing his way past a throng of soldiers heading towards the little battery. This was the assault force, the forlorn hope, and the companies that would follow to exploit the breach once it had been secured. That captain of the Forty-Sixth was about to become overwhelmed by this vast mass of soldiery and it would be an uncomfortable few hours at the battery before the mines were blown.

A straw mattress had been laid out for him under a makeshift tent and Walker greeted him with wine and a meal of salt pork roasted over a brush fire, ship's biscuit and a jar of preserved strawberries. He found that he was ravenously hungry and when he'd made a good supper, he fell onto the mattress without removing his shirt or trousers. He heard Walker shushing the chattering watch and then, as the first light of the new day started to tinge the walls of the Morro Castle he fell into a deep sleep.

He had an hour of blissful unconsciousness before he was woken by the enormous roar of a thirty-two pound cannon commencing the morning bombardment. The day was already warm and his shirt was sticking to his chest. He was just starting to think about how he'd refresh himself to look respectable when Walker opened the flap that covered the entrance to the tent and, bending low, for it was a small tent, laid out a basin of water and a tray with coffee and the inevitable biscuit. Carlisle gave a momentary thought to the labour that had brought a basin of fresh water to this parched plateau and then dismissed any feelings of guilt as he washed away yesterday's sweat and dirt. His waistcoat and trousers had suffered badly from the coral limestone of the glacis but Walker had sponged and dried the waistcoat and had a clean pair of breeches and stockings ready for him. Washed and breakfasted he felt ready to face the day and after a brisk walk to inspect his two batteries he started down the hill to meet Laredo at the landing site as he'd directed.

The landing was busy as always. It was in a good position, behind a fold in the hills, and it was completely invisible from the castle. Two small jetties had been erected and half a dozen ship's boats and flatboats bustled around, delivering stores, ammunition and the all-important water. He saw his own longboat approaching and waited for it to arrive.

Laredo was seated in the stern looking as though he'd been hustled unceremoniously from his sleep. He could also see a surprising number of *Dartmouth's* marines: Pontneuf, immaculate as always in his red coat, Francis Kemp, the second lieutenant holding a ten-foot staff with a canvas cover over the upper three feet, and Sergeant Wilson looking grim and competent with a file of three marines, each man with his long musket held vertically between his knees. Pontneuf had evidently got wind of a promising affair, the chance to be in at the kill when the Morro Castle fell, and Laredo's summons had given him the perfect excuse. Carlisle's first thought was to send them all packing, but on reflection he realised that he should have a body of his own people with him for this most dangerous mission. There was no knowing what would happen when he tried to find Velasco in what was hoped to be the ruins of the castle. Pontneuf didn't explain himself, but it was clear that he thought his place was with his captain and now that he had time to consider, Carlisle secretly agreed.

***

Their way lay along the sand between the sea and the low cliff to the Beach Mortar Battery that sheltered behind an old stone redoubt at the point where the bluff rose into craggy cliffs. The battery was presumably built by the

Spaniards in an earlier age to cover this line of approach to the castle, but it had been abandoned long ago. From there it was a scramble up the low cliff to Fuzer's Battery, where four twenty-four pounders were firing furiously at the castle over three hundred yards of cleared rocky scrubland. From there the path to the battery under the seaward bastion passed below a sap built of sandbags at the top of the cliff, because on that arid plateau there wasn't enough soil to either dig trenches or throw up earthworks.

'There's not much traffic here, sir, considering that this is the point where the breach will be made.'

'They all came up last night, Mister Pontneuf. It'll be a tight squeeze at the battery and a miracle if the Spaniards don't guess what's happening. At least the assault party went up at night. If they'd waited for this morning they'd have raised so much dust that the dullest Spaniard would know what was afoot.'

Carlisle glanced at Laredo who appeared lost in his own thoughts, and evidently didn't hear the mention of his own nation.

'I think, sir, that your action last night might have helped. It was quite a show viewed from the sea and must have been spectacular from the castle. They might guess, but all the activity since then could just as easily be reinforcements in case the Spanish bring heavier ships up next time.'

What had seemed like a tiny space in the darkness of the night, now revealed itself as an extensive area of dead ground where the glacis met the sea cliffs. The miners were scattered in small groups on the rocks, evidently they'd been withdrawn already, and that told Carlisle that the moment to fire the mines was close at hand. The storming party was nearest to the glacis, three sections of men, a mix of grenadiers and musketeers of the line companies, with a lieutenant in charge of each. Behind them the remainder of the assault party waited under the command of a lieutenant colonel, and further back the entire First Brigade was seated in company order with the men talking in low voices.

Old Bahama Straits

Brigadier-General Haviland, the commander of the army's First Brigade that had been assigned the task of taking the Morro Castle, was deep in conversation with General Keppel, seemingly oblivious to all around them until a staff officer pointed to Carlisle.

'Good morning, Captain Carlisle, and this must be Captain Laredo, good morning to you too, sir.'

Laredo's grasp of English had improved during his six month's captivity but still he understood little except that he was being welcomed and he bowed in reply, returning the greeting in Spanish.

'Does he speak any English, Carlisle?'

'Not much, General. We make do with my Spanish.'

'Well, I hope he won't be needed. Would you ask your marine lieutenant to escort him out of earshot?'

Laredo bowed again as he was dismissed. He'd learned the lessons of a prisoner, to accept those things that no amount of protest was going to change, and being dismissed by a major general certainly fell into that category.

'Unless something changes I'm going to blow the mines at two o'clock, that's three hours from now. I trust – I hope – that the covered way and the counterscarp will fall into the ditch and the scarp and a portion of the bastion too. At that point I'll decide whether we have a practicable breach and if we do, Colonel Stuart here will send in his storming party with the rest of the assault party close behind. As soon as they've cleared the breach, the remainder of the brigade will follow, company-by-company. I hope that will be enough to take the castle. If it isn't, if the breach isn't practicable or if the assault party is thrown back or even if Colonel Stuart's brigade gets stuck inside the castle, that's where Lord Albemarle believes you and the Spanish commander might be able to help. How do you see that happening?'

Carlisle had thought long and hard since yesterday and he was more-or-less ready with the answer.

'Velasco is a proud man and I've no doubt that he won't

give up the castle easily. The mere fact of a practicable breach won't be enough…'

'You've met him, I believe.'

Keppel was impatient, he wanted to get back to the technicalities of blowing the mines and releasing his assault party. This was the culmination of his career so far and he was anxious that nothing should go wrong.

'Yes, General, twice.'

Carlisle was irritated at being interrupted and made his point by waiting for Keppel to resume the conversation. The two men stared at each other until Keppel realised that he'd been at error.

'Pray continue, Captain Carlisle.'

Carlisle nodded, it wasn't quite a bow but would serve under the circumstances.

'In our last meeting I seeded the idea that he could surrender the castle with the honours of war, and hinted that the arrangement could be extended to the city at the point where it becomes indefensible. He rejected the offer, but it's quite certain that he saw its merit. Velasco's proud to the point of absurdity, but he's no fool. My instructions from Lord Albemarle are to make that offer again today, if it seems appropriate. Captain Laredo is under parole for as long as he's ashore so that he can help with any negotiations.'

'That's my understanding too, but not if we can take the castle out-of-hand without too much English blood being shed.'

'Just so, sir. Then if my party might be permitted to follow behind Colonel Stuart's assault force I can hold myself in readiness.'

'You have a parley flag, Captain Carlisle?'

'I do indeed, sir. The white is well hidden until we need it.'

***

Old Bahama Straits

The three hours passed slowly. Carlisle spent some time with Colonel Stuart, discussing the conditions under which the offer of terms should be made, but then it was just a matter of waiting under the baking sun. The soldiers each had their canteen and barrels of fresh water had been brought up to replenish them. At half-past-twelve a cold dinner of beef and bread and cheese was issued and at half-past-one a ration of rum. The men drank it down in one go almost as though they didn't really want it. Their minds were elsewhere now, thinking about those first few minutes when they would have to burst into the great Morro Castle.

Carlisle and his marines drew closer together and moved forward until they were immediately behind the assault force.

Two minutes to go by Carlisle's watch and a figure covered in dirt came scurrying out of the mine entrance and ran back to report to the General. A second scrambled over the ridge of rock that separated the ditch from the sea. Carlisle covered his ears with his hands and crouched low.

Boom!

The first explosion was quieter than Carlisle had anticipated, muffled by its distance underground, no doubt. A blast of hot air came rushing out of the mine entrance followed by a dense, black cloud of smoke that shot across the assembly area and out over the water. The very ground moved beneath Carlisle's feet and after the sound of the explosion he heard the distinct rumble of falling masonry and dirt, but much less than he'd expected.

Boom! Boom!

The second mine, the one under the bastion exploded in two separate blasts and the cloud of smoke shot vertically from the mine shaft across the ditch. This time the sound of cascading masonry was much louder and the shaking of the earth more prolonged.

Carlisle looked up to see Keppel and the brigade commander scrambling up the glacis to survey the damage. Five minutes ago that would have been unthinkable and would surely have resulted in an early grave for both of them, but a quick glance showed that the merlons around the fighting platform at the top of the bastion were cocked at a drunken angle, and that for a few minutes at least no response could be expected from the defenders.

Carlisle ran up the glacis to see for himself. If Keppel decided that the breach was impracticable then he knew that Admiral Pocock would want to know the reason from the only senior sea officer on the spot. For Carlisle was convinced that this was the last roll of the dice for this great expedition. If a breach had not been made then the Morro Castle would stand another day, and he very much doubted whether Albemarle's army had enough strength to continue the bombardment until it reached a conclusion or to delve further to lay another mine.

'D'you see, Captain…'

Perhaps because Keppel also knew that Sir George would have to be persuaded that the army had done its utmost, he was addressing his thoughts to Carlisle.

'… the covered way and the counterscarp have barely been touched, but there's enough of a fall there for the forlorn hope to scramble down.'

Carlisle dropped down onto the covered way and looked over the edge. A few desperate men might scramble down there but they'd be easy targets from the bastion, and the Spanish defenders would regain their wits soon.

'However, look at the bastion now, see how it's opened up. If we can get across that ridge of rock then the men can surely climb up there and through that breach. What do you think Haviland?'

The brigadier was studying the bastion below his shielding hand and nodding slowly to himself.

'A breach, sir. A practicable breach. My men can take that.'

'Very well…'

A shot rang out and a musket ball left a bright splash of lead on the rock between the two soldiers. They grinned foolishly at each other and hoisted themselves over the lip of the Glacis and trotted down to safety. Carlisle followed, barking his shins on the stone as he jumped down.

***

Carlisle had barely found his feet when a trumpet blared and half a dozen drums started to roll. A young lieutenant jumped onto the glacis that he'd just vacated and with a wave of his sword ran to the top and dropped down onto the covered way. His section of twelve men followed him, as he picked his way across the jagged ridge of rock with a steep drop of some sixty feet to the ditch on his left and a similar distance to the rocky shore on his right.

Much as General Keppel considered this assault the high point of his career, so the lieutenant saw this mad charge of his forlorn hope as the making of his. He'd pushed and argued and cajoled to be given this desperately dangerous task, and if the castle was taken he could expect an immediate promotion without the inconvenience of waiting for a vacancy or raising the purchase price. And so he charged forward ignoring the hail of musketry that was falling around him and his men. Carlisle saw two of them hit by musket balls and fall towards the sea, but the others continued. Behind them came another lieutenant also leading his twelve, and behind them another. A steady stream of men were jostling for position now on that wicked ridge of rock, scoured by musketry and with certain death only a missed step away.

The leading lieutenant reached the bastion and started scrambling upwards over the fallen masonry with his men hard at his heels. They were in the defenders' dead ground now and for a few seconds safe from the Spanish musketry. Carlisle saw them pause to regroup at the top just below the fallen masonry that made up the gun embrasures. It was less than ten seconds and then the lieutenant waved his sword again and launched himself onto the fighting platform and out of Carlisle's sight.

The three assault sections had all made it across the ridge

and were climbing up the bastion. Colonel Stuart and the rest of the assault force were on the ridge now, and a seemingly unstoppable tide of men was racing into the Morro Castle. Carlisle could see the last men of the assault force waiting their turn, leaving a gap that would soon be filled by the regular companies. Brigadier Haviland waved urgently at Carlisle; it was clear that he wouldn't wait long.

'Captain Laredo, follow me, if you please,' Carlisle said in Spanish.

He nodded at Pontneuf and Kemp and the little band ran forward to take their place before the brigadier.

Probably the musketry had ceased as the Spanish defenders had other things on their minds with the forlorn hope pouring through the breach, but Carlisle wouldn't have noticed if they were under fire. Pontneuf took the lead with Sergeant Wilson, then Carlisle and Laredo and finally Kemp and the three marines. The ridge was the trickiest part and it was difficult not to think of the deadly drop on either side. Four men had fallen, to Carlisle's certain knowledge, and two of them looked as though they had merely slipped, a missed footing that had cost them their lives. They couldn't hurry because of the press of men ahead of them and they couldn't fall behind because the main body of the force was hard on their heels. Every man was fired up by rum, and the example of their friends, and the pressing wish for anything to break the boredom of the siege, even this perilous assault on the strongest fortress in the western Caribbean.

The scramble up the broken stones of the bastion was easy too and they reached the fighting platform as the last of the assault force disappeared over the top. Pontneuf led the way in a slanting run towards the landward wall of the bastion, for what he saw convinced him that his captain and the Spanish officer needed to be out of the line of fire.

***

CHAPTER TWENTY-SIX

A Quixotic Hero

Friday, 30 July 1762.
The Morro Castle, Havana.

Colonel Stuart reached the top of the bastion and looked swiftly around. The three sections of the forlorn hope had run into trouble, that much was easy to tell by the red-coated bodies lying on the shattered platform and the small groups seeking the cover of the abandoned cannon and fallen merlons. The reason was evident; a stout, sandbagged wall, about three feet high rose twenty paces in front of him, with muskets and wall guns appearing along the top. They were firing wildly, not in volleys, but the Spanish muskets were finding their mark and a few of the attackers had already fallen before they'd made a step forward from the breach. He could see grenadiers, musketeers and what looked like Spanish seamen, all jostling for position to fire at the English invaders.

'Sergeant Major! Form a line, two ranks deep. Keep the men in order there.'

This is what he'd trained for, more than half of his life. His men rushed to either side of him, the sergeants pushed and prodded with their half-pikes and in a short time they'd made their line. He could hear the forlorn hope firing from his flanks, but they'd done their job, this was his turn. He looked along the line. Every musket had a bayonet and each was loaded, hardly a single man had disobeyed his orders by firing randomly as they reached the breach. He drew a deep breath. A wall gun fired from his right, scattering a handful of musket balls among the attackers, but he ignored it. They'd never reload it in time for another shot. He saw a few grenades thrown over the sandbags but they fell short and did no damage. They were useless in the open in any case.

'Volley fire by ranks!'

'Present your muskets!' shouted the sergeant major, 'take aim…'

The sergeants used their half-pikes to adjust the aim of the men who through excitement had forgotten to point at the target. A tip up here and a nudge to the left or right there. The sergeant major waited with the patience born of his long years of service to the colours. When all was ready he bellowed.

'…front rank, give fire!'

Crash!

A hundred muskets fired as one. It was a good volley, the sort that would have destroyed the enemy if they didn't have a breastwork for protection. As it was, most of the Spaniards had ducked behind the protecting wall and the volley was largely spent on the sandbags and on the empty space above. It didn't matter, the issue would be settled at the point of the bayonet in any case, the muskets merely asserted the attackers' superiority.

Success still stood in the balance; it only needed those Spanish defenders to rally, to stand and receive the charge, and they could yet push the invaders back through the breach. One Spaniard at least understood that. He was wearing a red waistcoat trimmed with gold that marked him out as a different corps to his fellows. It briefly crossed Stuart's mind that this must be the famous Captain Velasco, for the Spanish navy uniforms were trimmed with red. He was waving his sword wildly and by his example of furious energy forcing his men to stay at the breastwork. Stuart looked over his shoulder. Carlisle had seen him also and had started forward. Well, he wasn't going to stop while the momentum was with him and while the sergeant major was waiting for his word of command. He nodded and raised his sword.

'Rear rank, Sergeant Major.'

'Rear rank, give fire!'

Velasco, if that was who it was, had the right idea by

keeping his men at the breastwork, but he should have seen the second volley in preparation and had them all duck down again. At least two dozen men close to Velasco, at the right of their line, were standing when the sergeant major gave the order, and when the smoke cleared there wasn't a single one to be seen. Velasco and his red waistcoat had disappeared entirely. Now; this was the moment when destiny stood in the balance.

Stuart pushed through the ranks and drew his sword.

'Assault force will advance!'

The wall of bayonets swept forward, pouring over the sandbagged breastwork and right across the bastion's fighting platform, driving the furious defenders before them.

***

The group clustered around Carlisle had seen what had happened; they'd witnessed Velasco fall but still didn't know how badly he was injured. By one of those strange occurrences that happens in battle, the British bayonet charge had veered to the right, passing clear of the place where Velasco lay. They were pursuing the fleeing Spaniards who were crowding at the slope that led down from the fighting platform. Laredo looked at Carlisle and shrugged wordlessly. There would be no negotiated capitulation of the Morro Castle now, all that could be hoped for was that the castle could be quickly surrendered to avoid further bloodshed.

'Let's see what we can do Mister Pontneuf. Mister Kemp, bring that damned white flag with you but make sure it's out of sight, we might yet need it.'

At a word from Pontneuf, Sergeant Wilson and the file of marines ran forward to secure the area where Velasco had fallen. Wilson knew why he was there, it was to protect Captain Carlisle's life, not to take part in the capture of the castle, and with that in mind, he deployed his three marines in a line towards the ramp, bayonets fixed and muskets loaded, ready in case of a counter attack. Pontneuf led the way around the end of the sandbagged breastwork. It was a gory scene. A dozen or so dead and badly wounded Spanish soldiers and sailors were lying in dejected attitudes, some in the white of the line infantry, some in the blue of the artillery and grenadiers and some in the common dress of seamen the world over. Velasco lay beside another officer, a captain of the infantry by the look of him, and over him knelt another officer who looked up in anger at the red coated British marines and Carlisle's blue uniform. He scrambled for his sword but Pontneuf placed a booted foot firmly over its blade, and the officer stood, evidently ready to defend Velasco with his bare hands. It had become curiously still on the fighting platform. The assault force had gone, charging down the wide slope that was made for the movement of artillery but now was so useful to the attackers. Haviland's First Brigade hadn't yet made its way across the ridge of rock. Theirs was a much more deliberate approach after the hectic rush of the assault force.

Laredo stepped forward. Carlisle could see that he was deeply moved by the scene but he really didn't know what he'd say to this last of the Spanish officers on the bastion. Laredo could exhort him to fight on, but he didn't think it likely, and in any case, the man was effectively a prisoner already.

'Captain Montez, it is I, Ramon de Laredo.'

Carlisle could understand the Spanish, but Pontneuf and Kemp showed their ignorance in their blank faces.

Montez wiped his hand across his eyes. He'd seen Laredo when he and this same English captain – he recognised him now – had visited Velasco a week ago. It was oddly reassuring that Laredo was here, for he felt the weight of responsibility most keenly. He saw Velasco open his eyes and move his hand. Then the commandant was still alive, but that hole in his coat where a musket ball had passed through and into his chest suggested that he was not much longer for this world.

'The castle is lost, Captain Montez, you are the ranking

officer now that Captain Velasco can no longer command. You must surrender to preserve the lives of our brave soldiers. Captain Carlisle will leave a guard on Captain Velasco…'

He glanced at Carlisle who nodded in reply.

'…but we must hurry before much more blood is spilled.'

Montez knelt beside Velasco and whispered in his unresponsive ear.

'Forgive me Señor.'

***

'Then do you surrender this castle, Captain?'

Carlisle was speaking in careful Spanish so that he wasn't misunderstood. Montez stood up and Pontneuf handed him his sword, watching him carefully all the while.

'Captain Laredo,' Montez said thickly, controlling his emotions, 'perhaps you would do me the honour of introducing me to this gentlemen.'

Laredo bowed while Carlisle fought to restrain his impatience. This was an important moment, certainly, but every second of delay in surrendering the castle was costing lives, both British and Spanish. He kept it mercifully short.

'Captain Carlisle, this is Captain Montez of the Spanish army. Captain Montez, I have the honour of introducing Captain Edward Carlisle of the British navy.'

That was the shortest introduction in Spanish that Carlisle had ever known, but now they really must move on.

'It is a pleasure to meet you Captain Montez. Now, you must surrender this castle unconditionally to prevent the further effusion of blood. Your men will be treated fairly. Do you agree?'

Montez glanced at Laredo who nodded in return. There was really nothing else he could do. The time for resistance was when the assault force was at the breach. Now it was all too late, and the leading units of the First Brigade had started climbing through the rubble and forming in their half companies.

'I agree Señor.'

Montez bowed and handed his sword to Carlisle who passed it to Kemp.

'Now, Captain, we must hasten to make this surrender effective. The flag first, you must strike the flag. Lead the way, if you please. Mister Kemp, you stay with Captain Velasco and the file of marines and guard him in life and in death. Mister Pontneuf, Sergeant Wilson, come with me.'

They hurried down the ramp, past the scenes of carnage where Spanish and British bodies lay mixed in death. Montez knew the quickest way to the flagstaff where the white and red and gold of Bourbon Spain still flew above the castle. Sergeant Wilson hauled it down without ceremony while Montez stood bare-headed.

***

'You think he'll survive a boat journey, Carlisle? My apologies, that's not a fair question, I'll wait to hear what Mister Montgomery has to say.'

General Keppel had arrived hard on the heels of Haviland's brigade and was immediately confronted with the problem of a mortally wounded Spanish captain. It wouldn't usually have been a question for a general, but it had become clear that Velasco was a hero to the Havana garrison, and his name was known in the rank and file of the British army too. There was a humanitarian question of the care for a dying man, but Keppel was more concerned about how this could be turned to his own advantage and to that of the huge British expedition.

'A question for a physician for sure, sir, yet I've seen men transported from ship-to-ship by boat when they've been closer to death than Captain Velasco appears to be. There's a good, comfortable barge lying below the fort and I've sent for a boat crew from the batteries. I can have him in the hospital in Havana in an hour.'

'Do you think it'll do any good? I don't mean to Velasco himself, although I'm sure I wish him well, but will it bring the Spanish closer to a reasonable understanding that they must accept terms? God, I'm sick of this enterprise; if I see another soldier dying of a fever rather than his honourable wounds, I'll fall on my own sword.'

'It must be clear to the governor-general that Havana is doomed, sir. He's holding out for his own honour now, and to save his own neck from his King's anger, perhaps. Then, of course, the common Spaniards still think of us as pirates and heretics, capable of any kind of bestial behaviour, and they might choose to fight on. Yet they're tired of this siege and the prisoners tell me that supplies in the city are running short. A humane gesture such as sending Velasco back to Havana might turn public opinion in our favour.'

'You're right, Carlisle. I certainly don't want to keep him here if he's dying and it'll be a grand gesture to send him back. Ah, here's Montgomery now. Well, Doctor, what of the patient?'

Montgomery was the surgeon-general to the army and a man of consequence, not to be rushed, and yet even he could see the urgency to make a decision.

'There's a bullet lodged deep in his chest cavity, General. It passed through his left lung – it may still be in the lung – and I fancy it's damaged an artery close to the heart, or severed it completely. I regret that his survival is unlikely, whatever happens. He might last a week and be carried off by an infection, but it's odds-on that he won't see tomorrow's dawn.'

'What if he's sent to Havana by boat?'

'It can hardly make matters worse. If he's carried gently and not disturbed too much it might even hold off the infection. The sea air often has that effect. He should have a doctor for the journey though.'

'Good, then that's settled. Captain Carlisle, you'll oblige me by taking Captain Velasco to Havana under a flag of truce, I see you brought one with you. If you can speak to de Prado then try to bring him to his senses. Doctor Montgomery, you'll attend to Captain Velasco on his journey. Make sure that the Spaniards know your quality and the honour that we're doing to their hero. If they want you to stay, and if you think it'll help, then I'll leave it to your judgement whether you do so.'

Montgomery bowed, putting the best face on it that he could.

'May I raise the case of Captain Laredo, General?' Carlisle asked. 'He's done everything we asked and he's desperate to see to the safety of his wife during this siege. I'd like to offer him parole on the condition that he doesn't take up arms again in this war.'

Keppel considered for a moment.

'There's no time to consult Sir George, will you answer for his agreement?'

'I will, General. We've discussed the conditions for his parole already, and I believe I know the admiral's mind on this matter.'

'Very well, as you wish. I'll send a drummer and bugler down with you. Oh, and Carlisle, take those two marine officers of yours and that frightful sergeant, they'll look decent enough if they get a look at a clothes brush. I wouldn't want de Prado to think we're a band of ragamuffins.'

***

The barge rowed slowly and steadily across the channel. It was eerily silent now that the bombardment of the Morro Castle had ceased. The Spanish in Havana had not yet decided what they should fire upon and were presumably wondering what was to come next. The barge flew a union flag in the bows and a Spanish ensign and Kemp's white flag in the stern. The Spanish ensign had been Kemp's idea, to honour the stricken hero. It wasn't the great flag that had flown over the fortress – that was destined to be displayed in London and to end its days in Saint Paul's cathedral – but a smaller one that he'd found in the boat. The trumpet and drum sounded at regular intervals but muted, as befit their mission.

Old Bahama Straits

Word of Velasco's wounds had already reached Havana by the mouths of the handful of Spaniards who'd succeeded in escaping the Morro Castle by boat or the even fewer who'd swum the channel. They'd guessed the boat's errand and there was a sombre gathering waiting to take Velasco to the hospital. Carlisle watched him go, paying his own silent tribute. He was the only man in the British force to have known Velasco while he was still hale and hearty, and he privately mourned his imminent passing. For even if Montgomery chose to be equivocal, Carlisle had seen enough wounds to be certain of the outcome. The doctor was at least obeying Keppel's implied instructions and had offered his services, to find them gratefully accepted, and he left in the carriage that carried his patient.

Carlisle felt deflated, as though all his work had come to this, an inconclusive finale. He looked about but nobody seemed interested except for Laredo who hung upon him like a faithful spaniel, hoping that his treat would soon come. Well, he could do that at least, and give Laredo his parole. He'd carried the letter around for a week now and it only required Laredo's signature and a date to make it effective. Yes, that was the last act, and then he thought of his conversation with General Keppel. He was right, of course, this must end soon before the loss of life reached truly staggering proportions. Perhaps it would do no good, but at least he could try.

'Captain Laredo, can you arrange for me to meet the governor-general?'

Laredo looked doubtful, he wasn't used to dealing at that level of government.

Carlisle could see what was going through his mind and he took out the letter. Laredo knew just what it was and he'd been longing for this moment. He stifled a sharp intake of breath.

'That man over there will have a pen and ink,' Carlisle said, pointing at a black-suited person who was evidently a clerk of some kind, 'we can deal with your parole now and

I'll wish you well. I have one further request, that you make your best endeavours to arrange for me to speak to de Prado.'

***

The sun was setting over the western hills when Laredo returned with the news that de Prado would see the English captain. It was evident from Laredo's smile that he'd found the time to visit his wife, and clearly it had been a pleasant reunion. That was good, for Carlisle knew of many unexpected returns that had not gone so well. He'd grown to like Laredo.

De Prado met him in a small, austere office, part of a group of warehouses and suchlike buildings, and offered wine, it being too late in the day for coffee or chocolate. There were few preliminaries, this being at best an unofficial embassy, and in any case they'd met before in a more social gathering. Carlisle noticed – he could hardly not – that de Prado hadn't fared well in this siege. He'd lost weight and his skin had an unhealthy pallor, and he sweated more than was right.

'Well captain, I won't say it's a pleasure to see you again, but still, I must thank you for bringing poor Velasco back to us. I haven't seen him yet. I've heard the opinion of Lord Albemarle's physician and no doubt I'll soon hear others, but what's yours, as a man who no doubt has seen wounds before?'

Carlisle wondered what this was about. Was it just a preamble or was de Prado really concerned about this post-captain, one of many in the Barlovento Squadron?

'He has a ball through his lung, your Excellency, and there's some other bleeding that Doctor Montgomery daren't probe. I find it hard to believe that he will last another day, and I regret it, he's a brave man.'

'Yes, indeed, and you knew him, I understand.'

'Yes, your Excellency. I met him when I visited Havana in December and again when I tried to persuade him to come to terms last week.'

Carlisle could tell that de Prado knew this already, and he was just stalling before coming to the point of the meeting.

'Well, you've made a happy man of Captain Laredo, and I dare say he's done us both a service over the past few weeks; now what is it that you have come to say? I doubt whether I'll be as happy as Laredo, but perhaps we can try.'

Carlisle took a breath. He was speaking in Spanish and they had no interpreter at hand to ensure a full understanding. Yet it was wonderful how easy he found it after weeks of conversation with Laredo.

'You'll understand, your Excellency, that this is an informal embassy and that I serve Sir George Pocock and not Lord Albemarle. Even so, I believe I understand their minds, and they would want me to take this opportunity to express their hope that this siege can be brought to a swift conclusion without any more bloodshed.'

De Prado smiled slightly.

'Lord Albemarle and Sir George are at liberty to withdraw at any time, I won't hinder them. I'm sure they know that the hurricane season is upon us and I'm told that the yellow fever is already decimating your army, more than decimating it if my information is correct. Of course, the loss of El Morro is a serious matter but I believe I can reasonably hope that time is on my side. I am ready to receive a formal notice of cessation of hostilities at their earliest convenience, and a proposal for their orderly departure from Spain's domains. Perhaps you will be so kind as to take that message back to Lord Albemarle and your admiral.'

***

CHAPTER TWENTY-SEVEN

Obstinacy

Saturday, 31 July 1762.
Havana, Cuba.

Namur had anchored in full view of the small fort of La Punta on the opposite side of the channel from the Morro Castle, and de Prado could easily see Lord Albemarle's standard flying alongside Pocock's. Consequently, the letter had been sent to *Namur*, rather than to the army headquarters ashore. It had arrived soon after sunrise, advising the joint commanders that Captain Velasco, the heroic defender of the Morro Castle, had died during the night. His funeral Mass was to start at four o'clock and he was to be buried in the evening before six o' clock.

Carlisle had been hastily summoned and shown the letter. It was short but polite; de Prado had suggested that Albemarle might like to order his guns to fall silent for the period of the funeral Mass and the committal, and that was all.

'What do you think, Carlisle? You know de Prado and you knew Velasco, should we do as the governor-general requests or should we go further? Do you perhaps think this is a trick to gain some sort of advantage?'

Carlisle looked from Albemarle to Pocock. They both knew what should be done but they were in a hurry, losing a hundred men to sickness every day and there was still no sign of the second American convoy. Days mattered, but so did minutes when decisions were to be taken. Well, they wanted his opinion and he'd damned well give it, double-shotted.

'De Prado is fighting for his honour now, sir, regardless of his bullish statement yesterday. He won't ask for more than this two hours ceasefire for fear of being rebuffed. Yet Velasco's death is an important moment. He'd become the city's emblem, its source of good fortune, and they'll want to mark his passing with all the honours that they can. We can do more good today by generosity than ever we can by force of arms. I suggest an immediate ceasefire, my Lord, and a return letter stating that the army won't move and your guns will be silent until dawn tomorrow, in respect for Velasco…'

Albemarle looked as though he was about to interrupt. Pocock regarded both the general and Carlisle with a sombre gaze. Carlisle had one more thing to say and he knew that if he let the general speak, the moment would be lost.

'…and I suggest that you, my Lord, and Sir George, attend the funeral. De Prado will agree, I'm sure.'

'Well, the army will benefit from a day of rest,' Albemarle said, cautiously, 'although I'm reluctant to extend this siege any longer than absolutely necessary. Now, this very instant, would be an appropriate moment for the rest of your Americans to arrive, Carlisle. As things stand I find that I can only pause for the two hours of the funeral and then those guns must be hauled up to the Cabaña so that we can bombard the city and the fleet anchorage before a lack of men forces us to retire. That's the only way this expedition will reach its goal.'

The great cabin fell silent as the general and the admiral considered the options. There was a knock at the door and Harrison entered. He bowed to Albemarle but delivered his message to the admiral.

'*Bonetta's* come from the east, sir, and sent a boat with a message. There's a convoy reaching along the coast, it looks like the Americans, and the wind's fair for them to arrive this afternoon.'

Albemarle and Pocock just stared at each other and then both looked at Carlisle.

'I won't ask how you arranged this, Carlisle, but your timing is immaculate. However, I must stay here to bring in the convoy. What do you think, my Lord?'

'A most timely arrival. A ceasefire it is then, effective immediately until dawn tomorrow, and I'll attend the funeral. Can you spare Captain Carlisle to accompany me?'

***

Boom!

A single gun spoke from the beleaguered city and then the deep, profound, unaccustomed silence returned. Carlisle had grown used to the constant din of the British siege batteries and the answering Spanish guns, but this quietness, this intense stillness punctuated by the minute guns, made a statement in a way that the continuous thunder of cannon could never do.

Boom!

An answering gun from *Namur*, much closer at hand. The flagship's master gunner had a dozen of his thirty-two pounders loaded and run out so that he could answer Havana's guns that were to start their solemn salute promptly at three o'clock. This was no time to be saving powder by using mere sixes or twelves.

A letter had been sent in haste to de Prado, suggesting the ceasefire and requesting a truce for Lord Albemarle to come ashore. The response was fast, as though Albemarle's letter had been expected, and after some intense work on the admiral's barge it was fit to carry a peer of the realm to a funeral. The General, Captain Carlisle, and the general's aide, a major of infantry, were seated in the stern sheets as the barge's crew rowed long and dry for the harbour entrance. *Namur's* bosun had transformed the barge remarkably in the few hours that he'd been given. Albemarle's party sat below a black canopy and the oars, normally white, had been painted black for the occasion. Every man of the crew wore a straw hat with a black band and the general's personal standard flew from the stern.

Boom! Boom!

The guns came at regular intervals, marking the minutes to a hero's farewell.

***

Old Bahama Straits

Yesterday the massive chain that strung across the harbour entrance had been left in place, with only a tiny portion of it lowered for the boat carrying Carlisle and Velasco to creep in along the shore. Today, the whole apparatus had been lowered so that Albemarle's barge could row through the centre of the channel.

'Well, they clearly don't fear any treachery on our part, Carlisle.'

'No, my Lord.'

No treachery, certainly, but there was nothing in the conventions that prevented Carlisle taking note of the defensive arrangements. He knew all about the chain but it was the blockships that were of most interest. There were three of them, one of which had been Velasco's command, and they'd been carefully sunk to constrict the passage to a narrow, winding channel that would be difficult to negotiate under fire. Some of the masts had been left standing but most had been chopped down to disguise the positions of the ships.

A Spanish longboat was waiting for them and without word or signal it swung in front of the barge and started leading the way past the blockships.

The barge came alongside the same wharf where Carlisle had brought the mortally wounded Velasco only yesterday. They were met by a small party with de Prado at its head. The two men exchanged bows but otherwise didn't speak as they were handed into a carriage. After the general's aide had joined them, Carlisle was left for a moment at a loss as to how he was to make his way to the church. Then another carriage swung into the square and Laredo stepped out, looking resplendent in his carefully cleaned uniform. Apparently they were to travel together, but again, not a word was spoken. This was apparently the local custom at a solemn funeral. He glanced covertly at his pocket watch; fifteen minutes to four o'clock, perfect timing.

The bells of the grand church of Saint Ignatius started tolling as the carriages made their stately way through the city. Something was missing and it took a few moments for Carlisle to notice that the minute guns had stopped when the bells started.

Their way to the church was thronged with a great crowd of people, all standing in an eery silence. Hats were whipped off heads as the governor-general's carriage passed and there was not a sign of animosity towards the two representatives of the besieging force that they all must know were passing before them.

***

Carlisle had been to a Catholic Mass before with Chiara, so he had an idea of what to expect. However, on every other occasion he'd noticed the festive air, the feeling of joy at the holiday that would start after the religious obligations had been satisfied. He'd never been to a funeral Mass and certainly never to one of a man whose death was so mourned as Velasco's. The church was silent but for the occasional sob, and even the great organ was stilled for now.

Albemarle and de Prado were led to seats at the very front while Carlisle and Laredo were shown to a rank of seating immediately behind. Montgomery was already there with what looked like his Spanish counterpart. They looked old and tired, exhausted by their efforts to save Velasco.

It wouldn't do to stare about him, like a youngster on the Grand Tour, but he couldn't help noticing that Laredo was exchanging furtive glances with someone sitting in the seats at the side of the church, nearest their own. He risked a quick glance. A young woman, a startlingly beautiful young woman, even though the black lace mantilla covered her hair and her eyes, was looking steadily in their direction. She looked so much like a younger Chiara that Carlisle's heart skipped a beat and he had to clasp his hands to stop them shaking. If this was Laredo's wife, then he could readily understand the Spaniard's wish to be home, and if he recognised the woman's bold look, then he was right to be concerned at leaving her alone.

The funeral Mass was interesting in itself and Carlisle

knew enough to stand and to kneel at the appropriate points, and to look solemn as Velasco's body was brought in. He'd been to Masses with Chiara that lasted for two hours or more, but this one was brief, less than an hour, and the sermon was delivered in Spanish rather than Latin, so he could understand its sense. It was followed by the sombre but stirring notes of the *Dies Irae* on the organ.

He and Laredo remained at their seats as all the others joined the queue for the sacrament of the eucharist. He was aware of Laredo's wife's gaze fixed upon him and it made him strangely uncomfortable as he fought to keep his eyes on the altar.

***

Velasco was laid to rest in a grave close alongside the church and as the first shovel of earth was thrown onto the coffin, the city's minute guns boomed out again, answered by *Namur's* thirty-two pounders that could be heard easily across a couple of miles of water. What must it be like in a city under siege, hearing batteries of guns like that firing furiously day and night? He could just about imagine how it must play on one's nerves, and how a peaceful surrender of the city must soon become the dominant hope among the citizenry.

Carlisle could see that Albemarle wanted to discuss just that with de Prado, but the Spaniard seemed determined that no such negotiations should sully the solemnity of the day, and for want of an interpreter, for Carlisle was separated from the general, Pocock could only hold his peace. Had de Prado engineered this, so that there was no chance of Albemarle raising the subject of a capitulation?

They left the church and were taken in the same carriages back to the wharf. The barge was alongside ready to depart but Albemarle stood stubbornly beside the carriage until Carlisle stepped out beside him. In any case, he knew enough about naval protocol to have waited for Carlisle, the junior officer by many ranks, to have boarded the boat first.

'Carlisle, would you tell the governor-general that I'd

value a few moments of his time, with you to act as my interpreter?'

Carlisle nodded, stepped towards de Prado, and bowed carefully.

'Your Excellency, Lord Albemarle would be grateful for a few moments of your time, if you would be so gracious.'

De Prado glanced at Albemarle. It was clear that he wanted no such thing and would be delighted to have these enemies sent back to their ship. He'd deliberately not offered refreshment. In any other circumstances it would have looked like a gross insult to a guest, but he could justify it in the case of a funeral.

'I can act as your interpreter, your Excellency.'

An aide hastened up with an urgent look on his face. De Prado moved aside a few paces and the aide spoke in a low voice intending that the Englishmen shouldn't be able to listen. Carlisle didn't recognise him, he hadn't been with de Prado on the other occasions that Carlisle had met him, and that was perhaps why he assumed that Carlisle wouldn't understand any words that he should chance to hear. And Carlisle did hear, just enough to know that the aide was reporting the arrival of the second American convoy. Nothing showed on de Prado's face at this terrible news but he dismissed the aide with a curt nod.

Carlisle couldn't risk telling Albemarle what he'd heard, not in so public a place, but a significant nod to seaward told the general all that he needed to know.

De Prado knew that he was trapped, that much was obvious. Now that reinforcements had arrived to replace Albemarle's sickly soldiers, it was almost certain that he'd have to deal with the general at some point, in the next days or weeks, and it was better if they could do so in a gentlemanly manner.

'Please tell Lord Albemarle that I would be delighted to speak with him for a few moments. We can use the customs officer's house.'

***

Old Bahama Straits

It was stuffy in the little house, although better than the warehouse office that Carlisle had been offered. The customs officer had been given no warning that de Prado would need it. Still, it was a defining characteristic of customs officers the world over that they lived by order and regularity, and their habits reflected that fact. Stuffy it might have been but it was scrupulously clean and as if by magic the governor-general's aide produced a bottle and three sparkling glasses, looking as though they'd been polished for just this event. Perhaps the unknown and unseen customs officer had more prescience than was normal.

'Lord Albemarle,' de Prado started, 'I must thank you for the consideration that you've shown on this dreadful day.'

De Prado was clearly an old hand at speaking through an interpreter and Carlisle found it easy to repeat his words in English. It was just a little more difficult to render the English into Spanish and he could see de Prado wince momentarily at each awkward phrase.

'It has been my honour to bid farewell to such a gallant gentleman.'

A pause while each man waited for the other to start, it was evident that the one to speak first would be seen as the supplicant, and neither wished to be in that position. Albemarle had asked for the meeting but that was before the American convoy was reported to de Prado. Perhaps this was the moment that he'd realise that further resistance was pointless, and he gave the Spanish governor-general that opportunity. Nothing; de Prado just waited patiently for Albemarle to state his case. After a few seconds that seemed like minutes, Albemarle spoke without taking his eyes from de Prado.

'You may know already, your Excellency, that I have received further reinforcements today, and you can guess that they will replace those of my men who have succumbed to sickness. Tomorrow we will establish batteries on the Cabaña and then your city and the Barlovento Squadron will be defenceless under our guns. You might hold out for a few more days or weeks, but the end is inevitable. I can offer fair terms for a capitulation, advantageous terms even, but must with regret inform you that they will be necessarily less so with each day that you refuse to negotiate. I hope that we can be completely frank in this rare opportunity to meet face-to-face rather than communicating what is a necessarily delicate situation through letters and intermediaries.'

Carlise silently cursed the general for his obscure words and phrases. De Prado was much the plainer speaker of the two.

De Prado looked as though he was on the verge of a decision, but pulled himself back at the very brink of committing himself.

'My Lord, a few thousand more men will not affect the situation, and my opinion today is much the same as it was yesterday. This city and this country will continue to defy your forces until a point is reached where we can resist no further. However, I do not see that point in the near future, and it is more likely that your army, and these reinforcements, will wither away as the sickness spreads among your unsalted troops. Meanwhile, the season for hurricanes ripens each day. I have the greatest of hopes that Havana will survive, my Lord, and talk of capitulation is premature. However, I will be happy to cease disturbing your army at the instant that you send me notice of your intention to retire.'

Albemarle shrugged, a most ignoble gesture.

'Oh, say the right things to end the conversation, if you please, Captain Carlisle. I recognise obstinacy when I see it. He'll have to come to terms soon, for I shan't leave until this city is mine. Don't tell him all that, just a polite farewell.'

***

The barge rowed faster on its return to the flagship, and Albemarle kept a brooding silence except for a multi-headed question that became a statement.

'Do we have heroes like Velasco anymore, Carlisle?

Old Bahama Straits

Have we English made warfare too mechanical, too industrialised? If so, then it's to our everlasting shame. I would never have left Velasco to hold the Morro Castle with that pitiful garrison. I'd either have withdrawn and fortified the Cabaña or I'd have sent him enough men and guns to hold the place for a year. Perhaps Velasco is a sign of Spain's demise, a last brilliant flickering of the candle before it's extinguished forever.'

He stared abstractedly at the passing heights of the Cabaña.

'Have you heard the expression *to take a hammer to crack a nut*? Well, it's now our policy that a hammer – and the bigger the better – is precisely the correct implement to crack a nut, and God help us.'

Carlisle kept his peace and studied the blockships and the chain barrier as they passed through. Once into the cooler, clean sea the coxswain urged the oarsmen to their greatest efforts and the barge fairly flew towards *Namur*. And as they approached, the convoy showed clear upon their starboard side. *Richmond*, two other frigates and nine transports. There was a tale to tell there, for word had reached the squadron that fourteen transports had left New York. Somewhere on the many miles of sea they had contrived to lose five ships. That was nearly a battalion of infantry that wouldn't be available to replace Albemarle's exhausted army.

***

CHAPTER TWENTY-EIGHT

Capitulation

Friday, 13 August 1762.
Lord Albemarle's Headquarters, Chorera, Cuba.

Pocock's flag lieutenant had brought the message so early that Carlisle, a habitual early riser, had only just shaved by the light of a candle and had not yet had breakfast. Pocock clearly believed in seizing the day before it had a chance to seize him. The only evidence of the sun was its reflection against the low clouds out to the east, foretelling one of Cuba's rare overcast days. Either that or it was the first indication of a gathering hurricane; Carlisle shivered at the thought.

'From Sir George, sir. You'll find that there is some urgency and I'm commanded to wait for your response.'

Carlisle had become used to the flag lieutenant's confident manner and no longer gave it a thought, but he was damned if he was going to be rushed. He let Simmonds take the letter and without a word withdrew to the peace of his cabin, leaving the lieutenant to wait on the quarterdeck.

In haste indeed; Pocock had omitted the usual salutations and come straight to the point.

> *Lord Albemarle has informed me that the peace negotiations are progressing too slowly. In view of the personal connections that you have made with the defenders of Havana, he has requested your assistance to bring them to a swift conclusion. You are therefore, without delay, to attend Lord Albemarle at his headquarters in Chorera.*

Carlisle read the letter again, very carefully. He knew that Albemarle had again sent an offer of terms to de Prado but he hadn't been involved. It was said that the Spanish were considering the matter, and yet there was no indication of how his own intervention might bring de Prado to see sense. Nevertheless, Pocock's orders were unequivocal and there was nothing to be done but obey. Albemarle must have sent his request before there was more than a hint of daylight; clearly his staff was working around the clock.

'Call away my boat's crew, Mister Simmonds.'

Carlisle thought for a moment. He had little idea of what he was getting into, and it would be as well to be prepared for anything, but really he needed nothing. This affair wouldn't be assisted by either the pen or force of arms; it was to be a battle of wits.

'Walker, my best coat and my sword.'

***

'What do you think of those clouds, Mister Beazley?'

Carlisle looked to the east where the sun had now risen above the horizon. The boat's crew were waiting for him and the flag lieutenant had already left to tell the admiral that Carlisle was on the way.

'I've been watching them this past ten minutes, sir. Not a hurricane, I'm certain of that, but it'll be a gloomy old day and this breeze is fading fast.'

'Well, the season's upon us, so keep a close eye on the weather.'

The sailing master nodded and took another look at the lowering clouds.

'Mister Gresham, I hope I'll be back before sunset but in any case you have command in my absence. No doubt you'll have a demand for boats to move water from Chorera to the Morro Castle. If you have to send any of our own water ashore, make sure that you send an account to the flagship.'

Water for the army to the east of Havana was a perpetual problem and the squadron's reserves of drinking water were being depleted at an alarming rate. There was nothing to be done, of course. The siege batteries on the heights of the Cabaña couldn't be maintained without water for the gunners, and there was no fresh water on that side of the city. The main army camp had moved to Chorera to the west of the city and there they had a good supply of fresh water, but it was a long way from there to the Cabaña and the ships were ideally situated to send their boats ashore towing the vast barrels.

***

Souter didn't wait for any orders, and the moment that Carlisle was seated, the pinnace was sent skimming across the smooth water towards the beach at Chorera. At first, Carlisle couldn't place what was different, but of course it was the silence. For two months the thunder of the guns had been a constant accompaniment to each day. Sometimes they were few and far off and sometimes Carlisle was so close to them that his ears rang when they stopped. There had been only one break, when Velasco had been buried. After the Morro Castle fell to the British assault, the gunfire had slackened while the batteries on the Cabaña were being prepared and the army headquarters moved west to Chorera, in case the city must be taken by assault after all. Yet still, every day brought its share of gunfire.

The batteries on the Cabaña had been completed on the tenth of August. Forty-five pieces of cannon and eight mortars had been sited to fire down upon Havana and the ships in the anchorage. After a failed attempt at negotiating a surrender, at daybreak on the eleventh they had commenced firing. The little fort of La Punta and the city's north bastion were soon silenced and in the afternoon de Prado had sent an embassy requesting a ceasefire for twenty-four hours to prepare articles of capitulation. Carlisle was aware that the negotiations were taking longer than they should and suspected that de Prado was hoping for an act of God to save him; divine mercy in the form of a hurricane, perhaps. There was also the small matter of the Barlovento Squadron, and it was likely that Admiral de Hevia was hoping to secure its release.

***

Old Bahama Straits

Albemarle's forward headquarters was in a modest farming estate little more than a mile from Havana's western walls. From there the city looked tantalisingly close, as though one could reach out and touch it. Between the farm and the walls lay open fields where Carlisle could already see the start of the first approaches and parallels being cut. Even a sailor could see that it would take a long time for the city to fall if Albemarle's army had to dig its way yard-by-yard towards the walls. Surely these siege works were a sham to persuade de Prado to surrender, and yet a direct assault hardly seemed possible with the parlous state of the army. Almost every soldier that he could see had come with the American reinforcements, the original regiments had been so reduced by disease and battle that many of them were unfit for combat. For the Americans it was a blessed period of peace, for under the terms of the ceasefire, all operations of war were suspended, and the picks and shovels had been laid aside for the day.

'Ah Carlisle, I'm pleased to see you, and I hope you can do me and your country a service today.'

Carlisle bowed but said nothing. Albemarle must be in a very great hurry to have dispensed with the usual preambles.

'I want you to go and talk some sense into de Prado, and even more into Admiral de Hevia. Their twenty-four hours of grace is over; we've agreed on the city and the army but they're still arguing about the Spanish squadron. De Hevia seems to believe that its fate has nothing to do with whatever agreement the governor-general makes and he's insisting that it be allowed to sail away unmolested. Sir George naturally thinks otherwise and I agree with him. There are only four of the line left after they sank three as blockships and we sank one in the channel. You speak the language and you seem to be well known and trusted, do you think you can do any good?'

It was much as Carlisle had imagined. The governor-general and the squadron commander would be desperate to salvage something out of this disaster, and with no real naval activity they could make a logical case for de Hevia's remaining ships to be given safe passage to another Spanish port, Cartagena des Indies, perhaps. Yet it just wouldn't do. Pocock would be pilloried if he let the Spanish ships escape and with Anson gone – news of his death had reached the squadron a few weeks ago – the new First Lord wouldn't be satisfied with anything less than the complete destruction or capture of the Barlovento Squadron.

'There's a danger, my Lord, that Admiral de Hevia will set his ships alight rather than surrender them.'

'Yes, certainly, but that would be an operation of war, and a violation of the terms of the ceasefire. You must make that point most strongly, Carlisle. If the ships are destroyed by Spanish hands then I'll consider the ceasefire is over and they can expect an early assault on their walls. Then there'll be no agreement and they must accept that my army will adopt the normal custom of war for a fortress that holds out beyond any reason. These men have families behind the city walls.'

Carlisle nodded thoughtfully; he could see why he'd been summoned. With only the fate of the squadron standing in the way of a capitulation agreement, it would take a sea officer to break the impasse, and he had a number of personal contacts on both de Prado's staff and de Hevia's.

'Very well, my Lord.'

'Then God go with you, Carlisle, but mark this: at two o'clock the batteries on the Cabaña will continue their bombardment and the siege operations will be recommenced. That's twice the duration of ceasefire that we agreed and I won't give them a minute longer. If they reject the terms, they'll have no further embassy, and the next time they see a British uniform it will be charging through a breach in their walls with a bayonet before it, and they know what they can expect after that.'

***

There was no need for drummers and buglers, not with a ceasefire in place, and Carlisle was deposited before the city's land gate in a carriage that had been taken from one of the estates. The gate opened as he walked forward and was immediately closed behind him. A Spanish carriage was waiting for him and he was carried swiftly through the city to the governor-general's palace. Carlisle had the leisure to look around him. There was some evidence of destruction but mostly the business of the city seemed to be going on as usual. Of course the batteries on the Cabaña had principally fired at the walls and bastions and at the anchorage, leaving the city largely untouched. That would be a useful point to make; that the end of the ceasefire would see the heart of the city targeted as well as the walls.

The governor-general must have been told who was coming and the subject of the discussion must have been evident, for he'd summoned de Hevia and Laredo to join him.

'Captain Carlisle, it's a pleasure to meet you again.'

'The pleasure is all mine, your Excellency.'

De Prado bowed graciously.

'Of course you know Admiral de Hevia and Captain Laredo.'

It was Carlisle's turn to bow, and was that a hint of a welcoming smile that he saw on Laredo's lips. He'd dealt fairly with Laredo and he hoped that he'd be an ally in these discussions. For all the formality and the exchange of letters and solemn signatures, these agreements were made between people even though their effect was felt in palaces and ministries. Those people needed to trust each other at a personal level, and Carlisle could hope that each of these men was aware that they were dealing with an honourable opponent.

'Do you bear a letter from Lord Albemarle, Captain Carlisle?'

'I do not, your Excellency. Lord Albemarle views this as an informal embassy in order that there should be no misunderstanding between us.'

De Prado frowned and looked for a moment as though he'd dismiss Carlisle out of hand, but he glanced sideways at de Hevia who nodded slightly. To Carlisle's eye it looked as though the balance of power between these two had subtly shifted.

'Your Excellency, as I understand it you have agreed to the terms for the city and the army, and it is just Admiral Hevia's remaining four ships-of-the-line and a few frigates and sloops that are in question.'

De Prado said nothing, allowing the admiral to speak. Carlisle guessed that de Hevia, while under the general guidance of de Prado as the governor-general, had orders directly from the Escorial Palace for the preservation of his squadron.

'The Barlovento Squadron has not been engaged, Captain Carlisle, and I hope you can understand that I cannot surrender my ships without a fight. This siege has nothing to do with my squadron and it should be allowed to depart in peace for Cartagena des Indies.'

Carlisle watched the two men. They had no room for manoeuvre, no trump cards to play, and their only hope was that Albemarle had no stomach for prolonging the siege with the hurricane season advancing and with his soldiers falling sick daily.

'With respect, Admiral, I must point out that our two countries are at war and that your ships have no right to sail anywhere in peace, but by the nature of things must be prepared to fight for their very survival. As for your part in the city's defence, your fine squadron has been reduced by half in order to bolster the city's defences and without Captain Velasco's courage, the Morro Castle would have fallen weeks earlier. This siege has been extended by your squadron's actions, even though your ships have not met Admiral Pocock's on the open sea. Now, however brave and skilled your crews, they can't pass out of this harbour under the British guns on the Cabaña and El Morro. Even if they did so, Admiral Pocock has a strong detachment of ships-of-the-line that has provided neither men nor guns to the siege, and they are waiting for the Barlovento Squadron. The articles of capitulation that Lord Albemarle has offered apply equally to the city, the army and your squadron, or else they do not apply at all.'

'And if I do not choose to bind my squadron's fate to that of the city, Captain Carlisle, what then?'

'In that case Lord Albemarle will be forced to end the ceasefire without any agreement.'

De Hevia glanced at the governor-general who closed his eyes as though in pain, then spoke with a weary voice.

'How long do we have, Captain Carlisle?'

Carlisle looked from one to the other of the Spaniards. In a flash of empathy he realised that they were arguing not just for their own honour but for their very lives. King Carlos was unlikely to deal kindly with these men who had so publicly failed in their duty. He couldn't help feeling some sympathy. The size of the force that Pocock had brought to this remote place and that Albemarle had thrown against the city was greater than anyone could have imagined – indeed a hammer to crack a nut – and only luck could have saved them.

'Until two o'clock, your Excellency, that's twice the period that was agreed and Lord Albemarle feels that he can delay no longer than that.'

'Very well, would you wait with Captain Laredo for a moment?'

De Prado and de Hevia walked out of the room leaving him and Laredo alone. There was a short awkward silence before Carlisle spoke.

'Did you find your wife well, Captain Laredo? I believe I saw her at Captain Velasco's funeral.'

'Yes, sir, and she sends you her thanks for delivering me back to her.'

Carlisle nodded, then came to a decision.

'I find that it would have been improper to tell my country's enemies what Lord Albemarle plans to do, but perhaps you can be an intermediary.'

'I will do my best, sir, if it will help both sides to understand each other.'

'Good, then here's the situation as I see it. The governor-general and Admiral de Hevia are both trying to buy time in the hope that the weather will drive us away, or that our force will be so reduced by disease that we can have no hope of a successful conclusion to the siege, or that a relief force should come by sea. They are also relying on the need for a long siege to make a breach in the city walls, perhaps as long as that for the Morro Castle.'

Carlisle was watching Laredo's face and could see that his logic had struck home.

'I concede that a hurricane might end the siege, but there's no sign of one yet. As for the other circumstances, two convoys of reinforcements have arrived from America to replace the sick soldiers and Admiral Pocock has stationed strong detachments of ships-of-the-line to the east and to the west. The Comte de Blénac can't come to your aid, nor can any Spanish ships. And finally, there will be no long siege. If his Excellency doesn't agree to the terms before two o'clock, then he can expect an assault at any moment, and then the city will be subjected to the full rigours of war. The fresh soldiers from America are more than sufficient for the task. They must accept the terms of surrender, in their entirety, or bring down disaster upon the heads of all in Havana.'

Carlisle hoped that his bluff about an immediate assault wouldn't be understood for what it was. He knew how much the army disliked intemperate assaults on fortifications but he also knew that a long siege could indeed hand a pyrrhic victory to the Spanish defenders.

Laredo showed no emotion. Perhaps he'd already guessed all of this; certainly he'd spent enough time in *Dartmouth* soaking up the British way of thinking. He rose and bowed then motioned to an army captain who had been sitting quietly in a corner.

'Would you excuse me please, sir? The captain will take care of your needs while I am gone.'

***

Carlisle resisted the urge to look at his watch but he was acutely aware of the passing minutes. He attempted to make conversation with the Spanish captain, but the man was clearly overawed by being present at such important and delicate negotiations, so after a while he sat in silence, trying to assure himself that the longer they were gone the more likely it was that they were seriously considering what he'd said, and even more what Laredo had presumably relayed to them. The arguments were sound, he knew, and apart from the threat of an immediate assault they were all truthful, but surely it shouldn't take this long.

Just as he was starting to think that he'd failed, the door opened and de Prado walked in looking old and dispirited, followed by de Hevia and Laredo.

'Well Captain, Admiral de Hevia and I find your arguments persuasive and we both believe that in the interests of humanity we must agree to Lord Albemarle's terms. We still have three hours before the ceasefire must end so I will await his Lordship's proposal for the signing, but I hope you will assure him of our good will and our determination to abide by the terms.'

'Your Excellency is as wise as he is generous,' Carlisle said, bowing again, 'and I hope you will count on me as your friend.'

All three Spaniards bowed.

'There is one last point that I find that I must mention, your Excellency, to avoid any misunderstanding. The Barlovento Squadron of course will become a prize of war and it would be directly counter to the agreement if it was damaged in any way before its surrender to Admiral Pocock.'

De Hevia flinched and looked as though he was about

to protest that his honour was being questioned, but changed his mind.

'Certainly Captain Carlisle, that is understood.'

***

CHAPTER TWENTY-NINE

A Lee Shore

Monday, 29 November 1762.
Dartmouth, at Sea, Sandy Hook west 15 leagues.

The fresh northerly breeze gave *Dartmouth* a fine heel to starboard as she made her offing from Sandy Hook. Carlisle revelled in it as he walked the poop deck wrapped in a thick woollen cloak and protected from intrusion by the splendid isolation of a captain of one of His Majesty's ships-of-the-line. He looked over to windward where he could just make out Long Island in this sparkling clear weather and glanced at his watch. There were ten minutes left before the end of the afternoon watch when his clerk would remind him of the meeting that he'd called with his principal officers. He'd hardly been on board while the ship lay at anchor off Sandy Hook and he was already feeling out of touch.

Ten minutes. He should be thinking ahead to how he could preserve his creaking ship for another three weeks in a North Atlantic winter, but his thoughts kept returning to personal matters. He'd brought the American convoy back to New York, seen the depleted regiments disembarked from their anchorage off Sandy Hook, and bade farewell to the transports that had been his responsibility for the long passage from Havana. Then he'd called on the admiral in New York, but try as he might, he couldn't get orders to Hampton, or even orders to stay in New York. The admiral was right not to concede to his hinted requests, but that didn't help. *Dartmouth* was long overdue for a refit and at this time of year only Portsmouth would do.

Nevertheless, if this wind persisted or backed into the west, as it should, they'd be at Spithead in less than three weeks, and then into a dry dock. *Dartmouth* would be paid off, for sure, and without a doubt Carlisle would be cast upon the beach. That suited him perfectly. He'd make the right noises at the Admiralty, of course, but he doubted whether anyone would be fooled into believing that he wanted another ship. In any case, the talk was of peace and there would be plenty of captains clamouring for the few commands that would be left in service. It was well known that the fortunate post-captains that had been at Havana would make a healthy sum in prize money – although nothing like the real fortunes that Pocock and Albemarle would make – and there was no financial incentive to keep him at sea. He didn't even care about hoisting his flag. At the present rate of promotions it would be over twenty years before he came to the top of the post-captain's list, and in the meantime there was a life to be lived at his home in Virginia.

There was a question of political influence too. The Earl of Bute was the man of the hour now, the *Prime Minister* as some were calling him. Bute's cousin had never forgiven Carlisle after they'd had a difference of opinion – a very grave disagreement indeed – when he'd taken passage to Villa Franca in *Dartmouth* two years ago. It would take a strong First Lord at the Admiralty to stand up to King George's favourite when it came to allocating ships.

In time, perhaps, he'd apply for a ship, but for now he longed only for home and the delights of family life. Three weeks to Portsmouth, a month or two to clear his accounts at Seething Lane and visit the Admiralty and his banker and prize agent, then a passage for Hampton and home. He could see the first crocuses bloom on the Palace Green, and watch the sheep brought out to graze. Joshua was four years old and he longed to see him before he grew too much older.

And here was Simmonds, just at the first stroke of eight bells, and he really couldn't neglect his duties any longer.

***

'We've stores of all natures, wood and water for three months, sir. We're forty men short of complement and there are another thirty in the surgeon's care. We have two

Old Bahama Straits

tiers of powder remaining and shot to match.'

Gresham's report was short and to the point. He knew his captain's mood and this was no time for a detailed report of exact quantities of stores. They had all they needed to reach Spithead with a wide margin of safety and they could fight an action, if the need arose. He was only telling Carlisle what he knew already, because if there were any deficiencies he'd have raised the alarm while they could still apply to the yards in New York.

'I've given Mister Simmonds an exact accounting, sir. The doctor begs to be excused as he has two cases that are nearing the end.'

'Very well, Mister Gresham. Would you ask the doctor when it would be convenient for me to visit the sick bay, preferably before the two men depart this life? I presume those are both fever cases from Havana.'

'That's correct, sir. Snape and Outhwaite.'

There was nothing more to say about the sick. They'd lost five men since they left Havana, all from the delayed effects of yellow fever, and probably there would be more to come before they struck soundings in the Channel.

The bosun had a long tale of woe. It was the usual story after so long in the tropics: threadbare sails, worn shrouds, stays, halyards and sheets, and masts and spars that were nearing the end of their lives.

'I'm sure you'll do your best, Mister Hewlett. Now, Chips, what do you have to tell us?'

The carpenter wasn't a naturally cheerful man and now he tugged at his long face before answering.

'Well, sir, this old girl needs a dry dock and no mistake. We're making two foot of water every watch and it'll be more if we get a good blow. My mates have caulked everywhere they could while we were at anchor, but they can't get at the seams below the waterline, no matter what.'

'Oh, I'm surprised, Chips. Can your mates not swim underwater?'

There was a deathly silence as the carpenter considered

his captains attempt at a jest. His lips moved silently twice, then he thought better of it and his witty riposte died before it saw the light of day.

'The seams are no worse than can be expected, sir, but it's that old mizzen that worries me, after it was sprung...'

'Excuse me, Chips, but I saw you and Mister Hewlett refreshing the woolding before we sailed this morning, is there another problem?'

'We woolded it alright, as tight as we could, but it's sprung badly and by rights it's a job for a yard. Oh, it'll hold in this sort of weather, but we'll need to favour it if we get anything worse. I'd like to see that mizzen reefed until we reach Spithead and as for the mizzen tops'l, well, I'll let Mister Beazley have his say.'

Carlisle turned to the sailing master who was evidently prepared for this introduction.

'I've looked at the mizzen and I agree with Chips, sir. We need to keep the strain off the lower mast, so we shouldn't spread the mizzen tops'l nor either of the stays'ls. That'll allow us to show a reefed mizzen.'

'Will that be enough to keep our head off the wind, Mister Beazley?'

Carlisle already knew the answer but it was as well that Beazley should make a statement that Simmonds could record.

'It will, sir, in this wind, although there'll be a little lee helm, I expect. If it gets worse we can furl the jib, and that should be a better balance. But God forbid we should have to claw off a lee shore, sir.'

'Amen,' muttered Gresham and Hewitt, looking solemn as though in church.

***

Carlisle visited the sickbay as he'd done every day until they anchored off Sandy Hook. The two worst sufferers wouldn't last the night but the surgeon had hopes that the others might recover. It was the weakening effect of yellow fever in all but three cases, and what they really needed was rest and recuperation at the Haslar naval hospital at Gosport. That's what he was telling them, that they must hold on for three weeks until they anchored at Spithead, when it was a short boat journey to Haslar Creek.

He turned in early with *Dartmouth* still heading east to clear the Nantucket Shoals and Georges Bank before they could haul their wind to make some northing on the great circle route to the Channel. He dozed until he heard four bells in the first watch and then fell into a deep sleep, so deep that it took two attempts for the midshipman to wake him.

'Captain, sir. Captain, sir. Mister Beazley's respects, and the wind is veering and strengthening, sir. He believes he'll have to bear away a point.'

As soon as he stepped onto the quarterdeck Carlisle could see that the weather was changing. The wind hadn't picked up by very much, not enough for another reef in the tops'ls, not yet, but it had veered three points towards the northeast and the ship was only just managing to hold its course with the bowlines and the sheets bar-taut. He looked up at the lateen mizzen sail. It had been reefed, but it possessed only one line of reef points that ran diagonally upwards from the tack to the leech. To further reduce the sail area it would need to be brailed, and that was usually a temporary measure in fair weather, for in strong winds a brailed sail would flog and eventually destroy itself.

'We'll need to bear away a point, sir.'

Beazley made his report in a half-shout, studying the dog-vane all the while.

'Will it veer any further, Mister Beazley?'

'Probably, sir, and it'll blow some more before the morning.'

'Then let's not chase it around the compass. Bring her four points off the wind, set a course to the sou'east, Master.'

'Sou'east it is, sir. I'll call all hands, with your approval.'

Carlisle nodded distractedly. He'd seen nor'easterlies in

this stretch of water before, and he knew they had the potential to build up to a regular storm and veer right around into the east or the southeast. In that case *Dartmouth* was in danger of being embayed between Nantucket Island and Cape Hatteras. It was an immense stretch of ocean, nearly a hundred-and-fifty leagues from island to cape, and normally it would pose no difficulty other than an uncomfortable few days beating to and fro to claw to windward. However, in *Dartmouth's* present state, it could be serious. If he couldn't make any way to windward he was doomed to be pressed deeper and deeper in towards the coast. The obvious answer would be to make for the sheltered water behind Long Island, but with the wind in the nor'east and his ship unable to make any way to windward, that was already impossible. He looked at the straining canvas. Sandy Hook would be a death-trap tomorrow, so his present plan was correct. Sail a few points free so that the ship wasn't overburdened, and make for the open sea, clear of the lee shore that waited to the west.

***

Carlisle paced the deck for the rest of the night. His fears were confirmed and as the wind rose by degrees and became stronger it veered further and further until it was coming directly from the east. He ordered the tops'ls and the jib furled in the middle watch and started reefing the courses in the morning. By the middle of the forenoon they were thrashing southwards and Beazley was starting to become concerned about weathering Cape Hatteras.

'Wind's sou'east-by-east, sir,' he said with a look of grave concern.

'Is this the closest she'll lie?

'Aye sir, it is. I daren't show any more sail on the mizzen and that means I can't set the jib. I reckon we're making at least two points of leeway. If this wind doesn't change for another day we'll be ashore on the Cape, sir.'

'We can always buy time by tacking back up to the nor'east.'

'That we can, sir, but it'll be thick weather up there and my dead reckoning isn't worth a groat now, and I don't see much chance of a sun sight, not with this lot.'

Beazley waved his arm to the thick, dark blanket of cloud that totally obscured the sky.

'Very well, we'll stand on at least until tomorrow morning, Master. If there's no change I'll consider wearing – I assume we can't tack?'

'That's right, sir, we'll be in irons in a flash if we try.'

'Then until tomorrow morning.'

***

The day passed again into night while Carlisle paced the deck or dozed restlessly in his cabin. Half of his mind was taken up with his concern for his ship but one tiny portion wouldn't let go of the book that Ann had sent him. That poet fellow had used the word *impervious* to describe the horrors of a lee shore. Was he affirming that the shore couldn't be penetrated? Perhaps it was the very force of the word that commended it to the poet, regardless of its strict meaning. Whatever the word's meaning, Carlisle was fully persuaded of the horrors of this particular lee shore.

Beazley plotted his dead reckoning but really the ship's position was nothing better than an educated guess. Few of the seamen went below to their hammocks; it was evident to all but the most simple that the ship was in a very precarious position. If they couldn't weather Nantucket Island or Cape Hatteras then they must make for either Chesapeake Bay or Delaware Bay. Neither of the two were attractive in a sou'easterly storm when a furious breaking swell was certain to have built up at each entrance. Carlisle knew this very well, but every fibre of his being told him that he'd have to choose one or the other. If he knew anything about the seaboard of the Middle Colonies, he knew that this storm wouldn't blow through for a couple of days, and by that time *Dartmouth* would be a splintered wreck upon a long, white beach. The Chesapeake or the Delaware then, and he knew instinctively which it must be.

He'd only taken a ship past Cape May into the Delaware a few times, but he knew the entrance to the Chesapeake like the back of his hand. He could picture the stretch of water between Cape Charles and Cape Henry and he knew the extent of the shoals that blocked off the northern half. He'd have to leave Cape Henry between one and two miles off his larboard beam. Any closer or any further and he'd be in the breakers that he knew would have built into a ferocious sea by now. If only he could find the passage, but in this weather no navigator on earth could tell his ship's position with any accuracy.

Eight bells sounded the end of the morning watch and a cold grey day emerged from the blackness of the night. A succession of regular, steep waves marched remorselessly from the southeast and the long, white trails of spume bore witness to the length of time that the storm had already been blowing. There'd been no sight of the sun, nor of the moon, nor even the pole star, and Beazley scratched his head as he looked over his log where the course and the speed of the ship had been recorded every half hour. He'd made a careful calculation of *Dartmouth's* leeway, but under this unusual rig it could only be an estimate.

'Well, Mister Beazley? Where do you make us?'

'Best I can say is twenty leagues off Cape Henry, sir. In my opinion we should wear ship now, and hope that the wind shifts. Back or veer, either way will do, it can't be worse for us than it is now.'

Carlisle turned and walked up to the poop deck where he rested his hand on the mizzen and stood still for half a minute. He could feel the stresses in the mast, the minute vibrations that told of splintered wood rubbing against splintered wood as the mast worked with the ship's pitch and roll. He sensed that any undue leverage on the mast could snap it clean in two where it had been fished and woolded. Well, it would have to be tried, one last attempt to break free from the lee shore. He walked back down to the quarterdeck, unable to keep his deep concern from his face.

Old Bahama Straits

'Wear ship, Mister Beazley. Brail the mizzen before you do so, if you please.'

'Aye-aye sir.'

Beazley understood the gravity of the situation. If the mizzen should go they'd never be able to keep the ship's head to the wind and they'd be blown incontinently to leeward.

'When you're ready, Mister Beazley.'

Every man was on deck and all eyes were on Beazley. The sailing master stared to windward watching for the most advantageous sequence of waves, for a lull in the wind, but really it was hopeless in this appalling visibility and after a minute he gave up.

'Brail up the mizzen.'

Beazley could feel the ship wanting to bear away, that was good.

'Helm to windward, Quartermaster.'

Old Eli nodded at the chief steersman – there were four of them to manage the great wheel in this weather – and between them they hauled it over to starboard. *Dartmouth's* bows swung slowly to leeward until the wind was coming from dead astern and suddenly the ship was through the wind and its head was starting to move towards the north.

'Let go the mizzen brails.'

Beazley looked over his shoulder to see the mizzen filling; now the wind was acting on the fore stays'l and the mizzen to complete the manoeuvre. Then a steeper-than-normal sea passed under *Dartmouth's* quarter and the stern dropped into the trough behind it. A strong gust of wind caught the mizzen at the same time as the ship heeled far over to larboard. There was a dreadful crack and the whole of the ship shook as the huge mast broke clean in two, with the heel of the upper part resting on the lower.

'Brail the Mizzen,' Carlisle shouted, 'Furl the fore stays'l. I have the ship, Mister Beazley. Give me a course to pass a mile and a half off Cape Henry. Your best guess now.'

It was all that was left to them. They must find the tiny

gap between the Capes in this thickest and stormiest weather, and they must steer into a mile-wide gap between the sandbanks. Their very lives depended upon it.

'West-by-north, sir. Two-and-a-half hours at this speed.

***

Carlisle was thinking fast now, planning what he should do if he should miraculously find the sand dunes of Cape Henry on his bow at about six bells. He could see everyone making their own preparations, stuffing their pockets with their coins and anything they valued, for they all knew that the odds were against *Dartmouth's* survival. The surgeon was bringing the sick men up on deck and laying those that couldn't stand in the waist.

The steering was erratic, but Old Eli stood like a rock, directing the steersmen with oaths and hand movements. An hour passed, two hours, and still nothing. The visibility was perhaps three miles and if anything the wind was getting stronger. Carlisle could feel the waves getting steeper and more disordered as the ship moved from the deeps into shallower water.

'Land ho! Land on the larboard bow. It's Cape Henry, sir.'

Whittle was at his post of course, and he knew the landfall for his home better than any man on board. Beazley had performed a miracle, yet again. Carlisle could feel the tension falling away and some on the deck even started smiling. Fools! Cape Henry hadn't had its say yet.

'Breakers right ahead, sir, all across the bow.'

Whittle had to bellow to be heard above the wind's roaring.

'Where's the best passage, Whittle?'

'One point to larboard, sir.'

'Your course is west, Eli.'

'Aye-aye sir.'

Now Carlisle could see Cape Henry but Cape Charles was lost in the mirk on the starboard side. Yes, on this course they'd pass right down the deep channel.

Nevertheless, it was a frightful prospect with white water everywhere he looked.

'Stand by both bower anchors.'

Was it possible that the ship would be saved after all? Carlisle dared to hope, but his optimism was soon dashed. As the waves hit the shoal water they generated huge combers that roared into the bay. One of them – bigger than its fellows – lifted *Dartmouth's* stern and dropped it into the trough behind. With a frightful crash the upper part of the mizzen mast slipped off the stump and with nothing to stop it, it smashed through the thick oak planking of the poop deck, through Carlisle's cabin and onto the main deck below. *Dartmouth* took a terrible lurch to larboard.

'The helm's not answering, sir,' Old Eli said in a calm voice, 'the mizzen must have cut the cables.'

Carlisle could see there was nothing to be done. The wind had charge of the ship and the wind was determined to put it aground on the sand just to the west of Cape Henry.

A bump, and she was free, another bump, another and a dreadful cracking sound from below, then the great ship came to a sickening halt as all the masts went by the board. Carlisle opened his mouth to shout for axemen to cut away the shrouds and stays and then he felt a terrible blow across his shoulders and back, and the world turned dark.

***

CHAPTER THIRTY

Home At Last

Saturday 4 December 1762.
The Carlisle House, Williamsburg, Virginia.

'We were lucky, sir. She struck in a quieter spot in the lee of the Cape and after we cut away the masts she sat on that sandbank happily enough until the storm passed through. The bosun had brought everyone down from aloft so we didn't lose a man, not even any from the sickbay. We made the best of it until the morning when lo and behold, the wind dropped to a whisper and it would have been like a millpond out there, but for the huge great swell still coming in from the sou'east. It was quite a sight, sir. As the sun rose the boats started coming from Hampton and all the little places out that way. There were a lot of scavengers among them but Mister Pontneuf put sentries all around, and anyway the greatest number of the boats were coming to take us off. The doctor put you in a stretcher and you were in Hampton before noon, still insensible. It was the cro'jack yard that got you, sir.'

Gresham beamed at his captain. It was the first time that he'd seen him since *Dartmouth* had been cast ashore in the lee of Cape Henry, and he was pleased to see that he was recovering. In fact Carlisle had only really regained consciousness the day before and Chiara and the doctor had been keeping all the visitors away.

'Thank you, Mister Gresham…'

Carlisle's voice was thick and his speech was slurred. The doctor thought that his skull wasn't fractured but his collar bone was certainly broken in the same place as it had been five years before, when a Dutch pirate's musket ball had felled him.

'…but what of the ship? Can she be floated off?'

Gresham looked puzzled for a moment then

remembered that Carlisle had not heard any news of the wreck until this moment.

'Oh my word no, sir. She's bilged both sides and her keel is broken in both of the scarfs; there are sprung butt-ends from for'rard to aft and the tide flows in and out as though it owned the place. Her masts are all gone too and her rudder. The navy agent from Hampton is preparing a report and planning the salvage, but the old *Dartmouth* will never float again.'

Gresham bit his tongue while Carlisle digested this information. There'd be a court martial, probably in New York, and all of the officers would be asked their opinion on the circumstances of the grounding. It didn't seem likely that any blame would be attached to the captain or any of the officers, after all the reports on the ship's parlous state that had been sent to Pocock and the navy board for the past six months. *Dartmouth* could have been – should have been – sent to Port Royal for repair before embarking on an ocean passage in winter, but then every ship that had been at Havana was in a similar state. It was just bad luck that they'd suffered such a severe storm with no chance of making way to windward. Yet still, a court martial was always unpredictable. The doctor had told him not to agitate the patient but it was difficult to talk dispassionately about the wreck of his ship.

'The crew, Mister Gresham, are they being lodged decently?'

This was firmer ground and Gresham was quietly proud of the way he'd dealt with *Dartmouth's* people, except for one item.

'They're all billeted in houses in the villages inside the Cape, sir, all along the coast towards Norfolk. The agent has seen to it and I've inspected some of them, they're decent enough, in the main. The officers are taking turns to row guard upon the ship when the weather isn't too bad and Mister Pontneuf and his marines are patrolling the shore, just so that nobody thinks it's easy pickings. There is one thing though, sir, we've had some desertions.'

Carlisle almost laughed at his first lieutenant's concerned expression.

'It's the younger men, sir, those with no ties back at home. They can see the way the wind's blowing as well as anyone and with this war winding down they'd rather start afresh in Virginia than in England. I've given them some idea of the prize money that they're owed, but it doesn't seem to bother them. Short of locking them up there's not much that can be done.'

'Well, I can't say I'm surprised. Has Whittle joined them? I thought I detected a yearning for home when I last spoke to him.'

'Oh, bless you, no, sir. Haven't you been told? Whittle was certainly considering running, but he heard about the ancient custom that a ship's captain can take a few followers with him when his ship's paid off. Well, he and Old Eli, not wishing to miss their tide, jumped ship. They borrowed a boat and hired a carriage in Hampton, well more of a cart in fact, and they came here yesterday to apply to join your household. I thought they'd deserted at first, but they were only straggling. In any case, I didn't enter them as run, and they're keeping out of my way today. When you weren't able to see them, they applied to Mister Angelini who happened to be at hand, and he spoke to Lady Chiara. I hope you don't mind, sir, but you seem to have engaged two followers while you were sleeping, although how you'll employ Old Eli on dry land is more than I can tell.'

At that the door opened to reveal Chiara, who had clearly been waiting for Gresham's allotted time to expire; the doctor had been most insistent on that matter.

'Mister Gresham, I trust you can join us for dinner at three o'clock. Enrico will be here and I hope that with your help and Whittle and the other fellow – it's a strange name and I can't say it very well – we can manoeuvre Captain Carlisle out of this room for the first time, but that can only be achieved if he has some rest.'

'Thank you Ma'am. I have business with Mister Simmonds that will occupy me until then.'

'Ah yes, Mister Simmonds is in the small office at the back. I'll send some coffee.'

'Oh, one piece of cheerful news, sir. All of the ship's books were saved, every one of them, so there should be no difficulty in clearing the accounts, and there's a round letter arrived from Admiral Pocock promising an early distribution of the prize money. A tidy sum, sir, a tidy sum indeed.'

***

Chiara plumped up Carlisle's cushions and fussed around him for a few moments. She knew that he'd be anxious to be up and about now that he could think clearly, and this was perhaps the last chance to speak to him while he was at a disadvantage.

'I'm so glad that I waited for you to return before baptising Cecilia. Of course, I had the perfect excuse with no priest within a day's ride, but she's hale and hearty and a few weeks won't make any difference. Do you approve of the name, Edward? We can still change it if you really object.'

Carlisle shook his head and gazed fondly at his wife.

'No, Cecilia is a beautiful name and it sounds quite Italian. It's perfect.'

Chiara stood and looked out of the window where a leaden sky foretold snow.

'You know, you'll see more of little Cecilia than you did of Joshua at this age. Mister Fauquier called early this morning, just for word of your health. He left his regards but he couldn't stay. He told me that the peace negotiations with France and Spain have started again, and this time they have high hopes of a conclusion. That will mean you don't need to return to sea and you can stay here and be a Virginian again!'

Carlisle smiled as happily as he could and he hoped that Chiara would attribute any sign of ill-ease to his injury. She was right, of course. He wouldn't be fit for command for six months and in that time it was almost certain that the war would be over and with no war there was little chance of him being given a ship, at least for the foreseeable future. Then it was the life of a gentleman of means for him, with perhaps a role in colonial politics. Maybe he'd go into business. In any case there'd be no more hazarding his life on the ocean and yearning for the bosom of his family. After all, it was what he wanted, wasn't it?

***

HISTORICAL EPILOGUE

At Sea

The Comte de Blénac demonstrated that the French navy was still capable of limited action in defence of its territories. As well as threatening Pocock's invasion force throughout the summer of 1762, he savaged the second convoy of reinforcements from America, capturing five transports and nearly five-hundred desperately-needed soldiers, most of them from the Fifty-Eighth of Foot, a regular line regiment. He rounded off his squadron's deployment by successfully escorting Saint-Domingue's sugar harvest back to France. Nevertheless, the French navy was in a parlous state and although the shipyards were busy building replacements, they could not come fast enough to affect the course of the war. Spain's navy could offer little help. It had been slow to mobilise for war and the tight control of its movements hampered the squadrons that were already in the Caribbean, preventing their joining up to form a battle squadron that could oppose the invasion of Havana. In late 1762 the trade routes of the world were firmly under British control. With the death of Lord Anson in June, the old guard was changing at the Admiralty.

Western Europe

The war had proved that French strategy – like the war plans of all great nations – was constrained by its geography. The Pyrenees Mountains and its long-standing accord with Spain secured France's southern boundary, the Atlantic protected its western side while its eastern flank was guarded by the Alps and the Mediterranean. However, France's north had always been wide open to invasion, and it was there that King Louis' attention was focussed. He simply could not allow the bewildering array of Germanic states across the Rhine to coalesce into a great power that could threaten his realm, and in the rise of Prussia he recognised exactly that threat. France's geopolitical problem dominated the grand strategy of the Seven Years War and forced it to spend the bulk of its war chest on its army. Despite that extravagant spending, the war north of the Rhine was grinding into stalemate and all the European powers were fighting on with one eye on the peace negotiations.

History proved King Louis to be right, of course, and it was from the north and by those very same Germanic states that France was invaded at least four separate times in the nineteenth and twentieth centuries. We are all prisoners of our geography.

Central Europe

In Central Europe, Frederick of Prussia continued to raise new armies to hold his territorial gains against the combined armies of Austria and Russia. Nevertheless, a tactical mistake in the autumn of 1761 left the Prussian state on the verge of collapse and it was only saved by the death of Empress Elizabeth of Russia in January 1762. Her successor Peter initiated peace negotiations with Frederick, taking the pressure off his army and saving Prussia from defeat and destruction.

North America

French territory in North America was reduced to a few settlements in Louisiana and tenuously-held land in the centre of the continent to the west of the Ohio and south of the Great Lakes. The English-speaking people of the thirteen colonies were starting to come to terms with the idea that they were no longer threatened with enclosure by French soldiers and settlers moving down from Canada. Louisiana was so far away that it was of little concern except to the people of Georgia, who also worried about Spanish Florida on their southern border. The mood in America was one of expansion to the west, and they were impatient with the continuing war that they largely saw as none of their business. They felt increasingly constrained by the demands of their colonial masters in Whitehall and although it's difficult to find evidence of anyone openly considering independence, many were thinking of ways and means to loosen the leash.

The Long War

France had lost territory in North America, the Caribbean, West Africa, the East Indies and, most humiliatingly of all, their own home island of Belle Isle, and there was no consolation in Germany where they were no more than holding ground. Their only conquest that had any bargaining power in peace negotiations was Minorca, and they had already promised that island to Spain as part of the secret treaty. Meanwhile, Spain had lost Havana and — although the word had not yet reached Madrid — their eastern colonial capital of Manilla. Even Spain's invasion of Portugal had run into trouble as the Portuguese army was reinforced by regiments from its old ally, Britain. The Third Bourbon Family Pact had failed and soon the cousins would have to renew the peace negotiations from an even worse strategic position than King Louis had been in a year before.

***

Chris Durbin

FACT MEETS FICTION

The Old Bahama Straits

John Elphinstone in the frigate *Richmond* scouted the Old Bahama Straits for Sir George Pocock's ships in 1762, and I hope he would forgive me for appropriating his great feat of navigation to Edward Carlisle in *Dartmouth*. We previously met John Elphinstone as he was captured, along with George Holbrooke, on the beach at Saint-Cast in *Perilous Shore*.

William Goostrey

Cambridge's captain, William Goostrey, was killed by musket fire from the Morro Castle and John Lindsay – then captain of the frigate *Trent* – took over command while the battle was still in progress. It's such a dramatic story that I couldn't resist placing Edward Carlisle in John Lindsay's position.

Stirling Castle

James Campell appears to be a rare example of a post-captain who would not bring his ship into action. We'll never know what prevented him playing his part in the bombardment of the Morro Castle, but four days after Havana surrendered Admiral Pocock convened a court martial. Campbell was tried by his brother post-captains and dismissed from the service. Perhaps he was fortunate not to share Admiral Byng's fate.

The Defence of the Morro Castle

Luis Vicente de Velasco was rightly praised for his defence of the Morro Castle. His family was ennobled and his son was created a Marqués. Charles III decreed that a third rate ship-of-the-line then being built should be named *Velasco* and it was duly launched in 1764, followed by a series of other similarly named ships. Sadly the last *SPS Velasco* that I can find recorded was stricken from the Spanish Navy list in 1971. Captain Velasco has joined a growing number of foreign heroes from the great age of sail that I've discovered while writing this series of books.

The Durnford Battery

Elias Durnford was an ensign in the Corps of Engineers at the siege of Havana. He laid out many of the siege lines and, as was customary at the time, one of the batteries was named in his honour. *Durnford Battery* was manned by sailors and I've placed Edward Carlisle in command for a few days. Elias Durnford prospered after Havana, and he surveyed and laid out the city plan for Pensacola, Florida, most of which is unchanged to this day. Among other appointments, he became the governor of British West Florida.

Continentals

The continental regiments arrived late for the siege of Havana, but their arrival was nevertheless timely as they provided a vital injection of manpower just as Albemarle's army was suffering its worst from the tropical diseases. Those that survived the enemy and the yellow fever returned to their home colonies with a wealth of military experience and when the colonies fought for their independence from Britain, many of them answered the call and joined George Washington's army.

Prize Money

The prize money from Havana was enormous. The two commanders, Pocock and Albemarle, each received £122,697 which in the eighteenth century was a vast fortune. Augustus Keppel, as Pocock's second-in-command, was paid £24,539 and William Keppel as a major general of infantry was paid a somewhat lesser amount. In one stroke this restored the Keppel family fortune that had been squandered by their father, the second Earl. Lieutenant-General Eliott, as Albemarle's second-in-command, received the same share as Augustus Keppel, and to give some idea of its value, he was able to buy Bayley Park in East Sussex (now called Heathfield Park) and still have enough money to alter and enlarge it. Even a post-captain such as Edward Carlisle was enriched by £1,600. Meanwhile – and by modern standards, scandalously – an able seaman or an army private received less than four pounds.

Sickness and Disease

Sickness and disease were the defining features of campaigns in the tropics before the advent of modern medicine. It was widely assumed that yellow fever was caused by the night air, particularly as it rose from swampy ground, and in 1762 nobody attributed this and other tropical diseases to the real culprits, mosquitos. Britain lost 2,764 killed, wounded, captured or deserted during the siege of Havana, which is not abnormal for a campaign of this sort anywhere in the world. However, by October they had also lost 4,708 dead from sickness, and men continued to die in great numbers during the passage back to the American colonies and to Britain. Almost every land campaign in the Caribbean had similar proportions of men killed by the climate and – as we now know – by disease-bearing insects. From a twenty-first century perspective, and on a simplistic analysis, this seems a disproportionate death toll to satisfy the middle-class craving for sugar.

The Governor-General and the Admiral

Governor-General de Prado and Admiral de Hevia were tried and convicted of treason for failing to fortify the

Cabaña, failing to mount an effective counterattack, leaving the Barlovento Squadron idle and surrendering the ships intact instead of burning them, and not removing the royal treasury before the surrender. De Prado was sentenced to death, but was reprieved and died in prison. De Hevia was sentenced to 10 years house arrest and the loss of his office and titles, but was later pardoned and reinstated.

***

Chris Durbin

THE CARLISLE AND HOLBROOKE SERIES

There are now fifteen Carlisle and Holbrooke Naval Adventures. The series starts in the Mediterranean at the end of 1755 when Captain Edward Carlisle's small frigate *Fury* is part of the peacetime squadron based at Port Mahon to watch the French fleet at Toulon. Carlisle is a native of Virginia but in those days before American independence it was quite normal for well-connected men from the colonies to take the King's commission. In fact, there is an information board at Mount Vernon that records George Washington's wish to join the navy and his mother's refusal to allow it. Imagine how things might have been different if he'd found himself on the quarterdeck of a man-of-war instead of leading the allied armies to ultimate victory against the British during the war of independence.

Carlisle has a master's mate, George Holbrooke, who is the son of an old friend now retired in England. Holbrooke's heart isn't in the navy; he wanted to become a lawyer but the family finances wouldn't stretch that far. His performance is disappointing as a sea officer, to the extent that Carlisle is considering dismissing him. However, when war breaks out the following year Holbrooke rises to the challenge and as the navy struggles to mobilise for war he achieves rapid promotion and is soon in command of his own ship.

Each book in the series focusses on one of the two principal characters, either Carlisle or Holbrooke, and they take centre stage in alternate episodes. There are broadly two books for each year of the war and I hope to carry the series through the period of strained relations between Britain and its American colonies, into the war for American independence.

The series is available in Kindle, Kindle Unlimited and in paperback formats, and I plan to publish two new books each year. The easiest way to obtain a copy is through

Amazon.

I'm also releasing audio editions of the books and I hope they'll be published at the rate of three-or-four a year. The audio books are available through Amazon, Audible and iTunes.

BIBLIOGRAPHY

The following is a selection of the many books that I consulted in researching the Carlisle & Holbrooke series:

Definitive Text

Sir Julian Corbett wrote the original, definitive text on the Seven Years War. Most later writers use his work as a steppingstone to launch their own.

Corbett, LLM., Sir Julian Stafford. *England in the Seven Years War – Vol. I: A Study in Combined Strategy.* Normandy Press. Kindle Edition.

Strategy and Naval Operations

Three very accessible modern books cover the strategic context and naval operations of the Seven Years War. Daniel Baugh addresses the whole war on land and sea, while Martin Robson concentrates on maritime activities. Jonathan Dull has produced a very readable account from the French perspective.

Baugh, Daniel. *The Global Seven Years War 1754-1763.* Pearson Education, 2011. Print.

Robson, Martin. *A History of the Royal Navy, The Seven Years War.* I.B. Taurus, 2016. Print.

Dull, Jonathan, R. *The French Navy and the Seven Years' War.* University of Nebraska Press, 2005. Print.

Sea Officers

For an interesting perspective on the life of sea officers of the mid-eighteenth century, I'd recommend Augustus

Hervey's Journal, with the cautionary note that while Hervey was by no means typical of the breed, he's very entertaining and devastatingly honest. For a more balanced view, I'd suggest British Naval Captains of the Seven Years War.

Erskine, David (editor). *Augustus Hervey's Journal, The Adventures Afloat and Ashore of a Naval Casanova.* Chatham Publishing, 2002. Print.

McLeod, A.B. *British Naval Captains of the Seven Years War, The View from the Quarterdeck.* The Boydell Press, 2012. Print.

Life at Sea

There are two excellent overviews of shipboard life and administration during the Seven Years War.

Rodger, N.A.M. *The Wooden World, An Anatomy of the Georgian Navy.* Fontana Press, 1986. Print.

Lavery, Brian. *Anson's Navy, Building a Fleet for Empire, 1744 to 1793.* Seaforth Publishing, 2021. Print.

The Siege of Havana

I found a number of references to the campaign but only one comprehensive and readily accessible book, which I strongly recommend.

Greentree, David. *A Far Flung Gamble, Havana 1762.* Osprey, 2010, Print.

***

Chris Durbin

THE AUTHOR

Chris Durbin grew up in the seaside town of Porthcawl in South Wales. His first experience of sailing was as a sea cadet in the treacherous tideway of the Bristol Channel and, at the age of sixteen, he spent a week in a tops'l schooner in the Southwest Approaches. He was a crew member on the Porthcawl lifeboat before joining the navy.

Chris spent twenty-four years as a warfare officer in the Royal Navy, serving in all classes of ships from aircraft carriers through destroyers and frigates to the smallest minesweepers. He took part in operational campaigns in the Falkland Islands, the Middle East and the Adriatic and he spent two years teaching tactics at a US Navy training centre in San Diego.

On his retirement from the Royal Navy, Chris joined a large American company and spent eighteen years in the aerospace, defence and security industry, including two years on the design team for the Queen Elizabeth class aircraft carriers.

Chris is a graduate of the Britannia Royal Naval College at *Dartmouth*, the British Army Command and Staff College, the United States Navy War College, where he gained a postgraduate diploma in national security decision-making, and Cambridge University, where he was awarded an MPhil in International Relations.

With a lifelong interest in naval history and a long-standing ambition to write historical fiction, Chris has completed the first fifteen novels in the Carlisle & Holbrooke series, which follow the fortunes of a colonial Virginian and a Hampshire man who both command ships of King George's navy during the middle years of the eighteenth century.

The series will follow its principal characters through the Seven Years War and into the period of turbulent relations between Britain and her American colonies in the 1760s and 1770s. They'll negotiate some thought-provoking loyalty issues when British policy and colonial restlessness lead inexorably to the American Revolution.

Chris lives on the south coast of England, surrounded by hundreds of years of naval history. His three children are all busy growing their own families and careers while Chris and his wife (US Navy, retired) of forty-two years enjoy sailing their Cornish Crabber on the south coast.

Fun Fact

Chris shares his garden with a tortoise named Aubrey. If you've read Patrick O'Brian's *HMS Surprise* or have seen the 2003 film *Master and Commander: The Far Side of the World*, you'll recognise the modest act of homage that Chris has paid to that great writer. Rest assured that Aubrey has not yet grown to the gigantic proportions of *Testudo Aubreii*, though at his last weigh in, he topped one kilogram!

FEEDBACK

If you've enjoyed *Old Bahama Straits* please consider leaving a review on Amazon.

Look out for the sixteenth in the Carlisle & Holbrooke series, coming soon.

You can follow my blog at:

www.chris-durbin.com

Printed in Great Britain
by Amazon